GREEN

lena nottingham

To anyone who has ever felt a little out of place in this world.

➤➤

table of contents

➤➤

C H A P T E R ' 1

"This is perfect!" Paisley exclaimed, holding the heavy box tight against her chest and hurrying up the front sidewalk. "It is even prettier in person, Lo!"

Meanwhile, Shiloh struggled to keep her grip on the boxes in her arms, craning her neck to see overtop of them. Her graduation robe hung down behind her and she managed to get her foot caught, nearly sending her flying forwards. Once she regained her balance, the green eyed girl set the boxes down and brushed her hands off on her jeans.

"Remind me again why we decided to move on graduation day?" she asked, flinging her black cap off of her head and letting it land on the front yard. Paisley simply laughed and shrugged, tilting her head to the side slightly.

"Did you really want to be there for Ryland and Vanessa's graduation party?" the small girl raised an eyebrow, laughing when a look of realization spread across her girlfriend's face.

"Right," Shiloh nodded, crinkling her nose at the smaller girl before taking a step back to study the small house. "God, this place looks even worse than it did on the website," Shiloh grimaced.

"Hush," Paisley shook her head. "It is perfect," she said, just as she made her way up the wooden steps to the front door. The small girl gasped when one of the slabs cracked under her feet, and she quickly hopped to the side to avoid falling down the stairs.

"It just... needs a little love," Paisley nodded firmly, nudging the next stair cautiously. This earned a laugh from Shiloh, who moved forward to inspect the stairs.

"More like a lot of love," the dark haired girl teased, motioning to tell Paisley it was safe to go up the other stairs.

She tugged the key out of her pocket, turning it in the lock. After struggling with a stuck doorknob for a minute or two, they managed to open the front door.

Paisley immediately set her box down, hurrying to stand in the middle of the small room. A wide smile spread across her face and she turned back to Shiloh, clapping her hands together.

"This is ours," she smiled, spinning around in a circle and looking around the room. "It is perfect," the small girl laughed, running forwards and pulling Shiloh into a hug.

"You're perfect," Shiloh laughed softly, pulling away from the hug and planting a quick kiss to her girlfriend's lips. "I wish I could say the same for the house," she added, walking over to the curtains and shaking the dust off of them.

It'd been nearly four years since Paisley had shown up at their apartment in New York, sporting the same worn white converse that she had kept with her ever since. Things had gone pretty smoothly for them since their spontaneous trip to Miami. Paisley had continued improving at a slow pace, never failing to put a smile on her girlfriend's face.

Shiloh was ecstatic to hear that she had been offered a job straight after she graduated. In her junior year of college she had interned with a graphic design company, who were so impressed with her work that they wanted her back in a permanent position as soon as she graduated. Paisley was even more excited to find out that Toby had been offered the same position, meaning they'd still live close to Maia and her now-husband.

Their relationship never experienced the 'dry spells', as some people prefer to call them. They was still as excited to wake up next to each other each morning as they had been when they first started dating. No one could deny that the two shared a bond deeper than just the physical.

Shiloh's thoughts were interrupted when she heard Paisley's footsteps reenter the house. She turned around just as Paisley managed to get the cage door open, allowing the old white cat to wander out into the foyer and immediately spread out in the sun.

"Lazy butt," Paisley mumbled, setting the crate aside and bending down to smooth out Wolf's fur. Shiloh couldn't help but smile, remembering the days when Wolf was only a tiny kitten that Paisley had protected so fiercely.

"C'mon, lazy butt numero dos," Shiloh teased, nudging Paisley's shoulder. "The quicker we get these boxes inside the quicker we can unpack, and then the quicker we can redecorate, and then the quicker we c-,"

"Slow down there," Paisley laughed, standing up and following Shiloh towards the door. "One step at a time," the small girl added, grabbing another box that they had crammed into the back of the car.

"I'm just excited to move in, that's all," Shiloh shrugged, tediously carrying a stack of boxes on her hip, using her free hand to carefully open the front door.

"We are moving in," Paisley nodded curtly, brushing past Shiloh and setting the box on the floor. "What does it look like we are doing?" The small girl stood up and crinkled her nose.

"You're right," Shiloh sighed, rolling her eyes playfully. "As always," she added, moving forwards and wrapping her arms around Paisley's waist from behind. The small girl giggled, reaching up and tugging on her beanie.

"Are you planning on wearing that thing all summer again?" Shiloh asked, looking up at the beanie. Paisley furrowed her eyebrows and turned around.

"Of course," she nodded, a shy smile on her face. "I dunno, I just like it," the small girl shrugged, reaching up to smooth out her hair. "It feels weird to not wear it."

"Goofball," Shiloh muttered teasingly, causing Paisley to crinkle up her nose.

"You love me," the smaller girl huffed dramatically, crossing her arms and marching back outside. Shiloh rolled her eyes half-heartedly.

"Tell me something I don't know!" she called after her, before jogging to catch up to the smaller girl. Paisley just laughed softly, helping Shiloh retrieve the last of their boxes from the back of her car.

"That's it...?" Shiloh raised her eyebrows, eyeing the stack of boxes they had piled into the middle of the room. "I didn't realize how little we brought."

"We left the furniture at the apartment," Paisley noted, nudging one of the boxes with her foot. "You got the mattress delivered here, right?" she asked, venturing down the small hallway and peering into all of the rooms.

"Yeah," Shiloh nodded, jogging after her and watching as she disappeared into the bedroom. Sure enough, the mattress had already been placed on the bed frame that had come with the house.

"This is ours," Paisley repeated what she had said earlier, almost in disbelief. "It is all ours and it is only ours," she smiled, turning around and placing her hand on Shiloh's shoulders. "I could get used to this."

"Me too," Shiloh laughed, setting her hands on Paisley's hips and planting a quick kiss on her cheek. "Are you hungry?"

"Yes," Paisley nodded once. "I did not know how boring graduation was," she laughed softly, smoothing out the black satin of Shiloh's gown.

"Yeah, but did you see Ryland trip?" Shiloh smirked, causing both of them to burst into laughter.

"Her face turned red," Paisley noted, covering her mouth to try and hide her own amusement. Shiloh just rolled her eyes playfully and tugged her phone out of her pocket, heading back into the kitchen.

Soon enough, both girls sat in the middle of the foyer, a box of pizza open between them. Wolf sauntered over to the couple, sniffing Paisley's arm cautiously before rubbing up against the girl.

"He only loves me when I have food," Paisley mumbled, picking off a small piece of her crust and tossing it in his direction. Shiloh laughed softly.

"I love this," Paisley sighed, setting her plate down and lying back on the floor so she could stare up at the ceiling. "This is perfect."

"Goofball," Shiloh muttered jokingly as she got up to throw away their trash. Paisley hummed in defiance, giggling when Wolf padded over and stuck his nose in her face.

The girls found themselves in bed only a short while later. Both of them were exhausted from the long day, due to waking up early for the graduation ceremonies and then moving into their new home. The minute Paisley's arms snaked up the sleeves of Shiloh's sweater, sleep had washed over both of the girls.

Or so they thought. Shiloh was confused when she felt someone squeezing her hand, drawing her out of her slumber. Slightly worried, she wiped her eyes and hummed some sort of questioning sound. Paisley sat cross legged in front of her, squeezing her hand once more.

"I can not sleep," the small girl whispered, running her fingers through her dark brown hair. Shiloh immediately became concerned, knowing Paisley's old sleeping habits all too well.

"You didn't have a nightmare… did you?" Shiloh asked tediously. She was instantly relieved when Paisley laughed and shook her head.

"You are gonna laugh at me," Paisley mumbled bashfully, turning her head to hide her smile. Shiloh couldn't help but laugh at the adorable gesture, running her thumb over the back of Paisley's hand.

"I laugh at you anyway," Shiloh teased, sitting up and smoothing out her hair. "Why are you still up?"

"I am too excited," the small girl giggled, hiding her face in her hands. "This is... this is our house. It is all ours. It is crazy, Lo," she whispered, awe laced in her words. Shiloh couldn't help but smile.

Their conversation was interrupted by the sound of voices from the other room. Both girls immediately froze, looking at one another with wide eyes. Paisley's first instinct was to bury herself under the blankets, while Shiloh quickly hopped off of the bed and grabbed the bedside lamp.

"What are you doing?" Paisley hissed, peering out from underneath the covers. Shiloh held up a finger to signal for her to be quiet, before slowly slipping out into the hallway. The smaller girl gasped, rolling off of the bed and quickly scurrying to catch up with Shiloh. She clung onto the older girl's arm as she peered out from the hallway.

"What the hell?" Shiloh mumbled. Her fear was quickly replaced with confusion when she saw Wolf perched on top of the fireplace mantle, looking just as surprised as they were.

"How'd you manage to do that?" Shiloh laughed, shaking her head and setting the lamp down. Paisley watched as Shiloh approached the fireplace, picking up the small battery operated radio and studying it in her hands.

"He wanted music," Paisley giggled, slipping out from her hiding spot and joining Shiloh on the other side of the room. The green eyed girl just laughed, experimentally flipping through the stations out of curiosity.

"Recognize this one?" Shiloh asked in surprise, turning up the radio so Paisley could hear the song. The small girl listened for a moment before a wide smile spread across her face.

"Dance with me," Shiloh giggled, reaching out and grabbing Paisley's hand. The small girl laughed, practically tripping into Shiloh's arms when the girl pulled her towards her.

"I love you," Paisley giggled breathlessly, allowing Shiloh to grab her hand and spin her around. The older girl just smiled, leaning in to quickly steal a kiss.

Both girls sang at the top of their lungs, causing Wolf to tilt his head to the side questioningly. Shiloh laughed, lifting Paisley up and spinning her around in the dim moonlight-lit room.

Once the song ended, both girls caught their breath through their incessant laughter. Paisley reached up, giggling and connecting her lips with Shiloh's. She felt the older girl smiling into the kiss, and squealed when she was practically swept off of her feet and into Shiloh's arms.

"Let's go to bed, goofball," Shiloh laughed, planting a kiss on her girlfriend's forehead. Paisley hummed in acknowledgement, throwing her arms around Shiloh's shoulders and allowing the older girl to carry her into the bedroom. Both girls collapsed on the bed in laughter.

"I love you too," Shiloh whispered breathlessly, rolling over on her side and cupping the back of Paisley's neck to bring in her for a kiss. Paisley hummed happily, reaching out and running her fingers across Shiloh's jawline before she pulled the older girl down on the bed, curling up in her side.

"I love us," Paisley giggled, causing Shiloh to smile softly.

"Here's to us then, goofball," Shiloh whispered, pulling the blankets back over them for the second time that night.

CHAPTER 2

The next morning, Paisley woke up as confused as ever. After her eyes fluttered open, it took her a few moments to realize where she was. After remembering, she sat up and grew worried when Shiloh was nowhere to be seen.

Anxiously, Paisley quickly slid out of bed and hurried into the hallway. "Lo?" she called, tilting her head to the side and quickly padding into the living room. She couldn't help but breathe a sigh of relief when she caught sight of Shiloh in the kitchen.

"Good morning," Paisley hummed, smiling softly. She grew concerned when Shiloh didn't answer her. Instead, the green eyed girl continued to mumble something to herself and dig through the boxes she had spread across the floor.

"Lo?" Paisley tilted her head to the side. "What is wrong?" she asked softly, reaching out and placing a hand on her girlfriend's shoulder.

Shiloh immediately jumped, whipping her head around and looking at the girl behind her. Paisley flinched in return, taking a step backwards.

"I'm so stupid," Shiloh sighed, letting her shoulders drop as she turned back to the boxes. "I made cereal and I went to eat it, but guess what? We don't even have a table. I didn't even think to get a table," she threw her hands down at her sides and huffed in frustration.

Paisley couldn't help but giggle, thinking that Shiloh was ridiculously adorable when she got flustered over the smallest things. "It is no big deal," Paisley shrugged, moving closer to her girlfriend.

"Who forgets to get a table?" Shiloh shook her head, rolling her eyes at her own stupidity.

"You," Paisley giggled, moving forwards and pulling the frustrated girl into a hug. "Who cares?" she said softly once they pulled away. Shiloh simply shrugged.

"There's just so much to do," Shiloh confessed, leaning back against the counter and running a hand through her hair.

"And we will do it," Paisley shrugged. "We have a lot of time, Lo. It is only…." she glanced at the clock. "Eight a.m." she giggled, realizing just how early Shiloh had gotten up.

"But first, cereal," Paisley nodded curtly, grabbing the box of Lucky Charms she had packed specifically for herself.

"Come on, Lo," Paisley pouted when she realized Shiloh's face was still staring down at the floor. "This is an adventure," she smiled hopefully, using her free hand to grab Shiloh's. "Everything is going to be okay," she reminded the girl, locking their pinkies together where Shiloh's tattoo was.

The green eyed girl glanced down at their connected fingers and sighed. Paisley was right. "We can eat on the back porch?" Shiloh offered, causing Paisley to smile contently and grab her bowl of cereal.

"Grumpy pants," Paisley mumbled teasingly, earning a playful glare from her girlfriend. They pulled two of the plastic lawn chairs next to each other and sat down. What their house lacked in size, it made up for in landscape. The land behind their house extended out for miles, giving them a nice green yard and all the privacy they could ask for.

"I can hear the birds," Paisley said quietly, pointing to the trees that lined their yard. Shiloh nodded with a mouthful of food, causing her girlfriend to giggle.

Once they finished breakfast, both girls immediately got to work on unpacking their boxes. It wasn't Paisley's ideal way to spend the day, but she knew Shiloh was eager to get it over with, so she didn't complain.

Paisley waited for Shiloh to disappear down the hallway with a few of the boxes before she quickly retrieved the box she had marked with a small star. She slid it across the room, skidding to a stop in front of the fireplace.

The small girl paused for a moment, listening to make sure Shiloh was busy in the other room. She smiled widely, practically tearing the box open and admiring the collection of drawings and paintings that she had packed tightly.

She pulled them out one by one, taking the time to scan each piece of artwork. With a soft smile, she began arranging them together.

When Shiloh emerged from the hallway holding an empty box, she nearly choked on thin air. Paisley smiled, turning around from where she had just hung the last painting and motioning to the wall above the fireplace.

"Surprise," Paisley giggled softly. "I knew you would not let me do it if I told you," she admitted, biting her lip nervously. "But I like it."

Paisley knew Shiloh was insecure about her work. Shiloh always told her that a real artist was never satisfied with their pieces. But Paisley was. She was more than satisfied. She loved Shiloh's art. It told her things that Shiloh's words couldn't.

"If you do not like it I can take it down," Paisley added once she noticed the hesitant expression on her girlfriend's face.

"No, I just," Shiloh shook her head, moving across the room and squeezing Paisley's shoulder. "It's just weird," she admitted. "Like… this is our home."

"Even though it needs some love," Paisley added with a soft giggle. Shiloh rolled her eyes playfully and crinkled her nose at the smaller girl.

As if on cue, a screeching sound echoed throughout the apartment. Wolf scrambled across the hardwood floor, hiding next to the fireplace. Paisley's hands immediately went to her ears out of instinct, blocking out the awful ringing noise. Even Shiloh flinched.

"I think that's the doorbell," Shiloh mouthed to Paisley. The dark haired girl quickly jogged over to the door, and sure enough, there on the front porch stood her three best friends. The screeching sound of their broken doorknob soon died down and Shiloh made a mental note to get that fixed.

"Cheechee!" Paisley chimed, flying past Shiloh and tackling Ryland into a hug. "I missed you," she giggled, pulling away and fixing the beanie on her head.

"It's only been a day, loser," Ryland stuck her tongue out at the smaller girl. She held up a bottle of wine, tossing it to Shiloh, who scrambled to catch it. "We brought a housewarming gift."

Shiloh laughed softly, turning the bottle around in her hands before jogging back into the kitchen to set it down. When she turned back around, Paisley had already allowed their former roommates to enter the small house.

"It needs some love," Shiloh explained, grimacing at the mess of boxes they had thrown all over the floor. "It'll be just like new the next time you see it," she laughed softly.

"I'll take your word for it," Vanessa laughed, pulling Shiloh into a hug. "My babies are growing up," she teased, pretending to wipe a tear from her eyes.

"Shut up," Shiloh mumbled as she elbowed Vanessa's side. "Don't remind me."

"And do not ring the doorbell next time," Paisley blurted out, remembering what had happened earlier. Shiloh couldn't help but laugh as she watched Paisley try to comfort a traumatized Wolf.

"Why'd you guys come all the way out here?" Shiloh asked, suddenly remembering that they were an entire hour away from each other.

"I was bored," Ryland shrugged, twirling her car keys around her finger. "And hungry. And it's always more fun to go out and eat when we're all together."

"You drove out here just so we could get food?" Shiloh laughed in disbelief.

"We can leave if you want," Leah smirked.

"No!" Paisley hopped into their conversation with Wolf cradled in her arms. "I am hungry," she giggled, realizing how desperate she had sounded.

"Well then get your hungry butt in the car, Chanch," Ryland laughed, reaching up and snatching Paisley's beanie from her head. The smaller girl pouted, setting Wolf down and running after Ryland to retrieve her beloved beanie. Shiloh rolled her eyes.

"Children," Leah whispered, making the green eyed girl laugh softly. The other three followed them out to the car, making sure to lock the door behind them.

A short drive later, the five best friends sat crammed into a booth at a small diner they had found on Main Street. Paisley hummed softly to herself, sharing her menu with Shiloh.

"What are you getting?" Paisley asked, looking up at Shiloh with a soft smile. The green eyed girl continued to scan the menu.

"Is it bad that I kinda want pizza?" Shiloh whispered, making Paisley laugh softly and shrug.

"You read my mind," the smaller girl giggled. "Should we just get a pizza?" she turned to the other girls, who all shrugged in agreement.

Soon enough, Paisley was taking her first bite of her slice of pizza and watching Shiloh do the same out of the corner of her eye. She giggled, reaching out and wiping a small dab of sauce on Shiloh's chin.

"Ew, love," Vanessa gagged from across the table. Ryland joined in, earning the middle finger from Shiloh.

"Be nice," Paisley teased, grabbing Shiloh's hand.

"So, Leah..." Vanessa raised an eyebrow, turning to the oldest girl next to her. "When is Troy going to put a ring on it?"

The small girl's face immediately turned bright red and she quickly brought her hands up to hide her eyes. Paisley giggled, smiling up at Shiloh before turning her attention back to the other girl.

"Come on, Hernandez," Ryland rolled her eyes playfully. "You've been dating for almost three years now and you're gonna tell me you haven't thought about it?"

Leah slowly lowered her hands with a soft shrug. "I mean, we've talked about it..." she admitted, flinching when both Ryland and Vanessa squealed in excitement.

"I want to be the first to know when he proposes," Paisley gave Leah a playful glare, trying to let make her feel comfortable.

"Okay, so define talking about it," Ryland nodded, leaning in closer. "We're all ears."

"You guys," Leah mumbled bashfully, hiding her face back in her hands. Paisley just giggled, taking a sip of her drink as the two girls interrogated her friend.

"That'll be us one day," Shiloh laughed, glancing at Paisley. The small girl nearly choked on her drink, her eyes widening. She looked over at her girlfriend, but Shiloh hadn't even given a second thought to what she had said.

Paisley repeated the words over and over in her head, feeling a small smile form on her face. Yeah, she'd like that one day, she decided. The small girl hummed contently, turning her attention back to her food.

As the meal came to a close, Paisley's attention was suddenly drawn away from the table. Meanwhile, Shiloh was listening to Vanessa and Ryland talk about the new dance studio they were interning at. She didn't even notice when one of the kids at the table near them started crying. Paisley did.

"Pais, did you hear th-?" Shiloh paused when she turned around and Paisley wasn't next to her. Her eyes immediately widened and she frantically searched the restaurant.

"Shy," Vanessa nudged the green eyed girl, pointing out Paisley across the room. Shiloh breathed a sigh of relief, watching as Paisley held the crying boy in her arms while his mother scrambled to clean up the drink he had just spilled all over himself.

The green eyed girl couldn't help the affectionate smile that spread across her face as she watched Paisley make funny faces at the baby to keep him entertained. The mother quickly got the table cleaned up, thanking Paisley over and over. Shiloh watched at her girlfriend shrugged it off, handing the child back over to his mother and waving goodbye to the small boy.

Paisley met Shiloh's eyes as she made her way back over to the table and smiled shyly. Shiloh wrapped an arm around her once she sat back down, kissing the side of her head.

"What made you do that?" Shiloh asked. Paisley simply shrugged, taking a sip of her drink once more.

"She needed help," Paisley laughed softly. "And so I helped her. No big deal."

"God I love you," Shiloh laughed, kissing Paisley's cheek and making her giggle. This was followed by gagging noises from across the table from the other three girls.

"Shut up," Paisley mumbled, hiding her face in her hands. Shiloh flicked them off when she wasn't looking, earning gasps of fake shock from her friends.

"So what's in store for you guys?" Leah asked, turning the topic of conversation over to them. "I mean, you've got the house. Shiloh's got a job. Paisley's got... well, you know. What's next?"

Paisley furrowed her eyebrows while Leah spoke, wondering why the girl hesitated when her name was mentioned. What was she going to do? The small girl bit her lip, looking up at Shiloh for an answer.

"Who knows," Shiloh laughed with a shrug. Paisley glanced down at her hands shyly. "I guess that's just part of the adventure," Shiloh said softly, reaching over and grabbing Paisley's hand when she sensed her nervousness. Paisley gave her a thankful smile, glad that Shiloh understood her so well.

Once Leah had spilled all the details of their relationship and the girls had split the bill for their meal, they dropped the two girls back off at their small house and said their goodbyes.

"Think we can finish the living room tonight?" Shiloh turned to Paisley, feigning excitement once they got inside. Paisley groaned.

"Come on," Shiloh laughed, abruptly scooping Paisley into her arms and spinning around. The small brunette laughed, quickly holding onto Shiloh's shoulders so she wouldn't fall.

"The world is ours!" Shiloh laughed setting Paisley down and twirling her around. "The possibilities are endless, kid! Embrace it!"

"What was in your pizza?" Paisley giggled, pausing for a moment to regain her balance. Shiloh just laughed, running her hands through her wavy brown hair.

"I just love you a lot," Shiloh admitted, laughing and catching her breath. "And I'm excited to spend the rest of my life with you," she smiled, placing her hands on Paisley's waist and pulling her close.

"You and me?" Paisley whispered, a shy smile playing at her lips.

Shiloh nodded, reaching up and brushing Paisley's hair out of her face. "Me and you, babe. Forever and always," she whispered before leaning in and connecting their lips, feeling the familiar feeling of sparks igniting in her fingertips.

CHAPTER 3

"I am hurrying!" Paisley laughed softly, digging through her clothes until she found her signature baby blue beanie. She smiled at herself in the mirror before tugging the soft material atop her head. "I am ready!" she called, hearing Shiloh gathering her things in the other room.

Paisley giggled when she jogged into the kitchen and found her girlfriend frustratingly shifting through the stacks of paper on their counter.

"The fucking keys," Shiloh muttered, shaking her head and looking up. Paisley couldn't help but laugh, pointing to the wall by the door.

"You hung that up last night," Paisley reminded her. Shiloh brought her palm to her forehead, hurrying over to the door and grabbing the keys off the small hanger she had installed near the door. Paisley just laughed, quickly tugging on her shoes as she hopped down the front stairs after Shiloh.

"Why are you so worried?" Paisley asked once they were on the road. She noticed how Shiloh was gripping the steering wheel so much that her knuckles were turning white. Reaching out, the small girl laid her hand on top of Shiloh's. "Calm down. They already gave you the job."

Shiloh sighed, knowing Paisley was right. "I know," Shiloh nodded, loosening her grip under her girlfriend's touch. "I just want to make sure I keep the job. I really like this position."

"You will," Paisley hummed, retracting her hand and resting back into the seat. "They already love you. That is why they gave you the job. Duh." She giggled, crinkling her nose.

"I thought I would've gotten rid of Ryland once we moved out," Shiloh teased, reaching over and taking

Paisley's hand. "Besides, I've got my good luck charm," she winked, making Paisley laugh.

"Like the cereal," Paisley nodded happily.

"That's Lucky Charms, goofball," Shiloh laughed, nudging her girlfriend's side playfully. "Nice try, though."

"Shush," Paisley muttered, feigning disappointment. Shiloh simply stuck her tongue out at her girlfriend once they pulled into the small parking lot outside her offices.

"It'll only be like ten minutes, and then we can go," Shiloh promised once they got inside, nodding towards the small waiting room down the hallway. Paisley nodded, leaning forwards for a quick kiss before the couple went in opposite ways.

Paisley sat down in one of the soft chairs, folding her legs beneath her and busying herself by aimlessly flipping through a magazine. Paisley slowly dozed off, nearly falling asleep until she heard a frustrated groan from across the room.

The brunette lifted her head, watching as the small girl across the room balled up a piece of paper and tossed it into the trashcan. The girl then tore another paper out of her notebook and laid it out in front of her, tapping her pencil impatiently against the table.

"What are you doing?" Paisley asked, tilting her head to the side slightly. The girl jumped when she heard Paisley address her, quickly turning her head around and glancing questioningly at the other girl.

"I have to write a stupid essay," the girl huffed, rolling her eyes. "And I can't think of anything to write about," she mumbled, curling her fingers around her pencil and turning back to her paper.

Moments later, Paisley was pulling her chair over beside the girl's, shyly glancing over at her paper. "I can help you," Paisley offered quietly, earning a questioning look from the girl. She studied Paisley's face, deciding that the other girl could be trusted.

"My teacher says I have to write about something I'm passionate about, but I don't even know what that means," the girl sighed, moving the blank paper between them.

"When you are passionate you are... you are doing something because you love it," Paisley explained, drumming her fingers on the table as she thought. "It is something you would fight for."

Paisley's lips curved into a smile when she noticed the girl's shirt, and she pointed to the horseshoe logo in the corner. "What is that?" she asked, watching as the girl looked down.

"I got this at the stables," the girl nodded happily. Paisley immediately noticed how her face lit up. "My sister got one just like it, too."

"The stables?" Paisley inquired, earning an excited nod from the girl.

"Yeah! Me and my sister go there every weekend, and we get to ride the horses," she smiled, turning around and pointing to the cartoon horse on the back of her shirt. "See?"

Paisley nodded. "Tell me more," the small brunette smiled, grabbing a pencil and tapping it against her arm.

"Well, it's super fun," the girl continued, a wide smile on her face. "It's called Happy Trails Stables, and everyone there is super nice. That's where me and my sister learn how to ride."

"We have to wear a heavy helmet and boots to keep us safe in case we fall," she nodded happily. "And then this girl named t helps us put the saddles on our horses. It's really complicated," she giggled. Paisley jotted something down.

"I always ride a horse named Isaac. He's dark brown and he has white on his nose," she laughed softly, pointing to her own nose. "Sometimes he doesn't like to listen, though. Hey, what are you doing?" she leaned in, looking at what Paisley was writing down.

"You can write about that," Paisley explained, pointing to the list she had made on the paper. "Three paragraphs," she nodded, tapping the paper. "One about the farm, one about the people at the farm, and one about Isaac," she smiled shyly, handing the pencil back to the girl and looking to her for approval.

"That makes it way easier!" the girl gasped, grabbing her pencil and looking back down at her paper. "Now I actually know what I'm gonna write about," she laughed, earning a proud smile from Paisley. "Thank you!"

"Angie, c'mon, we're gonna be late to your brother's game."

A voice appeared from behind them and Paisley turned around, watching as the girl shoved her things back into her backpack and threw it over her shoulder.

"Mom, look! She helped me!" the girl smiled, holding out the paper and pointing to Paisley. The woman raised an eyebrow, looking over the paper.

"That's nice of her," the woman scanned the paper before handing it back to her daughter. "Do you have kids?"

Paisley shook her head when the woman turned to address her. "I was just trying to help," she said softly.

"Well, you know, my son's preschool is looking for teacher's assistants, if you're interested, I mean," the woman grabbed her daughters hand to stop her from knocking over a plant. "They've been searching forever for someone to fill that position."

"I..." Paisley hesitated, biting her lip.

"Here," the woman dug into her purse and pulled out her card, handing it to the other girl. "That's their phone number, in case you decide anything," she smiled, bidding her goodbye before hurrying down the hallway after her daughter.

Paisley looked down at the card in her hands, scanning over the small font. She quickly tucked it up into her beanie when she heard the click of Shiloh's shoes approaching back down the hallway.

"I'm so sorry," Shiloh breathed, running a hand through her hair once she caught sight of Paisley. "They got to talking and we didn't even look at the time," the girl apologized.

"It is okay," Paisley shook her head, giving her girlfriend a comforting smile. "How was it?" she asked before hopping to her feet and following Shiloh back out to their car.

"Intimidating," Shiloh laughed. "They were all older than me. I don't think I even spoke a word when I was in there," she rolled her eyes jokingly. Paisley frowned.

"Why not?" she tilted her head to the side. Shiloh just shrugged as they pulled out of the parking lot.

"You should talk next time," Paisley nodded softly. "You have good ideas." Shiloh smiled over at her.

"I'll try," she nodded. "I'm just afraid they'll think I'm some huge idiot who doesn't have a clue what she's doing."

"You are," Paisley giggled, crinkling her nose. Shiloh nudged her playfully and pointed down the road.

"Are we still going?" she asked, looking over at Paisley. The small girl nodded happily, leaning back in her seat.

It'd been years since Paisley had ever had the need for a phone. Most of the time she was at the apartment, and if she wasn't, she was with Shiloh. Not to mention, she wasn't quite equipped to handle one when she first showed up.

But now, a few years later, Shiloh realized that they would need a way to stay in touch. With Shiloh starting her job, and Paisley being a naturally adventurous person, the green eyed girl decided it was time to get Paisley a phone.

Paisley didn't really care either way. Shiloh was definitely the more technology dependant one in the relationship. But Paisley liked the idea of being able to call Shiloh whenever she wanted. And she liked the games.

So an hour and a lot of decisions later, Paisley happily followed Shiloh out of the store with her iPhone, complete with a bright yellow case.

"Gimme your phone," Paisley hummed once they got in the car. "I need to add everyone," she laughed softly, looking over at Shiloh. The green eyed girl couldn't help but laugh as she passed her phone over to Paisley, who immediately opened to her contacts and began transferring everyone's numbers onto her phone.

"Ryland says hi," Paisley giggled a few minutes later, handing Shiloh's phone back over to her. Her girlfriend laughed, rolling her eyes playfully as they pulled into their small driveway.

"Lo, wait!" Paisley quickly grabbed Shiloh's arm once they got back inside. "I have to show you something."

Shiloh, confused yet curious, followed Paisley as the smaller girl led her over to the couch. She watched as the girl reached up into her beanie and pulled out a small slip of paper.

"I want to get a job," Paisley said quietly, handing the small business card to the other girl on the couch. "As a teacher's assistant."

"You do?" Shiloh looked back up at her with a soft smile. Paisley nodded slowly, somewhat scared yet excited.

"Is that okay?" Paisley asked, tilting her head to the side.

"Of course," Shiloh laughed, reaching out and brushing Paisley's hair out of her face. "Why wouldn't it be?"

Paisley instantly smiled, taking the card back from Shiloh and running her fingers over the dark numbers. "Do you think I can do it, though?" she asked, her disposition changing once more.

"Of course you can," Shiloh laughed in disbelief, pulling Paisley into her side. "You're my girl. And I know my girl can do anything she puts her mind to."

Paisley blushed, biting her lip and looking down at her hands. "I want to do it," she smiled, pulling her phone out of her pocket and beginning to dial the number from the card.

Shiloh just smiled proudly. She leaned back on the couch and rested her head on Paisley's shoulder while the small brunette held the phone up to her ear, waiting nervously for someone to answer.

"Hi."

Shiloh quickly sat up, watching as Paisley anxiously drummed her fingers on her lap. She reached out, grabbing her girlfriend's hand to calm her down.

"I, uh, I heard you are looking for a teacher's assistant?" Paisley asked biting her lip.

"Yeah."

Shiloh felt Paisley's grip on her hand tighten and she gave her a supportive smile. The small girl looked over at her, crinkling her nose playfully.

"Tomorrow?" Paisley glanced at Shiloh, who quickly nodded. "Yeah, tomorrow works," she smiled, biting her lip nervously.

"Paisley," she answered quickly. "Paisley Lowe."

Shiloh couldn't help but giggle when she saw an excited smile creep on her girlfriend's face.

"Thank you," Paisley smiled widely, nodding a few times before quickly saying goodbye and hanging up the phone. She immediately turned to Shiloh. "They want me to come in and help out tomorrow. They said we will go from there," Paisley failed to hide her excitement.

"This is so exciting!" Shiloh giggled, pulling Paisley into a hug and planting a soft kiss on her cheek. "We're growing up."

"Ew," Paisley giggled, crinkling her nose. "Why would we want to do that?"

Shiloh rolled her eyes playfully. "If you get this job, you're gonna be able to play with little kids all day. You're practically made for that position."

Paisley couldn't help but laugh when Shiloh hopped off of the couch, pulling Paisley up with her and spinning around. "I love you, Pais," she whispered, wrapping her arms around her girlfriend's waist and planting a kiss to the bridge of her nose. "I love you and I'm so so proud of how far you've come."

"You are a dork," Paisley mumbled shyly, hanging her head down. Shiloh simply giggled and used one of her hands to tilt Paisley's chin upwards, meeting her eyes.

"Say you love me," Shiloh huffed playfully, making Paisley giggle. "Say it!"

"No!" Paisley squealed, laughing as she tried to escape Shiloh's grip. The green eyed girl wrapped her arms around Paisley's waist and picked her up, carrying the laughing girl into their bedroom and falling back on the bed.

"You have to say it," Shiloh teased, rolling over so she had Paisley trapped under her arms. "Or else I'm gonna tickle you."

"No!" Paisley continued to fight, trying to wiggle out of Shiloh's grip.

"You asked for it," Shiloh hummed, reaching in and tickling the smaller girl. Paisley squealed, holding her hands up to try and push Shiloh away.

"I surrender!" Paisley giggled, trying to catch her breath. Shiloh paused her motions to raise a playful eyebrow at the girl.

"You've gotta say it," Shiloh laughed softly, wiggling her eyebrows. Paisley sighed, holding her hands up in defeat.

"I love you," Paisley mumbled with a soft giggle, watching as Shiloh pumped her fist in victory and feel back onto the bed beside the girl. Paisley took advantage of the opportunity, rolling over so now she had the upper hand.

"Say you love me."

CHAPTER 4

Paisley brushed her hair out of her face and studied herself in the mirror next to the door, reaching up to fix the signature beanie on her head. She spun around once before smoothing out the mint green sweater she had chosen to wear. The small girl jumped when she felt a pair of arms wrap around her waist.

"Stop overthinking it, babe. Y'look adorable," Shiloh whispered, her morning voice prominent. Paisley blushed, looking away when her girlfriend kissed her shoulder gently.

"I'm serious," Shiloh giggled, using one of her hands to tilt Paisley's chin so she was looking straight into the mirror. "Look at yourself. You're absolutely beautiful. Every inch of you," she pressed a kiss to Paisley's cheek.

"Now get your butt into the car before you're late to your first day of work," Shiloh teased, removing herself from Paisley so she could grab her keys from the hanger near the door. Soon enough, their car was pulling out into the street.

It was easy to tell that Paisley was nervous. Shiloh could see by the way she was digging her nails into the denim material of her jeans and tapping her foot impatiently. The green eyed girl reached over and took her hand to calm her down.

"There's nothing to be afraid of," Shiloh said softly. Paisley glanced over at her, her bottom lip drawn inbetween her teeth. "Really, Pais. It's okay to be nervous. But don't freak yourself out, yeah? Kids love you. You'll do great."

"And if you think it's too much for you, we'll find you something else, okay? Relax," Shiloh smiled, bringing Paisley's hand up to her lips and pressing a soft kiss on the back of her palm.

"Promise?" Paisley laughed softly, holding up her pinky. Without hesitation, Shiloh locked their pinkies together, a tradition they'd had for what felt like forever.

"Promise," Shiloh nodded. Paisley kept their pinkies interlocked, bringing her hand back into her lap and sighing softly. She was feeling a mix of nervousness and excitement. Surprisingly, her excitement was overruling any anxiety she was feeling.

Paisley sat up slightly when Shiloh pulled into the small school parking lot. She couldn't help but smile when she saw the colorful playset, which was currently empty. Shiloh glanced over at her girlfriend, watching her taking in all the surroundings.

"Do you want me to come in with you?" Shiloh asked, squeezing Paisley's hand.

"I got it," Paisley laughed, leaning over and kissing Shiloh's cheek. "Noon, right?"

"Yep," Shiloh nodded, beginning to realize just how much her girlfriend had grown in the past few years. "You've got your phone?"

Paisley rolled her eyes playfully, pulling her phone out of her pocket to show the girl in the driver's seat. Shiloh gave her a thumbs up.

"Call me if you need anything," Shiloh reminded her, earning another eye roll from Paisley. "Okay, fine, maybe I'll just let you live here with the kids if you're gonna be so sassy," Shiloh teased. Paisley just stuck her tongue out, leaning in to plant another kiss on her girlfriend's cheek before she stood up.

Shiloh watched as the smaller girl fixed the beanie on her head, taking a deep breath before slipping inside the school building. She couldn't help but wait a few minutes to make sure Paisley didn't change her mind. The green eyed girl jumped when her phone buzzed.

[My Girl - 7:55] i love you. i forgot to tell you today

Shiloh couldn't help the blush that spread across her cheeks. She raised her eyebrow when seconds later, Paisley's message was followed by another, which only contained the turtle emoji. Another message appeared shortly after.

[My Girl - 7:56] that was supposed to be a heart

Shiloh laughed, rolling her eyes as she quickly typed a reply.

[Lolo - 7:56] I love you more. Get to work, goofball.

Paisley giggled, sending Shiloh the correct heart emoji before silencing her phone and slipping it back into her pocket. She took one last deep breath before entering the small classroom.

The teacher immediately looked up when Paisley closed the door behind her. "Oh, hi!" she smiled, immediately getting up from her desk and making her way across the room. "You must be Paisley. I'm Mrs. Stephanie," she held out her hand.

Paisley quickly shook her hand, offering the woman a shy smile. She seemed exceptionally cheery for someone who was up this early. "Nice to meet you," Paisley nodded softly.

"Oh my god, sorry, I'm using my teacher voice," the woman laughed, her voice lowering back down to a normal octave. "Class starts in like five minutes. Honestly all you have to do is keep them entertained during activities and make sure they don't run off and get themselves into trouble. You'll figure it out as you go," she laughed, looking around the room. "Any questions?"

Paisley bit her lip, scanning the room for a few moments. All the children were distracted with the various toys. "I, uh," Paisley cleared her throat and turned her attention back to the teacher. "I was in an accident when I was younger," she said softly, bringing her hand up and knocking on her skull. "So... I can be a little... slow, sometimes," she said nervously, forcing herself to maintain eye contact.

"And I can't cook to save my life," the woman laughed, earning a look of confusion from Paisley. "We've all got our problems. It's no big deal. The kids will love you, don't worry about it," she shrugged, patting Paisley on the back. A wave of relief washed over the smaller girl.

"I better get that," she laughed, jogging over to the front of the room where a few parents were waiting to drop their children off. Paisley bit her lip, taking a few steps back and leaning against the wall.

She watched as a few children ran happily into the room, immediately busying themselves with the toys. She was so distracted by watching a little girl knock over a block tower that she didn't even notice Stephanie practically handing her a little boy. Paisley inhaled sharply, turning and quickly taking a crying child into her arms.

"This is Jeremiah," she said softly. "He doesn't like it when mommy leaves," she added in a whisper. Before Paisley could say anything, she was gone, and the small girl was left holding the crying boy.

"Uh," Paisley bit her lip, looking around the room. She quickly found an empty corner and hurried over to sit down, adjusting the boy in her lap.

"Hey," Paisley said softly, looking down at the boy who had his head buried in his hands. "Hey, you do not have to cry," she whispered. Reaching out, she gently moved his hands away from his face. "Your mommy will be back soon."

The boy simply shook his head, burying his head back in Paisley's shoulder and remaining quiet. Paisley bit her lip, looking around the room desperately. She caught sight of something on the colorful shelf next to her.

Paisley scooted over, reaching out and grabbing the small colorful piano from the shelf. She eyed it questioningly before flipping the power switch.

Tapping a few random keys, Paisley glanced down at the boy in her arms. "Twinkle twinkle little star," Paisley whispered quietly, tapping the keys in the order that she remembered. "How I wonder what you are."

The small boy looked up, furrowing his eyebrows together and looking back and forth from Paisley to the toy piano. Paisley glanced up at him, smiling softly.

"Up above the world so high, like a diamond in the sky," Paisley laughed softly, watching as he turned around to observe her piano playing. "Twinkle twinkle little star, how I wonder what you are."

"Again."

Paisley couldn't help but smile when the little boy scooted out of her lap so he could sit next to her by the piano. "Want to help?" Paisley asked, internally patting herself on the back when he nodded excitedly.

"Okay. See these three keys?" Paisley took his hand, moving his small fingers to the keys and playing them in order. "Play them like this... 1, 2, 3," she explained. Once she moved her hand away, he imitated the pattern.

"See?" Paisley smiled, moving her hands to the other end of the small keyboard. "Do it again, and keep going," she nodded softly. He smiled up at her before looking down at the keyboard in concentration.

Once he started playing, Paisley joined in. She smiled, remembering when her and Shiloh had played the same song a few years ago. It had been when she first gotten her piano.

"Good job!" Paisley clapped her hands together once they finished. The small boy giggled shyly, smiling up at Paisley.

"What's your name, lady?" he asked, tilting his head to the side. Paisley couldn't help but laugh.

"Paisley," she smiled. "What is yours?"

"Jeremiah," he nodded, grimacing. "I don't like my name. It's an old grandpa name."

"Then I will give you a cool name," Paisley giggled. "How about... JJ?"

"JJ?" he giggled, thinking about it for a few moments. "Yeah," he nodded with finality. "I like it."

Paisley smiled, holding out her fist in front of the little boy. His eyes lit up and he eagerly bumped Paisley's fist. The older girl made an exploding noise with her mouth, which made the small child burst into laughter. This drew the attention of a few of the other kids.

Pretty soon, she was surrounded by all the small children, pestering her for fist bumps. The small girl wondered why she was ever nervous in the first place.

About four hours later, Paisley struggled to get Jeremiah to go back to his mother when it was time for the students to be picked up. She finally was able to convince him to go home, promising him that she'd be back tomorrow to play.

When she stood back up, she smoothed out her shirt. She bit her lip nervously when she came face to face with the teacher.

"The job is yours if you want it," she smiled. Paisley immediately relaxed. "You're a natural. The kids love you."

"I... Thank you," Paisley took a deep breath. "I had fun," she laughed softly.

"So I'll see you tomorrow?" the woman asked hopefully. Paisley nodded.

"Of course," the small girl laughed, fixing the beanie on her head. She bit her lip to try and hide her smile. She couldn't wait to tell Shiloh all about her day.

A few minutes later, Paisley was eagerly heading back out to the parking lot. She smiled widely when she saw Shiloh's car, but grew confused once she approached the car and realized it was empty. Paisley quickly looked around.

Her lips curved into a smile when she saw the dark haired girl sitting on one of the benches by the playground, a tiny blonde girl sitting cross legged beside her. Shiloh had her sketchbook in her lap, sketching something while the small girl babbled incessantly.

Paisley watched with a soft smile on her face as Shiloh tore a page out of her sketchbook and handed it to the small child. The girl smiled widely, clutching the drawing to her chest and hopping off of the bench. She gave Shiloh a big hug before scurrying back off to the playground, proudly showing her drawing to a woman who Paisley assumed to be her mother.

Shiloh looked up from her sketchbook, immediately spotting Paisley standing at the edge of the parking lot. She gave her a soft smile, closing her sketchbook and jogging over to greet her girlfriend with a quick kiss.

"So? How was it?" Shiloh asked hopefully, reaching out and fixing Paisley's beanie for her. The small girl giggled excitedly.

"I got the job," Paisley said softly, trying to contain her own excitement. Shiloh didn't, though. The green eyed girl squealed happily, pulling Paisley into a hug and spinning her around.

"I told you there was nothing to worry about," Shiloh laughed softly, kissing Paisley's forehead. "C'mon, I've got a surprise."

"A surprise?" Paisley raised an eyebrow as Shiloh led her over to the car. The green eyed girl simply nodded, refusing to give her any details as they pulled out onto the road.

Paisley pestered Shiloh for the entire car ride, but the girl held out. The small girl finally gave up, resorting to drawing patterns on the condensation on the window while Shiloh drove.

"We're here," Shiloh laughed softly when Paisley immediately perked up, practically leaping out of the car. The green eyed girl quickly grabbed her things from the back of the trunk,

Paisley raised an eyebrow when she saw the basket in her girlfriend's hand.

"Figured we'd have a picnic," Shiloh laughed, pulling Paisley into her side. "To celebrate."

"I love you," Paisley giggled, allowing Shiloh to lead her up the small dirt pathway. Her smile widened when she saw the small clearing in the woods. It looked like something out of a movie. The sun shone right through the trees, illuminating the small patch of grass and practically making it glow. Paisley hummed contently.

"I love you more," Shiloh laughed, spreading out the blanket in the grass and motioning for Paisley to join her. The small girl smiled widely, hurrying to sit down next to the dark haired girl. When she met Shiloh's eyes, she couldn't help but think that her girlfriend looked like an angel. Especially with the sun hitting her light skin and causing her to glow.

Paisley reached out, running her fingertips over Shiloh's jawline. The green eyed girl paused what she had been doing to look up at her girlfriend, who was looking at her as if she were the finest piece of art she'd ever seen.

"You are beautiful," Paisley whispered, almost in awe. "I hope you know that."

Shiloh couldn't hide the blush that spread across her face. She reached up and placed her hand on top of Paisley's, bringing it down and lacing their fingers together. "You make me feel beautiful," she said softly.

"I guess we are good for each other, then," Paisley giggled, looking down shyly. "You do the same for me."

"Goofball," Shiloh giggled, leaning over and connecting their lips. It was then that she realized that there was no better feeling than that of feeling someone smile into a kiss.

C H A P T E R ' 5

Paisley doesn't like Fridays.

She decided this after her first week of work was over and Shiloh wasn't waiting for her in the parking lot. The small girl trudged grumpily over to Leah's car, tossing her backpack over her shoulder and sliding in the passenger seat.

"I forgot she had a meeting," Paisley huffed when Leah gave her a questioning look. Leah just laughed and rolled her eyes as they pulled out of the parking lot.

The apartment all five girls had once shared was now only home to Vanessa and Ryland. When Shiloh and Paisley moved about an hour away to Tarryton, Leah moved in with Troy, leaving her about halfway between Tarryton and the old apartment.

And now Paisley sat in Leah's car, staring absentmindedly out the window as she pondered what they would be doing that weekend.

"I bet Nala will be excited to see you," Leah laughed, raising an eyebrow at Paisley. Paisley's eyes widened, realizing that she hadn't been able to see Troy's dog since they'd moved.

"I am supposed to tell him to propose to you," Paisley giggled, looking up from her phone where she had just received a few detailed texts from Ryland. Leah rolled her eyes and scoffed, making Paisley laugh even more. She quickly bent down to reply to Ryland.

"What about you and Shiloh?" Leah asked, raising an eyebrow. Paisley paused for a moment, quickly sending her text to Ryland and then looking back up at the girl.

"Yes. What about us?" Paisley tilted her head to the side.

"You know," Leah chuckled. "It's legal in all 50 states now," she wiggled her eyebrows. Paisley pursed her lips in thought.

"Marriage?" Paisley bit her lip when Leah gave her a quick nod. The small girl hummed in question, tilting her head to the side and turning back to look out the window. "I do not even get marriage," Paisley spoke softly.

"What's there to get?" Leah stole a glance at Paisley, who had since turned to face the older girl. "It's just... marriage."

"That is it?" Paisley tugged on her beanie and thought for a moment. "Then what is the big deal?"

"It just means you love that person and you want to be with them for the rest of your life, that's all," Leah shrugged. Paisley crinkled her nose in confusion.

"But I love Lo and I want to be with her forever, and we are not married," Paisley nodded softly. "What is the difference?"

Leah furrowed her eyebrows, not sure how to answer Paisley's question. "Girls like a big fancy wedding," the older girl laughed softly. "The long dresses, pretty flowers, the first dance..." Paisley noticed the longing look on Leah's face. "Us girls like that stuff, I guess. Marriage just seals the deal."

Paisley giggled, nodding before quickly typing another text to Ryland. She hurried to follow Leah once they pulled into the apartment parking lot, tossing her phone back into her bag and practically sprinting past Leah and into the living room to greet Nala.

"Well hello to you too," Troy laughed when the younger girl slid to her knees beside the small dog to greet her. Nala hopped up to plant slobbery kisses all over Paisley's face, making the girl giggle.

"Wait!" Paisley quickly stood up, grabbing Troy's arm before he could greet Leah. She stood on her tiptoes, furrowing her eyebrows when she was still too short. "I need your ear," she laughed shyly.

Once he bent his knees slightly, Paisley leaned in. "Leah wants you to propose to her," the small girl whispered, hopping backwards once she was done to watch his reaction. The older boy raised an eyebrow, glancing from Paisley to the kitchen, where Leah had disappeared into.

"Really?" he laughed, somewhat nervous. Paisley nodded quickly before fixing the beanie on her head.

"She said so," Paisley said softly, try to hide the smile that was threatening to spread across her face. "So you should do it soon. She wants a big wedding with pretty flowers and a fancy dress." Paisley internally applauded herself for remembering what the older girl had said in the car.

"I'll work on it," he laughed, fist bumping the smaller girl before sauntering into the kitchen. As soon as he was out of her sight, Paisley dived back down to grab her phone out of her backpack and text Ryland to let her know that their mission had been accomplished.

Paisley still didn't like Fridays when the next week rolled around. She was woken up that morning by a hungry Wolf, who wouldn't allow her to go back to sleep until she fed him. Then, she practically had to roll Shiloh off of the bed to get her to wake up. (Which she didn't mind too much, because she loved Shiloh's voice in the mornings.) And then, when she drew open the curtains in the kitchen, she was met with big gray clouds rolling in over their house.

Sure enough, just as both girls pulled into the parking lot at the preschool, the faint sound of raindrops began to cover the roof of their car. Paisley sighed, shaking her head and glancing out the window.

"Toby and Maia are picking you up today," Shiloh reminded her. Paisley nodded, a small smile on her face.

"And Lucas," the brunette added. Shiloh laughed and quickly nodded.

"And Lucas," she confirmed. "God, it's weird. It seems like just yesterday we were helping Toby glue his sculpture for Art History back together. And now they're parents..."

"Hopefully he does not drop the baby like the sculpture," Paisley laughed softly. Shiloh grew confused when her girlfriend leaned over the center console, searching around in the back seat of the car.

"What're you looking for?" Shiloh tilted her head to the side.

"I got it," Paisley mumbled, finally locating the paper bag and pulling herself back into the passenger seat. She smiled softly and presented the brown paper bag to her girlfriend, who took it cautiously.

"I made you lunch," Paisley laughed softly. "For your meeting."

"Oh shit, yeah, I didn't even think about that," Shiloh laughed softly, glancing into the bag. "Thank you, babe," she giggled before setting the bag down so she could lean in for a kiss.

"I'll see you around dinnertime," Shiloh nodded, reaching out and fixing Paisley's beanie. "I love you."

"I love you too," Paisley hummed, giggling when Shiloh playfully motioned for her to get out of the car.

"Have fun with the children!" Shiloh called after her. Paisley turned around, thinking for a few moments.

"Have fun with the... the... the people!" Paisley giggled, causing her girlfriend to burst into laughter. Paisley waved one last time before jogging into the building to avoid the rain, which was beginning to pick up speed.

The minute Paisley set foot in the classroom, she was practically tackled to the ground by a horde of pre-schoolers.

"One at a time!" Paisley giggled, quickly regaining her balance and kneeling down so she could provide each child with their 'mandatory' fist bump.

"Miss Paisley, you have to come to our salon!" One of the small girls, Kelsey, took Paisley's hand and quickly tugged her over to the back of the room, where another small blonde was intently organizing a kit of fake brushes.

Before Paisley could argue, one of the small girls was taking off her beanie and running one of the small plastic brushes through it. Paisley watched as the other child grabbed her hand and began 'painting' her nails with a magic marker.

"We have to talk about boys," Kelsey proclaimed, nodding curtly. "That's what ladies do in salons."

"I'm getting married," the other girl giggled, standing up proudly. "Frankie gave me a ring and everything, see?" she held up her hand to display a half eaten ring pop.

"Gregory is gonna ask me to marry him once he asks his mom," Kelsey giggled, twirling a strand of Paisley's hair around her finger. "But for right now he's just my boyfriend."

"What about you, Miss Paisley, do you have a boyfriend?" the small girl looked up curiously once she finished coloring Paisley's nails purple. Paisley shook her head.

"We can help you find one!" Kelsey clapped her hands together. The other girl quickly joined in, beginning to list off men they knew that didn't have wives.

"I do not think my girlfriend would like that," Paisley giggled. Both girls immediately froze, looking at one another and then looking at Paisley in confusion. The older girl suddenly became nervous, opening her mouth to explain herself. Before she could, though, both girls plopped down in front of her and looked up at her hopefully.

"What's she like, Miss Paisley? Is she pretty?"

Paisley couldn't help but blush when she nodded, and both of the girls giggled excitedly. "She loves her!" Kelsey nodded excitedly, turning to the other girl while pointing at Paisley. "Look at her face!"

Paisley laughed shyly and brought her hands up to cover her face. Both girls squealed and reached up to grab Paisley's hands away.

"What's her name?"

"Shiloh..." Paisley said shyly, letting her hands fall back to her sides. Both girls looked at her hopefully.

"Are you gonna marry her, Miss Paisley?" Kelsey asked, smiling excitedly. At the same time, Paisley's face dropped slightly. She didn't quite know the answer to that question.

"Why?" Paisley asked, unsure of how to respond. The girls looked at her in shock.

"If you love her, you have to ask her to marry you. You have to get a big sparkly ring too, and then she'll say yes," Kelsey nodded. Paisley felt her heart speed up at the thought of getting married to Shiloh.

"My mommy and daddy got married in Paris," the other girl, whose name was London, smiled proudly. "It's the city of love. They said so."

"And you can take her on a honeymoon! They put rose petals on the bed, I think. It's super fancy. It's like a vacation, but only for big kids," Kelsey nodded, sure of herself.

Paisley bit her lip. She didn't know marriage came with all these regulations. How was she supposed to do all of that? She didn't have much money. Hell, her and Shiloh had both just started new jobs. They struggled to get groceries on a weekly basis.

Paisley couldn't get the nagging thoughts out of her head for the rest of the day. She tried to distract herself with work, but the thought was always in the back of her mind. Was Shiloh disappointed because of her?

A few hours passed and soon Paisley found herself padding out into the parking lot and looking around for Toby's truck. She smiled softly when she saw Maia holding her son's hand, keeping him steady as he took a few wobbly steps down the sidewalk.

"Almost there," Paisley giggled softly, catching Maia's attention. She smiled widely when she saw the girl, handing her son off to Toby and pulling Paisley into a hug.

"How are you?" Paisley asked, glancing behind Maia where Toby was making funny faces at the small boy in his arms.

Maia's pregnancy had taken everyone by surprise. Especially the young couple. But everyone had fallen in love with Lucas from the moment they met him.

"Exhausted," Maia laughed and rolled her eyes, nodding towards her son. "He kept me up all night. Was he crying? Nope," she shook her head. "He talks to himself. He literally just lies there and babbles for hours when he's supposed to be sleeping."

"Takes after his mom," Toby mumbled under his breath, making Paisley burst into laugher. Maia just rolled her eyes playfully at both of them, taking Lucas from Toby so she could buckle him in the backseat.

"You up for Café Terra?" Toby turned to Paisley, who nodded softly. She slid into the backseat beside Lucas, leaning over and smiling widely at him in greeting.

"Hi buddy," Paisley giggled when he reached his hand up. She allowed him to hold onto her index finger, clutching it in his tiny fist and making an untranslatable noise. Paisley laughed softly and continued making funny faces to entertain him as they drove.

Soon they were all seated at a booth in the small café, with Lucas in the high chair next to Paisley. The girl had insisted that Maia take a break for once. Besides, Paisley liked babies.

She set a few pieces of macaroni in front of him, giggling when he struggled to get it in his mouth and smeared cheese all over his face. The small girl grabbed a napkin, distracting him by wiggling her eyebrows before quickly wiping the mess off of his face.

"You're gonna make a good mom someday, fuchsia," Toby chuckled. Paisley crinkled her nose at the nickname, which she had earned in art class when she couldn't pronounce the name on the tube of paint, resulting in a collection of hilarious failed attempts.

"He's right, though," Maia nodded, reaching into her bag to hand Paisley a small toy to keep Lucas entertained. "Kids love you."

"I can not just buy a kid from the kid store," Paisley shrugged, turning back to them and poking at her pasta. "It does not happen."

Maia tilted her head to the side. "What do you mean?"

"Me and Shiloh..." Paisley reached over and covered Lucas' ears. "We do not have a penis."

Toby choked on his water, practically spitting it all over the table. Paisley quickly moved to hand him a napkin, sitting back down nervously.

"There's other ways to get a baby, Paisley," Maia nodded, trying to hold in her laughter at Paisley's innocence. "Married couples like you guys have tons of options."

Paisley furrowed her eyebrows. There was that word again. "We are not married," Paisley sighed, slumping down in her seat. Their conversation was cut short when Lucas dropped his toy and started crying, but Paisley couldn't kick the nagging thoughts out of the back of her head.

CHAPTER '6'

"How did you propose?" Paisley bit her lip. The small girl sat on the floor of Maia and Toby's living room, with Lucas next to her. The small boy was busying himself with Paisley's shoelaces.

"He put the ring on a rose and when he handed it to me, the ring slid down onto my finger," Maia laughed softly. "It was literally perfect." Paisley furrowed her eyebrows, scooting forwards and taking Maia's hand to look at her ring.

"How much did it cost?" Paisley looked up at Maia, who simply giggled. Paisley furrowed her eyebrows and glanced at Toby. "I am serious."

Toby laughed, looking over at Maia before bending down and whispering something in Paisley's ear. The small girl gasped, cupping her hands over her mouth and looking up at him in shock. "Are you serious?" Toby nodded. Paisley let her shoulders drop.

"What about the wedding?" Paisley asked hesitantly, scooting back and holding up a toy to keep Lucas occupied. Toby and Maia exchanged questioning glances.

"We were just planning on eloping once we found out about Lucas," Maia shrugged. "But you know my dad. He and my mom planned a huge wedding. Flowers and fancy dresses and all," she rolled her eyes.

"This one took it upon herself to splatter paint the train of her dress," Toby laughed. Paisley looked over at Maia, who wore a proud smirk.

"You can take the girl outta' the art but you can't take the art outta' the girl," Toby laughed, leaning over to ruffle his wife's hair. Paisley giggled from her spot on the floor before pulling a sleepy Lucas into her lap.

"Why all the marriage questions, fuchsia?" Toby looked back over to Paisley. "Did Shiloh pop the question?"

Paisley furrowed her eyebrows. "Pop the question?"

"Like did she ask you to marry her?" Maia laughed softly, explaining the phrase to the smaller girl. Paisley shook her head slowly.

"Just thinking, that is all," the small girl shrugged and turned back to making funny faces at Lucas before the couple could question her any further.

About an hour later, Lucas had managed to fall asleep on Paisley's stomach as she lay back on the carpet. Paisley herself had nearly dozed off when Maia knelt down and nudged her shoulder.

"Shiloh asked us to drive you home. Do you mind carrying him out to the car?" the small brunette asked, giving Paisley a soft smile.

Paisley nodded, sitting up carefully and holding the sleeping child against her chest. Maia extended a hand to help the girl to her feet, earning a thankful smile.

Carefully supporting Lucas with one arm, Paisley held her backpack with the other and followed Maia down the front steps of their small patio. She gently laid the sleeping baby in his car seat and managed to buckle him in without disturbing his slumber, which earned a congratulatory high five from Maia. As soon as Paisley slid into the passenger seat, both girls were on the road.

As they were driving, Paisley eyed Maia's hand that rested on the center console. Gently, she reached out, looking up at Maia for approval and slowly slipping the ring off of her finger. Paisley studied it in the light.

"That is a lot of money for such a little thing," Paisley laughed softly, sliding the ring back onto Maia's finger and sighing softly.

"Is there something you wanna talk about, Paisley?" Maia raised an eyebrow, pulling into their small neighborhood. Paisley shook her head, too nervous to make eye contact with the other girl.

"I'm only a text away, yeah?" Maia turned to Paisley after pulling into her driveway. Paisley nodded, giving her a thankful smile. She hopped out of the car, holding up a finger to signal for Maia to wait.

"Bye little dude," she giggled, circling around the back of the car and leaning in to say goodbye to Lucas. "Be quiet for your mommy tonight. I will be back to play soon," she laughed softly, kissing his forehead and smoothing out his hair.

"Thanks for hanging with us today, Paisley," Maia nodded, giving her a small wave as Paisley padded over to the front of her house. She made sure to avoid the broken step, waving as Maia backed out of the driveway.

Wolf immediately greeted Paisley at the door, rubbing against her legs and begging for attention. Before Paisley could bend down to pet him, Shiloh practically came sprinting into the foyer, grabbing Paisley's shoulders.

"You're not allowed inside yet," Shiloh shook her head. Paisley crinkled her nose, looking down at the striped apron her girlfriend had on. She couldn't help but giggle.

"Don't judge," Shiloh laughed, positioning Paisley on the front step. "Ring the doorbell," she raised an eyebrow, nodding towards the small button on the side of the house. "Do it," she laughed when she noticed Paisley's hesitation.

Paisley couldn't help but giggle at Shiloh's excitement. She reached up, gently pressing the doorbell. A melodic ringing noise echoed around the small house and Paisley's lips curved into a smile.

"It doesn't even scare Wolf," Shiloh nodded proudly, taking Paisley's hand and leading her into the house. "I bought two different ones and tested them out just in case. I also made dinner, which is... which is probably burning!" she realized, letting go of Paisley's hand and scrambling into the kitchen.

Paisley giggled, rolling her eyes playfully and following Shiloh into the kitchen. She watched as her girlfriend pulled a pan out of the oven, swatting the steam away with her free hand. Setting it on the stove, Shiloh turned to Paisley with a dorky smile on her face.

"Homemade pizza," Shiloh laughed softly, motioning towards the pan. Paisley couldn't help but smile, and she hurried forwards to plant a soft kiss on her girlfriend's lips.

"It is wonderful," Paisley said softly. "Lucas says hi, too," she nodded, making Shiloh laugh. "He fell asleep on me today," she added with a quiet giggle.

"How is the little booger?" Shiloh asked, stealing another kiss from Paisley before she turned back to the pan on the stove to cut the pizza into slices.

"He can almost walk on his own," Paisley nodded happily, leaning against the wall as Shiloh slid their food onto two plates. She took it upon herself to grab them two drinks from the fridge. "And he makes a lot of noises," she laughed.

Both girls sat in the middle of the living room, which was yet to have much furniture. Paisley didn't mind, though. She liked the open space. The sun streamed in through the windows and gave it an almost eerie calmness.

"You're beautiful."

Paisley furrowed her eyebrows, looking up at Shiloh with a mouthful of food. The green eyed girl couldn't help but laugh. She leaned over, brushing Paisley's tousled hair out of her face. "I mean it, y'know," she said softly.

Confused, Paisley tilted her head to the side.

"You're beautiful, Pais," Shiloh scooted forward and slid Paisley's beanie off of her head so she could run her fingers through her long hair. "I just wanna make sure you don't forget that," she whispered, slipping the light blue beanie back onto her head.

Paisley grew shy, looking down to hide how much she was blushing. She mumbled a thank you, which made Shiloh laugh softly.

"One day, I want you to be able to look in a mirror and say 'I'm beautiful, and no one's gonna tell me otherwise'," Shiloh nodded, reaching out and squeezing Paisley's shoulder.

"One day," Paisley laughed softly. She looked up slowly, studying Shiloh when the girl wasn't paying attention. "Do you know, Lo?" Paisley whispered, tilting her head to the side.

"Hm?" Shiloh looked up, wiping her mouth and giving Paisley a look of confusion.

"You are beautiful, too," Paisley nodded. She giggled when Shiloh's face grew as red as hers had. "Everything, Lo. Every single thing about you," Paisley pushed her plate aside and scooted forwards so she could gently run her fingers over Shiloh's cheek.

"You know what?" Paisley furrowed her eyebrows, coming up with a sudden revelation. She didn't want for Shiloh to answer. "You are like a good book, Lo." She couldn't help but laugh when she saw confusion spread across Shiloh's face.

"Stay here," Paisley nodded once, scrambling to her feet and running into the bedroom. Moments later, she reemerged with a book in her hands. Paisley knelt back down in front of Shiloh and set the book inbetween them.

"This is a very good book," Paisley nodded softly, running her fingers over the red and gold embellished cover. "But it is not because the cover is pretty." She shook her head.

Paisley opened the book slowly and traced her fingers over the small words. "It is good because of what is inside. The words and the lessons. That is what matters, Lo," she slid the book forwards in front of Shiloh.

"Where do you get this from?" Shiloh laughed softly, placing a hand on the book and looking up at Paisley. "I feel like you've done this whole 'life' thing a few times before. There's too much wisdom in that lil' body of yours," she smiled, reaching out and lacing their fingers together.

"Can we go for a walk?" Paisley asked softly, looking out the window. "The sky is golden."

"Sure," Shiloh laughed, grabbing their plates and bringing them into the kitchen. Paisley smiled, padding over to the front door so she could tug on her shoes.

"Loooo," Paisley giggled, holding one of her feet up and looking at Shiloh hopefully.

Rolling her eyes, Shiloh bent down to tie her girlfriend's shoes. "I told you I can teach you how to do it on your own," Shiloh looked up at her, but Paisley simply giggled and shook her head.

"I like it when you do it," Paisley crinkled her nose. Shiloh ruffled her hair playfully before slipping her own shoes on and heading out the front door. Paisley fixed her beanie, hurrying to catch up with Shiloh.

"Wolf can come too," Paisley nodded, holding the door open for the fluffy white cat.

"Paisley! He's not gonna f-," Shiloh was cut off when Paisley padded towards her, Wolf sticking right by her side.

"What was that?" Paisley smirked, raising an eyebrow at her girlfriend. Shiloh just rolled her eyes playfully.

They continued their walk with Wolf right by Paisley's side, leaning against her leg for guidance most of the time. Paisley ended up carrying him part of the way back when he lay down on the sidewalk and refused to move.

Once they got back to the apartment, both girls were exhausted. They now lay in bed, staring up at the ceiling in comfortable silence.

"I like this," Paisley whispered, blinking a few times to let her eyes adjust to the darkness. "It just feels right."

"It's meant to be," Shiloh laughed softly. She pulled Paisley into her side, feeling the small girl lock their pinkies together and snake her free hand up her sleeve.

"Sing?" Paisley whispered, looking up at Shiloh hopefully.

"Only for you," Shiloh whispered.

Shiloh smiled softly when she realized Paisley was already asleep. Or so she thought. The green eyed girl lay her head back and allowed sleep to wash over her.

It was only when Shiloh was awoken by the distant rumbling of thunder that she realized something was missing. Paisley.

C H A P T E R ' 7

Shiloh walked slowly down the hallway towards the soft whispers she had heard. Peering into the living room, she blinked a few times as lightning flicked through the home and lit it up for a few moments.

The scene in front of her was almost angelic. Paisley sat in the middle of the room, clad only in her underwear and what Shiloh made out to be one of her sheer white blouses. She couldn't help but smile when she realized Paisley must have just grabbed the first item of clothing she found to throw overtop of her sports bra.

Besides the glow of the moon though their windows, the only other thing lighting up the room was the dull light coming from the laptop placed in front of Paisley. The small girl mumbled something under her breath, gently pushing Wolf away when he tried to gain her attention.

Shiloh raised an eyebrow, taking a few steps out from behind the hallway to make her presence known. Paisley, however, was too focused on the task at hand to notice the green eyed girl until her soft voice filled the room.

"What'cha up to?" Shiloh whispered, kneeling down next to her girlfriend. Paisley gasped, her hands immediately grabbing the laptop and turning away from Shiloh.

"Nothing," Paisley whispered. She looked up at her girlfriend nervously. "Why are you awake?"

"I could ask you the same thing," Shiloh said quietly, concern laced in her words. "Is something wrong? Did the storm wake you up?"

Paisley shook her head, looking down at the laptop screen anxiously. "You should go to bed," she whispered. Shiloh tilted her head to the side.

"What's going on?" Shiloh asked, suddenly becoming more concerned. She scooted forwards to try to see the laptop but Paisley quickly moved it once more. Shiloh raised an eyebrow.

"Nothing," Paisley shook her head once more. It was then that the green eyed girl saw tears forming in the younger girl's eyes, threatening to spill over.

Paisley grew confused when Shiloh quietly got to her feet and disappeared out of the room. She quickly turned back to the laptop, wiping her eyes and trying to focus through her blurred vision.

It was only when she heard footsteps reproaching that she looked up to find Shiloh kneeling next to her, placing two glass on the hardwood floor.

"Let's talk," Shiloh nodded softly, taking the bottle of wine Ryland had given them out from under her arm. She poured a small amount in each of the glasses, gently sliding one to Paisley. "What's got you up this late?"

Paisley studied the glass, cautiously wrapping her fingers around it and bringing it to her lips. Shiloh watched as the small girl took a sip, running her tongue over her teeth a few times to capture the taste. The green eyed girl breathed a sigh of relief once Paisley lifted her glass for another sip.

"It is nothing, Lo," Paisley shook her head, swallowing the lump in her throat. Shiloh gave her a look that only Paisley understood. A look that said 'I know better than to believe that.'

Gently, Shiloh reached out and placed one hand on the laptop, looking up at Paisley for approval. When the small girl simply hung her head down, Shiloh slid the laptop in front of her and leaned down to study the screen.

"What is this?" Shiloh tilted her head to the side. She set her wine down and moved the cursor around the screen. "Surveys?" The girl looked up at Paisley, who was hanging her head down guiltily. "I don't understand," Shiloh said softly.

"I need money," Paisley whispered, almost inaudibly. Shiloh almost didn't catch the small girl's words, but when she did, she grew even more confused.

"Money for what?" Shiloh asked. "We have money. We both just started jobs."

"I need a lot of money," Paisley said softly, shaking her head. Shiloh raised an eyebrow.

"Well I hate to break it to you but online surveys aren't gonna make you a lot of money anytime soon, goofball," Shiloh laughed softly. She instantly regretted it, though, because moments later Paisley let out a frustrated sigh and brought her hands up to wipe her eyes once more.

"No, baby, I didn't mean to upset you," Shiloh quickly shook her head, shutting the laptop and pushing it aside so she could wrap an arm around her girlfriend. "I'm just trying to figure out why you think you need money."

"I need..." Paisley took a deep breath, shaking her head and looking down at her hands in her lap. "I need a ring."

"A ring?" Shiloh asked, tilting her head to the side. Things started to fall into place when Paisley stole a shy glance at her and nodded. "A ring... for what?" Shiloh watched as Paisley's eyes widened and she looked back down.

"For something," Paisley mumbled. Shiloh sighed, reaching out and taking Paisley's hand in hers.

"You know we can talk about anything, Pais. Anything," Shiloh emphasized her words. A vague idea of what Paisley had been doing was forming in her head, but she wanted to hear Paisley say it first.

"I..." Paisley couldn't help but laugh nervously. She shook her head and looked down. "I wanna..."

"Say it, Pais," Shiloh squeezed her hand, feeling a mixture of confusion and excitement.

"I want to marry you," Paisley whispered, the words finally spilling off of the tip of her tongue. She didn't dare to look up at Shiloh. She was scared of how her girlfriend would react.

"You could've just said that in the first place," Shiloh giggled, which took Paisley by surprise. She looked up, finding the green eyed girl with a shy smile on her face. Shiloh was thankful it was dark so Paisley couldn't see how badly she was blushing.

"You're serious, though?" Shiloh asked softly, tilting her head to the side. "You really want to... you know?"

Paisley nodded, but let out a soft sigh. "I am sorry," she mumbled, looking down at the ground. Seeing Shiloh's excitement only made it worse for her.

"Sorry for what?" Shiloh furrowed her eyebrows in concern.

"I can not get a sparkly ring," Paisley shook her head, letting her hair fall somewhat in front of her face. "I can not get a beautiful dress or lots of flowers or-,"

She was cut off by Shiloh, who squeezed her hand and pressed a finger against her lips to silence her. "Pais," she laughed softly and shook her head. "All that stuff? It doesn't matter," she brushed her hair out of her face.

"But they said..." Paisley whispered. Shiloh shook her head.

"It doesn't matter what they say, Paisley. It never does. You know what matters?" Shiloh reached out, tilting Paisley's chin up so she could see the smaller girl's face. "What we say. That's all that matters."

"And you know what we say when we get married? For better or for worse, for rich or for poor," Shiloh cupped Paisley's cheek, running her thumb across the smooth skin.

"If you want to get married, I'm not gonna let some stupid ring stop that from happening. Money doesn't buy love."

Paisley looked up when the realization washed over her, a shy smile on her face. "So we can do it, then?"

"Get... get married?" Shiloh laughed softly, still somewhat in shock that Paisley wanted something like that. Paisley nodded softly. "Are you sure?"

Paisley giggled, nodding once more. "Yes, I am sure," she rolled her eyes jokingly. "I would not say it if I was not." She couldn't help but laugh when Shiloh just stared at her in disbelief.

"I mean it, Lo," she laughed softly, crawling forwards and sitting directly in front of Shiloh. She cupped her face, forcing the other girl to look her in the eyes.

"If it is not about the ring, or the fancy dress, then it is just about love, right? We have that, Lo," Paisley nodded softly. "It will not change anything, right? It only... it only brings us together, right?"

"Right," Shiloh whispered. Paisley had a way of taking the most complex situations and breaking them down into the simplest ideas. It was one of the many things Shiloh loved about her.

"So you really want to get married?" Shiloh asked, a nervous smile on her face. Paisley bit her lip.

"Do you?" Paisley whispered.

"It would be an honor to be your wife, Paisley Lowe," Shiloh whispered, leaning in and placing a kiss on the bridge of her girlfriend's nose.

"That is it?" Paisley giggled. "You and me?"

"Me and you, goofball," Shiloh laughed, excitement bubbling in her stomach. Paisley smiled widely and leaned in to connect their lips in a soft yet passionate kiss.

Once the kiss pulled away, Paisley couldn't contain the excited smile on her face. "We are getting married, Lo," she whispered, bursting into laughter moments later.

Shiloh giggled and stood up. Paisley furrowed her eyebrows, watching as the girl retrieved her phone and scrolled through it for a few moments.

"We have to practice for our first dance, right?" Shiloh smiled softly, setting her phone down and turning up the volume. Paisley's eyes widened when she recognized the song.

"C'mere," Shiloh laughed, holding out her hands and helping Paisley to her feet. "Do you know how to dance?"

"No," Paisley giggled, shaking her head and looking away shyly.

"Hey, hey, it's okay," Shiloh laughed, taking Paisley's hands and placing them on her shoulders. "Just follow my lead, yeah?" she gently laid her hands on Paisley's waist and slowly guided her torso to move in time with her own.

"I love you," Shiloh whispered. Paisley nodded, wrapping her arms further around Shiloh's neck and closing the gap between them. Their lips met, making butterflies erupt in Shiloh's stomach. There was something different about this kiss, as if it was sealing the deal.

"C'mon, goofball," Shiloh laughed, bending down and scooping Paisley up into her arms. The smaller girl giggled when Shiloh carried her into the bedroom and laid her back on the bed. With a heavy sigh, Shiloh collapsed on her back next to the girlfriend.

"We are getting married," Paisley giggled. She couldn't get enough of those words. "I love you. I want to spend the rest of my life with you. Forever and ever and ever," she rolled on her side so she could face Shiloh.

"Lo?" Paisley whispered, suddenly feeling nervous. There was something different in the air. She couldn't put a name to it, thought. Shiloh sat up slightly, sensing the change.

"Can I kiss you?" Paisley asked softly, scooting forward and feeling her breathing slow down. Shiloh nodded, their faces only inches apart. "Okay," Paisley whispered. "I am going to kiss you now," she reached up to cup Shiloh's cheek, closing the gap between them.

C H A P T E R   8

Shiloh woke up the next morning when she felt Wolf rubbing his face against hers, making the green eyed girl crinkle her nose and blink her eyes open in confusion. She laughed softly, rolling over and coming face to face with a sleeping Paisley. Her lips curved into a smile when she saw the smaller girl's nose twitch slightly.

She reached out, cupping Paisley's cheek and running her thumb over the girl's smooth skin. Studying the girl's peaceful face, Shiloh moved her hand up to comb her fingers through her girlfriend's hair.

She pulled away when the girl's eyes fluttered open. Paisley whimpered, giving Shiloh a sleepy smile and reaching out to move the green eyed girl's hand back to her hair. Shiloh couldn't help but laugh when Paisley sighed contently and sank back down into her pillow.

"M'not gonna play with your hair all morning," Shiloh whispered, making Paisley laugh softly. The small girl opened her eyes once more, reaching up to cover her mouth before yawning softly. She rolled onto her back, staring up at the ceiling and humming contently.

"How'd you sleep?" Shiloh asked, scooting next to her and draping her arm across the smaller girl's stomach. Paisley giggled and turned her head to look at Shiloh, who crinkled her nose playfully.

"Really good," Paisley admitted, her cheeks turning slightly red. Shiloh raised an eyebrow at her.

"Yeah?" the green eyed girl laughed. She lifted her head, planting a kiss to Paisley's temple. "And why was that?" What Shiloh had intended as a playful question instead caused Paisley to sit up slightly, furrowing her eyebrows in thought.

"I sleep a lot better now," Paisley nodded softly, pursing her lips. "I think... I think it is because I feel... safe. Or comforted. I can not explain it. It is like with you, nothing can hurt me. So when I sleep, there are no worries to keep me awake. Does that make sense?"

Shiloh couldn't wipe the smile from her face, because it was the exact same way that she felt. "It makes perfect sense," she smiled. Just as she was about to lay her head back down, both girls' attention was caught by the sound of meowing coming from the doorway. Paisley giggled when Shiloh groaned, sitting up and facing the culprit, who impatiently pawed at the carpet in front of him.

"You're worse than Paisley when it comes to food," Shiloh muttered. The small girl beside her huffed, sitting up and giving her girlfriend a playful glare.

"Okay, fine, make me feed the child," Shiloh teased, crinkling her nose at Paisley before swinging her legs off the bed and following an eager Wolf into the kitchen.

"You just have to have your food, don't you?" Shiloh mumbled, looking at the cat who sat perched expectantly on the counter. The green eyed girl laughed to herself as she placed his bowl in front of him.

Shiloh took a few minutes to make herself a cup of coffee, leaning against the counter and gazing out the window.

She used to hate mornings. But when she met Paisley, it was practically impossible to sleep in with the energetic girl constantly getting into trouble. And then, she found herself growing to love mornings. She loved the peaceful silence. It was like a new beginning each time, setting the tone for the rest of her day. And mornings were always wonderful with Paisley by her side.

She wasn't even surprised when she heard soft footsteps behind her, feeling a pair of small arms wrap around her waist. Paisley laid her head in the crook of Shiloh's neck, humming softly. Shiloh couldn't help but set her coffee down and spin around so she could place her hands on the smaller girl's shoulders.

"We're getting married," Shiloh whispered, watching as Paisley's eyes glimmered in the golden sunlight streaming in through the windows. "I'd kiss you but I need to brush my teeth," she added with a soft giggle.

"Me too," Paisley crinkled her nose, quickly pecking Shiloh's cheek before disappearing into the bathroom. Meanwhile, Shiloh grabbed two bananas from the pantry, figuring they'd work for breakfast.

Soon enough, Paisley had convinced Shiloh to sit on the back porch while they ate. The small girl laid back on the porch swing, her head in Shiloh's lap so she could gaze up at the sky.

"We are getting married," Paisley giggled, breaking the comfortable silence between them. Shiloh raised an eyebrow and glanced down at her.

"You've said that like ten times this morning," the older girl laughed, absentmindedly running her fingers through Paisley's hair.

"That is because I am excited," Paisley laughed and gazed up at Shiloh, studying her face. "It still does not seem real, Lo. It seems like it is a dream. Is it like that for you?"

"A little," Shiloh nodded softly. "It's not a bad feeling, though."

"No, of course not," Paisley shook her head and sighed contently. "I just do not want to wake up."

"Me neither," Shiloh giggled, leaning down and kissing the bridge of Paisley's nose. "Tell you what, if somehow, somewhere, this is all a dream…. we've got to promise to find each other again when we wake up, yeah?" she held up her pinkie in front of Paisley, who locked their fingers without hesitation.

"What is meant to be, will be," Paisley nodded simply. Moments later, she realized what she had just said. Her eyes shot open and she sat up quickly, looking at Shiloh with wide eyes.

"My mom used to say that," Paisley whispered in disbelief. Shiloh tilted her head to the side and she bit her lip.

This would still happen every so often. Small details of Paisley's past would suddenly lace themselves into her memory once more, making themselves known in moments such as this. They always seemed to take the smaller girl by surprise.

Shiloh reached out, gently taking Paisley's hand in her own. There was no telling how the smaller girl would react. Luckily, Shiloh was able to let out the breath she had been holding when Paisley laughed softly.

"What's meant to be, will be," Shiloh whispered. "I like that."

"Me too," Paisley nodded. Her face slowly fell when a sudden realization washed over her. She pulled her legs underneath her and let her head hang down.

"What's on your mind?" Shiloh asked quietly. Paisley brushed her hair out of her face and shrugged.

"I just wish they could have been here for all of this. They never got to meet you… they will never get to meet our kids…" Paisley sighed.

"Woah, woah, who said we're having kids?" Shiloh laughed, raising an eyebrow. She instantly regretted it when Paisley quickly shook her head and looked down. "Hey, Pais, I was joking," she sighed, scooting closer to the girl.

"They will never see us get married," Paisley whispered. Shiloh sighed softly leaned over, resting her head on Paisley's shoulder.

"That's kind of a bummer, huh?" Shiloh said quietly. Paisley nodded, leaning her head against Shiloh's. The green eyed girl ran her thumb over Paisley's hand.

"You know how you said they never got to meet me?" Shiloh asked after a few moments of silence. Paisley lifted her head slightly, nodding.

"Well, at least I got to meet them," Shiloh shrugged softly.

"But-," Paisley opened her mouth to speak but Shiloh raised a finger to tell her to wait.

"I mean, obviously not in person," Shiloh continued, reaching out and resting her arm across Paisley's shoulders. "But though a person, yeah. I've met them countless times through you."

"I see how you always try so hard not to hum along to a song, but you always fail," Shiloh laughed softly. "They gave you a love of music."

"Your dad taught you how to hold a paintbrush the right way, I can tell," Shiloh nodded softly. "There's some things that even an accident of your caliber can't take away from us."

"But most importantly, I see the compassion they instilled in you. I see the way your eyes light up whenever you have an idea, I see the way you struggle to sit still when you're looking forward to something, I see the way your eyebrows twitch slightly when you're thinking really hard about something," she reached up and teasingly poked the girl's eyebrow. "I see how much they loved you, because I see the way you constantly give love without asking for anything in return.

"So yeah, I've met them. And they're pretty fucking incredible people, even if the only notable thing they ever did in their lives was raise you," Shiloh nodded.

"And if it means something to you, we'll tie a wedding invitation on a balloon and send it up to them," Shiloh whispered with a soft laugh. Paisley smiled shyly, nuzzling her head into the crook of Shiloh's neck.

"Y'know, I think there's two other people that would like to hear the news, though..." Shiloh looked down at Paisley, a small smirk playing on her face.

At first, Paisley furrowed her eyebrows in confusion. But the moment it hit her, she hopped to her feet and smiled widely. She held up a finger to signal for Shiloh to wait before hurrying back inside.

Shiloh watched as Wolf strolled out the open door, immediately finding a sunny spot in the grass and sprawling out contently. Shiloh couldn't help but roll her eyes.

A minute or so later, Paisley reappeared holding her bright yellow iPhone. Laughing softly, the small girl quickly reassumed her position next to her girlfriend and glanced up at her for approval before beginning a Facetime call with Shiloh's parents.

Paisley quickly handed the phone over to Shiloh when it started ringing, growing shy. Shiloh giggled and switched the camera on them. She held her arm out, raising her eyebrows at Paisley nervously when it began connecting.

"Hey, what's up?" Matthew immediately answered. "Oh, hey Paisley." The smaller girl waved shyly.

"Is mom there?" Shiloh asked, running a hand through her hair.

"Uh, yeah, I think she's down here," Matthew nodded and glanced at the door behind him. "Why? Is everything alright?"

"Yeah," Shiloh laughed nervously, stealing a shy glance at her girlfriend. "Can you get her? We have something to tell you."

"Uh oh," he laughed, grimacing. "Is it bad?"

"Daaaad," Shiloh whined, making Paisley giggle next to her. "Just get mom. Please."

"Colette?!" he yelled, setting the camera down for a moment. Shiloh took the opportunity to lean over and press a quick kiss to Paisley's cheek. The smaller girl blushed, immediately moving her hands up to hide her face when Shiloh's father picked up his phone once again.

"What's going on?" Colette leaned over Matthew's shoulder, looking into the camera. "Are you girls okay? Did something happen? Is there a-?"

"Mom, mom, we're fine, I promise," Shiloh laughed, pulling Paisley into our side. "But we do have something to tell you..." She glanced at Paisley, winking subtly and then making a pouty face. Paisley got the message, containing her laughter and quickly letting her face fall. Shiloh turned back to the camera and sighed, feigning nervousness.

"Oh god, what is it?" Colette looked at Matthew worriedly. Shiloh could tell by the way Paisley was drumming her fingers on her knee that she was struggling to keep her poker face. "Shiloh, are you guys okay?"

"I guess we should just say it," Shiloh sighed, turning to Paisley and nudging her playfully out of the camera frame. The smaller girl nodded slowly. "Here it goes..." Shiloh mumbled, squeezing Paisley's hand and tapping the back of her palm to count down.

"Shiloh, you've g-,"

"We're getting married," Both girls blurted out at the same time. Paisley only made it halfway though, though, before practically choking on thin air.

"Oh my god, are you okay?" Shiloh laughed, forgetting about her phone for a moment and turning to Paisley, who was still coughing into her elbow.

The small brunette nodded, hitting her chest a few times before bursting into laughter. "I-I think a bug flew into my mouth," she giggled, swatting her hair out of her face.

"Shiloh Michelle!"

Both girls immediately froze and Shiloh clamped her mouth shut, widening her eyes as she slowly picked up the phone in her lap. "Yeah?"

"You're getting married?!" Shiloh winced, unable to decipher her mother's reaction.

"I... Yeah," Shiloh gulped. She felt Paisley take her hand and looked over at the smaller girl, who looked just as anxious as she was.

"I told you!"

Shiloh practically dropped the phone when her father stood up from his chair, leaving the phone propped up on his desk. She inhaled sharply.

"That's no fair!" Colette huffed, shaking her head.

"What's not fair?" Shiloh bit her lip. Matthew burst into laughter, clapping his hands together and giving his wife a smug smile.

"She thought you guys would tie the knot after this year. But I told her that you guys were too in love to wait," he nodded proudly. "And who was right?" Matthew turned to his wife. "Me," he smirked.

Shiloh and Paisley both exchanged glances before letting out relieved sighs. It was only then that Wolf looked up from his spot in the grass, wondering what all the commotion was about.

"We're so happy for you two," Colette smiled, turning back to the camera. "We really are. I think marriage will suit you both quite nicely," she laughed. Matthew nodded in agreement.

"I love you," Paisley whispered, leaning her head on Shiloh's shoulder and smiling contently. She let her eyes wander out to the yard, taking in the golden glow of the morning and feeling her heart flutter. Everything was falling into place.

CHAPTER 9

"Don't be so nervous," Shiloh laughed, watching as Paisley continued to try and stack the envelopes perfectly in her lap.

It had been about a week since the girls had first told Shiloh's parents that they were getting married. Since then, things had begun falling into place. After talking about it, both girls decided they were eager to just get married and get on with their lives.

A small, intimate wedding sounded just right to them. After some discussion with Shiloh's parents, Paisley now held a stack of pastel yellow envelopes in her lap, running her fingers over Shiloh's cursive handwriting on the front.

The girls had already sent out invitations to a few of Shiloh's close family members. Now, all that was left was the handful of envelopes in Paisley's lap, with the names of their closest friends scrawled on top.

They'd yet to tell their friends, simply because they wanted to be able to present them with the invitations in person. So now, both girls sat in the parking lot of their old apartment complex, trying to work up the courage to go inside.

"Right back at you," Paisley mumbled, a shy smile playing on her lips. Both girls were waiting for the other to get out of the car, too nervous to make the first move.

"Why are we so nervous?" Shiloh laughed, turning to the smaller girl who was fiddling with her cracked yellow nail polish. Paisley looked up and studied the building in front of them.

"I am excited," she nodded softly. "But I am also nervous. Do you think they are going to be surprised?" The small girl looked over at Shiloh curiously.

"I honestly have no clue," Shiloh laughed softly, checking the time. "Are you sure that Leah's in there?"

"Ryland said she was making her come over to make them lunch," Paisley giggled, holding up her phone to show Shiloh.

"Might as well get it over with," Shiloh laughed softly, squeezing Paisley's hand before sliding out of the car. The smaller girl fiddled with the invitations in her hands as they waited for the elevator to reach the top floor.

Paisley followed Shiloh down the hallway, exchanging glances with the girl once they reached the apartment and she didn't make a move to knock on the door. Giggling, Paisley reached out, walking straight into the apartment without bothering to knock.

"That's one way to do it," Shiloh mumbled under her breath, causing Paisley to giggle. They exchanged glances when the living room was empty. Paisley smirked, hearing voices coming from the kitchen.

Before Shiloh could stop her, the smaller girl was tiptoeing quickly around the corner. Shiloh caught up to her just in time to witness Paisley jumping onto Ryland's back and throwing her arms over the girl's shoulders.

"Holy shit!" Ryland gasped, turning around and trying to shake the intruder off of her. When she heard Paisley giggle and saw Shiloh standing across the room, she let out a relieved sigh and brought her hand to her heart.

"Oh my god, don't ever do that again," Ryland unlocked Paisley's arms from around her neck as the smaller girl hopped back down to the ground. "Wait, what the hell are you guys doing here?"

Paisley's eyes immediately widened and she quickly took her spot back beside Shiloh. The green eyed girl elbowed her, giving her a look that feigned playful annoyance. "Uh, where's Nessa and Leah?" Shiloh bit her lip.

"They're out on the balcony. What's up?" Ryland placed a hand on her hip, noticing the girl's nervousness.

"Can you go get them?" Shiloh ran a hand through her hair. Paisley glanced up at her, struggling to hold back an excited smile.

"We have a surprise," the smaller girl added. Ryland raised an eyebrow at the couple, but made her way around the back of the apartment to get the other two girls.

Pretty soon, all five best friends sat in the living room. Vanessa, Leah, and Ryland were all squished onto the couch, while Shiloh sat in the small chair with Paisley perched precariously on the arm rest.

"You're not like... dying, right?" Leah asked, genuine concern spreading across her face. Paisley couldn't help but giggle, shaking her head and looking over at Shiloh once more. She had the envelopes tucked in the large pocket of her hoodie, waiting for the right moment to reveal them to her former roommates.

"Nope. We're perfectly healthy," Shiloh laughed. Ryland cocked her head to the side, while Vanessa just stared at them in confusion.

Paisley took this as the perfect opportunity, looking at Shiloh for approval before hopping to her feet and padding over to the couch. She pulled the envelopes out, quickly handing the correct one to each girl. Biting her lip nervously, the small girl hurried back over to Shiloh's side.

"What is this? The stone age?" Ryland laughed, holding up the envelope. "Why didn't you just text us?"

"Who even sends letters anym—?" Vanessa began, but was cut off when Leah squealed and startled the other girls. The oldest girl hopped up from the couch, crossing the room in record time and practically tackling the girls into a hug.

"The fuck?" Ryland and Vanessa both exchanged confused glances before racing to get their envelopes open. Moments later, Vanessa's jaw practically dropped to the ground and Ryland gasped, bringing the card up closer to her face to make sure she'd read it correctly.

"Falling!" Paisley squealed, suddenly losing her balance on the arm of the couch and stumbling backwards. Luckily, she caught herself before she fell to the ground, but by the time Vanessa and Ryland caught up to her and wrapped her in a hug, she tripped over her own two feet and ended up sending all three of them down to the ground.

Paisley burst into laughter, allowing Ryland to help her back up to her feet. She glanced over at Shiloh, who was still being held in a tight hug by Leah. When the girl pulled away, Vanessa and Ryland immediately wrapped Shiloh in a hug while Leah held her arms out for Paisley.

After the five girls finally pulled away, Shiloh and Paisley stole a quick glance at one another. Paisley giggled giddily, looking shyly down at the ground.

"I can't believe it's been almost four years," Vanessa laughed, shaking her head. "I never would have seen this coming if you told me four years ago, that's for sure." Paisley blushed, scooting closer to Shiloh and leaning against her girlfriend.

"What's going on with the wedding?" Vanessa asked, picking up the invitation and studying it once more.

"It's in Miami. We're just doing a small little ceremony in my parent's backyard. Nothing too fancy," Shiloh shrugged, pulling Paisley into her side.

"We'll be there," Ryland nodded, pulling Shiloh into another hug. "Look at us, growing up and shit," she laughed and crinkled her nose. "Pretty soon you'll be popping out babies."

Paisley's eyes widened, remembering her conversation with Maia and Toby. She decided on keeping her mouth shut, though, knowing the reaction she had earned from her other friends.

"Let's just focus on one thing at a time," Shiloh laughed, squeezing Paisley's arm when she noticed the smaller girl stiffen. "Now all we have to do is find you two dates and then we can all get married and wreck havoc in suburban New York," she teased, winking at Vanessa and Ryland.

The five girls ended up going out to lunch together, which turned into Vanessa, Ryland, and Leah all gushing about how romantic their wedding was going to be. Both girls couldn't seem to keep the smiles off of their faces.

Now, both girls were in the car once more, headed back home. Well, at least to their home town. They had two more envelopes to deliver, which Paisley had resting neatly in her lap.

"Why were we nervous for that?" Paisley laughed softly, drumming her fingers on her lap and looking over at her girlfriend. Shiloh shrugged, crinkling her nose at the smaller girl.

"Now telling Maia and Toby should be easy, yeah?" Shiloh raised an eyebrow. Paisley considered this for a moment, looking down at the cards in her lap before shaking her head.

"No. I am still nervous," she confessed, making Shiloh laugh softly. At the same time, they both reached for each others hands. Both girls exchanged glances, causing Paisley to giggle shyly when Shiloh laced their fingers together.

Soon enough, both girls were parked in front of Maia and Toby's house. Paisley suddenly gained an idea, quickly handing the cards to Shiloh.

"We have to get them back," Paisley giggled, clapping her hands together. When Maia and Toby had gotten pregnant with Lucas, they had pulled a prank on the other couple to inform them of their engagement.

Paisley and Shiloh had been sitting in art class when Toby came in, feigning anger. He had given them a long, made up story about how Maia had found out she was pregnant and practically fled the state. Both girls had been in shock, and Paisley was nearly in tears until Maia jumped out behind them, causing Paisley to actually start crying tears of relief.

Since then, the couple had always joked about getting revenge on them. And now was the perfect time. Shiloh watched in confusion as Paisley grabbed a water bottle and poured a few drops onto her palm, before dotting small tear sized amounts around her eyes. The smaller girl then proceeded to rub her eyes a few times to make it appear as she had been crying.

"Someone's been planning this," Shiloh laughed softly when Paisley studied her reflection in the window and jutted out her bottom lip slightly.

"Come on," Paisley whispered, hopping out of the car and motioning for Shiloh to follow her. "You stay here," she grabbed Shiloh's hand, making her duck down next to the door so she couldn't be seen.

"What are y—?" Shiloh quickly clamped her jaw shut when Paisley pressed a finger up to her lips. The small girl took a deep breath before knocking softly on the door.

Paisley quickly hung her head down when she heard footsteps approaching the door. A few seconds later, the door was pulled open slightly. Maia peered out, opening the door more when she saw Paisley.

"Paisley?" Maia asked softly, noticing the girl's composure. "Is something wrong?" She pushed the door wide open, balancing Lucas on her hip.

"L-lo left," Paisley whispered, trying to hide the smile that was threatening to play at her lips. Shiloh watched from her hiding spot, feeling her heart ache at how genuinely sad Paisley sounded.

"She what?" Maia tried to hide her shock, not wanting to startle Paisley any more. The smaller girl nodded, squeezing her eyes shut.

"We broke up," Paisley mumbled, shaking her head and looking down. "She... she left this," she added, reaching into the pocket of her hoodie and willing herself not to ruin it. The smaller girl slowly handed the envelope to Maia, which she had already ripped open before to make it more believable.

"Oh my god..." Maia whispered. She quickly handed Lucas off to Toby, who had appeared behind her. Paisley bit her lip, watching as the other girl slipped the card out of the envelope.

"What the...?" Maia narrowed her eyes, leaning in to study the words closer. "Oh my god!" she gasped, the card falling out of her hands. It was only then that Paisley broke character, bursting into laughter and clapping her hands together.

"You're getting married?!" Maia asked in disbelief. Paisley nodded furiously, a wide smile on her face. "Where's Shiloh?"

Moments later, the green eyed girl slipped out from her hiding spot with a playful smirk on her face. Paisley high fived her, leaning into her side and smiling proudly. "Got you," the smaller girl teased, crinkling her nose.

"You're really getting married?" Maia asked in disbelief. Toby jogged back into the room after putting Lucas in his swing, just as shocked as Maia was.

"In Miami," Shiloh nodded softly. "We don't expect you guys to be there because of the baby and work and stuff, but we just figured we'd let you know in person," she laughed when Toby gave them a playful glare.

"Okay, we kind of deserved that," Toby admitted, rolling his eyes. Maia pulled them both into a hug.

When the hug pulled away, Paisley sniffed, bringing her hands up to wipe her eyes. Shiloh grew confused when she saw the tears on her girlfriend's face.

"Wait, Pais, are you actually crying?" Shiloh asked, concern laced in her voice. Paisley bit her lip, nodding softly.

"I do not like thinking about you leaving," she admitted, looking up at her girlfriend. "Even if it is fake."

"I don't think you're gonna have to worry about that," Shiloh pulled the girl into her side and kissed her cheek. "We're getting married. You can't get rid of me that easy, goofball." She couldn't help the red blush of her cheeks when she felt Paisley giggle softly beside her.

C H A P T E R   1 0

"Psst. Lo," Paisley whispered, peering her head out from the door across the hallway. She bit her lip, awaiting a response from her girlfriend.

"What?" Shiloh's voice rang out from the opposite room. She moved closer to the door, fumbling with the hem of her dress.

"Can you braid my hair?" Paisley giggled shyly.

"I thought it was bad luck if we see each other before the wedding?" Shiloh called out, setting her curling iron down and moving towards the mirror to gently comb her fingers through her hair.

It had only been a few weeks, but everything had fallen together so quickly. Now, both girls were in Miami, accompanied by their three best friends. Currently, Paisley and Shiloh were getting changed in separate rooms. Downstairs, a handful of their closest family and friends were waiting patiently for the wedding to begin.

The girls hadn't wanted anything big. In fact, they had originally planned to simply get eloped and then have a small celebration with their family. But Shiloh's parents had convinced them to have a small ceremony in the backyard.

The small white archway with flowery vines running up the sides sat in front of a few rows of white wooden chairs, all thanks to Shiloh's father. When the girls had first seen the simple setup, Paisley couldn't stop talking about how perfect it was.

They'd finally managed to get their three former roommates to leave them alone so they could finish getting ready. Ryland and Vanessa had deemed themselves the couple's personal stylists for the day, while Leah was downstairs helping set up the small table of refreshments.

"You really believe that?" Paisley giggled and rolled her eyes. She was aching to see her fiancé, wishing that the girl would just open her door.

"I dunno," Shiloh laughed, taking one last look at herself in the mirror. "Wait, what do you need again?"

"I wanted you to braid my hair..." Paisley laughed shyly. "You know, the fancy way that you do it." The small girl opened her door even more, frustrated that Shiloh was still in the closed bedroom across the hall.

"Just give me a second!" Shiloh called out, hurrying over to the other side of the room and digging though her suitcase until she found the small white flower crown she had brought with her. She carefully placed it atop her head, fixing her hair in the mirror one more time before making her way over to the door.

"Opening the door in 3..." Shiloh warned, smiling when she heard Paisley giggle on the other side. "Two...." She gripped the door handle, slowly turning it open. "One..." she whispered, stepping out into the hallway and instantly having her breath taken away when she saw Paisley.

The smaller girl wore a simple white sundress, which flowed down to her knees. She looked like an angel, Shiloh realized as she scanned her up and down. When she met Paisley's eyes once more, she realized the smaller girl was staring at her in exactly the same manner.

Shiloh had opted for a white romper, and Vanessa had insisted upon one with subtle lace embellishments. She'd curled her hair, simply allowing it to hang freely with the small flower crown on top of her head.

"We are getting married," Paisley finally breathed out in disbelief, smiling shyly. "Wow."

Shiloh laughed, moving forwards and brushing Paisley's hair out of her face. "You want me to braid it?" she asked softly, which earned a nod from the smaller girl.

The green eyed girl led her over to the bed, making her sit down so she could kneel behind her and run her fingers through her hair. Paisley shivered, glancing at their reflection in the mirror.

"You nervous?" Shiloh asked, leaning over to grab a brush from the nightstand. She gently began separating Paisley's hair into sections, brushing through it a few times before starting a simple French braid at the top of her head.

"Nope," Paisley shook her head slightly. Shiloh raised an eyebrow.

"You aren't?" the girl asked, surprised by Paisley's answer. She began leading the braid to the side, allowing it to fall over Paisley's shoulder as she tied it off with a clear hair tie.

"It just seems like this was supposed to happen," Paisley shrugged, watching as Shiloh loosened the braid slightly. "I do not think I have anything to be nervous about. Do I?"

Shiloh couldn't help the small smile that tugged at her lips. "I guess you're right," she laughed softly, letting the braid rest on her shoulder and turning the smaller girl so she could see herself in the mirror. "I never thought about it that way."

"Now get your butt downstairs before Nessa and Ryland come up here and yell at us," Shiloh laughed, squeezing Paisley's shoulder. The smaller girl leaned in for a kiss, but Shiloh dodged her, holding up a finger and shaking her head. "Save it for the wedding, goofball," she giggled, carefully adjusting the front of her dress and making sure her braid lay perfectly against her shoulder. A few stray strands of hair hung down, framing her face and making her look even more perfect.

"Let's go get married," Shiloh laughed softly, nudging the girl towards the door. Paisley held up a finger to signal for her to wait, quickly hurrying across the hallway. Shiloh stood in the doorway curiously, watching as Paisley reappeared moments later with a small daisy tucked behind her ear from the arrangement of flowers in the bedroom.

"Perfect," Shiloh laughed, reaching up and running her thumb over Paisley's cheek. "They're gonna yell at us if we keep them waiting any longer, c'mon," she gently took the girl's hand, giving her a shy smile before leading her towards the stairs.

"Do you, Shiloh Everest, take Paisley Lowe to be your partner in life and your one true love? Will you cherish her friendship and love her today, tomorrow and forever? Will you trust and honor her, laugh with her and cry with her? Will you be faithful through good times and bad, in sickness and in health as long as you both shall live?"

Shiloh failed to hide the smile that tugged at her lips when she looked up and saw Paisley's eyes already on her. She squeezed the girl's hand and nodded softly. "Of course I do."

Paisley laughed softly, looking down to hide her blush. Shiloh glanced out at the rows of chairs, immediately noticing Leah taking pictures of them while Ryland and Vanessa waved excitedly at her.

"And do you, Paisley Lowe, take Shiloh Everest Lowe to be your partner in life and your one true love? Will you cherish her friendship and love her today, tomorrow and forever? Will you trust and honor her, laugh with her and cry with her? Will you be faithful through good times and bad, in sickness and in health as long as you both shall live?"

"Duh," the smaller girl looked up. Her eyes immediately widened when she realized what she had said, and she glared over at Ryland when the girl burst into laughter. "I do," Paisley giggled, looking back at Shiloh and biting her lip to hide her smile.

"Well then, by the power vested in me, I now pronounce you wife and wife."

"You're supposed to kiss me now," Shiloh whispered when Paisley just stood there with a dorky smile on her face. She couldn't help but giggle when the smaller girl's eyes widened in realization.

Paisley quickly took a step forwards, interlocking her pinkie with Shiloh's before leaning in and using her free hand to cup the back of Shiloh's neck. She kissed her gently, smiling into the kiss when she heard Ryland and Vanessa cheering for them.

As if they had planned it, both girls immediately brought their interlocked pinkies up and kissed their hands when the kiss pulled away. They both burst into laughter when they realized what they'd done.

At that point, Ryland couldn't contain her excitement anymore. She jumped up from her chair, running up to pull both of the girls into a hug. Moments later, both Leah and Vanessa followed.

Pretty soon, both girls were whisked away in different directions to greet their friends and family members. Currently, Paisley sat outside with Shiloh's siblings while her now-wife was being engaged in conversation with their family friends.

Maggie, now 8 years old, sat on the bench beside Paisley, swinging her legs back and forth as she gazed out at the yard full of guests. She glanced over at Paisley, furrowing her eyebrows together.

"So now that you're married, what's that mean?" the small blonde asked, tilting her head to the side. Paisley turned to face her, carefully tucking her hair behind her ear as she tried to think of a response.

"It just means that we are married," Paisley shrugged with a soft laugh. "I think it matters more to everyone else than it does to us. We already knew we would be together forever. All this..." she motioned around the yard. "All of this was just to let everyone else know."

"Like what Daxton did!" Maggie laughed, turning to her older brother who immediately tried to hush her. Tara burst into laughter, which only confused Paisley even more.

"What?" Paisley tilted her head to the side. Daxton rolled his eyes and sighed, leaning back in his chair and turning to Tara to tell the story.

"Daxton got in trouble at school because he beat up this kid that was talking all this shit about these two girls that just started dating," Tara laughed, looking over at Daxton who just shook his head.

"I don't see why it's such a big deal," he muttered. Paisley tilted her head to the side.

"I think they deserved it!" Maggie nodded with finality, causing Paisley to laugh softly. She couldn't help but nod in agreement.

"Why are you mad?" Paisley raised an eyebrow, figuring the boy would have been bragging about what he had done. Tara turned to him, expecting an answer.

"It's stupid that I should even have to do something like that," Daxton scuffed his shoes against the patio absentmindedly. "He shouldn't have anything against them in the first place. If it had been my sister I would've-," he paused when he saw Paisley's face fall slightly.

"Not you," he quickly shook his head, nudging Paisley's knee with his own. "You're different. She looks at you different," he laughed.

"It is okay," Paisley nodded softly. "We apologized. It is just hard to think about sometimes," she shrugged. "But good job," she added with a soft laugh.

"Thanks," Daxton chuckled. Maggie giggled, hopping up and stealing the hat off of his head. Before he could react, she was taking off across the yard. Rolling his eyes, he quickly got to his feet to run after her.

"Children," Tara scoffed jokingly, turning back around once her siblings disappeared out of sight. "I have to ask, Miss Paisley Lowe-Everest... what's next for you guys?"

"What do you mean?" Paisley tilted her head to the side slightly and watched as Tara glanced over in Shiloh's direction, who was tapping her foot impatiently as her aunt continued talking.

"Like... what happens now? More cats? Kids?" she wiggled her eyebrows, causing Paisley to laugh softly and shrug.

"One step at a time," the older girl said softly, smiling when she saw Shiloh glance over in her direction and flash her an apologetic smile. "Maybe one day," she whispered softly, turning back to Tara with a shy smile.

A little while later, Paisley sat with Ryland and Vanessa, who were having a contest to see who could fit the most grapes in their mouth. Paisley watched, her stomach hurting from laughing so hard at her former roommates' struggle. She paused, though, when she saw a pair of green eyes seeking her out from the other side of the yard.

Paisley sat up slightly, looking in Shiloh's direction. An excited smile spread across her face and she quickly excused herself from the table. She watched as Shiloh disappeared around the side of the house. Waiting a few moments, Paisley made sure no one was watching her before following suit.

"Finally," Shiloh laughed when Paisley hurried around the front of the house. She grabbed her wife's hands, pulling her in and planting a soft kiss on her lips. "Do I even need to ask?"

Paisley shook her head. Both girls already knew exactly what they were doing. The green eyed girl laughed, grabbing the smaller girl's hand and leading her towards the car.

"I love you, by the way," Shiloh whispered once they got in the car, leaning across the center console to steal another kiss. "I always will," she added with a soft smile before backing out of the driveway and heading towards their destination, her fingers interlocked with Paisley's.

C H A P T E R 1 1

"Hurry up!" Paisley laughed, already halfway up the hill by the time Shiloh had gotten out of the car. She nearly tripped backwards, quickly catching herself and pouting when Shiloh burst into laughter.

"Not funny," Paisley mumbled, crossing her arms and playfully jutting out her bottom lip. Shiloh couldn't help but laugh even more, jogging up the hill to catch up with her wife. She paused for a moment. Wife. She liked the sound of that.

"Someone's eager," Shiloh laughed when Paisley grabbed her hand, pulling her the rest of the way up the hill. Both girls stood still for a moment once they reached the top, gazing ahead at the wrought iron gate.

Paisley took a deep breath, giving Shiloh a shy smile before leading her down the familiar pathway. Shiloh kicked a stone as they walked while Paisley's eyes scanned their surroundings. When she spotted the tree, she led Shiloh off of the pathway and immediately knelt down to brush off the two graves.

Meanwhile, Shiloh dug a blanket out of her backpack, laying it out in the glass underneath the tree. Paisley turned around, giving her a questioning look.

"I planned ahead," Shiloh laughed, sitting cross legged in the middle of the blanket. She patted the space next to her and motioned for Paisley to join her. With a soft smile, Paisley padded over to the blanket and sat down, leaning against Shiloh's shoulder and sighing contently.

"If there were here they would be super happy," Paisley whispered, causing Shiloh to laugh softly. "They were always happy. Even if everything else sucked."

"I wonder where you get it from," Shiloh giggled and nudged Paisley's shoulder. The smaller girl hid her face in the crook of Shiloh's neck, accidentally knocking her elbow and causing her to lay completely flat on her back. Paisley couldn't help but laugh, and she lay back so her head was resting on Shiloh's abdomen.

Shiloh moved her arms behind her head, staring up at the sky as the wind gently rustled the leaves on the tree above them. She smiled when she felt Paisley take one of her hands in her own, cupping it between hers and resting it under her chin.

"There are so many stories here, Lo," Paisley whispered, keeping her gaze focused on the sky.

"Stories?" Shiloh propped herself up on her elbows, looking down at Paisley, who nodded eagerly.

"Just think about it," Paisley pursed her lips in careful thought. "Everyone here once had a story. And now there's millions and millions of stories here. I wish I could know them all."

"I don't," Shiloh said absentmindedly, gazing at the sky while Paisley played with her fingers. The smaller girl furrowed her eyebrows and looked up at Shiloh.

"Why not?"

"Because the best story of all is ours," Shiloh whispered, tracing her eyes back down to the small girl. "You're my whole book, Paisley. It starts with you and it ends with you. No other stories exist in my world."

"Ours is my favorite, too," Paisley said softly, looking up at the girl with adoration filled eyes. "I will tell our story forever and ever. I promise," she locked their fingers together.

"I couldn't ask for anyone better to be my leading lady," Shiloh laughed, crinkling her nose. Paisley reached up to run her fingers through Shiloh's hair. The two girls locked eyes and Shiloh leaned down to plant a soft kiss on Paisley's lips.

"We're married," Shiloh laughed, lingering in front of Paisley's face. The small girl couldn't help but giggle, sitting up and crossing her legs underneath her.

"It feels the same," Paisley toyed with the end of her braid. "Everyone acted like it was a big deal but it did not feel like that to me."

"Is that bad?" Shiloh tilted her head to the side. Paisley quickly shook her head.

"No. It is a good thing. It means that kind of stuff does not matter to us," she shrugged.

"What do you mean?" Shiloh asked, still somewhat confused. Paisley just smiled softly and leaned against Shiloh's shoulder.

"It means that we do not need fancy rings or big ceremonies to make us happy. We just are. Just being with you is good enough for me," she nodded softly, allowing her eyes to absentmindedly follow a butterfly that fluttered around the graves.

"Remember how you said we had Chemistry?" Shiloh asked, raising an eyebrow at the younger girl. Paisley looked up at her in confusion.

"Yeah..?" Paisley tilted her head to the side.

"We still do," Shiloh giggled, crinkling her nose and leaning in to quickly steal a kiss from the smaller girl.

"Lame," Paisley teased, laughing when Shiloh pouted playfully and crossed her arms. She reached out to take Shiloh's hand, but the green eyed girl scooted out of her reach with a playful smirk. Just as Paisley was about to reach for her again, Shiloh gasped and held up a finger, signaling for her to wait.

"I have something for you," Shiloh nodded, pulling her backpack into her lap. "For us, actually," she added as she dug around. Paisley watched curiously.

Shiloh hummed happily when she found what she was looking for, pulling out a small glass mason jar. Paisley tilted her head to the side, leaning in to study it closer when Shiloh held it between them. She grew even more confused when she saw a collection of dollar bills stored inside.

"It's out honeymoon fund," Shiloh nodded softly, turning the jar around in her hands. "I know we agreed on nothing fancy, but I thought we could put any extra money we have in here towards a honeymoon one day. I think you deserve one."

"I like that idea," Paisley laughed quietly, gently taking the jar out of Shiloh's hands and smiling when she saw the small flowers she had painted around the edges. She ran her fingers over the smooth glass and looked up at Shiloh with a soft smile on her face.

"There's one more thing," Shiloh added, biting her lip nervously. Paisley immediately sensed something was up by the way Shiloh avoided eye contact.

"So I know we said no rings or anything, but..." Shiloh cleared her throat and grabbed something from the front pocket of her backpack. "I did some digging of my own and found this," she whispered, taking Paisley's hands and placing something between them.

Paisley instantly felt the cool metal against her palm. She glanced up at Shiloh for approval before slowly opening her hands. Her heart jumped when she saw the familiar silver locket. She held it up in front of her, studying the intricate design carved in the metal. Her eyes flickered over to meet Shiloh's, feeling a bittersweet nostalgia filling her chest.

"How...?" Paisley whispered, holding the locket tight against her chest. "How did you find this?"

"My dad knows one of the officers that was at the scene of your accident," Shiloh nodded softly, watching as Paisley ran her thumb over the heart shaped locket. "I talked to him and then he got in contact with the branch that handled your parent's accident. They recovered this at the scene. I figured it was important."

"It is," Paisley nodded almost immediately. She bit her lip, glancing up at Shiloh before carefully opening the silver heart to reveal a worn black and white picture.

Shiloh leaned in to get a better view, watching as Paisley's grip on the necklace tightened. It was hard to make out details in the picture, but Shiloh could see the faint image of three figures.

"I am the little one," Paisley smiled shyly. "I could not even walk yet," she traced the outline of the heart. "This was at Aunt Susie and Uncle Tom's wedding."

"My dad got it for my mom for their anniversary," Paisley nodded softly. "She never took it off. She always said it was good luck."

The smaller girl held the necklace to her chest before glancing over at the graves. Shiloh watched as Paisley took one last look at the picture before closing the locket.

Without exchanging any words, Paisley gently handed the locket to Shiloh, who automatically knew what she wanted. She moved to kneel behind the smaller girl, gently moving her hair out of the way before reaching over her to lay the necklace across her chest. Once she clasped it back together, Shiloh watched as Paisley held her hand against her chest with a soft smile.

"What happens now?"

Shiloh lifted her head when she heard Paisley break the comfortable silence between them. They'd been lying on the blanket for a while. The sun had already made its way behind the trees, leaving them in the dim glow of the moonlight.

Paisley looked up when Shiloh didn't answer her, finding the green eyed girl looking at her in confusion.

"I mean... what is next? For us?" Paisley bit her lip. Shiloh reached out, beginning to undo Paisley's braid absentmindedly. She ran her fingers through her hair, thinking for a few moments.

"I guess that all depends on what we want," Shiloh shrugged. Paisley lay back, resting her head in Shiloh's lap while the girl aimlessly played with her hair.

"What do we want?" Paisley gazed up at her, realizing just how beautiful her wife looked with the moonlight against her soft skin. Shiloh shrugged softly.

"Happiness," Shiloh said simply. "In whatever form that may come in."

"So like..." Paisley bit her lip, looking away shyly and shivering when Shiloh combed her fingers through her hair. "Kids?"

"I don't see why not," Shiloh said, a soft smile spreading across her face. "I can definitely see us having kids one day."

Paisley sighed contently, happy with the fact that Shiloh agreed with her. "I am gonna be the best mom ever one day," Paisley nodded softly.

"And why's that?" Shiloh giggled, leaning back on one of her hands and looking down at the smaller girl, who had her body laid out on the blanket with her head in her lap.

"Because I am gonna make sure they have everything they need. And that they are good people," Paisley nodded. "And I will never hurt them. I will give them everything."

Shiloh felt her heart flutter upon hearing how passionately Paisley was speaking. There was no doubt in her mind that her wife would be the best mother to their children.

"They're gonna be the luckiest kids in the world," Shiloh whispered, looking down at Paisley and noticing how her eyes reflected the moonlight. "I know that for a fact."

"They are gonna be lucky because they have you for a mother," Paisley nodded softly. "You will show them so much. Like you have shown me."

"I guess we'll make a pretty good team then, yeah?" Shiloh laughed, squeezing Paisley's hand. The smaller girl nodded, reaching up and cupping the back of Shiloh's neck so she could pull her into a gentle kiss.

"I love you," Paisley whispered when they pulled away, running her thumb over Shiloh's cheek and trying to convince herself that the girl was actually real. She seemed like a dream. If she was, Paisley never wanted to wake up.

"I love you too," Shiloh laughed, shivering at Paisley's touch. She lay back, pulling Paisley closer into her side so the girl's arm was draped across her waist and her head was resting on her shoulder.

"What do you wanna do now?" Shiloh asked, tracing circles on the back of Paisley's palm. The smaller girl gazed up at the sky and shrugged.

"Lay with you some more," she whispered, content on just existing alongside the girl.

"Sounds good to me," Shiloh laughed, pulling Paisley closer into her side and kissing her forehead.

"Sing?" Paisley giggled, looking up at her wife hopefully. Shiloh nodded softly, reaching out to brush Paisley's hair out of her face.

"Only for you."

———————————————

Shiloh gazed down at Paisley once she finished the song, well aware that the girl had already fallen asleep. Something in Shiloh always pushed her to finish the song, though. So once she finished singing, she gently pried herself off of the girl so she could stand up.

Soon enough, Paisley's sleeping figure was in Shiloh's arms as they green eyed girl made her way back to the car. She laid her wife in the passenger seat, pausing for a moment to simply admire how beautiful she was even when she wasn't trying.

"I love you," Shiloh whispered, reaching out and tucking a loose strand of hair behind her ear. "It's you and me. Forever."

C H A P T E R 1 2

"Remember, Shiloh, this is our day! Okay?" Maggie leaned out the car window, watching as Shiloh dug through the trunk of the car. The black haired girl tossed two beach towels in Paisley's direction and glanced up at her sister, whose blonde hair was flowing gently in the wind.

"I know, dork," Shiloh laughed, nudging her sister's shoulder as she moved around the front of the car to help the smaller girl carry the beach bag. "I told you, I have errands to run. Besides, I don't even want to spend time with you," she teased. Maggie scowled playfully, sticking her tongue out at her older sister.

"You sure you're gonna be okay?" Shiloh asked, turning to Paisley. Her wife had promised to spend a special day with Maggie while they were still in Florida. Paisley saw Maggie as her own sister and nothing less.

"I am sure," Paisley laughed, taking the bag from Shiloh and shifting it on her shoulder. "I am sorry you can not come with us," she glanced over at Maggie with a small smile on her face. "She wanted it to be just us."

"I get it," Shiloh rolled her eyes playfully, pulling Paisley into her side. "I can't share you very well, can I?" she laughed and kissed her cheek.

"Now get outta' my car, weirdo," Shiloh turned back to Maggie, who opted for crawling out of the window instead of using the door. She smiled widely, taking the towels out of Paisley's arms to help her carry.

"I'll be back in two hours, call me if you need anything, okay?" Shiloh eyed both of the girls, making sure Paisley had her phone with her. Once they said their goodbyes, Maggie took off down the beach, prompting Paisley to run after her after sneaking a quick kiss on Shiloh's cheek.

Shiloh laughed softly, watching as Maggie almost immediately shed her cover up and ran into the water. Paisley carefully laid down the towels, which made Shiloh laugh even harder when she saw how meticulous she was about making sure everything was neat.

The green eyed girl couldn't help but watch them for a few minutes as Paisley followed Maggie down to the edge of the water, holding her hand and helping her keep her balance as they walked further into the waves, until the water reached their knees.

Shiloh didn't consider herself protective. She was just... careful. Okay, sometimes a little bit more than careful. But who could blame her, really? She had known Paisley when the girl could barely crack an egg, let alone take care of herself and a child. But things had changed. Shiloh still couldn't help but look out for her, though. She still remembered the small girl that sought comfort in her room after having a nightmare.

So, it was hard to blame her when she decided that her errands could wait. She told herself she would only stick around for a few minutes, just in case they changed their minds. Maybe the water was too cold, or the sand was too hot. Maybe Shiloh was just making excuses.

But that didn't stop her from slipping into one of the small beach stores when Paisley wasn't looking in her direction. She figured she'd browse for a few minutes, and then if Paisley and Maggie were still okay, she'd be on her merry way.

The green eyed girl ran her fingers through her hair, absentmindedly walking up and down the aisles and browsing through the random tourist merchandise. Finding nothing interesting, she turned to leave, but paused when she heard a voice.

Not just any voice, either. At first, she couldn't figure out who it was. But she knew that voice. It resonated deep within her.

Scott.

Just as Shiloh made the realization, the owner of the voice entered her aisle and nearly ran into her. She stumbled a few steps backwards, memories flashing through her head of all the pain this man had caused Paisley. Her Paisley.

But she had to be tactical about this. She couldn't just punch him. Well, she could. But she needed answers first.

"Wait, do I know you?" Shiloh asked once she composed herself, putting on her best innocent face and praying that he didn't know much about her. Scott paused, turning around and scanning Shiloh up and down.

"I do!" Shiloh nodded quickly. "We went to high school together, right. I'm Shiloh. You're..." she played dumb. "Scott, right?"

"Oh, right," he nodded, turning around and running a hand through his hair. Shiloh struggled to contain the look of disgust on her face.

"Hey, you got in that car accident, didn't you?" Shiloh asked, continuing her act.

"Uh, yeah, I did," he chuckled. Shiloh bit down on her lip when she saw how lightly he took it.

"I haven't seen you around," Shiloh furrowed her eyebrows, pursing her lips and feigning confusion. "I mean, I've seen almost everyone I knew from high school around here at one point or another. Did you move?"

"Nah, I live with my parents a few minutes away," he shrugged, laughing and cupping the back of his neck. "It's a funny story actually. There was all this drama with one of the girls that was in the car and I skipped town until her case was closed or whatever. The freak ended up killing her uncle and p—,"

Before he could finish his sentence, Shiloh's fist was balled tightly in his collar, pushing him up against the wall.

"You know that 'freak' you're talking about? Yeah, she's my wife," Shiloh snarled, tightening her fists. "And if you're looking for the freak, stop looking at everyone else but yourself," she leaned in closer. "If you ever... ever even go near her, I w-,"

Shiloh was cut off by the ringing of a bell to signal that someone else had entered the store. Before she had time to react, she was met with Paisley and Maggie's wide eyes, frozen at the end of the aisle.

Paisley quickly ran to Shiloh's side, pulling her away from the wall. Scott scoffed, glaring at Shiloh from a few feet away. Meanwhile, the green eyed girl stood frozen, expecting everything to come crashing down.

Instead, Paisley pushed her a few steps back, placing her hands on her shoulders and giving her a soft nod. Unsure of what was going on, Shiloh watched as Paisley turned back around to face Scott. Her breath caught in her throat.

"I forgive you," were the first words that left Paisley's mouth, making Shiloh's jaw practically drop to the floor. "You may break a person, but you can never destroy them," her voice was low, years of anger and anguish boiling in the back of her throat.

"I hope you are happy," Paisley's voice faltered for a moment, prodding Shiloh to reach out and grab her hand. "I hope you are happy because I am. You do not have any power over me anymore."

Without another word, Paisley let go of Shiloh's hand and practically marched out of the store, calling for them to follow. Instead, Shiloh stood frozen, replaying what had just happened over and over in her head.

Before Shiloh even had a chance to follow up Paisley's words with a snide comment, a small blonde stormed down the aisle. Without even looking at her older sister, Maggie turned to Scott, landing her knee right inbetween his legs and causing the man to double over in pain.

Shiloh gasped, looking down at Maggie who looked more than pleased with herself. "Margaret Everest!" she gasped, trying to not to laugh but failing when she saw just how serious the smaller girl was.

"I'm so s—," she turned to Scott, realizing what she was about to say. Pausing for a moment, she glanced back at Maggie before shaking her head. "Actually, I'm not sorry. You deserved that." She grabbed Maggie's hand. "C'mon."

Maggie was the first to break into laughter when they exited the store, and Shiloh quickly followed.

"I know I'm not supposed to promote violence but he had it coming," Shiloh whispered, grabbing her sister's hand and tugging her away from the store before Scott could come after them. Her first instinct was to find Paisley and make sure she was alright.

She immediately spotted the small girl on the beach, sitting in the sand with a towel wrapped around her shoulders. Slowly, Shiloh knelt down beside her. Maggie understood, smiling softly at her sister and sitting down on the other side of Paisley.

"Are you okay?" Shiloh asked, placing a hand on Paisley's thigh. The brown eyed girl looked up and shrugged softly.

"That was weird," Paisley admitted with a soft laugh. Shiloh breathed a sigh of relief. At least Paisley wasn't traumatized. "What did I see in him?" The smaller girl crinkled her nose and shook her head.

"It is weird," Paisley's voice got softer. She ran her fingers through the sand absentmindedly. "Very weird."

"I'm sorry, you shouldn't have had to see him at all," Shiloh shook her head and looked down. Paisley, however, looked up at Shiloh and furrowed her eyebrows.

"Why?" Paisley tilted her head to the side. "He does not matter anymore. He never really did," she laughed softly and glanced over at Maggie. "He is the past. You…" she turned back to Shiloh, reaching up and brushing her hair out of her face. "You are the present. And the future." Paisley shrugged. She didn't think it had been that big of a deal.

"Are you sure?" Shiloh asked, meeting Paisley's eyes and trying to search for any sign of fear. Instead, the smaller girl just laughed and shook her head. Before Shiloh could say anything, though, Paisley's eyes shifted to something behind them.

Moments later, Paisley's lips were against hers, pulling her into a kiss. Shiloh's breath caught in her throat but she didn't argue. She brought a hand up to Paisley's cheek, separating them when she needed to catch her breath.

"What was th...?" Shiloh trailed off when she saw Paisley craning her neck to see behind them. Raising an eyebrow, the green eyed girl turned around, immediately seeing who Paisley was looking at. Scott stood down the beach, his eyes wide after what he had just seen.

Before Paisley could come to her own defense, Shiloh smirked, making direct eye contact with Scott before cupping the back of Paisley's neck and pulling her into another kiss. Paisley giggled against her lips, hearing Maggie laugh proudly from beside them.

Right before the kiss pulled away, Shiloh flashed her middle finger behind Paisley's back, causing Maggie to laugh even harder. Paisley took a deep breath once the kiss broke, feeling her cheeks burn bright red.

"Once more for good measure," Shiloh whispered, stealing another quick kiss from her wife. When they looked behind them once again, Scott quickly turned his head away, causing all three girls to erupt into laughter.

"I'm proud of you," Shiloh said softly, squeezing Paisley's hand. "And I hope you know that every single word you said in there was one hundred percent true."

"I learned from the best," Paisley giggled, leaning her head on Shiloh's shoulder. The green eyed girl couldn't help but notice how her eyes kept flickering over in Scott's direction, though.

"You don't really wanna be at the same place as him," Shiloh laughed, shaking her head. "C'mon," she whispered before standing up and gathering their things. Paisley watched in confusion.

"Why don't we go roller skating? It's too hot outside anyway," Shiloh raised an eyebrow. She saw Paisley smile in relief and offered her wife a hand, helping her to her feet.

"Let's go!" Maggie squealed, hopping to her feet and taking off towards the car. Shiloh couldn't help but laugh as she shoved everything into their beach bag.

"Come on," Paisley whined playfully, grabbing Shiloh's hand. The green eyed girl raised an eyebrow at her wife, tossing the bag over her shoulder and eyeing Maggie, who was waiting expectantly by the car.

"Hop on," Shiloh laughed turning around and holding out her arms. Giggling, Paisley hopped onto Shiloh's back, allowing the older girl to hook her arms under her legs to hold her in place.

"I love you, by the way," Paisley whispered as Shiloh trudged up the beach, carrying the smaller girl on her back. The brown eyed girl leaned her head down to place a kiss on Shiloh's cheek.

"I love you more," Shiloh laughed, letting the bag slip off of her shoulder once they reached the car. Paisley hopped off of Shiloh's back and began helping them load their things back into the car.

Shiloh, however, took a step back. She watched as Paisley ruffled Maggie's hair, causing the smaller girl to pout playfully and earn an apologetic hug from her. She couldn't help but laugh.

They had come so far from where they first started. Paisley's compassion and understanding continued to shock her, and she'd come to terms with the fact that she would never truly get used to it. And surprisingly, she was alright with that.

C H A P T E R   1 3

"Have fun!" Shiloh called as Paisley hurried down the sidewalk. They'd been so caught up in tossing a toy back and forth with Wolf that morning that both girls didn't realize they were going to be late for work.

Just as Shiloh went to start the car once more, she caught sight of someone running back towards the car. She grew confused when Paisley motioned for her to roll down the window, tapping on the glass hurriedly.

"Are you going home?" Paisley asked, out of breath. Shiloh nodded, raising an incriminating eyebrow.

"Good," Paisley nodded. She bit her lip to hide her excitement. "Look in the guest bedroom."

Before Shiloh could even ask her wife what she meant, the smaller girl took off down the sidewalk and disappeared into the building. Shiloh furrowed her eyebrows together, suddenly curious as to what Paisley was talking about.

She hurried home, tossing her jacket aside by the door and startling Wolf when she accidentally pulled the door shut with a bit too much excitement. The cat sat up from his perch on the counter as Shiloh headed down the hallway.

They had been so busy with the wedding the week before that they hadn't had time to pay much attention to their house. The only two rooms they occupied most of the time were the kitchen and the bedroom, so the two empty rooms at the end of the hallway had yet to be lived in.

Or so she thought.

Shiloh was confused as soon as her fingers curled around the doorknob to the guest bedroom and she came face to face with a completely different room. Her breath caught in her throat and she allowed her eyes to scan her surroundings.

On the opposite side of the room sat a brand new easel, right in front of the large window that held the perfect view of their large backyard. On the adjacent walls, there were string lights and random pictures the girls had gathered over their time as a couple. Rows upon rows of shelves held all of her art supplies, organized neatly together.

Shiloh couldn't find her words. When had this happened? The green eyed girl took a step forwards, allowing her eyes to scan over the various photos that had been hung on the walls.

Out of the corner of her eye, she caught sight of something pinned to her easel. Raising an eyebrow, the green eyed girl crossed the room and carefully took the lined paper into her hands.

Lo, Please don't be mad.

When we got married, we both said we did not want to do anything big. But I had to do something. Because you deserve big things.

I do not know what I am supposed to say. Happy wedding? That sounds funny. But I am happy because we are married. I wish I could really show you how happy I am. I can not even put it into words, Lo. I love you.

So please do not be mad. I know how sometimes you do not like when the attention is on you. But I needed to do something. And you should not be mad, because I think this is like a present for me, too.

I wanted you to have somewhere that is all yours. You know? A space where you can paint amazing things and listen to your favorite songs as loud as you want.

And I like to watch you paint. It is one of my favorite things. You love it, and I love you. So it works out. I hope you like it.

I love you.

- Paisley

Shiloh couldn't help the dorky smile that spread across her face. There was just something so special about Paisley. She couldn't explain it.

She folded up the note and tucked it in her pocket, making a mental note to never get rid of it. The green eyed girl slowly looked around the room once more. It fit her. Paisley knew her too well. There was a blue tapestry hanging on the wall by the door and Shiloh had a feeling the color wasn't just a coincidence.

Her eyes landed on her leather bag full of paint, which had been hung from one of the shelves. Without thinking twice, Shiloh grabbed the bag and emptied its contents onto the large wooden table next to the easel.

In one hand she grabbed a tube of yellow paint. But her eyes also landed on a tube of blue. Before she even realized what she was doing, she was squeezing equal amounts of both onto a clean palette and mixing them together.

Moments later, the yellow and blue dissipated into a calming shade of green. With a paintbrush in one hand and her palette balanced on her hip, Shiloh didn't think twice when she brought the brush to the white wall and got to work.

Shiloh drew her bottom lip in between her teeth as her brush glided quickly against the wall. She began to hum softly, becoming lost in her own little world.

Her two favorite things in the world were Paisley and art, she decided. But technically, Paisley was art. Paisley always seemed to work her way into every aspect of Shiloh's life. And she didn't mind.

Once she was finished, she took a few steps back and admired her work. Holding her brush inbetween her teeth, Shiloh used her free hand to retrieve her phone from the table and snap a picture of her creation. She immediately sent it to Paisley.

Meanwhile, on the other side of town, Paisley had a small child cradled in her arms. The little girl had fallen asleep in her lap during 'circle time', and according to her mother she hadn't slept a wink all night. Paisley decided against waking her up, so now she sat in the back of the classroom with the sleeping girl in her arms while the other kids were out on the playground.

Just then, she felt a buzzing in her pocket. The small girl carefully freed one of her hands so she could check her phone. A wide smile immediately crossed her face when she saw the picture Shiloh had sent her.

The outline of a large heart was slathered onto the plain white wall. Paisley could tell Shiloh had drawn it. The green eyed girl's hearts always came out slightly lopsided. She had complained about it to Paisley before. In the middle of the heart, Shiloh had carefully painted "KCC + LMJ" in her cursive handwriting.

Even though they were married now, little things like that still made Paisley's heart flutter. She was constantly in a state of disbelief that Shiloh was hers.

Shiloh was in that same state of shock, at that exact same moment. She sat at the stool by her easel, taking in the room. Maybe she was overreacting, but she had always dreamed of having her own art studio as a child, and somehow Paisley had just known. For her it was as if things had come full circle for them.

Her phone buzzed a few moments later and she smiled when a picture popped up on her screen and she was presented with yet another reason why she loved her wife.

[My Girl - 11:58] i love you lo

[My Girl - 11:58] so much

Attached was a picture Paisley had taken with the front camera. Her hair was tousled from her beanie, which she had used as a pillow under the small girl's head, which rested on her shoulder. Paisley had her lips curled in a soft smile and her big brown eyes filled with adoration.

In that moment, Shiloh realized that nothing was as beautiful as being in love with someone who looks like love itself.

[Lolo - 12:01] Ethereal.

[Lolo - 12:02] That's what you are.

Shiloh locked her phone, sliding it back into her pocket and taking another long look at the room. When her eyes landed back on the easel, she gained an idea.

Paisley hurried out to the car once she passed the sleeping girl off to her mother. Work had been relatively calm that day and she had nearly fallen asleep herself. Though that didn't stop her from smiling widely when she saw Shiloh's car parked out front, waiting for her.

Paisley grew confused when the moment she got in the car, Shiloh was already starting the engine and pulling out of the parking lot. She furrowed her eyebrows together, unable to read the expression on her wife's face.

"Lo?" Paisley tilted her head to the side. She had expected something completely different when she saw Shiloh. She wanted to know what the girl thought of her present. But instead, she saw something in the girl's eyes that she hadn't seen much of in a while. Nervousness.

"I, uh..." Shiloh stumbled over her words and Paisley had to hold back her smile due to how cute the girl was when she didn't know what to say. "I have a surprise for you... kinda," Shiloh bit her lip and glanced over at the girl in the passenger seat.

"Is it bad?" Paisley asked. A lot of the surprises she had encountered in her lifetime had been anything but good. But when Shiloh quickly shook her head, Paisley calmed down slightly.

"Just trust me," Shiloh laughed softly. She reached over, lacing their fingers together, which made Paisley relax. She trusted Shiloh with every fiber of her being.

"I do," Paisley nodded. "Is it a-?"

"No questions," Shiloh giggled and held up a finger to quiet the girl. "You'll see," she nodded softly, her voice growing quieter. She was somewhat nervous, even though deep down she knew she didn't have to be.

Paisley remained quiet for the rest of the ride while absentmindedly playing with Shiloh's fingers. Once they got back to the house, she immediately greeted Wolf at the door, cradling him in her arms and cuddling him in the crook of her neck.

"C'mon," Shiloh laughed, tossing her jacket aside. "I need your help with something."

Paisley grew confused, setting Wolf back down. She didn't argue, though. The smaller girl followed Shiloh down the hallway and into the guest bedroom. She couldn't help but smile when she saw their initials painted on the wall.

"I love it, by the way," Shiloh whispered, pulling Paisley over to the easel. "It's perfect. Absolutely perfect." She leaned in, planting a soft kiss on the smaller girl's lips.

Before Paisley even had a chance to reply, Shiloh was suddenly moving across the room and rearranging her supplies. Paisley watched as Shiloh took her wooden stool and moved it in front of the easel. "I wanna paint you," she whispered shyly.

"Me?" Paisley felt her cheeks flush red. Shiloh nodded softly and reached out to take Paisley's hand.

"Is that okay?" she asked quietly. Paisley quickly nodded and gave her wife a soft smile. God, she was in love.

"Awesome," Shiloh laughed in relief, squeezing her hand and leading the brown eyed girl over to the stool by the window. "You can just... sit," she shrugged softly. Paisley couldn't help but giggle at how nervous Shiloh appeared to be.

The room was hot, so without even thinking about it, Paisley shed her leggings. She was wearing one of Shiloh's sweaters that was big on her, and it came down to the middle of her thighs anyway. Tossing the leggings aside, the small girl climbed onto the stool and somehow managed to sit cross legged.

"Here," Shiloh whispered, still nervous. She was comfortable around Paisley, obviously. But she was worried that she wouldn't be able to capture the girl's beauty the way it deserved to be captured. She moved forward, brushing Paisley's hair out of her face and giving the girl a soft smile.

"You really like it?" Paisley asked once Shiloh smoothed out her sweater and began gathering her paints together. She took the time to study the studio once more, happy with the way it had turned out.

"Of course I do. I love it," Shiloh nodded. She pulled her hair up into a messy ponytail before setting a clean canvas on her easel. She took a few steps back, studying Paisley intently. This caused the smaller girl to giggle, becoming bashful under her wife's watchful eye.

"How am I supposed to do this?" Shiloh laughed, shaking her head. "You're already a work of art."

Paisley's cheeks turned red and she looked away shyly. There was nothing in the world that could ever lessen the effects of Shiloh's words on her. Nothing.

"I'll try my best," Shiloh concluded, causing Paisley to laugh softly. The green eyed girl moved back over to her easel.

Paisley loved watching Shiloh paint. It was as if the moment Shiloh took the brush in her hand, she became a different person. There was a whole new level of confidence present in her when she painted, Paisley realized.

She watched as the green eyed girl furrowed her eyebrows in concentration, bringing the brush to the canvas and beginning to paint in small, light strokes. Paisley could sit there forever, she decided. Watching Shiloh exist was her favorite pastime.

And she was perfectly fine with that.

CHAPTER 14

Paisley was a work of art.

Shiloh decided this while she was painting the smaller girl. Every brush stroke, every single detail on the canvas contributed to making her favorite creation yet. There was just something about the real Paisley, though. Something Shiloh couldn't capture with a paintbrush.

But she tried her best. Because Paisley deserved to be immortalized. Whether it was through painting, or writing, or some other art, the girl needed to be remembered.

It was the direct middle of the day, meaning that the sun was high in the sky and sending beams of light searing through the window and making Paisley appear as if she was glowing.

There was one part of the painting that Shiloh focused on the most, though. Paisley's eyes.

The smaller girls brown eyes were so expressive. Shiloh didn't know that someone's eyes could hold so much emotion until she met Paisley. Whenever she saw her wife's brown orbs, she was met with solace and adoration.

So Shiloh spent extra time on Paisley's eyes, mixing together various shades of brown and trying her absolute best to capture their depth. She leaned in so close to her canvas that her nose was almost touching the material. Using small strokes of her brush, she looked up every few moments to study Paisley's eyes before turning her attention back to her painting.

When she finally managed to create the perfect shade of brown, Shiloh began adding in the smaller details. The crinkles around Paisley's eyes when she smiled, the specific shape of her lips, the small strands of hair that fell down her shoulders. With every stoke of her brush, the painting became more and more defined.

She had nearly finished painting when her phone buzzed on the table between them. Paisley leaned forwards to grab it, furrowing her eyebrows.

"It is Maia," she nodded softly and held up the phone. Shiloh motioned for her to answer it, setting her brush down and wiping her hands on her jeans. Paisley brought the phone up to her ear.

"Hello?" the small girl tilted her head to the side. Shiloh was so busy nitpicking her painting that she didn't notice the way Paisley's eyes widened a few moments later.

"Got it," Paisley nodded quickly. She set the phone back down and hopped off of the stool, scrambling to tug her leggings back on under her long sweater. It was only then that Shiloh turned around and raised an eyebrow at her.

"What are you doing? What'd she say?" Shiloh asked in confusion. Paisley shook her head and grabbed her jacket from the corner of the room.

"We need to go," Paisley bit her lip nervously and looked up at Shiloh. "She said that there is an emergency. She needs someone to watch Lucas."

"Wait, what?" Shiloh's eyes widened. Paisley grabbed her hand, pulling her out of the room and towards the front door. Shiloh quickly caught up with what was going on, hurrying to slip on her shoes before jogging out to the car after Paisley.

"Did she say anything else?" Shiloh bit her lip. Paisley sat in the passenger seat next to her, tapping her foot anxiously as Shiloh quickly pulled out of their short driveway and took off down the road.

"No," Paisley muttered, shaking her head. "I am worried," she ran a hand through her hair and turned to Shiloh, her big brown eyes searching for some sort of reassurance.

"It's okay," Shiloh quickly grabbed her hand and squeezed it. "I'll get us there as fast as we can, yeah?" She made a sharp turn, driving a little faster than usual to get them to their destination quicker.

Paisley tapped her foot impatiently the entire drive, so many possible scenarios cycling through her mind. The second the car pulled up in front of the house, Paisley practically leaped out of her seat and sprinted to the front door. Shiloh followed close behind.

"Come in!"

Both girls exchanged worried glances after Paisley rang the doorbell. The smaller girl grabbed Shiloh's hand and pulled her inside, growing confused when the living room was empty. She glanced at Shiloh worriedly, who took the lead and led them towards the kitchen.

She fumbled around for the light switch, and moments later the room was lit up and Paisley was stumbling back a few steps.

"Surprise!"

Shiloh quickly grabbed Paisley to keep her from falling backwards. Before either of the girls had a chance to realize what was going on, they were both practically tackled into hugs.

"You're married now!" Ryland yelled, squeezing both girls tightly. Paisley was the first to burst into laughter, relieved that there wasn't actually an emergency.

Shiloh, on the other hand, took a few extra seconds to realize what was going on. "Wait... this is for us? Are you guys okay?" she pulled out of the hug and hurried over to Maia and Toby, who were leaning against the counter with proud smiles on their faces.

"We had to get you over here somehow," Maia laughed. Shiloh took a deep breath, holding her hand against her chest.

"You scared the shit out of us," she shook her head and shoved Maia in fake anger. "I hate you guys," she mumbled. Paisley raised an eyebrow from across the room, padding over to Toby and taking Lucas out of his arms.

"Hey buddy," she giggled, balancing the baby on her hip. "Did you do this?"

Shiloh couldn't help but laugh as she watched Paisley interact with Lucas. Kids were just drawn to the brown eyed girl for some unexplained reason.

"Hey Paisley," Toby smirked, nudging the smaller girl and raising an eyebrow. "Did she like it?"

Paisley tilted her head to the side, turning to Toby and thinking for a few moments. Her face spread into a smile and she nodded softly, glancing at her wife.

"She said she loved it," Paisley nodded. "Thank you for helping me, by the way."

"No problem," Maia smiled, reaching out and ruffling Lucas' hair. "You're the one who had the idea."

Shiloh listened to their conversation, a shy smile on her face. She watched as Paisley brought Lucas into the living room to lie him down on his blanket.

"You're married," Leah smiled, turning to Shiloh once Ryland and Vanessa followed Paisley into the other room. "How's it feel?"

"The same," Shiloh laughed, shrugging. "More official."

"Toby got some fancy grill so we thought we'd have a cookout and celebrate your wedding since we couldn't be there," Maia smiled softly. Shiloh pulled her into a hug.

"Thank you for not actually having an emergency," the dark haired girl laughed as she pulled away.

"Sorry about that," Maia rolled her eyes and glanced at Toby. "He thought it would be the only way to get you guys over here quick enough."

"Well it worked," Shiloh laughed. She smiled when she heard the baby giggling from the other room, following Maia, Toby, and Leah when they headed into the living room.

Paisley was sitting cross legged on the floor with Lucas in front of her, pinching her cheeks and making a funny face to try and get him to laugh again. She looked up when she saw Shiloh, her face turning bright red in embarrassment.

"Watch this," Shiloh laughed softly, kneeling next to Paisley and getting the baby's attention. She flipped her hair over so it was covering her face and leaned down to Lucas could see her better. "Where'd I go?" she giggled, feeling the toddler grab a handful of her hair and try to move it out of the way.

"Boo!" she laughed when he revealed her face. Moments later, Lucas burst into laughter and Paisley had to grab onto him to keep him from teetering over and losing his balance.

"Y'know, Lucas needs a friend," Toby spoke up from the couch with a mischievous smirk on his face. "Someone his age that he can hang out with."

Paisley glanced at Shiloh before looking up, furrowing her eyebrows in confusion. Ryland and Vanessa both laughed while Leah looked at them questioningly.

"I agree," Maia laughed, rolling her eyes at Toby playfully. "Someone better hurry up and give Lucas a friend before he gets too lonely."

"Yeah, Leah," Shiloh spoke up with a smirk. Both Toby and Maia exchanged glances, knowing their plan had taken a wrong turn. "You and Troy better bring us a little baby sunshine."

Paisley bit her lip, pulling Lucas into her lap and thinking about what Toby had said. Distracting herself, she picked up one of Lucas' rattles and waved it in front of him, catching his attention.

"We painted his bedroom yesterday," Maia spoke up, changing the subject after everyone started pestering Leah. "We couldn't agree on a color so we did two."

"Gray and blue," Toby nodded. "It actually looks pretty cool."

Pretty soon, everyone was following Maia and Toby upstairs and into the small bedroom. Paisley was so engrossed in entertaining Lucas that she didn't even notice.

"No, do not eat it, silly," she giggled, pulling the rattle away from him. When she set it down, she caught sight of something yellow out of the corner of her eye. It peaked her interest, and she stood up, bringing Lucas with her as she padded out onto the back patio.

"Look," Paisley whispered, pointing to the pale yellow butterfly that had landed on one of the small bushes. "See it, Lucas?" she knelt down next to the plant and eyed the small creature.

"That is a butterfly," she nodded softly when she saw Lucas' eyes widen. "Hey, you have to be gentle," she reminded him when he reached out for it. "See? Like this."

Meanwhile, Shiloh leaned against the doorway in Lucas' bedroom, listening as Maia and Toby explained how they were going to set up the toddler bed once he was old enough. She glanced around the room, suddenly realizing what was missing.

"Hey, where's Paisley?" Shiloh interrupted their conversation, glancing at the empty hallway behind her. She bit her lip nervously.

"She's downstairs with Lucas, I think," Maia raised an eyebrow, watching as Shiloh quickly turned around and hurried down the staircase. The other girls and Toby followed.

"Guys, she's not d——," Shiloh started, pausing when something caught her eye. "Nevermind," she said quietly, glancing out the window and watching as Paisley held her finger out in front of Lucas, a small yellow butterfly perched atop it.

"Look at her," Shiloh glanced back at them, nodding towards the window. "Look how cute she is," she added in a whisper, not even realizing what she was saying.

"She's so good with kids," Shiloh laughed, sitting down on one of the couches next to Maia. Toby headed outside to start the grill.

"Then get to it!" Ryland smirked, wiggling her eyebrows at the green eyed girl from across the room. "You heard what Toby said."

Shiloh's eyes widened and she glanced outside once more. Paisley had the butterfly now sitting on her nose, her eyes crossed slightly to see it. Lucas was watching her intently while Paisley tried not to giggle. Shiloh smiled softly.

"I don't know if she even wants kids," Shiloh mumbled, turning back to them but stealing a glance at her wife every few moments. "We never really talk about it."

"Are you blind?" Maia laughed, nudging her shoulder. "She works at a school, for god sakes. And look at her now," she pointed to Paisley, who now had Lucas in her lap, gently letting the butterfly crawl up his arm.

"When do you know if it's the right time? What if she doesn't even w—?" Shiloh was cut off when Ryland plopped down next to her, cupping her hand over her mouth to silence her.

"You're thinking way too hard about this," Ryland laughed, rolling her eyes. "Stop thinking and start doing," she nudged the green eyed girl.

"But--," Shiloh started, but immediately clamped her jaw shut when she heard the back door open. Paisley padded into the room, humming softly and bouncing a content Lucas on her hip.

She paused when she realized all eyes were on her, immediately silencing and growing embarrassed.

"Dinner's ready!" Toby called, setting the last plate of hamburgers on the kitchen table. Shiloh smiled softly at Paisley, giving Ryland a warning glare before hopping to her feet.

"I'll take the baby," Shiloh laughed, holding out her arms to Paisley. "You go eat."

"I can get him," Maia raised an eyebrow, appearing beside Shiloh. Both girls shook their head at the same time.

"You get him all day. I've got it," Shiloh nodded, reaching out to take the baby from Paisley. "Go eat."

"No," Paisley giggled, turning away from Shiloh before she could take Lucas. "I want him."

"I want him," Shiloh pouted playfully, making Paisley laugh. "You've had him all day, take a break."

"You take a break," Paisley teased, looking down at Lucas and sticking out her bottom lip. "He is my best buddy. Not yours. Right Lucas?"

"Still believe what you said earlier?" Ryland smirked, wiggling her eyebrows at Shiloh before walking out of the room, confident that her job was done when she saw Shiloh's face turn bright red.

CHAPTER 15

"Goodnight, Lo," Paisley whispered, rubbing her eyes and curling up in the older girl's side. As always, she snaked her hands up Shiloh's sleeves. It was just a natural part of their sleeping position now.

"Night, Pais," Shiloh yawned and gazed at Paisley as she melted into her. The smaller girl was always the first to fall asleep. Not that Shiloh minded. She always slept easier with Paisley by her side.

But for some reason, tonight was different. Just as she would start to fall asleep, her body would jerk itself awake again. When this happened multiple times, Shiloh groaned and rolled onto her back.

She gazed up at the ceiling, trying to will herself to fall asleep. Unfortunately, she was wide awake, and nothing she seemed to tell herself could help her fix this.

Sighing, Shiloh carefully peeled herself from Paisley's sleeping figure and adjusted the blankets back over the smaller girl. She made sure to be quiet as she slipped out of the room and down to the guest bedroom.

Flipping on the lights in the art studio, Shiloh plugged in her phone and turned on her painting playlist. Paisley had helped her put it together one afternoon when the smaller girl decided they needed music for when Shiloh painted.

'Team' by Lorde came on first, and Shiloh hummed along softly as she gathered her paintbrushes together. She kept the lights dim, enjoying the blue moonlight that came in through the windows.

Just as she started thinking of things to paint, a small meow distracted her. She groaned, hurrying over to the door to make sure Wolf didn't get in. But when she turned around, she realized the white cat had made himself at home atop the stool where Paisley had previously sat. Rolling her eyes, she raised a finger in warning at him before returning to her easel.

In her nighttime delirium, Shiloh absentmindedly dipped her brush into purple and swirled it around on the canvas. She wasn't quite sure what she was doing, but it kept her occupied for quite a while. She got so lost in her painting that she didn't even notice when the playlist ended.

What she did notice, though, was the clap of thunder that sent Wolf flying down the hallway. Furrowing her eyebrows, Shiloh lifted her head and glanced out the window, where rain was pouring down relentlessly. A flash of lightning lit up the room for a split second.

Biting her lip, Shiloh set her paintbrush down and made her way back down the hallway. She was surprised when she opened the door to the bedroom slightly and found Paisley still fast asleep, with Wolf now curled up in her side.

Maybe she just hadn't heard the thunder. Shiloh knew how badly Paisley hated storms. She remembered the days back at the apartment when Paisley would practically hide at the sign of a storm.

Another large boom of thunder disproved her theory, though. Both Shiloh and Wolf jumped when the house practically shook, but the smaller girl just shifted slightly in her sleep, hair sprawled across her pillow.

Shiloh raised an eyebrow, unsure of how to feel about this. Glancing at Wolf one last time, she closed the door quietly and headed back down the hallway, flinching when another clap of thunder echoed throughout the house unexpectedly.

The green eyed girl put on music once more, turning it up louder to try and drown out the storm raging on outside. She turned back to her painting, trying to concentrate as best as she could, but failing. She was too bothered by the thoughts circling through her head.

What if Paisley didn't need her anymore?

Shiloh thought it was crazy, at first. But as she pondered the subject even more, she found herself setting down her brush and leaning against the table for a moment, deep in thought.

What if Paisley only was with her because she needed her? What happened when Paisley was perfectly fine on her own? Would she realize that she didn't need Shiloh anymore?

Another clap of thunder sent Shiloh stumbling backwards, nearly falling over. Being snapped out of her thoughts, she grabbed her paintbrush, turned her music up even louder, and forced herself to continue painting.

A few minutes later, Shiloh found herself gripping the paintbrush so tightly that her knuckles were turning white. Just as she leaned into work on the smaller details, a loud crash behind her sent her reeling backwards.

"Oh my g-," she breathed, cutting herself off when she saw the small girl standing in the doorway. Paisley shook her head, quickly kneeling down to try and pick up the jar of paintbrushes she had knocked over.

"No, no, it's fine," Shiloh shook her head, sliding down on her knees beside the girl and helping her gather up the brushes. "What are you doing up?" she asked, glancing up at the smaller girl.

"I-I woke up and it was storming, and you were gone, and then I came to try and find you and you were painting, and... and... I just like to watch you paint," Paisley let her words spill out of her mouth in one giant breath, causing her to gasp for air when she was done. Another clap of thunder made Paisley jump and instinctively grab onto Shiloh's arm. "I do not like storms," she laughed nervously, biting her lip.

"I came in to check on you and you were asleep," Shiloh said softly. When she saw Paisley glance nervously at the window, she sat down and patted the space next to her. "Are you okay?"

"Yeah," Paisley said softly, biting her lip. A flash of lightning made her eyes widen and she looked at Shiloh anxiously. "Can you… can you just… hold me?"

"You don't have to ask that," Shiloh laughed softly, scooting closer to Paisley and placing an arm around her shoulders. She ran her fingers up and down the smaller girl's arm, trying to comfort her. "I couldn't sleep so I came in here to paint."

"What are you-," Paisley jumped when there was another clap of thunder, prompting Shiloh to pull her closer. "What are you painting?"

"Wanna see?" Shiloh asked, finding Paisley's hand and lacing their fingers together. The smaller girl nodded and bit her lip. Shiloh squeezed her hand, helping the girl to her feet and walking her over to the easel.

"What is it?" Paisley tilted her head to the side, eyeing the combination of blues, purples, and blacks. She watched as Shiloh grabbed her paintbrush and continued blending in the background.

"Celestial bodies," Shiloh nodded softly, motioning to the clusters of small yellow dots that almost appeared as if they were shining. Paisley leaned in closer.

"What is that?" Paisley asked, tilting her head to the side. Shiloh held her paintbrush inbetween her teeth and took a step back to admire her painting.

"The things in the sky. Like the stars," Shiloh nodded softly and began working on another section of the painting.

"They are shaped like people," Paisley noted, giggling and reaching up to wipe a dot of paint off of Shiloh's cheek.

"Two people," Shiloh affirmed, pointing to the two shapes that appeared as if their arms and legs were entangled.

"You know, it's like… how connections and souls can extend out of our bodies," she bit down her lip and paused to focus on blending two dark colors together. "How when you have a bond with someone that's so incredibly special, there's more there than just the physical."

"Oh," Paisley nodded softly and reached out to help Shiloh keep the canvas still while she worked on one of the corners. "It is pretty."

"Thanks," Shiloh laughed softly, glancing up at the smaller girl. "Can you hand me a blue? Like a dark blue. Like... galaxy looking blue." Paisley nodded, digging through the tubes of paint before choosing the best one and handing it to Shiloh.

"I like it," Paisley nodded and watched as Shiloh began mixing another color. "It reminds me of us."

"That's what I was aiming for," Shiloh laughed, giving Paisley a shy smile before turning back to the canvas and continuing to add touch ups in the background. Paisley jumped slightly when another low rumble of thunder interrupted the silence.

Before she could say anything, the smaller girl was being pulled into Shiloh's side, held close against the girl. Shiloh kissed her forehead, running her hand up and down Paisley's arm. "Some things just never change, do they?" she asked softly.

"I hate storms," Paisley mumbled, biting her lip when the room was illuminated with lightning for a split second. "I always have."

"Why do you hate them so much?" Shiloh set down her paintbrush, and tilted her head to the side.

"I just do," Paisley shrugged and looked around the room. "They are so... big. And powerful. I can not control them." She looked down at the floor, biting her lip. "When you are little, you can cry and throw a fit until your parents give in... but... but no matter what you do, you can not change a storm."

"You can't change a storm..." Shiloh nodded, thinking over Paisley's words. "Why would you want to? I mean... there's just some things we don't have control over. Why waste your time worrying about something you can't change?"

"I-I don't know," Paisley whispered, more distracted by the strong winds that were picking up inside. She scooted closer into Shiloh's side, biting her lip nervously.

"If you could control storms, would you still stay here?" Shiloh asked quietly, holding onto the girl as they both watched out the window. Paisley looked up at her in confusion.

"Why would I leave?" Paisley bit her lip and focused on Shiloh, now more concerned on the meaning of her question than the storm.

"I just... I mean..." Shiloh shook her head. "If you had nothing to be afraid of. Or... or like... no worries or anything. Where would you go?"

"Why would I go anywhere?" the smaller girl tilted her head to the side. "I have everything I need here," she shrugged off Shiloh's question, taking a step forwards to inspect her painting closely.

Shiloh stood still, somewhat in shock. Paisley was oblivious to the weight of the question she had just answered. But the outcome had been more than enough for Shiloh. A soft smile had permanently etched itself onto her face.

"Lo?"

Shiloh snapped out of her thoughts, looking up at Paisley and tilting her head to the side.

"I said, where would you go?" Paisley asked, walking up to the window and pressing her fingertips against it as the rain began to slow down. "If you could control everything."

"To wherever you are," Shiloh walked over to the window and traced a spiral in the condensation. "There really isn't anything else that matters." She saw a small smile creep on Paisley's face, but it was quickly hidden when the girl looked away bashfully.

"I love you, you know," Paisley whispered, lifting her head. "Sometimes I think you forget that," she took a step forwards and reached out to cup Shiloh's cheek.

"You should remind me more often then," Shiloh laughed softly, shivering under Paisley's touch. It was impossible for her to hide the effect that Paisley had on her.

"I will. All the time," Paisley laughed softly, leaning against Shiloh's shoulder and gazing out the window. Only moments later, a loud clap of thunder sent her stumbling backwards and away from the window. Even Shiloh jumped.

"It sounds like the s-sky is breaking," Paisley mumbled, bringing her hand up to toy with her bottom lip. Shiloh glanced around the room once more before drawing the blinds shut and leading Paisley back into the bedroom.

"What about the painting?" Paisley tilted her head to the side. Shiloh shrugged, dramatically falling back onto the bed and motioning for Paisley to lay down next to her.

"I'm tired anyway," Shiloh shrugged, pulling the blankets over her feet and waiting for Paisley to join her.

Paisley opted for crawling onto the bed, burrowing her way under the covers. The smaller girl jumped when another clap of thunder filled the room, and Wolf quickly joined them. Shiloh groaned, pushing the cat aside until he finally gave up on lying in between them and settled for curling up at their feet.

"Sing?" Paisley whispered, immediately curling up against Shiloh's side and tangling their legs together.

"Only for you," Shiloh nodded, pressing a kiss to Paisley's forehead just as lightning flashed throughout the room.

C H A P T E R   1 6

Shiloh woke up the next morning in an empty bed.

At first, she panicked. She sat up quickly and looked around their shared bedroom to try and find Paisley. She immediately calmed down, though, when she heard soft humming coming from the other room. Judging by the towel hanging next to their dresser, Paisley had already been up and showered for a while.

Yawning, Shiloh rolled out of bed and gazed at her reflection in the mirror. She crinkled her nose, noticing her tousled hair and the streak of dark paint that had dried just above her jawline. The green eyed girl slipped into the bathroom, turning on the shower and going over her plans for the day while the hot water soothed her muscles.

About fifteen minutes later, Shiloh tugged on a pair of jeans and a white t-shirt, throwing her hair up into a high ponytail before wandering out into the kitchen. Paisley was rummaging around in the drawers, not even noticing Shiloh had woken up.

"What's that smell?" Shiloh asked, leaning against the counter and causing her wife to jump. Paisley nearly dropped the bowl in her hands.

"Hi," she giggled, setting the bowl down and motioning for Shiloh to come closer. "I made cupcakes. I think," she pointed to the oven. "I had to start over, because I forgot eggs in the first batch. But I think I did it this time."

"And why are we making cupcakes at 7 in the morning?" Shiloh asked, laughing softly and bending down to peer into the oven.

"Because today is Jeremiah's birthday," Paisley nodded softly as she began to rinse out the mixing bowls in the sink. "And he has to go to his mom's house tonight, and he does not like his mom's house because his big brother ignores him. So we are going to have a birthday party for him. With cupcakes," she smiled, pointing to the oven once more.

"Well that's thoughtful of you," Shiloh couldn't help but smile when Paisley looked up at her shyly. "What kind of icing did you get?"

Paisley's head shot up and she looked at Shiloh with wide eyes. Both girls realized at the same time, and before Paisley could panic, her wife quickly shook her head and held a hand up.

"We can make it from scratch, yeah?" Shiloh hurried over to the stack of boxes by the door, rummaging through them until she found one of her mother's old recipe books. Paisley watched as she flipped through the pages, setting the book down on the counter. "Can you grab the mixer and plug it in?"

Paisley nodded, giving Shiloh a thankful smile. The rest of their morning was spent mixing the ingredients (which took a few tries) and decorating the cupcakes with pink icing (Jeremiah's favorite color) and rainbow sprinkles.

A little over an hour later, Shiloh was pulling into the parking lot while Paisley held the platter of cupcakes steadily on her lap. Shiloh would look over and laugh every few seconds at the look of sheer concentration on her wife's face as Paisley focused intently on making sure none of her treasured desserts got ruined.

"Eat a cupcake for me, yeah?" Shiloh teased, hopping out of the car to grab Paisley's door. Paisley carefully stood up, holding the plate tightly and giving Shiloh a soft nod.

Shiloh leaned into plant a kiss on the smaller girl's lips, but Paisley nearly stumbled backwards. "Do not drop them!" she giggled, quickly regaining her balance. Shiloh fake pouted, settling for reaching out and tucking a loose strand of hair behind the girl's ear.

Paisley laughed and crinkled her nose. "See you at 12?"

"See you at 12," Shiloh nodded. "Love you," she whispered, squeezing Paisley's shoulder and circling back around the car. Paisley gave her a small smile before carefully making her way into the building.

Shiloh sighed softly, sitting back in the car for a moment and gazing up at the sky. They were just beginning to get into a routine and she couldn't be happier with the way her life was turning out. The buzzing of her phone interrupted her thoughts.

[My Girl - 8:34] i forgot to say i love you

[My Girl - 8:34] i never forget in my head though

[My Girl - 8:35] but i love you a lot

Shiloh giggled, sending Paisley back a series of heart emojis before locking her phone and heading back to the house.

It's funny how things fall apart so unexpectedly.

After dropping Paisley off at work, Shiloh made her makeshift office at their newly purchased kitchen table and got right to work.

The green eyed girl enjoyed her job. She and Toby got assigned a lot of projects together, and they had no problem meeting deadlines and coming up with ideas.

She was thankful to have the flexibility of her job, too. Both she and Toby got to give a lot of input, which was all taken seriously. She'd heard horror stories of graphic designers being doomed to spend their entire careers whitening teeth in Photoshop, but luckily that wasn't the case for her.

Currently, she was on the phone with Toby, working on a brochure they had been assigned to finish for a haunted house. She sat back in her chair, feet propped up on the table with her laptop on her lap.

"Pumpkins aren't scary," Shiloh laughed, rolling her eyes and leaning forward to glance at her emails. "It's supposed to be the 'scariest night of your life.' I don't think pumpkins are going to convince people of that."

"Luke is scared of pumpkins," Toby argued. "He totally burst into tears when we tried to take a picture on the front porch because there was a pumpkin next to him."

"Is Luke going to the haunted house?" Shiloh raised an eyebrow. Silence.

"Didn't think so," she laughed and scanned the email once more. "What about zombies?"

"I know! I can be little bo peep and Lucas can be my sheep!" Maia's voice could be heard in the background, and Shiloh rolled her eyes half-heartedly.

"Sheep are lame," Toby scoffed, becoming distracted by his wife. "I say we dress him up as a bodybuilder. We can give em' fake tattoos and everything."

"Toby! We are not dressing our son up as a bodybuilder for his first Halloween!" Maia laughed. Shiloh held her phone against her ear with her shoulder and scanned through her emails.

"Ow!" Toby whined on the other line. "That hurt!"

"It was a diaper, get over it," Maia giggled. Shiloh rolled her eyes when she heard Toby gasp.

"Was it dirty?! Maia! You c—,"

"It wasn't dirty, you idiot," Maia laughed. "Now take the baby so I can get his lunch ready."

"I'm working here," Toby muttered half-heartedly.

"Doesn't look like there's much work getting done," Maia snapped back jokingly. Shiloh heard rustling on the other line that signaled that Lucas had been passed off to Toby.

"Shiloh, come on, what's so bad about a bodybuilder?" Toby turned his attention back to the phone. This time, though, Shiloh was the distracted one. She heard a faint noise coming from the other room and furrowed her eyebrows.

Holding the phone against her ear, she peered into the living room. "Really Wolf?" Shiloh groaned. Everything that had once been on the mantle was now spread across the floor.

"Shiloh? I asked you a q—"

"Do whatever, Toby. I've got to go," Shiloh nodded, quickly hanging up the phone and bending down to pick up the potted plants before Wolf made an even bigger mess. The small battery operated radio had been switched on, emitting a bothersome static noise.

Shiloh stood up and began to place their things back onto the mantle, keeping an eye on Wolf. He tentatively pawed at the radio, confused by the noise it was making. When he realized it posed no threat, he tapped it again, sending it skittering across the floor.

The static noise stopped and suddenly a grainy voice came into earshot. Shiloh ignored it, grabbing their broom and sweeping up the dirt from the potted plants.

"—at a New York school. The shooter has not been identified, but families h—,"

Shiloh froze, listening to the radio for a few moments. When the sound disappeared again, due to Wolf pawing at the radio once more, Shiloh threw the broom aside and quickly retrieved the radio from its spot on the floor. She turned the dials, trying to get back to the station.

"--students. Again, nothing else is known at the time but we will keep you updated as soon as we get new information. In other news, the a—"

Taking a deep breath, the green eyed girl stood up and glanced around the room. There were hundreds of schools in New York, she told herself. She was probably just overreacting.

But she couldn't will herself to sit back down at continue working. She knew this was going to eat at her until she had answers. So, grabbing her bag, she decided showing up to her meeting an hour early would be worth it if she got to drive past Paisley's school.

Shiloh tapped her fingers on the steering wheel impatiently as she headed down the street, forcing herself not to slam her foot down on the accelerator to get there as fast as she could. It was nothing, she told herself. She was just going to her meeting. Everything was fine.

Everything wasn't fine, unfortunately.

The moment Shiloh saw the red and blue flashing lights as she made it to the top of the hill, her heart dropped in her chest. The parking lot was blocked off and she quickly swerved to park across the street.

She practically sprinted over to the school, weaving her way through the crowd of distraught parents. Just as she was about to break free, she felt a hand grab her shoulder and pull her back.

"No one's allowed any further," the officer motioned to the caution tape draped across the parking lot.

"But my w—," Shiloh began, but was cut off.

"Everyone has someone in there, I understand," he nodded, letting of her shoulder. It took everything in the green eyed girl not to run once more. "Please just be patient."

Shiloh nodded softly, biting down on her bottom lip so hard that she feared she could draw blood. She dug her nails into her palms, staring at the doors of the building and praying that Paisley was okay.

Minutes passed, each ticking second sending another pang of anxiousness into Shiloh's chest. She watched as multiple officers entered the building, but none came out.

Then, as if a switch was flipped, an officer came out holding the hand of a small boy, who was holding the hand of the small girl behind him, and so on. A long string of students silently made their way out of the front of the school building, and the parents around Shiloh all pushed forward to retrieve their children.

Shiloh held her breath, narrowing her eyes and watching as the kids continued to file out of the buildings. They immediately clung onto their parents, who were all practically in tears.

And then the last child exited the building. And it was silent. And Shiloh's heart stopped.

And then it all hit her at once. The green eyed girl took a step forward and crumpled down to her knees, burying her head in her hands and trying to contain her sobs. This wasn't happening.

The sounds of families being reunited flooded the parking lot and she heard the cries of kids, clinging onto their parents out of fear. Shiloh couldn't squeeze her eyes tight enough to get the noise out of her ears.

And then it all went silent.

The green eyed girl lifted her head when she heard a murmur of shock move through the crowd. She blinked a few times, wiping her eyes to clear her vision.

And then she saw it. Well, her.

Paisley.

The small brown eyed girl took small, hesitant steps forwards as she scanned the people surrounding the building. Clinging to her shoulders was a small boy, who Paisley was holding protectively against her chest, despite her own fear.

Paisley stopped walking, standing quietly and looking around at the crowd of people staring at her. Her eyes were wide with fear and when the officer approached them, the small boy in her arms lifted his head.

Moments later, the child wiggled himself free from Paisley's grip and hurried across the parking lot, jumping into his mother's arms, who was now sobbing in relief instead of sorrow. Paisley, however, still stood frozen, bringing her arms up to hug them around her torso.

Shiloh, who was still in a state of shock, slowly stood up. The moment her brain caught up with her body, she was sprinting across the parking lot, dodging the officer that attempted to stop her.

"Oh my god," Shiloh breathed out, pulling Paisley into her arms and holding her tight. She was alive. She was okay. She was breathing. Tears were still pooling in Shiloh's eyes and she quickly pulled away, holding Paisley by the shoulders and studying her face.

"Are you okay?" Shiloh asked, looking into Paisley's eyes and trying to draw some sort of answer out of her wife. Paisley blinked a few times and looked down at her hands.

"Ouch."

C H A P T E R   1 7

"Ouch."

In that very moment, Shiloh felt her heart practically stop. She looked down at Paisley's hands and gasped when she saw the crimson substance smeared all over her palms.

"Oh my god," Shiloh shook her head, suddenly patting down Paisley's arms and frantically searching the girl to see if she had been hurt. The brown eyed girl remained frozen, staring down at her hands.

"Are you hurt?" Shiloh grabbed Paisley's shoulders, trying to draw some sort of reaction out of the girl. Everything was moving in slow motion and she felt sick to her stomach. Paisley blinked.

"It's not hers."

Shiloh froze, flinching when she felt a small hand tug at her sleeve. She whipped her head around, looking down at the little boy who had pushed his way back through the barrier. She recognized him as the child that Paisley had been carrying.

"She tried'ta help the bad guy. That's why her fingers are red," he nodded, holding up his hands to try and explain it to Shiloh.

"We really need you guys to clear the area," a masculine voice appeared from behind them, causing both Shiloh and Paisley to jump. The green eyed girl instinctively grabbed Paisley's hand, trying her best to ignore the way she felt the smaller girl tense up under her touch.

As the crowd began to disperse, the reality of what had just happened hit Shiloh. She turned back to Paisley, studying the small girl up and down. The smaller girl couldn't seem to peel her eyes away from her own hands, and

Shiloh grimaced when she realized the blood was now staining hers as well.

Without thinking twice, the green eyed girl shed her jacket and cleaned off her own hands before grabbing Paisley's and doing the same. The smaller girl just watched her, her eyes wide.

Shiloh didn't have time to think about what exactly was going on. All she knew was that she had to get Paisley out of there. She grabbed the smaller girl's hand, pulling her through the crowd. Thankfully, Paisley trailed behind her, slowly looking around at all the people surrounding them.

The drive home was silent. Shiloh forced herself to keep her eyes on the road. She knew if she said a word that she'd get emotional, and then she'd be in no state to drive.

Paisley followed Shiloh into the house, standing quietly in the foyer. Shiloh bit her lip, running a hand through her hair. She didn't know what to do.

"I'll get you something to drink," Shiloh managed to stutter out, turning and hurrying into the kitchen. She quickly filled a cup with water, turning around and gasping when Paisley appeared only a few feet away from her.

"I, uh, here," Shiloh said softly, handing the cup to the smaller girl. Paisley took it, studying it for a few moments. Shiloh wasn't sure how she was supposed to feel. Especially after Paisley's hands started shaking so badly that the cup slipped out of her grip and came crashing to the floor.

The smaller girl didn't even flinch, she just slowly stared down at the water that was now pooling around her feet.

"It's okay," Shiloh blurted out, bending down and grabbing the cup. She grabbed a dish towel and began wiping up the water. Her heart was beating so fast against her chest that she genuinely wondered if that was what a heart attack felt like.

"Stupid."

Shiloh froze when Paisley's voice broke the silence between them. She was hallucinating. She had to be. Her grip on the rag tightened and she stood up, looking at the smaller girl worriedly.

"Stupid," Paisley mumbled again, her hands curling into fists. This was all too familiar to Shiloh.

"Fuck," Shiloh cursed under her breath, shaking her head. "Fuck, fuck, fuck!" she threw the dish rag to the ground, bringing her hands up to her head and pacing back and forth. What was she supposed to do? What was even going on?

She was brought out of her panic when she heard heavy breathing. She quickly turned around, finding a terrified Paisley backing away from her. Don't say it.

"Please," Paisley whispered, holding her hands up in front of her. Shiloh's mind suddenly went into protective mode, and she quickly shook her head.

The second she took a step towards Paisley, though, the smaller girl held her hands out even further. Shiloh grabbed her hands, trying to move them away from her face to show her that she meant no harm.

Paisley's hands shook as she tried to keep Shiloh away, shaking her head frantically. "Please," she whimpered.

"Paisley," Shiloh whispered, trying to get the girl's attention. Paisley was still trying to push Shiloh's hands away but the green eyed girl had laced their fingers together and was holding them in place. "Paisley, look at me," she repeated herself.

"Please!" Paisley raised her voice, digging her heels into the ground and trying to push Shiloh away from her. She continued to shake her head, squeezing her eyes shut.

"Paisley!" Shiloh snapped, raising her voice along with the girl. Paisley immediately froze, her eyes snapping open and she stared at Shiloh in terror.

"It's me! It's Shiloh!" the older girl's voice grew raspy as she shook Paisley's hands, trying to get it into her head that she wasn't going to hurt her. Paisley stayed frozen, her eyes wide.

"I'm not going to hurt you," her voice grew calmer, her eyes pleading into the smaller girl's. Paisley's eyes softened and she relaxed her arms, allowing Shiloh to move closer to her.

"Paisley, look at me," Shiloh brought her hands up to cup the smaller girl's cheeks, lifting her head to meet her eyes. "You're safe. We're home. No one's going to hurt you."

Paisley stared at her blankly, which made Shiloh's heart drop.

"Please say something," Shiloh whispered, shaking her head and looking into the girl's eyes, begging her to tell her that this was all just some sort of joke. When silence enveloped them once more, though, it took everything in Shiloh to fight the new round of tears that threatened to spill over.

"Okay," Shiloh took a deep breath, squeezing her eyes shut and forcing herself to think about this rationally. "Let's just... let's just go lie you down for a bit," she said quietly. When Paisley didn't protest, Shiloh grabbed her hand and led her into the bedroom.

"Just try and calm down a bit, okay?" Shiloh asked softly, making Paisley sit down on the edge of the bed. "I'm going to make you something to eat. I'll just be in the kitchen." When Paisley nodded softly, Shiloh gave her a sympathetic smile and slipped out of the room.

Moments later, though, she heard rushed footsteps behind her. When she turned back around, Paisley was right behind her, looking up at her nervously.

"Paisley, go lay down," Shiloh nodded towards the bedroom. The smaller girl just glanced at the door before turning back to Shiloh. Sighing, the older girl allowed Paisley to follow her into the kitchen.

Shiloh dug through the pantry, trying to find something easy to make. When she turned back around, Paisley was standing in the doorway, watching her silently.

Taking a deep breath, Shiloh moved to the fridge. She heard soft footsteps behind her once more, turning around to Paisley a few steps closer to her.

The smaller girl's eyes met Shiloh's pleadingly. At this point Shiloh gave in, closing the refrigerator and turning around. She bit her lip, slowly holding out her arms. Paisley's eyes flickered between Shiloh's arms and her eyes before she hesitantly moved forward, allowing Shiloh to wrap her arms around her.

Shiloh held Paisley close against her chest, stroking her hair to try and calm her down. It was at this point that she felt how much the smaller girl was shaking.

"C'mon," Shiloh sighed, attempting to take Paisley's hand and lead her into the living room. Paisley stayed glued to Shiloh's side, though, so the older girl wrapped an arm around her waist and led her slowly to the couch they'd just gotten a week before.

Shiloh sat down, waiting for Paisley to do the same. The smaller girl looked at her nervously, but eventually sat down next to her. Shiloh watched as Paisley's wide eyes slowly took in her surroundings.

The green eyed girl was terrified. Okay, more than terrified. She wasn't sure if there was a word to describe how she was feeling. Seeing Paisley in this state was only bringing back an onslaught of memories that she thought she'd never have to face again.

Paisley was still shaking tremendously. Shiloh watched as the smaller girl tried to fold her hands in her lap, but resorted to hugging her arms around her torso and looking down at her legs.

"It's gonna be okay," Shiloh whispered, turning slightly to face Paisley. The smaller girl gazed at her, tilting her head to the side slightly. "No one's gonna hurt you when I'm around."

Paisley brought her knees up to her chest, nodding her head softly. Moments later, though, she inhaled sharply, nearly falling off of the couch.

Shiloh was confused at first, but then she saw Paisley's phone on the ground with a new message on the screen, she realized what had scared Paisley. She quickly turned to the smaller girl, placing her hands on her shoulders.

"Can you stay here while I go grab you something to eat?" she asked softly, trying her best to assure the smaller girl that she was safe. Paisley nodded hesitantly, and Shiloh lingered for a moment to study her eyes, wishing with everything in her that she could have a glimpse into the smaller girl's mind at that moment.

She gave Paisley's shoulder a reassuring squeeze before swiping the girl's phone from the carpet and dialing Ryland's number. She disappeared into the kitchen, tapping her foot impatiently as she leaned against the counter. Ryland picked up on the first ring.

"Paisley, oh my god, you're okay," the light haired girl sounded worried, and Shiloh bit her lip.

"Uh, it's... it's Shiloh," the green eyed girl moved over to the fridge, searching for something to give Paisley to eat.

"Where's Paisley?" Ryland's voice was laced with panic.

"The living room," Shiloh said quietly, holding the phone against her ear with her shoulder as she dug through the back of the fridge, retrieving a container of yogurt.

"Is she okay?" Ryland asked. "We heard about the shooting at her school... Me and Nessa just saw the news and-,"

"Ryland..." Shiloh whispered, her voice cracking as she tried to fight tears. She heard the other girl pause on the end of the line.

"Don't tell me she's hurt," Ryland's voice changed.

"She's... she's fine... I mean, like... physically," Shiloh swallowed the lump in the back of her throat and shook her head. "But not... not..."

"We're on our way," Ryland blurted out, noting that her best friend was on the verge of tears. "Do you need us to pick up anything on the way over?"

Shiloh bit her lip, glancing around the kitchen. "We have like... no food," she said softly.

"On it," Ryland nodded curtly. "Just hang tight until we get there, okay? Tell Paisley we love her."

"I will," Shiloh nodded, saying goodbye to Ryland and willing for the girls to get there fast. Alone, she wasn't sure what she was supposed to do.

She took a deep breath, splashing her face with cold water in the sink before grabbing a spoon and heading back into the living room. She paused under the archway, studying the scene in front of her.

Paisley was curled up on the couch, cradling Wolf in her arms and staring straight ahead. The white cat didn't seem to mind being trapped in Paisley's grip, he only rested his chin on her shoulder and sighed contently. Shiloh somehow found comfort in this.

"I, uh, I got you yogurt," Shiloh said quietly, walking over to sit back down. "The banana kind that you like."

Paisley's eyes followed her, but she made no move to take the plastic cup when Shiloh held it out in front of her. Shiloh met her eyes pleadingly, holding up the spoon and trying to get her to take the food.

When Paisley shook her head, Shiloh sighed and set the yogurt down. She leaned back on the couch, looking over at the younger girl who was watching her silently.

"I don't know what to do," Shiloh admitted, her voice cracking. She glanced over at Paisley, silently praying for some kind of reaction. But the smaller girl just gazed back at her with eyes full of anxiety.

"I promised you," Shiloh whispered, shaking her head. "I was supposed to keep you safe and I didn't."

At that point, Shiloh realized that she was completely powerless.

C H A P T E R   1 8

Both girls sat in silence for a good 30 minutes. Paisley had Wolf cradled in her arms, looking down at the floor nervously. Shiloh's heart ached when she saw how badly the smaller girl was shaking, but she didn't know what she was supposed to do.

She couldn't help the sigh of relief that left her lips when she heard soft knock at the door. Paisley tensed, but Shiloh practically scrambled to let Ryland and Vanessa in.

Upon opening the door, Ryland gave Shiloh a knowing look and made a beeline for the living room. Just as Shiloh turned around to follow the girl, she felt a hand grab her wrist and pull her in the opposite direction.

"What the—?" Shiloh stumbled when Vanessa tugged her into the bedroom. "What are you…?"

"Breathe," Vanessa laughed, placing her hands on the other girl's shoulders. "I just need to make sure you're alright."

Shiloh sighed, leaning back against the door and trying to push past all the conflicting emotions she had running through her head. Vanessa studied the other girl, well aware that she wasn't 'alright.'

"I don't know what you expect me to say," Shiloh said quietly. "She won't even talk to me."

"It's that bad?" Vanessa's jaw opened slightly, and the dark skinned girl struggled to hide her shock. Shiloh nodded, swallowing the lump in her throat.

"You know how she was when she first… you know?" Shiloh's voice grew quiet. Vanessa nodded hesitantly.

"She's… like that," Shiloh choked on her words, cupping her hand over her mouth and turning around to try and hide her tears. Vanessa wasn't having any of it, though, and she grabbed Shiloh's shoulder to turn her around.

"Like what?" Vanessa prodded, needing answers. Shiloh took a deep breath and shook her head.

"I don't know!" Shiloh threw her hands down at her sides and gave up on trying to hold back her tears. "Everything is 'ouch' or 'please' or 'stupid' or... I just... she won't even talk to me!"

"Woah, woah, okay," Vanessa grabbed Shiloh's shoulders and carefully led her over to sit down on the edge of the bed. "I didn't expect it to be that bad..." she confessed.

Shiloh bit her lip, nodding before letting her head drop into her hands, trying to stop herself from crying any harder than she already was. This was literally causing her physical pain.

"All we heard is that there was a shooting and that they got the guy, but her was like, already dead," Vanessa reached out to rub circles in Shiloh's back, trying to comfort her friend.

"She had blood..." Shiloh breathed in deeply "...on her hands."

"What?" Vanessa froze, leaning over to try and see the expression on Shiloh's face. "Was she hurt?"

Shiloh shook her head, digging her nails into the material of her jeans and willing herself to stop crying. She hated acting like this in front of other people.

"I don't know what to do..." Shiloh admitted, burying her face back into her hands once more and taking a deep breath. "I can't... I just... seeing her like this again was my biggest fear and now..." she gave up on trying to hide her emotions, inhaling sharply as a sob escaped her lips.

"Hey, hey, let's not jump to conclusions," Vanessa shook her head and scooted closer to Shiloh. "Can't you call her doctor? Yeah... let's.... let's do that first. That's the first step."

Shiloh wiped her eyes, looking up at Vanessa when she felt the girl lean behind her to grab her phone from the nightstand. "What's his name under?" the girl asked, looking to Shiloh for an answer.

"I can do it," Shiloh sniffed, wiping her eyes once more before taking the phone from Vanessa's hand. The dark skinned girl eyed her questioningly, but once Shiloh dialed the number and held the phone to her ear, Vanessa placed a supportive hand on her friend's shoulder.

"Uh, hi," Shiloh bit her lip. "It's Shiloh Everest, Paisley's wife.... yeah," she glanced over at Vanessa nervously, but the other girl just gave her a soft nod to encourage her to go on.

"I don't know if you've heard about the... the incident at the school...?" She bit her lip and let her hair hang in front of her face. "Oh okay, well... yeah... Paisley was there..."

Shiloh's eyes widened and she sat up slightly, looking at Vanessa with an unreadable expression. She held the phone tightly against her ear and nodded. "Uh, yeah, actually... yeah," she bit her lip.

Vanessa noticed Shiloh's disposition change when she went silent. The green eyed girl fought back tears for the second time and her grip on the phone tightened.

"Yeah..." Shiloh whispered, biting her lip. She avoided eye contact with Vanessa, knowing it would just cause her to start crying again. "As soon as possible, yeah."

"Alright," she nodded softly, digging her nails into her palm. "Thank you."

She ended the call, tossing the phone aside and immediately shaking her head. Vanessa gave her a questioning look.

"What'd he say?" the girl asked, unsure if she even wanted to know the answer. Shiloh took a deep breath and abruptly stood up, throwing her hands down at her sides.

"This was supposed to be over!" Shiloh raised her raspy voice, her tone laced with desperation. "This isn't supposed to be happening!"

"Woah," Vanessa jumped to her feet and grabbed Shiloh's hands, trying to get to her calm down. "Breathe, Shy, breathe," she met her eyes, looking at her seriously.

Shiloh fought back her tears, trying to listen to Vanessa by taking a deep breath. A sob escaped her lips and she quickly used one of her hands to cover her mouth, squeezing her eyes shut and letting out a shaky breath.

"Now try and tell me what he told you," Vanessa placed her hands on the green eyed girl's shoulders.

"He said..." Shiloh coughed, turning her head away for a second and taking a deep breath to compose herself. "He said it happens... her PTSD can like... be triggered.... I don't know," she shook her head.

"He thinks it triggered something?" Vanessa raised an eyebrow in confusion.

"It's common apparently," Shiloh whispered, her vision still blurred by her tears. "If they experience something traumatic they can... like... regress and shut down when they don't know how to handle it..."

"You mean like..?" Vanessa paused when Shiloh shook her head, holding up a hand to get the other girl to stop talking. The green eyed girl walked back over to the bed, sitting down and burying her head back into her hands.

"Oh..." Vanessa breathed out, hit with the reality of the situation. She sat back down next to Shiloh, placing her arm around her friend's shoulders and sighing softly.

"He's changing her appointments back to once a week," Shiloh's raspy voice made a reappearance. "But he said... I mean, there's not much we can do besides that...." she paused for a moment to collect herself. "It's something that she has to... just... work through... on her own..."

"With us," Vanessa corrected her. "She'll have you by her side."

"What if I can't..?" Shiloh's voice cracked and she felt as if someone had her heart trapped in their fist. "What if she doesn't...?"

Vanessa shook her head, stopping Shiloh before she went any further. "She will, Shiloh. Okay? It's just another bump in the road."

"More like a fucking sinkhole," Shiloh mumbled, resting her head back in her hands and exhaling slowly. It was as if just when she had been getting better, something else had to come along and screw everything up once more.

"Okay, you need a nap," Vanessa sighed, standing up. "We've got Paisley for now, okay? You rest."

"No, what I need is to take care of her," Shiloh rebutted, standing up and moving towards the door. Moving quickly, Vanessa blocked her way out.

"No, Shiloh. You can't take care of someone else when you're like... this..." she motioned to the distraught girl. "DJ and I can take care of it for now. You sleep."

"But-,"

"I mean it," Vanessa gave her a look that meant business, one that Shiloh knew better than to argue with.

"You're so annoying," Shiloh mumbled half heartedly, sitting back down on the bed. Vanessa gave her a playful smile, flipping off the lights as she slipped out of the bedroom.

The tears came easy after that. Especially when Shiloh's eyes landed on the picture of her and Paisley that sat on the bedside table.

Feeling miserable and utterly discouraged, Shiloh burrowed under the covers and willed for this to all be a dream.

Meanwhile, Vanessa headed back into the living room. Her and Ryland exchanged glances, and judging by her friend's facial expression, she knew Shiloh hadn't been exaggerating.

Paisley sat on the far end of the couch, now hugging her knees to her chest and staring blankly at the floor. Wolf was perched on the arm of the couch, refusing to leave the smaller girl's side.

"She's barely moved," Ryland whispered when Vanessa sat down on the coffee table between them. "She won't even talk to me," Ryland's voice was laced with confusion.

"It's not just you," Vanessa shook her head, reassuring the other girl. "Shy called the doctor and apparently this kind of thing happens," she said quietly so Paisley couldn't hear them.

Wolf pawed at the smaller girl's knee and Paisley turned her head slightly, staring at the cat quietly. Vanessa and Ryland exchanged glances.

"Well what do we do?" The light haired girl whisper-yelled, growing even more worried than she had been before. Both Paisley and Wolf glanced over at her.

"I don't know if there's much we can do," Vanessa admitted, biting her lip. "I don't-,"

"We're her friends first, right?" Ryland questioned, glancing over at Paisley who was now studying them intently. "Maybe she just needs her friends right now."

"Yeah…" Vanessa nodded softly, moving to sit a few feet away from Paisley. She noticed the yogurt Shiloh had brought out, grabbing it and glancing back to the smaller girl.

"Hey Paisley," Vanessa said softly, holding up the small plastic cup. "Do you wanna eat something? You probably should."

The smaller girl's eyes traced over Vanessa's face, making sure she wasn't a threat. She shook her head softly before resting her chin back on her knees. Ryland and Vanessa exchanged glances.

"Well I'm ordering pizza, I'm starving," Ryland stole Vanessa's phone, dialing the number before the older girl could stop her. Paisley perked up slightly, lifting her head to watch the light haired girl.

"You'll eat pizza?" Vanessa asked, noticing this. Paisley turned her attention over to the older girl, a pleading look in her eyes. Vanessa understood, nodding softly.

"We heard about what happened," Vanessa said quietly, leaning against the couch and looking over at Paisley. "Ryland and I figured we'd come over and keep you guys company for a bit. Strength in numbers, right?"

Paisley simply gazed at her with wide eyes, scanning her surroundings once more. She was constantly on edge, wary of any possibly danger. Her nails were dug into the material of her jeans to try and steady her shaky hands.

"Hey," Vanessa whispered, reaching out and placing a hand on Paisley's knee. The smaller girl tensed and looked at her with panic in her eyes, but Vanessa quickly shook her head. "You're okay, Paisley, just breathe."

Paisley's shoulders relaxed slightly and she bit her lip, bringing her hands up to smooth out her hair. She looked at Vanessa and then scanned the room in confusion when she realized who was missing.

"She's taking a nap," Vanessa quickly explained, causing Paisley to look at her questioningly. "She's just really... tired."

"Pizza's on its way," Ryland announced, coming back from the kitchen with two water bottles. "Drink up, Chanch," she tossed one in Paisley's direction.

Vanessa was just about to yell at the other girl, but to her surprise Paisley caught the bottle gently, looking up at Ryland before turning it around in her hands a few times. Ryland plopped down beside Vanessa, noticing the girl's warning glare. "What?"

"You could've freaked her out or something," Vanessa hissed. Ryland just shrugged.

"She doesn't want to be babied. She never did," Ryland took a sip from her own water bottle before offering Vanessa some. "Just give her some time to cool down and keep her company while she sorts herself out. If we make a huge deal out of it she'll do the same," Ryland nodded once.

Vanessa understood, glancing back at Paisley who was taking small sips from the water bottle and holding up the bottle cap for Wolf to inspect. She sighed softly.

"Shiloh's pretty upset," Vanessa whispered out of earshot. "I made her lay down for a bit. She was crying."

"She never cries," Ryland noted. She paused, looking over at Paisley who was now staring down at her shoes, a blank expression on her face. She bit her lip.

"I'm worried," the light haired girl confessed quietly. Vanessa nodded in agreement, watching as Paisley buried her head inbetween her knees and willed herself to stop shaking.

CHAPTER 19

Thirty minutes later, Ryland plopped back down on the couch beside Paisley, offering her a plate. The smaller girl glanced at her tentatively before reaching out to take it.

Ryland laid a piece of pizza on Paisley's plate, giving her a soft smile before leaning forwards beside Vanessa. The dark skinned girl had found Shiloh's laptop and was currently trying to log onto their Netflix account.

"This has got to be the only time I'm not going to complain about watching Friends," Ryland whispered, glancing back at Paisley, who was holding the plate up and studying her piece of pizza.

"Don't push it," Vanessa said quietly, her eyes fixed on Paisley, who had picked off a small piece of the crust and popped it into her mouth. The two girls high fived subtly, relieved that they'd managed to get the girl to eat something.

"Which one is the funniest one?" Ryland asked, pushing Vanessa aside and taking over control of the computer. She scrolled through Friends episodes, looking to Vanessa for an answer.

"How am I supposed to know?" Vanessa whispered, shaking her head. "Just pick a random one," she nudged Ryland's shoulder.

"Fine," the light haired girl clicked a random episode and tilted the laptop, making sure Paisley could see it from where she was sitting. The two other girls scooted back onto the couch.

Paisley didn't audibly acknowledge their choice in shows, but she did lean forward slightly so she could see the screen. Ryland and Vanessa exchanged glances before leaning back on the couch and pulling out their phones.

Both girls weren't paying much attention to the episode, which is why they were taken by surprise when rather loud noise echoed through the room. They both jumped, but when they realized it was the computer, they didn't think much of it.

That was, until they heard a whimper come from the other end of the couch. Paisley had her head buried in her knees, her arms wrapped tightly around legs to make herself as small as possible.

Vanessa immediately hopped forwards to pause the show, where one of the characters was scrambling to clean up the large piece of furniture he had knocked over. Ryland, on the other hand, quickly scooted towards Paisley and gently placed a hand on her shoulder.

"Hey, hey, it's alright, it was just the s-," Ryland began, but was interrupted when Paisley practically dove forwards and buried her head in Ryland's shoulders.

Ryland quickly moved to wrap her arms around the smaller girl in an attempt to comfort her. She couldn't even tell if she was crying, all she knew was that Paisley was shaking worse than she'd ever seen, and the smaller girls breathing was short and rushed.

"Paisley, Paisley," Vanessa quickly shook her head, shutting the laptop and moving on the other side of the couch to rub circles in the girl's back. "Hey, Paisley, you're okay. Deep breaths."

"Her heart..." Ryland mouthed, nodding to get Vanessa's attention. "She's like... terrified," the light haired girl whispered. Paisley's hands clung tightly to the back of Ryland's hoodie, balling the material into her fists.

Vanessa bit her lip, giving Ryland a sympathetic look. Neither of them liked seeing their friend like this.

"Look, Paisley," Vanessa hopped to her feet. Ryland watched as her roommate quickly locked the front and back doors, drawing all the blinds shut and trying to get Paisley's attention. "Look, we're safe here," she sat back down on the couch, placing a gentle hand on the smaller girl's shoulder.

"Do you have like... classical music?" Vanessa turned to Ryland.

"You're kidding, right?" Ryland scoffed, raising an eyebrow at the girl.

"I don't know!" Vanessa whisper yelled, scanning the room once more. "I just thought it would help... I don't know, calm her down or something."

"Check Shiloh's phone," Ryland nodded towards the table. "She's all sappy and lame like that."

"Good idea," Vanessa nodded, retrieving the girl's phone and sitting back on the couch. Paisley had calmed down slightly, but she was still holding onto Ryland for dear life, with her head buried in the other girl's shoulder.

"Shit," Vanessa groaned. "She has it password protected."

"Give it here," Ryland rolled her eyes. Vanessa complied, watching as Ryland studied the phone for a few minutes before tapping 4 numbers. Moments later, she was scrolling through the music app.

"How come she told you her password?" Vanessa gaped, crossing her arms.

"She didn't," Ryland laughed, looking up. "Her password was Pais. It wasn't that hard to guess."

"Oh," Vanessa said softly, looking down at Paisley. Ryland had one hand around the smaller girl, and her free hand was scrolling through Shiloh's phone.

"Of course," Ryland laughed, rolling her eyes. When Vanessa raised an eyebrow at her, she held up the phone.

"She has a playlist dedicated to getting Paisley to sleep," Ryland rolled her eyes and studied the phone once more. "How lame."

"Well let's hope it comes in handy," Vanessa snatched the phone out of Ryland's hands, earning a half-hearted glare from the older girl. She pressed play, and 'Gracious' by Ben Howard quietly filled the room.

The minute the song began playing, Paisley lifted her head slightly. Ryland glanced down at the girl before looking over at Vanessa in surprise.

"She's calming down," Ryland mouthed slowly, using her free hand to point to Paisley. The smaller girl sighed softly, resting her head back on Ryland's shoulder and squeezing her eyes shut.

"Nope, no way," Ryland shook her head. "She is not falling asleep on me," the light haired girl tried to lift Paisley off of her, but the smaller girl looked up at her innocently.

"Ugh, fine," Ryland glared at Vanessa when she laughed. Sighing, the youngest girl leaned back against the couch and allowed Paisley to rest her head back on her shoulder.

About an hour or two later, all three girls had fallen asleep. Surprisingly, Paisley had managed to doze off for a while.

It didn't last long, though. She was woken up by a loud ringing in her ears, making her bolt upwards and gasp for breath. The smaller girl's hands shook and she frantically looked around the room, finding the other two girls dead asleep on the couch.

Her heart was pounding against her chest as she stood up slowly, hugging her hands around her torso. The room was nearly pitch black and she was biting her lip so hard that she thought she would draw blood.

Paisley gazed pleadingly at the two sleeping girls, willing for one of them to wake up. The smaller girl whimpered, squeezing her eyes shut and taking a slow step forwards.

She paused and opened her eyes cautiously, scanning the room. When nothing jumped out of the shadows, she took a few quick steps forwards. Pause. Look around.

She felt her way through the darkness, jumping slightly when Wolf brushed against her leg. His eyes reflected the light in the darkness, making them glow slightly. Paisley watched as he pawed at one of the hallway doors, slipping into the room. She followed.

The room was dimly lit by the moonlight coming through the window. Paisley narrowed her eyes, tracing the outline of the figure on the bed. Shiloh.

The smaller girl bit her lip, slipping into the dark room and standing still for a few moments. Quietly, she retrieved Shiloh's blanket that had fallen on the floor and gently laid it back over the girl.

Paisley looked down at her hands, holding them up in front of her and watching how much they were shaking. She couldn't seem to calm down no matter how hard she tried.

Unsure of what else to do, and not wanting to wake Shiloh, the small girl carefully circled the bed, crawling onto the opposite side and sitting cross legged. She looked over her shoulder, studying the moon that was glowing high in the sky.

She flinched when Shiloh moved slightly in her sleep. Paisley whipped her head back around, afraid that she had awoken the girl. She sat frozen for a few moments until she concluded that the girl was still asleep.

Paisley studied her, watching as Shiloh's chest rose and fell slowly. Subconsciously, she began to breathe along with Shiloh, mimicking the older girl.

Paisley gasped when something brushed against her arm, quickly calming down when she realized it was only Wolf. The old white cat nudged her hand, demanding attention.

Biting her lip, the smaller girl tore her eyes away from Shiloh and scratched behind Wolf's ears. The cat sprawled out beside her, yawning widely and claiming his spot on the bed.

Paisley gazed back over at Shiloh, admiring how content she looked. The smaller girl allowed her eyes to scan the room absentmindedly. Big mistake.

Paisley whimpered. Everything around her had the potential to be something bad. The shadows appeared as if they were moving and she inhaled sharply, scooting further onto the bed.

She stole a glance at Shiloh, who was still fast asleep. Hesitantly, she let her hand slip off of her lap and inch towards the girl. She kept an eye on the shadows while she found Shiloh's hand, locking their pinkies together gently.

The small girl held her breath, scared that she had awoken the older girl. When Shiloh didn't stir, Paisley exhaled slowly and forced herself to keep her eyes on Shiloh, away from the shadows.

Shiloh was awoken the next morning by a beam of sunlight invading her eyelids.

She groaned, rolling over and covering her face. The green eyed girl grew confused, though, when she felt a blanket covering her legs. Paisley always stole the blankets in the middle of the night.

Paisley.

Shiloh sat up quickly, rubbing her eyes and cursing herself for falling asleep for so long. She looked around the room, feeling her heart drop in her chest when she realized Paisley hadn't joined her.

She pulled her hair up into a ponytail, hurrying out of her bedroom. She nearly missed the figure sitting on the floor across the hallway, and she nearly screamed out of shock.

"Oh my god," Shiloh caught her breath and brought her hand up to her heart. "Wait... Paisley?" she whispered, eyeing the small girl that was sitting across from her door. Wolf was curled up in her lap, and Paisley glanced up at Shiloh anxiously.

"Hey," Shiloh softened her voice, looking down at the smaller girl. "Uh, is it okay if I... join you?" She motioned to the floor next to the girl.

Paisley gazed up at her before scooting over slightly. Taking this as her approval, Shiloh slid down against the wall next to the girl and pulled her legs underneath her.

"How'd you sleep?" Shiloh asked after a few moments of silence. Paisley's eyes traced her up and down. The smaller girl shrugged slightly.

"Good?" Shiloh tilted her head to the side. Paisley blinked a few times before shaking her head.

"Bad?"

Paisley shook her head again, making Shiloh furrow her eyebrows together.

"Did you sleep at all?" Shiloh suddenly realized what Paisley was alluding to. The smaller girl bit her lip and looked away, which was enough of an answer for Shiloh.

"Hey, it's okay..." Shiloh whispered, she reached out but caught herself, drawing her hand back. "Hey Pais?"

The smaller girl looked back up at Shiloh quietly.

"Is it okay if I.... you know... touch you?" she asked softly, unsure of what her answer would be. She didn't want to do anything wrong and scare the smaller girl even more.

Paisley nodded softly, already scooting closer to the older girl. Shiloh let out a sigh of relief.

"I called your doctor yesterday," Shiloh said softly, gently wrapping an arm around Paisley's shoulders and pulling her into her side. "Is it okay if we like... go talk to him today?"

Paisley tensed, looking up at Shiloh nervously. She shrugged ever-so-lightly, telling herself to trust Shiloh's decision.

"I just... I don't really know..." Shiloh sighed and shook her head. Paisley looked at her in confusion but the green eyed girl just dismissed her words and leaned her head on Paisley's shoulder.

"We'll figure something out," Shiloh whispered, hoping her words would prove to be true. Paisley took a shaky breath, fighting the tears that were threatening to spill over.

CHAPTER 20

Shiloh sighed and gazed up at the ceiling, running her fingertips up and down Paisley's arm lightly. She hated seeing the smaller girl like this. She hated that they had to be back in this situation again.

But she loved Paisley. And that's why she stayed.

For Shiloh it wasn't even a decision. She never considered leaving. She would never even bring herself to think about it. Just the thought of being separated from Paisley made her feel sick to her stomach.

Granted, they were technically separated slightly now that Paisley wouldn't utter a word, but Shiloh had dealt with the girl at her lowest points already. She would walk through fire for Paisley time and time again. She just would.

Shiloh glanced over at the smaller girl, who was trying so desperately to keep her eyes open. Biting her lip, Shiloh reached out and gently placed her hand under Paisley's chin, lifting her head to face her.

"Do you want to lie down for a bit?" Shiloh asked quietly. Paisley jumped slightly, but quickly calmed down. She looked at Shiloh, uncertainty flickering in her eyes.

"I'm not gonna leave you," Shiloh shook her head. Her words held a heavier meaning for both of the girls. "I'll sit with you while you try to sleep, okay? You don't have to worry."

Paisley bit her lip and nodded softly. Relief washed over Shiloh, and the older girl stood up slowly, holding out a hand for Paisley. She took her hand gently.

"Here," Shiloh handed Paisley a clean sweatshirt once they got into the bedroom. When she smaller girl made no move to take it, Shiloh stepped forward and gently helped her change. Paisley yawned quietly and Shiloh couldn't help but smile.

"C'mon," Shiloh whispered, sitting down on the bed. Paisley crawled next to her and glanced up at her, a hopeful look flickering in her eyes.

"You want me to... you know...?" Shiloh asked quietly.

Paisley gave her the slightest of nods, and Shiloh decided this was a glimmer of hope. She gave Paisley a soft smile and scooted up on the bed, pulling the blanket over the girl once she lay down.

Paisley faced the wall, gazing out the window blankly. Shiloh sat behind her, reaching out and tracing patterns on the girl's upper arm absentmindedly.

"Only for you," Shiloh whispered, almost inaudibly.

Shiloh finished singing, taking a deep breath and looking down at Paisley once more. She expected the smaller girl to at least have her eyes closed, but instead Paisley was looking up at her with a distant look in her eyes.

For some reason, Shiloh pulled her hand away, shaking her head and looking down at the smaller girl.

"Don't do that," Shiloh whispered, exhaling slowly. Paisley's eyes widened in confusion.

"Don't," Shiloh shook her head and got off the bed, causing Paisley to sit up and tilt her head to the side.

"Stop... just... stop staring at me like I'm supposed to do something..." Shiloh's voice cracked and she brought her hands up slightly.

It was silent for a few moments before Shiloh cracked, throwing her hands down at her sides and no longer fighting the tears that blurred her vision. "I don't know what I'm supposed to do, Paisley!" she yelled.

At this point, Vanessa had been stirred awake by the noises. Upon realizing where she was, she rolled over to try and shake Ryland awake as well.

Paisley's eyes were wide in fear when Shiloh's mood suddenly changed. She sat up on the bed and eyed the girl in confusion, feeling her heart start to speed up. She didn't understand.

"Can't you just say something? Anything?" Shiloh's tone changed once more, desperation laced into her words. "Please just say something!" she begged, looking at Paisley pleadingly as she tried to hold back her tears.

Paisley just stared at her, not breaking the silence. Her eyes begged for the older girl to not be mad at her. But before anyone had a chance to do anything else, the bedroom door burst open.

"What the hell is going o-?!" Ryland started, whisper-yelling. She paused when she saw a distraught Shiloh, who was now just realizing what she was doing. The green eyed girl brought her hands up to cup her mouth, looking back and forth from Ryland to Paisley.

Without another word, Ryland grabbed Shiloh's arm and pulled her out into the hallway. Shiloh glanced back just in time to see Vanessa give her a sympathetic look before slipping into the bedroom.

"What the hell?" Ryland whisper-yelled, pulling Shiloh into the art studio and closing the door behind them. "What was that?"

"I... I..." Shiloh stumbled over her words, shaking her head and looking away from Ryland. The light haired girl wasn't having any of it, though.

"Listen, Shy, I don't appreciate waking up this early in the first place, so you better get to telling me what the hell you were yelling at P—,"

"Why did this have to happen again?!" Shiloh blurted out, throwing her hands down at her sides. Her elbow accidentally collided with her easel, sending it flying to the floor. Both girls jumped, but Shiloh continued speaking before Ryland could do anything.

"I just... we just... it was all going so well, and now... we just... why does it always have to happen to her?! What did she ever do to deserve any of this!?" Shiloh shook her head. "What am I supposed to do?! I couldn't be there for her and n-!"

"Stop trying to fix her!" Ryland grabbed Shiloh's shoulders, trying to get her to stop rambling. The green eyed girl froze, staring at Ryland in confusion.

"Shiloh," the light haired met the her eyes, giving her a look that meant business. "This is not your fault. Quit telling yourself that right now."

"Listen to me," Ryland drew out her words, slowly letting go of Shiloh's shoulders as the green eyed girl composed herself slightly. "You can't fix her. We all learned that years ago. She doesn't need you to be her doctor, or her therapist. She already has those. She needs you to be you. She needs Shiloh. And you're the only person that can fill that role."

"So stop trying to fix her, and just be there for her," Ryland lowered her voice as Shiloh calmed down. The green eyed girl swallowed the lump in her throat and nodded softly.

"You're right," Shiloh whispered. She wiped her eyes, glancing back at the door and biting her lip. "I just hate seeing her like this again..."

"It's not fun for any of us, trust me," Ryland sighed, reaching out and squeezing her friend's shoulder. "But what she needs is her friends."

Shiloh laughed, shaking her head and looking down. "You said to me when she first showed up," she said quietly before Ryland could question her.

"Well..." Ryland shrugged, running a hand through her hair. "We're still learning."

"Yeah," Shiloh whispered, glancing back at the door. She sighed, feeling guilt for having yelled at Paisley, even if it hadn't been directed at her.

Before either girl could say anything else, they were both distracted by the door opening slightly. Vanessa peered into the room and glanced at both of the girls.

"I, uh..." Vanessa pushed the door open more, revealing a small Paisley standing next to her. Moments later, the brown eyed girl was moving forwards. Before Shiloh could react Paisley had wrapped her arms around her torso, burying her head in the crook of Shiloh's neck.

Shiloh's eyes widened and she looked at Vanessa questioningly. When she felt Paisley's hands cling onto the back of her shirt, she quickly brought her arms around the smaller girl and held onto her tightly.

"I don't know," Vanessa whispered. Shiloh nodded softly, feeling her heart drop when she realized the smaller girl was crying.

"Thank you," Shiloh mouthed, turning to Ryland. Her friend gave her a sympathetic smile, nodding towards Paisley.

"We've got to get to the studio," Vanessa reminded Ryland, poking her head in the door once more. "I mean... unless you..." she turned to Shiloh and bit her lip, but the green eyed girl quickly shook her head.

"I've got it," Shiloh nodded, smoothing out Paisley's hair and looking down at the girl, whose head was still buried in her shoulder. "Thank you guys, really, you-,"

"Save it," Ryland laughed and rolled her eyes playfully. "You know we're always here."

"Text us after the doctors," Vanessa added. After saying their goodbyes and gathering their things, the two girls left Shiloh and Paisley alone in their small house.

Shiloh took a deep breath, gently separating them and looking down at the smaller girl. Paisley shook her head, bringing her hands up to cover her mouth in an attempt to stop her tears.

"Hey…" Shiloh said gently, reaching out to pull Paisley's hands away from her face. She cupped the smaller girl's cheeks and used her thumbs to wipe away her tears. "I'm so sorry," she whispered, leaning her forehead against Paisley's and sighing.

Paisley squeezed her eyes shut, breathing out slowly. Her eyes flickered back up to meet Shiloh's and she looked away nervously.

"I wasn't yelling at you, you know," Shiloh said softly, Paisley's eyes met hers once more. "I just… I don't like how these kind of things keep happening to you. You don't deserve it at all."

Paisley lifted her shoulders slightly, letting them drop in a small shrug.

"C'mon," Shiloh sighed softly, leading Paisley back into the bedroom. The smaller girl stood hesitantly at the door when Shiloh sat down on the bed, patting the space beside her.

"Here," Shiloh perked up, remembering something. She hurried over to their closet, pulling out one of their moving boxes and digging through it. Paisley watched in confusion.

"Will this help?" Shiloh laughed nervously, holding up a familiar yellow stuffed dog. Although Paisley didn't crack a smile, her eyes widened slightly and she nodded quickly. For Shiloh, that was progress.

Paisley took a few steps forward, taking the stuffed animal from Shiloh gently. Sunny. His name was Sunny. She knew that. Clutching it tightly, the smaller girl followed

Shiloh over to the bed and sat down on the very edge, looking at her nervously.

"C'mere," Shiloh scooted back on the bed and held her arms out. Paisley crawled next to her, to which she was pulled into the older girl's side. She was able to relax slightly with Shiloh around.

"Y'know, Paisley," Shiloh said softly, looking down at the smaller girl. "If I could wave a magic wand or pay a lot of money and make things better for you, you know I would..."

Paisley nodded softly, picking at her fingernails nervously. A few moments of silence passed between them before Shiloh spoke once more.

"But I can't do that," Shiloh finally said with a soft sigh. Paisley glanced up at her. "But if it helps, I can try to help you get rid of the scary things."

Paisley looked up at Shiloh, studying her face for a few moments. Biting her lip, the smaller girl looked down at their hands and gently laid hers overtop of Shiloh. She looked back up at the older girl for approval.

Shiloh couldn't help the hopeful smile that spread across her face when she felt Paisley's hand on top of hers. She leaned down to press a soft kiss to the girl's forehead. Maybe things could get better.

C H A P T E R   2 1

"Can you try and tell me what happened that day, Paisley?"

Shiloh and Paisley sat on a less-than comfortable white couch in the doctor's office. It had taken the older girl a while to convince Paisley to leave the house. Paisley had had a death grip on Shiloh's arm for the entire car ride.

Now, Paisley squirmed under the doctor's watchful eye. Shiloh bit her lip and glanced back and forth from the doctor to her wife, wondering if she should interrupt.

"Talking about it will help, Paisley," the doctor glanced down at her file, tapping his pen against the desk. "Keeping it all to yourself is only going to make it harder on you."

Paisley hung her head, shuffling her feet against the floor nervously. The smaller girl kept her head down even when the doctor sighed and turned his attention back to her file.

"It's really all up to time," he said after a few moments of silence, now addressing the green eyed girl beside Paisley. "It's all up to her. When she feels ready to talk, she will. Otherwise we can't really do anything besides bring her back to therapy each week."

Shiloh's shoulders dropped slightly. She watched as Paisley kept her head down, afraid of being ridiculed. The green eyed girl let out a soft sigh and turned back to the doctor, giving him a soft nod.

"Medicine is always an option," he added. "But it says here you didn't really have a good experience with that the last time you tried it?"

Shiloh shook her head quickly. "Yeah... I mean, no. No medicine," she bit her lip. She didn't want to have a repeat of what had happened last time they put Paisley on medicine.

"Alright," the doctor wrote something down. "At the most, we can talk about giving her something to help her sleep if this continues. For now, we've just got to wait it out."

"You okay?" Shiloh whispered, reaching out and placing a hand on Paisley's shoulder. The smaller girl looked up uneasily.

"We get to go home now," Shiloh nodded towards the doctor. "He just wanted to check up on you."

Relief washed over Paisley and she stood up quickly, standing by the door and looking at Shiloh expectantly. After thanking the doctor, the green eyed girl followed Paisley back out to the car.

"Hey, hey, look at me," Shiloh reached over the center console and took Paisley's hand in hers. "You're okay. Breathe," she whispered softly, running her thumb over the back of Paisley's hand. The brown eyed girl met her eyes, giving her a slight nod.

They drove in silence for a while, which was only broken when Shiloh took what Paisley believed to be a wrong turn. The smaller girl sat up quickly, her eyes moving around the car frantically.

"Woah, woah, calm down," Shiloh laughed softly, pulling into a small parking lot. "You know where we are, goofball."

Paisley paused, peering out of the window and calming down slightly when she realized where they were. Shiloh grew disappointed, though, when the smaller girl didn't show much of a reaction.

"I figured we'd get froyo as a little distraction, yeah?" Shiloh asked hopefully. Paisley glanced over at her, giving her a hesitant nod. Realizing that was all she was going to get, Shiloh slid out of the car. Paisley immediately appeared at her side, holding onto her arm nervously.

Shiloh couldn't help the pang of guilt she felt when she saw how on edge the smaller girl was. She wasn't sure how to fix this, though, so she settled on squeezing Paisley's hand and leading her into the small store.

Paisley's eyes widened when they stepped inside, suddenly surrounded by a crowd of people who had the same idea as them. She bit her lip, pausing and taking the time to survey her surroundings.

Shiloh watched Paisley for a few moments, noticing how she was intently scanning the people around them, as if she were making sure none of them posed a threat. The thought made Shiloh feel sick to her stomach.

"Come on," Shiloh whispered, tugging Paisley's hand and forcing the smaller girl to follow her. Shiloh grabbed two cups, offering one to the smaller girl. When Paisley just gazed at her, Shiloh sighed and resorted to sharing a cup with the smaller girl.

"Banana?" Shiloh asked, pointing to the machine in front of them. She saw a glimmer of hopefulness in the smaller girl's eyes, and took that as a yes.

Shiloh moved towards the cash register, but grew confused when she felt small fingers curl around her wrist to stop her. When she turned back around, Paisley bit her lip, nodding towards the toppings bar.

"Oh," Shiloh laughed softly, following Paisley over to the bar. She set the cup down in front of Paisley, silently urging her to get what she wanted.

Biting her lip, Paisley looked around before plucking two gummy bears from the candy section. She bent down slightly to make sure she placed them perfectly on top of the ice cream.

Glancing around once more, the smaller girl quickly swiped a banana slice and popped it into her mouth, making Shiloh laugh. Paisley just gave her a soft shrug before following the older girl over to pay for their food.

Now, they sat at a small round table. Paisley had scooted her chair as close to Shiloh's as possible, holding tightly to the plastic yellow spoon the girl had given her.

"Breathe," Shiloh said softly, placing her hand on Paisley's arm and making the smaller girl look over at her. "Just try to relax, okay? Clear your head."

Paisley nodded, looking down at the ground and scuffing her shoes against the floor. Her eyebrows furrowed together when she looked up and came face to face with Shiloh's spoon. The green eyed girl giggled, jutting out her bottom lip.

Tentatively, Paisley opened her mouth, taking the small spoonful of froyo into her own mouth. Shiloh laughed softly, picking off the gummy bears and setting them aside. She knew Paisley wouldn't want to eat them.

Paisley didn't eat much, Shiloh noticed. The smaller girl was more focused on scanning everyone around them. She was wary of every passing stranger, and the thought put Shiloh on edge.

"Are you done?" Shiloh broke the silence between them. Paisley jumped, turning around to face the other girl. She nodded softly, biting her lip and hoping Shiloh wouldn't be disappointed in her.

"Alright," the green eyed girl nodded softly. Paisley followed behind her as they headed back to the car, still keeping an eye out for anything that could possibly cause them harm. Shiloh noticed this, too.

"Not everyone is bad, y'know," Shiloh spoke up as they pulled out of the parking lot. Furrowing her eyebrows, the smaller girl turned to face Shiloh once more.

"You can't live your entire life trying to find the negative in everyone," Shiloh explained, glancing over her shoulder as she backed out. "You'll drive yourself crazy that way."

"There's some much more good in the world. I mean, sometimes it takes a while to find, but it's there. You just have to look," Shiloh nodded softly, stealing a glance at her wife once they were safely on the road.

"I was thinking about this the other day, actually," Shiloh said shyly, glancing over at an attentive Paisley. "If you break everything down, you're left with 'good'... and you're left with 'bad.'"

"But nothing will ever be 100% good, or 100% bad. Ever. So even if it seems like the world is crumbling down around you, there will still be at least 1% of... goodness out there," she reached out and took Paisley's hand gently.

"And I guess they like to say that everything happens for a reason. It's hard to believe sometimes," she nodded softly. "But I mean... look at us, you know? I never thought I'd be here with you. Especially when all that shit happened in high school. So maybe all this bad is just here to make us appreciate the good a bit more."

Paisley turned in her seat slightly and nodded. For now, that was enough for Shiloh. She squeezed the smaller girl's hand as they pulled into their driveway.

"Do you wanna try and sleep?" Shiloh asked, holding the door open and watching as Wolf scurried over to rub against Paisley's legs. The smaller girl bent down to cradle him in her arms before turning to Shiloh and tilting her head to the side.

"You haven't slept for like two days now, aren't you tired?" Shiloh asked. Paisley looked down at Wolf before shrugging.

Sighing, Shiloh nodded. "Well, you should at least lay down for a little bit." She saw hesitation in Paisley's face and quickly held up a finger. "I'm not taking no for an answer."

Paisley sighed, following the older girl into the bedroom and setting Wolf down on the bed. The white cat immediately found his perch atop one of the pillows, yawning and stretching out.

"I'm just gonna be right in the living room, okay? I have some work to get done," Shiloh reached out to smooth out Paisley's hair, giving her a soft smile.

With a soft nod, Paisley crawled onto the bed and immediately burrowed under the covers. Wolf tilted his head to the side and pawed at her arm, but Paisley sighed and gently pushed him away.

Biting her lip, Shiloh forced herself to turn off the lights and leave the smaller girl alone. Spotting her phone on the counter, she quickly grabbed it and snuck back into the room, turning on her music softly and placing it beside the bed before exiting the room for the second time.

With a heavy sigh, the green eyed girl retrieved her laptop and sat down on the couch, keeping an eye on the bedroom door just in case.

Realizing she didn't have her phone, she quickly searched around until she found Paisley's. She dialed Toby's number, putting the phone on speaker and hurrying to check her emails. Her inbox was overflowing, seeing as to she hadn't done any work in a few days.

"You've reached Tobias the single father of one, how may I help you?"

Shiloh rolled her eyes, leaning back in the couch and scrolling through her emails. "Where's Maia?"

"She went to visit her parents and left me with the kid for two days," Toby feigned annoyance. Lucas was making noises in the background, which caused Shiloh to laugh softly. "Where have you been?"

"Oh right..." Shiloh breathed out slowly and bit her lip. "Did you hear about the... you know...?"

"What?"

"The shooting," Shiloh sighed, wincing at her words. There was silence on the other end of the line.

"Don't tell me it w-,"

"It was," Shiloh interrupted him, wanting to get the conversation over with as quickly as possible. "She's not hurt. Just a little shaken up. Well, more than a little, but... yeah," she exhaled slowly.

"Well if you ever need something to do, you two can come over and entertain the devil baby," Toby joked, understanding that Shiloh didn't want to talk about it much.

"I'll keep that in mind," Shiloh laughed half-heartedly, scanning her emails once more. "So...."

"So..." Toby mimicked her, making Lucas laugh in the background.

"I was thinking for the Gagery project that we could get H-," Shiloh began, but was interrupted.

"Woah, woah, woah, we're working?" Toby laughed. Shiloh raised an eyebrow in confusion. "Dude, don't stress yourself out."

"It needs to be done," Shiloh shook her head. "It's fine."

"No it's not," Toby rebutted. "Take a break, Shy. I can handle it from here. The Gagery project isn't even due for another month."

"But-,"

"I'm serious. Otherwise I'm gonna send Lucas over to slobber all over you," Toby laughed. Sighing, Shiloh shut her laptop.

"Are you sure?"

"I'm sure. I can handle it for now, I promise," Toby laughed at Shiloh's hesitancy. "Go... take a nap or something. Just give yourself a break."

"Thanks," Shiloh laughed softly. After saying their goodbyes, the green eyed girl sighed, bringing her hands up to her forehead and rubbing at her temple. She, too, was exhausted.

Quietly, the green eyed girl tiptoed down the hallway and back into the bedroom. She silently celebrated when she found Paisley asleep, one of her legs dangling off the bed. Wolf sat beside the smaller girl protectively, tilting his head to the side when he heard the door creak open.

Shiloh remained silent, sitting down on her side of the bed and letting out the breath she'd been holding. Wolf padded over to her, sniffing her hand tentatively. Once he confirmed it was Shiloh, he hopped off the bed and headed into the hallway, content that he had left Paisley with someone trustworthy.

Sighing, the green eyed girl ran a hand through her hair. She felt the bed move behind her, but just as she was about to turn around, a pair of arms snaked around her waist.

The smaller girl scooted forward behind Shiloh, resting her chin on the older girl's shoulder and sighing softly. Shiloh was frozen for a few seconds, shocked by Paisley's actions.

"Did I wake you up?" Shiloh asked softly, turning her head slightly to try and look at the girl. Paisley just shrugged, closing her eyes and leaning her head against the older girl's.

"I love you," Shiloh whispered, letting out a tired sigh when Paisley didn't respond. She caught sight of their reflection in the mirror and bit her lip.

Gently, Paisley moved one of her hands to find Shiloh's, slowly tracing a heart on the back of her palm. She lifted her head to see if the older girl understood.

Shiloh glanced down at their hands and then over at Paisley, smiling softly. She took the younger girl's hand in hers, repeating the action by tracing a heart on her palm before kissing it, gently curling Paisley's fingers into a fist.

Yeah, things would get better.

C H A P T E R   2 2

Shiloh wanted answers.

She'd never push them out of Paisley, granted. But that didn't stop her from lying awake at night and wondering what exactly was going on in Paisley's mind. What had happened inside that building? What had Paisley seen?

It was only a day later, but time was passing so slowly that Shiloh felt as if it had been an eternity. They'd spent the day at home. Shiloh had convinced Paisley to go for a walk in the late afternoon, and now the green eyed girl was cleaning up from dinner while Paisley got ready for bed.

Shiloh sighed softly, glancing out the window above their sink and catching sight of the sun disappearing just behind the trees. Paisley still hadn't spoken a word that day. Luckily, the two had a bond that surpassed just their words, but Shiloh was growing tired of one sided conversations.

She just wanted things to work out for them for once, she decided as she rinsed off their dishes. It was as if every time the two girls would just start to settle down, something would come along and turn their whole world around.

Just as Shiloh dried off the last of their dishes, Wolf came romping into the foyer. She peered out of the kitchen and moments later their doorbell echoed throughout the house.

Raising an eyebrow, the green eyed girl quickly dried off her hands and jogged over to the door. Her heart dropped in her chest when she saw two uniformed police officers standing on their front porch.

Unsure of what else to do, Shiloh slowly pulled open the door and nervously ran a hand through her hair.

"Paisley Lowe?"

"Uh…" Shiloh shook her head. "That's not me… That's my wife," she glanced back to the hallway, just as Paisley appeared, tugging one of Shiloh's old t-shirts on over her head.

The smaller girl froze when she saw the two men in the doorway. Taking a deep breath, Shiloh turned to her, holding out her hand. Paisley's eyes widened and she shook her head, refusing to meet anyone's eyes.

"That's her," Shiloh said softly, biting her lip and turning back to the men.

"We're investigating the shooting, is she okay with answering a few questions about what she saw?" one of the men asked, glancing at the smaller girl over Shiloh's shoulder.

"I, uh…" Shiloh looked back to Paisley, who had taken a timid step backwards. "If you… well, she's been pretty affected by it. I don't know if she'll answer, but…"

"We'll just ask yes or no questions, then," the man chuckled, looking down at the small notepad in his hand. "We just need as many perspectives on the situation as possible," he shrugged.

Shiloh nodded softly, allowing the two men to step into the house. Wolf immediately rushed over to them, sniffing at their feet and then moving protectively to Paisley's side. The smaller girl stood quietly, her eyes locked on her hands.

"Pais," Shiloh whispered, jogging over and placing a hand on the smaller girl's shoulder. "They just wanna ask a few questions about… what happened. Is that okay? You don't even have to talk. You can just nod your head yes or no."

Paisley bit her lip, glancing up at Shiloh nervously. When she saw that the green eyed girl didn't appear to be too anxious, the smaller girl nodded hesitantly.

Five minutes later, the smaller girl was seated on the couch in their living room. Wolf immediately hopped up on the arm of the couch beside her.

"Were you in the school at the time of the shooting?"

Shiloh studied Paisley's face from her spot next to her. When she saw the smaller girl furrow her eyebrows and look down, Shiloh reached over and took her hand.

"All you have to do is nod or shake your head," Shiloh reminded her. Paisley glanced from Shiloh to the police officers before nodding softly.

"And you're a teacher's assistant for morning preschool, am I correct?"

Paisley nodded once more.

"Were you in the classroom when you first heard gunshots?"

The smaller girl's eyes widened. Shiloh grew confused when Paisley's grip on her hand tightened drastically. The police officers didn't push her, though, which Shiloh was thankful for.

A few moments later, taking everyone by surprise, Paisley shook her head slowly.

"Wait what?" Shiloh glanced over at the police officers while one of them quickly wrote something down.

"Okay... were you outside on the playground?" one of the officers offered Shiloh a shrug, letting her know they were just as confused as she was.

Furrowing her eyebrows, Paisley shook her head once more.

"The bathroom?" Shiloh offered. Upon hearing this, Paisley nodded slowly. Her eyes flickered over to meet Shilohs nervously.

"Okay, so you were in the bathroom when you heard the gunshots. Were you alone?" the officer looked up from his notepad. Keeping her eyes on the ground, Paisley shook her head.

"You were with a student?"

Paisley nodded softly. One of the officers flipped to another page in the notebook and studied it for a few moments. Shiloh gave Paisley's hand a comforting squeeze.

"Was this in the bathroom just across the hall from your classroom?"

Paisley shook her head, earning a look of confusion from the two men. One of them stepped forward, placing a piece of paper between them and handing Paisley a pen.

"Can you show us where you were?" he asked, pointing to the map. "This is the entrance of the school, and this is the classroom you work in," he reminded her by pointing out the small boxes on the map.

Nodding quietly, Paisley took the map and studied it quietly. Shiloh held her breath when the smaller girl gently took the pen and circled the outline of a bathroom in another hallway. The green eyed girl felt her heart speed up as soon as she saw the red 'X' that was also placed in that same bathroom. Both officers exchanged glances.

"Okay..." the officer in front of them took the map back from Paisley, who glanced up at him nervously. The other officer had disappeared out to the front yard, dialing something on his phone.

"So you were taking a student to the bathroom?" the other officer asked, trying to keep Paisley calm. "Was this the same student you brought outside with you? The young boy?"

Paisley glanced at Shiloh pleadingly.

"Was it Jeremiah?" Shiloh asked, recognizing the smaller boy that had approached Shiloh once Paisley had made her way outside with him. Paisley nodded, thankful that Shiloh understood.

"It was," Shiloh turned back to the officer. "Jeremiah."

"So you were taking him to the bathroom when you heard the gunshots. What direction did you hear them coming from?" the officer pointed back to the map.

Paisley gazed down at the paper in her hand, feeling her memories all of a sudden become fuzzy. She bit her lip, looking at Shiloh pleadingly.

"I don't think she knows," Shiloh said softly, squeezing Paisley's hand once more. The officer nodded.

"That's okay," he said, jotting something else down. "Did the shooter come into the bathroom, Paisley?"

Immediately, Shiloh felt the smaller girl's grip on her hand tighten considerably. Paisley looked down at the ground, giving the slightest of nods. Shiloh's heart dropped in her chest.

"Did he see you? Or were you hiding?"

Paisley's grip on Shiloh's hand tightened even more, and the smaller girl furrowed her eyebrows together. She glanced at Shiloh with a conflicted look on her face.

Paisley nodded, unsure of herself. But moments later, she quickly shook her head once more. The memories were fuzzy. She couldn't remember.

Shiloh and the officer both exchanged glances. He scanned his notes one more.

"Did he say anything, Paisley?"

The smaller girl's eyes widened and she pulled her knees up to her chest, burying her head in between them to stay hidden. Shiloh bit her lip. She didn't know how far she could push Paisley for answers.

"I think that's enough for now," the officer nodded, earning a thankful look from Shiloh. "We have other people to get to anyway. If she remembers anything else, give us a call?"

Shiloh nodded, taking the business card from the officer and thanking him. She led the man over to the door, glancing over at Paisley before lowering her voice so the smaller girl couldn't hear her.

"Did they catch the shooter?" Shiloh asked quietly. The officer turned back to face her and raised a questioning eyebrow.

"They didn't need to," he shrugged. Now it was Shiloh's turn to be confused.

"You mean he's still out there?" her eyes widened.

"Oh..." the officer shook his head. "No. He wasn't. They pronounced him dead at the scene."

"You mean...." Shiloh felt her heart drop in her chest. "You think she...?"

"We're not sure yet," the officer shook his head, understanding what Shiloh was hinting at. Shiloh bit her lip nervously and tried her best to stay calm, just now realizing the intensity of the situation.

"Either way, he was the one at fault," the man added. "Even if she did... you know... it's self defense."

Shiloh was comforted by this fact. She nodded softly, glancing back at Paisley only to realize the smaller girl was gone. Panicking, she quickly bid the officer farewell and hurried back into the living room, which was now empty.

"Paisley?" Shiloh called, trying to hide the panic in her voice. She hurried down the hallway and poked her head into the bedroom. Nothing.

"Pa—!"

Shiloh quickly clamped her mouth shut when a quiet noise caught her attention. She held her breath, listening intently. A small meow echoed from across the hallway and she quickly hurried over to where Wolf sat, pawing at the bathroom.

"Pais?" Shiloh pressed her ear against the door. Her suspicions were confirmed when she heard the smaller girl's shaky breathing. Cursing herself for leaving her alone, Shiloh gently placed her hand on the doorknob.

"Paisley, I know you're in there," Shiloh said softly. "I'm coming in."

The green eyed girl grew confused when she attempted to open the door but couldn't get the handle to budge. Realizing she'd been locked out, Shiloh bit her lip nervously.

"Paisley..." Shiloh shook her head. "Can you please unlock the door? The police left...."

A muffled 'no' came from the other side of the door, shocking Shiloh. Furrowing her eyebrows together, the green eyed girl scanned the hallway before sighing and sitting down, her back pressed against the door.

"I'm just gonna sit here until you come out then," Shiloh nodded with finality, leaning her head against the door and sighing. She heard Paisley take a deep, shaky breath and felt a pang of guilt.

Absentmindedly, Shiloh began humming quietly to herself. She grew confused when she heard the smaller girl shift on the other side of the wall, but quickly realizing Paisley had her ear pressed against the crack in the door.

A soft smile spread across Shiloh's face and she folded her legs underneath her. Wolf wandered over to her, pawing at her lap just as Shiloh began to sing.

Shiloh's voice slowly trailed off at the end of the song and she glanced down at Wolf, who had curled up beside her. It seemed to be that the cat only agreed with her on one thing, and that was keeping Paisley safe.

"Are you gonna let me in now?" Shiloh sighed softly, leaning her head against the door. When she was met with complete silence, a sneaky smile crept its way onto her face.

Shiloh quietly got to her feet, hurrying across the hallway and swiping a bobby pin from their bedside table. Doing her best to remain quiet, the green eyed girl knelt back down beside the bathroom door and worked the small pin into the lock, turning it a few times before the door clicked open.

Gently, Shiloh pushed her way into the bathroom, met with a sleeping Paisley slumped against the wall. She couldn't help but be grateful that despite all the madness, Paisley still looked completely content when she was asleep.

Shiloh bent down, carefully taking the smaller girl into her arms. Wolf hurried beside her as she carried Paisley into the bedroom and laid her down on the bed. Just as Shiloh got up to leave, the smaller girl stirred slightly. In her sleepy delirium she rolled over, grabbing Shiloh's hand.

"Stay."

CHAPTER 23

"Stay."

Shiloh's breath caught in her throat and she looked down at the smaller girl, who had curled her fingers around her wrist. Paisley bit her lip.

"You want me to...?" Shiloh trailed off as soon as Paisley nodded.

"Are you okay?" the green eyed girl whispered, scooting back on the bed. There were still so many questions running through her head, but her first priority was always Paisley. As long as Paisley was okay, her questions could wait.

Instead of responding, the smaller girl just tugged on Shiloh's arm, making her lay back on the bed. The moment she did, Paisley was curled up next to her, burying her head in her shoulder.

It was at this point that Shiloh realized how scared the smaller girl appeared to be. She quickly wrapped her arms around the girl, feeling how fast her heart was beating.

"Hey, Pais, breathe," Shiloh whispered. The smaller girl lifted her head, anxiety flickering in your eyes. "What are you so afraid of?"

Paisley immediately shook her head and buried it in Shiloh's shoulder once more. Biting her lip, the green eyed girl propped herself up and scooted back so she was leaning against the headboard with Paisley in her arms.

"It's just us," Shiloh said softly, absentmindedly running her fingers through the smaller girl's hair. "You can tell me anything, y'know."

"I know," Paisley mumbled against Shiloh's shoulder. This comforted the green eyed girl somehow. At least Paisley was talking. At this point, that was progress.

"I just wanna help you," Shiloh sighed, leaning her head back and gazing up at the ceiling. Paisley didn't respond. The smaller girl just took a deep breath and squeezed her eyes shut.

Shiloh couldn't remember how long they laid there for. The comfortable silence between them had nearly lulled Shiloh to sleep. But, just as it began to get dark outside, but girls were startled by the knock at the door.

Paisley's eyes immediately widened, causing Shiloh to grab her hand to reassure her she was okay. The smaller girl met her eyes with a panicked expression.

"Just relax," Shiloh whispered, slowly standing up and running a hand through her hair. "I'll be right back," she leaned down and pressed a kiss to the smaller girl's forehead.

Paisley watched with eyes full of fear as Shiloh disappeared from the bedroom. Wolf immediately appeared at her side, nudging her hand to demand her attention.

Meanwhile, Shiloh ran a hand through her hair as she jogged over to the door. The second she turned the doorknob, someone practically pushed the door the rest of the way open.

"What the—?" Shiloh began, moments later being cut off by a small blur that whizzed past her.

"Jeremiah what did we talk about!?"

Shiloh jumped, whipping her head back around to look at the older woman that stood on the front porch.

"I'm so sorry," the woman breathed, shaking her head. "I don't know what's gotten into him."

Still utterly confused, Shiloh glanced back to the hallway where the young boy had disappeared down. She bit her lip, turning back to the woman in the doorway.

"I... I don't understand..." Shiloh admitted, furrowing her eyebrows together.

"Oh my god, I'm sorry," the woman quickly shook her head. "My son, Jeremiah, is in Paisley's class. He's-,"

"Is he okay?" Shiloh interrupted, suddenly remembering how Paisley had been the one to carry the smaller boy out of the building. Her heart dropped in her chest at the thought.

"He was pretty shaken up," the woman admitted, running a hand through her short hair. "But Paisley took good care of him, I suppose. By the time the police came over to question us he was more than willing to give them answers."

"The police talked to him too?" Shiloh asked, glancing back to the hallway where the boy had disappeared and biting her lip.

"Yeah. Just now, actually. Once they left he insisted on coming over her to tell Paisley something," the woman laughed somewhat nervously, making Shiloh even more confused.

Meanwhile, Paisley was sitting nervously on the edge of the bed with Wolf at her side. She perked up slightly when she heard footsteps coming down the hallway, but when the door was flung open, she jumped.

It wasn't Shiloh. Looking down, Paisley became even more confused when she saw the small boy standing in the doorway. Jeremiah. Something in her was comforted by the fact that he was okay after what had happened.

But then, she was reminded of what had happened.

"Miss Paisley! You're the good guy!" Jeremiah interrupted her thoughts, scrambling over to the bed and making even Wolf tense slightly. Confused, the smaller girl looked down at the boy standing in front of her.

"You're not the bad guy!" Jeremiah continued, trying to get his point across. Paisley tilted her head to the side slightly.

"You're a good guy, Miss Paisley! You saved me!" Jeremiah grabbed her hand. "You saved us from the bad guy!"

"What?" Paisley asked quietly. Nervousness flickered in her eyes. Jeremiah's enthusiasm had taken her by surprise.

"You kept the bad guy away," Jeremiah nodded quickly. "And you even tried to help the bad guy!"

"Oh," Paisley whispered, memories flickering before her eyes. She bit down on her lip to try and keep herself calm.

"You're like a superhero," Jeremiah's eyes widened at his new analogy. He crawled up on the bed, taking Paisley by surprise. "Did you know that, Miss Paisley? You're a superhero. A real life superhero."

"I am?" Paisley raised an eyebrow.

"Yeah," Jeremiah nodded proudly. "I think you're even cooler than Spiderman!"

Meanwhile, Shiloh stood in the foyer with Jeremiah's mother, discussing what they'd heard about the shooting. Both girls were just as equally clueless when it came to what exactly went on in the building.

Shiloh paused mid-sentence when she heard noises coming from down the hallway. She exchanged glances with Jeremiah's mother before taking a few steps towards the source of the noise, holding her breath.

Paisley was laughing.

Shiloh bit her lip to hide her smile. She'd missed that sound. The green eyed girl jumped when the bedroom door flung open once more, and she quickly moved away to pretend like she hadn't been listening.

"I told her, mommy!" Jeremiah ran back out into the living room with a proud smile on his face. "I told her she wasn't the bad guy!"

"What?" Shiloh spoke up, causing the small boy to turn around and look her up and down.

"Are you the princess?" he asked, tilting his head to the side innocently. Shiloh raised an eyebrow.

"Am I what?" she asked, looking over at his mother, who was just as confused as she was. Jeremiah giggled and shook his head.

"The princess, silly! Paisley's princess!" Jeremiah rolled his eyes, as if this was supposed to be common knowledge. "She has flowers right here," he pointed to his shoulder, nodding excitedly.

"And she also has magic powers," he lowered his voice, as if what he was about to say was top secret. "She's made out of the ocean because she's so beautiful and powerful. But sometimes, if you look at her eyes for long enough, you can see the ocean in them," he nodded proudly.

Shiloh's cheeks turned bright red and she was thankful it was dark enough outside to hide her blush.

"Who told you that?" Shiloh asked, glancing back down the hallway. She stifled a laugh when she saw Paisley's head quickly disappear back into the bedroom.

"Miss Paisley did," he nodded. "She always tells us stories before naptime. The princess story is my favorite because she's not a boring princess."

"Oh..." Shiloh bit her lip and nodded softly.

"So it is you!" Jeremiah gasped, jumping up and pointing at Shiloh. The green eyed girl was confused at first, until she saw her hoodie had slumped down slightly to reveal the very top of her tattoo. Her eyes widened, but she quickly composed herself.

"Maybe," she smirked, raising an eyebrow at the younger boy. "But if I told you, that would ruin the magic of it all," she winked. Jeremiah giggled.

"I get it," the small boy glanced back to his mother before turning to Shiloh and returning the wink. Giggling, he moved closer for her and tugged on her sleeve, signaling for her to bend down. Shiloh did so, and he stood on his tiptoes to cup his hand around her ear.

"At the end of the story, after the ocean princess defeats the evil troll, she saves the flower princess from her tower and breaks the spell the evil troll put on her," Jeremiah pulled away to glance at his mother, making sure she couldn't hear them. "And then she kisses her," he whispered, an excited smile on his face.

Shiloh failed to hide her bashfulness. She stood up quickly, running a hand through her hair and biting the inside of her cheek to keep herself from smiling like an idiot.

After saying her goodbyes to Jeremiah and his mother, Shiloh took a few moments to calm herself down before slowly heading down the hallway. Wolf followed after her, nearly tripping her as he weaved between her legs.

She pushed the bedroom door open slightly, finding her wife sitting on the edge of the bed with her head hung down. Paisley's hair brushed past her shoulders, falling in front of her face.

Shiloh instantly grew concerned, and she slowly sat down on the bed next to Paisley. Placing a hand on the smaller girl's shoulder, she gently brushed the hair out of her face.

Paisley was smiling.

Shiloh let out a sigh of relief, unable to stop the smile that spread on her own face. She'd missed that. What had changed, though?

"Well that was unexpected," Shiloh laughed softly, making Paisley look up at her quietly.

"I am the good guy," Paisley nodded softly. "I remember."

"What?" Shiloh raised an eyebrow, suddenly becoming confused. She watched as Paisley's face fell slightly.

"I-I..." Paisley quickly shook her head. "I do not want to talk about it right now."

"Later?" Shiloh asked hopefully. Paisley looked up, scanning her wife's face hesitantly. She sighed and gave her a soft nod. Shiloh struggled to hide her relief.

Yawning, the green eyed girl laid back on the bed. Paisley turned around and sat cross legged, studying Shiloh's face. She was still playing everything over in her head.

Shiloh could tell Paisley wasn't fully in the moment. She was off somewhere in her head, she could tell by the distant look in her eyes. Biting her lip, a mischievous smile spread across her face.

"So a princess, huh?"

Paisley's eyes widened and she snapped her head back over to look at Shiloh, who couldn't help but laugh.

"What?" Paisley tilted her head to the side, even though she had already heard what Shiloh said. The green eyed girl raised an eyebrow.

"Tell me about this ocean princess Jeremiah told me all about," Shiloh laughed softly. Paisley's cheeks grew bright red and she hid her face.

Giggling, Shiloh sat back up and gently pried Paisley's hands away from her face. The brown eyed girl bit her lip, trying to look down and hide the soft smile that had graced her lips.

"*C'monnnn,*" Shiloh whined playfully, reaching up and kissing the bridge of Paisley's nose. "I wanna hear about this princess."

"She is pretty," Paisley said quietly, making Shiloh smile.

"Yeah?" the green eyed girl sat up and laced their fingers together, prodding Paisley to go on.

"Yeah," Paisley nodded, a soft smile forming on her face. "But... but that is not all."

"It isn't?" Shiloh raised an eyebrow.

"She is pretty on the outside because she is pretty on the inside, that is how it works," Paisley smiled shyly when Shiloh squeezed her hand.

"And... she is the ocean princess. But only some people know that, because she lets them see the ocean in their eyes," Paisley reached up and traced her fingertips across Shiloh's cheek.

"What about the flower princess?" Shiloh giggled. Paisley's face grew bright red.

"She.... uh... she..." Paisley shook her head and looked away to hide how flustered she was. "She lives in a tower. But a bad troll guards it, and he put a spell on the tower so no one can get in."

"But then one day, the ocean princess sees through the windows of the tower and she sees the flower princess. And the flower princess is sad, because the troll is mean," Paisley bit her lip. "But then, the ocean princess saves the flower princess from the tower, because she has the seal of the flower on her shoulder, and she is the only person who can break the spell on the tower."

"The troll comes after them, but the ocean princess teaches the flower princess how to fight the troll. And they live happily every after," Paisley nodded softly, looking up and meeting Shiloh's eyes once more.

"That's funny. I think you forgot a part," Shiloh whispered, a small smile forming on her face as she leaned in slightly. "Don't you?"

"I dunno," Paisley giggled shyly, involuntarily lifting her shoulders. "What is it?"

"I recall a kiss happening," Shiloh squeezed Paisley's hand, now only inches away from the girl's face. "Prior to the happily ever after, that is."

"That would make it a good story," Paisley giggled, her eyes flickering down to Shiloh's lips.

"We'll have a happily ever after one day, Paisley. I promise," Shiloh whispered, locking their pinkies together before cupping the back of her neck and pulling her into a gentle kiss. She felt Paisley smile against her lips and couldn't stop herself from doing the same.

C H A P T E R   2 4

"It's later."

Shiloh and Paisley lay on their bed, the dull moonlight from the window serving as their only source of light. Shiloh had an arm around the smaller girl, holding her protectively against her side.

Paisley had calmed down considerably since Jeremiah had left. Shiloh wasn't sure what had happened, but she was grateful that it did. Paisley was actually talking to her.

"Huh?" Paisley lifted her head upon hearing her wife's words. She blew a loose strand of hair out of her face, prodding Shiloh to reach out and tuck it behind her ear.

"You said you'd tell me later," Shiloh said softly. She didn't want to push anything on the girl, but she was also painstakingly curious about what had changed.

Shifting slightly, Paisley turned so she could face the older girl. The entire energy in the room was different now. A nervous tension had fallen over both of them. Shiloh held her breath.

"I remember," Paisley whispered. She felt comforted by those words, signifying that the murkiness of her memories had now faded away, replaced with a somewhat comforting clarity.

"You do..." Shiloh repeated. "Is it bad?"

Paisley quickly shook her head.

"I am the good guy," Paisley bit her lip. "Jeremiah said so. And then I remembered."

"Care to share?" Shiloh laughed nervously. She'd made it a habit of studying Paisley's hands. Whenever the girl was nervous, she'd wring out her fingers, or twiddle her thumbs back and forth. For Shiloh, it was a tell tale sign not to push her much. But now, the smaller girl had one of her hands laced with Shiloh's, and the other was aimlessly tracing the shape of her flower tattoo.

"You will not be mad?" Paisley looked up. She met Shiloh's eyes, finding nothing but comfort in them.

"Of course not," Shiloh practically scoffed in disbelief. Paisley nodded quietly.

"Okay..." the smaller girl whispered. She took a deep breath, preparing her words. Shiloh waited patiently, well aware that Paisley needed time. She was more than willing to give her that.

"It was Jeremiah's birthday," Paisley nodded softly. "And we made the cupcakes, remember?"

Shiloh nodded softly. Paisley sat up, causing the older girl to shift her weight slightly so the smaller girl could lean partway against her and partway against the headboard.

"And we did not have napkins, so we had to go get paper towels," Paisley nodded softly, almost as if she was confirming it to herself as well.

"But Jeremiah wanted to get them himself, and he could not reach the machine thingy in the first bathroom, so we went to a different one," Paisley explained. She kept an eye on Shiloh's face as she spoke, not wanting to upset the girl.

"Go on," Shiloh nodded.

"Can you reach?" Paisley asked, tilting her head to the side. Jeremiah nodded furiously, grabbing one of the small footstools and scrambling atop the counter to collect a handful of paper towels.

"Is this enough?" the small boy turned back around to show Paisley the tall stack of napkins he'd managed to gather. Just as Paisley opened her mouth to speak, a deafening noise echoed from down the hallway.

It's funny how things can change in the span of a second.

When the noise rang in Paisley's ears, her mind immediately threw her back to a few years prior, where the sound had been all too familiar.

But, one thing stopped her from completely retreating into the past. And that was the small boy standing in front of her with wide eyes.

Acting upon instinct, Paisley grabbed the boy from the countertop just as another shot rang out, now closer to them.

"Are those bad guys?" Jeremiah asked worriedly.

Unable to concentrate on anything else, Paisley hurried to bring them both into the stall.

"Quiet," Paisley shook her head and held a finger to her lips once she placed the smaller boy on the back of the toilet. Luckily, Jeremiah seemed to sense the seriousness in Paisley's voice and he stayed silent, pressing his hands against the sides of the stall to keep himself balanced.

The smaller girl rushed to pull the door of the stall closed, locking it just as another round of shots sounded off. Jeremiah whimpered, quickly catching Paisley up to speed.

"Shhh, it is okay," she said, trying to believe her own words. Her heart was pounding so hard against her chest that she was genuinely fearful it would break its way out of her ribcage. But her one mission right now was to make sure the smaller boy was okay.

There was an eerie silence taken over them. Paisley took a deep, shaky breath, thanking the gods that this toilet had a lid. Placing it down, she cautiously climbed atop it, pressing her hand against the two sides of the stall to keep herself level. She didn't want their feet showing beneath the stall.

"It is okay," Paisley whispered, feeling one of Jeremiah's hands lower to cling onto her shoulder. His back was pressed against the wall behind Paisley, higher up on the back of the toilet.

"I'm scared," Jeremiah whispered. Paisley carefully reached up to place one of her hands atop his, flinching when she heard another gunshot, even louder this time.

"Let's talk about the princesses," Paisley whispered. Her voice was barely audible, even quieter than the irregular dripping coming from the faucet outside the stall. She squeezed her eyes shut and forced herself to stay calm.

"The flower princess?" Jeremiah whispered, growing interested. Paisley was glad she had somehow managed to distract him.

"And the ocean princess," the small girl nodded.

"Did they ever get their happily ever after?" the boy asked quietly. Paisley took a shaky breath, unable to calm her beating heart. She nodded slowly.

"Everyone gets a happily every after," she whispered, biting down on her bottom lip and willing herself to stay calm.

"How do you know?" Jeremiah asked. Paisley winced when she felt his grip on her shoulder tighten.

"I just d-,"

Paisley's breath caught in her throat when she heard the unmistakable creaking noise of the bathroom door. She felt Jeremiah freeze above her and quickly squeezed his hand, offering him some type of silent comfort.

Slow, meticulous footsteps entered the room. They seemed to echo on for forever, each one sending a pang of fear through Paisley's chest. She held her breath.

"Fuck."

Paisley jumped when a masculine voice broke the tense silence. Slowly, she craned her neck to peer through the crack in the stall. What she saw made her heart drop in her chest.

Clad in baggy jeans and dark t-shirt, the man (no younger than 30) clutched a silver revolver in his right hand.

Paisley curled her toes in her converse, feeling fear radiate through every nerve ending in her body.

"Fuck."

The man cursed again, and Paisley watched as he began pacing back and forth in front of the mirror, bringing his free hand up to clutch his hair.

Paisley found herself surprised by the emotions laced in her voice. He didn't sound like a "stone cold killer," and although he wore an emotionless expression, his voice seemed to tell otherwise. She sensed anger, but most importantly, fear. Fear? The smaller girl furrowed her eyebrows.

Then, Paisley watched in utter shock as the man brought his arm up, pressing the end of the revolver against his own forehead with a shaky hand. Her eyes widened.

Without thinking, the smaller girl squeezed Jeremiah's hand before quickly hurrying out of the stall. She pressed her back against the door to hide the smaller boy inside, coming face to face with the larger man, who immediately whipped his head around when he heard commotion from behind him.

"What the f-?"

"Do not do that," Paisley shook her head furiously, locking eyes with the gun in his hand. Her heart was beating like crazy by now, and she could faintly hear Jeremiah's rushed breathing from behind her.

But she couldn't let another person die. She'd been responsible for that one too many times.

"You don't understand," his voice growled, low in the back of his throat. It pierced through Paisley and sent chills down her spine. The smaller girl had to force herself to keep her feet planted firmly in the ground.

"Give me it," Paisley's voice came out slightly shakier than she had indented, but she held out her unsteady hand and nodded towards the gun in his hand.

Moments later the cold ring of silver was pressed bluntly against Paisley's forehead, causing her to stumble backward and inhale sharply. Fear flickered in her eyes and she looked at the man pleadingly.

This only lasted a few seconds, though, because soon the man took a step away and pressed the end of the gun to his own temple.

Paisley squeezed her eyes shut just as the final shot rang through the building.

"B-but I was the g-good guy, right?" Paisley whimpered, looking up at Shiloh nervously. Tears welled in her eyes which she quickly reached up to wipe away.

"Of course you were, baby," Shiloh whispered, giving in and pulling the smaller girl into a hug. Paisley lost the battle to her own tears at this point, the emotions had grown too overpowering. She wrapped her arms around Shiloh's torso and buried her head in the older girl's torso.

"I'm so glad you're okay," the green eyed girl said softly, fear even laced in her words. The thought of losing Paisley and having to go on without her was completely paralyzing.

"I could not," Paisley murmured, her voice muffled against the girl's shoulder. She shook her head and squeezed her eyes shut as more tears streamed down her face.

"You couldn't?" Shiloh asked quietly. She gently pried them apart, placing her hands on Paisley's shoulders and holding her steady. The smaller girl reached up to wipe her eyes.

"I could not, Lo," Paisley insisted, shaking her head. "I tried, I really did. I swear, I tr-,"

"Tried to what?" Shiloh cut her off, growing worried.

The smaller girl let out a defeated sigh. Her shoulders dropped and she squeezed her eyes shut, forcing more tears to roll down her face.

"I could not save him."

The brown eyed girl's voice came out as a raspy whisper, which left Shiloh feeling like she'd been hit in the chest. She quickly shook her head.

"No, no, Pais, that's not true," she scrambled to pull her wife into another hug.

"But he... h-he..." Paisley choked on another sob.

"Shh, babe, I know," Shiloh whispered against the top of her head, rubbing circles into Paisley's back to calm her down. "None of what happened is your fault. He made the decision to do what he did, not you."

"But I could h-,"

"No, Paisley," Shiloh shook her head. She couldn't stand to see Paisley trying to make excuses. "The sad truth is that we can't save people. We can only love them and hope that they save themselves."

Paisley let out a defeated sigh against Shiloh's sweatshirt, bringing her hands up to curl under Shiloh's arms and grasp her shoulders. The green eyed girl felt physical pain from seeing Paisley this torn.

"You did save someone, though," Shiloh reminded her. Paisley lifted her head in confusion, looking at her wife through blood shot eyes.

"Jeremiah," Shiloh nodded softly to answer the girl's silent question. "You kept him safe, didn't you?"

Paisley nodded slowly. Shiloh could have predicted what happened next.

"But—,"

"No, Paisley, stop that," Shiloh held her finger up to Paisley's lips to silence her. "Stop downplaying your successes just because things didn't turn out exactly as you wanted them to."

Paisley clamped her jaw shut slowly, brown eyes meeting green hesitantly. Shiloh sighed and shook her head.

"This may sound really selfish of me to say, but right now all that matters to me is that you're safe," Shiloh confessed. She reached out to cup Paisley's cheek in the pale moonlight, using her thumbs to wipe the tears away.

"And next time, stay in the stall, yeah? For my sake," Shiloh laughed softly. "You've got a heart of gold and sometimes it can put you in danger."

Paisley nodded softly. She was constantly shocked by Shiloh's patience. She knew she should have been used to it, but every time she expected the older girl to grow annoyed, she was only met with gentle touches and kind words. It was comforting for her to know that someone was willing to put up with her, even at her worst.

"I love you," Paisley whispered, reaching up to wipe her own tears from her face. She yawned and noticed how Shiloh looked at her adoringly.

"I think what we both need is a good night's sleep, yeah?" the green eyed girl raised an eyebrow. Paisley nodded in agreement, making Shiloh laugh softly.

"Can you sing?" Paisley asked, crawling up on the bed beside Shiloh as she laid back. The older girl shot her a surprised look after not having heard those words in longer than usual.

"Of course," Shiloh nodded softly. She held out her arms and motioned for Paisley to join her, pressing a soft kiss to her wife's head when she lay in her arms. "Only for you. It's always for you."

CHAPTER 25

Shiloh didn't expect things to go back to normal right away.

Even though Paisley had been able to vocalize what she had experienced to her, Shiloh was well aware that the smaller girl was still dealing with the aftershocks of what happened. That was just how Paisley handled things. One step at a time.

It had been a week or so since the police showed up at the door. The weather had taken a considerable turn, trading the splintering heat of the summer for the slight comfort of the autumn breeze. The leaves in their backyard had only just begun to turn colors, prompting Paisley to go on and on about how beautiful their yard would look in a month's time.

Shiloh had been able to get back to work, and currently she and Toby sat in the middle of his living room. A collection of papers were sprawled out between them, and the two graphic designers were taking their time to look over each one.

Meanwhile, Paisley sat on a blanket on the floor beside them, entertaining Lucas by rolling a ball to him and prompting him to roll it back. Each time, she'd clap her hands and cheer him on, and the small child would laugh hysterically. Thankfully, Shiloh and Toby somehow managed to stay focused despite the chorus of giggles that erupted every few moments.

"I like the color scheme on this one better," Shiloh leaned forward and pointed to one of the brochures set in between them. "But the font isn't scary enough."

"I'm so tired of doing these stupid Halloween projects," Toby groaned, tossing the handful of papers he had in his hand down to the ground. "Why does New York even have that many haunted houses?"

"Who knows," Shiloh laughed and shook her head. She grabbed another stack of brochures and began sifting through them. "I'm gonna be so glad once that holiday comes and goes."

"I'm dressing Lucas up and taking pictures and that's it," Toby nodded, giving up on their work and lying back on the carpet, supporting his head with his hands.

"Decided on a costume yet?" Shiloh laughed and raised an eyebrow.

"We compromised," Toby rolled his eyes, earning a questioning gaze from Shiloh.

"He's gonna be a puppy," Toby grumbled.

"Sounds like that wasn't much of a compromise on your part," Shiloh smirked, gathering up the brochures and stacking them together. Toby mumbled something under his breath as Shiloh turned around to steal a glance at Paisley.

The younger girl clapped her hands together to get Lucas' attention. When the toddler looked up, she crinkled her nose and gently rolled the ball towards him.

"Catch it!" she cooed, giggling when the smaller boy nearly fell over when he reached for the ball. Once he retrieved it, though, Paisley's face lit up and she applauded him. Lucas giggled softly, concentrating on pushing the ball back over to Paisley.

"She's got a knack for kids," Toby spoke up, causing Shiloh to turn back around and look at him with a raised eyebrow.

"What? She does," Toby held up his hands as if he were surrendering. Shiloh glanced back at her wife once more before turning her attention back on him.

"I can't argue with you there," she laughed, biting her lip to hide her smile when she heard Paisley burst into laughter from behind her. "She's a kid at heart. That's why. She understands them."

"So is it gonna happen soon?"

Shiloh jumped when Maia appeared, just waking up from her nap. The brunette sat down next to Toby, ruffling his hair playfully and stretching out her arms.

"Is what gonna happen soon?" Shiloh asked in confusion. She grew even more confused when the married couple across from her exchanged knowing glances.

"Well, you know..." Maia laughed, glancing at Paisley. "You guys... kids? I mean, it's only a matter of time, right?"

Shiloh's eyes widened and she hurriedly glanced back at Paisley, her face growing bright red in the process. "I don't... I..." she mumbled, shaking her head once she turned back around. This earned looks of confusion from Maia and Toby.

"I thought you wanted kids?" Maia asked, recalling the conversations she and Shiloh had had over the years once they found out the brunette was expecting.

"I do, I mean... I do," Shiloh nodded to quickly correct them. "Of course I want kids... I just..." she paused to glance back at Paisley once more, watching as she scooped Lucas up into her arms, causing him to erupt into laughter.

"Paisley doesn't?"

"No! I mean... no, I don't know. I think she does, at least," Shiloh turned back around and bit her lip. "I just... don't know if it's the right time yet, you know?"

"Okay, Shy, let me tell you something right now," Toby leaned forward, beating Maia to saying something. "If there's one thing I've learned from... this," he motioned between Maia and Lucas. "Is that there's no right time. Ever."

Shiloh furrowed her eyebrows, still somewhat confused by his words.

"Think about it," Toby continued, sitting up and slinging his arm around Maia's shoulders. "When you say "right time," do you have an exact idea in you mind of when it might be?"

Thinking for a moment, the green eyed girl slowly shook her head.

"Exactly," Toby nodded once. "Because there isn't a right time. If you're waiting for the perfect timing, you're going to be waiting forever. Don't worry too much about the outside factors that don't matter. You'll know when it's time."

"And if you don't..." Maia glanced at Toby, laughing softly. "Sometimes the best things come in the form of a surprise," she nodded in Lucas' direction.

"But luckily you guys don't really have to worry about surprise babies," Toby added, earning a playful shove from Maia and causing Shiloh's face to turn bright red.

Just as Shiloh opened her mouth to reply, Maia held up her hand to signal for them to be quiet. Shiloh watched in confusion as the other girl quickly retrieved her phone out of her pocket.

"Hello?"

Toby and Shiloh exchanged looks, but before the green eyed girl had the time to ask any questions, Maia gasped and quickly hopped to her feet. Worriedly, Toby followed suit.

Both Shiloh and Paisley exchanged confused glances when this happened. Paisley stood up, taking Lucas into her arms and holding him on her hip. Shiloh did the same, watching as Maia's eyes widened and she quickly nodded.

"Okay, okay, yeah, I'll be there," Maia nodded and turned to Toby, brushing past him to grab her shoes from the door. "Love you too."

"What's going on?" Toby stepped forward once Maia hung up her phone. The girl shook her head, letting out a sigh of frustration.

"She's in the hospital," Maia hurried to slip her shoes on. "Dad says she fell again." The girl stood up, worry laced in her words.

"Woah, woah, calm down," Toby grabbed Maia's shoulder. "I can drive you there. You literally just woke up." Maia nodded softly, moving forwards to take the baby from Paisley's arms.

"We can watch him," Paisley blurted out, taking everyone by surprise.

"We can?" Shiloh turned back to look at her wife, who glared at the green eyed girl and nodded.

"Go," Paisley shrugged, looking down at Lucas in her arms. "Do not worry about him." All eyes turned to Shiloh now, who was glancing back and forth from Paisley to Maia.

"Oh, I, uh, yeah," Shiloh quickly shook her head. "We've got him. Got nothing else planned today anyway," she shrugged and glanced back to Paisley, earning a thankful smile from the younger girl.

"Are you sure?" Maia bit her lip.

"Oh shut up with the politeness," Shiloh laughed, reaching out and squeezing her shoulder. "Lucas is practically free babysitting for Paisley. Go," she joked, earning a half hearted gasp from the smaller girl behind her.

"Thank you so much," Maia sighed, pulling Shiloh into a hug and giving Paisley a thankful smile from over her shoulder.

"Send her our best," Shiloh nodded, watching as the couple quickly disappeared out the door. When she turned back around, Paisley bit her lip nervously and looked down at the boy in her arms.

"We've got this," Shiloh attempted to comfort Paisley, but the smaller girl quickly shook her head.

"I know that," Paisley rebutted, adjusting Lucas in her arms. "I am just worried about them," she nodded out the window, where Toby's car was backing out of the driveway.

"Oh," Shiloh nodded in understanding. "Well... let's just try and keep Lucas happy right now, yeah?"

"Yeah," Paisley nodded softly, glancing at the clock and then back at the baby in her arms. "Do you think he is hungry?"

"Uh..." Shiloh furrowed her eyebrows. "I mean, yeah, right? It's almost dinnertime. I can make him something."

"M'kay," Paisley nodded softly. She sat back down on the blanket with Lucas, watching as Shiloh disappeared into the kitchen. Moments later, though, the dark haired girl reappeared.

"What the hell does he even eat?"

Paisley giggled, looking down at the small boy and shrugging. "He likes mac and cheese. Maia makes it for him."

"I can do that," Shiloh nodded, giving Paisley a bashful smile before slipping back into the kitchen for the second time. The smaller girl couldn't help but laugh at her wife's confusion.

"Babe, where's the m—?!"

"Blue box!" Paisley called back, answering Shiloh's question before she could even finish her sentence. She heard the green eyed girl laugh from the other room and smiled softly to herself.

"Aha! Got it!" Shiloh retrieved the box from the pantry, silently patting herself on the back. Meanwhile, Paisley sat Lucas down on the blanket and pulled over a few of his toys, trying to keep him entertained.

Ten minutes later, Shiloh was perched on the counter, swinging her legs back and forth and waiting for the last few minutes of the timer to pass.

"No!"

Shiloh jumped when she heard Paisley's voice echoing from the living room, immediately hopping to her feet.

"No no no!" Paisley shook her head. "Sit back down!"

"What's going on?" Shiloh ran into the living room, growing confused when she was met with a flustered Paisley and a even more confused Lucas.

"He walked!" Paisley huffed, pulling Lucas into her lap and shaking her head.

"He what?" Shiloh gaped. The tone in Paisley's voice and the news she just presented her had taken her off guard.

"He walked!" Paisley threw her hands in the air. "I told him to go get the toy and he stood up and walked to get it!"

"Oh my god," Shiloh laughed, relieved that nothing awful had happened to either of them. She bent down, scooping Lucas out of Paisley's lap and smiling widely at him.

"Did you walk, bud?" she asked, ruffling the small tuft of hair on his head. Paisley huffed, pushing herself up to her feet and glaring at Shiloh.

"What?" Shiloh laughed, confused by Paisley's annoyance.

"He walked and they did not see!" Paisley pointed to the now empty driveway.

"Did he really walk?" Shiloh asked, setting Lucas down and helping him gain balance on both feet. She ignored Paisley's groan of frustration from behind her.

"C'mon, bug, come here," Shiloh backed up a few steps before kneeling down and holding out her arms. Lucas watched her before tentatively setting one foot in the other. Moments later, he was toddling over into her arms, greeted by an excited Shiloh.

"He really did walk!" Shiloh smiled widely in surprise, scooping the small boy back into her arms and kissing his forehead.

"And they did not see!" Paisley reiterated her point.

"That's not our fault," Shiloh shrugged, bouncing Lucas on her hip. Paisley just huffed and plopped back onto the couch. She crossed her arms, upset that she hadn't gotten to share the moment with his parents. Shiloh sighed, moving over to sit beside her.

"If you want, we can send them a video?" she offered, pointing to Paisley's phone on the table. Paisley raised her eyebrows, leaning forward and retrieving the device.

"Really?" she asked, a small smile forming on her face.

"Really," Shiloh nodded once. She paused, though, when a sound from the other room caught her attention. She quickly passed Lucas off to Paisley, running back into the kitchen. "As soon as I finish making his dinner!"

C H A P T E R   2 6

With the changing colors of the leaves also came the colder weather. As always, Paisley was more than excited for the upcoming holidays. Halloween hadn't even passed and the smaller girl was already planning for Thanksgiving.

With only a few days left until Halloween, Paisley and Shiloh were busy with putting the finish touches on their house. Vanessa and Ryland had insisted that they come to their Halloween party. The two girls were notorious for completely covering the apartment in decorations and getting more than their share of noise complaints from the neighbors.

Currently, Paisley was balancing on a chair on the front porch, reaching up to hang a string of pumpkin lights from the roof. Shiloh was in the art studio as usual, slaving over a painting she'd been working on for over a week.

Wolf was perched on the edge of the porch, sticking near Paisley as always. The smaller girl finally was able to plug in her string of lights, clapping her hands when the front of the house lit up. She moved onto the fake cobwebs, which she found surprisingly difficult to maneuver.

Meanwhile, Shiloh had her painting playlist on full blast. There was a paintbrush tucked behind her ear and another in her mouth. Her white t-shirt was a mess of reds and yellows, and a streak of purple went unnoticed on her chin. She was so lost in her work that she didn't even realize what time it was.

Her current project was one of her favorites. The idea had been inspired by Paisley (although she didn't know it). Shiloh liked to think of it as the calm after the storm. She leaned in closer to her canvas and began adding in the smaller details onto the ocean, making sure to give extra attention to her shadows.

After a few minutes, Shiloh paused and rubbed her arms. The air had gotten exceptionally cold. Scanning the room, she snatched an old flannel from the table and tossed it over her shoulders. Without another thought, she went back to work.

Only a few minutes later, though, she felt a thin trail of sweat forming on her upper lip. Fanning herself off, she tossed the flannel aside and turned her attention back to her painting.

An hour or so passed and Shiloh found herself freezing cold once more. Shimmying back into the plaid flannel, she held her brush in her mouth and jogged across the hallway to check their thermostat. She was surprised when she saw that the temperature was completely normal.

But because she was Shiloh, and sometimes she was a little too determined, she ignored the slight ache in her head and continued to work on her painting.

Some time passed, and now Paisley stood on the sidewalk in front of their house, admiring her handiwork. It was just the right amount of scary and decorative. Even Wolf enjoyed batting around a balled up piece of caution tape.

Proud with her handiwork, Paisley retrieved the old cat from the front porch and made her way inside. She kicked off her boots and tossed her jacket aside, making her way down the hallway.

The first thing she heard was Shiloh sneezing. Raising an eyebrow, the smaller girl peered into the studio. Shiloh's hands were practically covered in paint, and when she used one of her cloths to wipe her nose, she was met with a long streak of blue right above her lip. Paisley tilted her head to the side.

"You sound sick," Paisley noted, making Shiloh jump at the sudden interruption. The smaller girl stood shyly in the doorway, her hair a windblown mess from how long she had been outside. Her cheeks were tinged red from the chilly fall weather, and Shiloh couldn't help but smile.

"Not sick, just allergies," Shiloh shrugged, sniffing and turning back to her canvas. "Hey, can you turn up the thermostat? I think there's a draft in here."

Paisley furrowed her eyebrows and glanced at the thermostat behind her. Knowing better than to believe her wife, she walked over to the windows and felt around the edges. No draft whatsoever.

"I will make you soup," Paisley nodded. Shiloh turned around in confusion.

"But I'm not s—,"

"I will make you soup," Paisley gave her a look, and Shiloh knew arguing with her wasn't going to get her anywhere. Sighing, the green eyed girl just shook her head and turned back to her painting.

With a victorious smile, Paisley made her way back down the hallway and into the kitchen. Wolf followed close behind, hopping onto his side of the counter. (Yes, he has a side of the counter.)

"Soup," Paisley mumbled to herself, glancing at the cat on the counter. "Where do we keep the soup, Wolf?"

When she didn't get an answer, the smaller girl moved to the pantry, digging through the various food items. After the occurrence at the school, Ryland and Vanessa had gone grocery shopping for them. Paisley could have sworn they had brought a few cans of soup over.

Of course, she was right, and soon the small brown eyed girl was heating up Chicken Noodle Soup. Next to it she was boiling another pot of water for tea. She knew Shiloh liked tea, and tea made Shiloh sleepy. And if Shiloh was sick, she would rather her sleep than complain.

About ten minutes later, Paisley found herself carrying a small tray into the art studio. A bowl of soup, a cup of green tea, and a few crackers were arranged nicely on a plate. Paisley was proud of her creation.

"I made you soup. And tea," Paisley said softly, knocking on the doorframe to alert Shiloh of her presence. The green eyed girl looked up from her painting as Paisley made her way in and set the tray down on the table. Paisley noticed how her wife had pulled yet another flannel on, but was somehow still sweating.

"Do you have a fever?" Paisley took a step forward and tried to feel Shiloh's forehead, but her hand was lazily batted away.

"I'm fine," Shiloh shook her head, glancing at the tray Paisley had brought her. "Really."

"I made you soup," Paisley reminded her. "And tea."

"I'm not really hungry right now, I told you," Shiloh shrugged. Paisley frowned slightly, her eyebrows stitching together as Shiloh reached up to rub her eyes.

"Are you getting sick?" Paisley asked, tilting her head to the side.

"No, Paisley," Shiloh's voice grew colder and the smaller girl bit her lip. "I'm fine. I told you. I'm just trying to get this fucking painting done." The girl sniffed and wiped her nose once again, turning back to the canvas in front of her.

Paisley nodded softly to herself, leaving the tray on the table and padding out of the room. Becoming distracted by Wolf, who had gotten one of his toys stuck under the couch, Paisley soon found herself involved in an intense game of keep away with the fluffy white cat.

It was only about ten minutes later, when she heard rushed footsteps in the hallway, that she forgot about her game and hurried to see what the commotion about.

She skidded to a stop in front of the bathroom just as Shiloh lifted her head from the toilet, coughing and exhaling shakily.

"Here," Paisley whispered, grabbing one of the hand towels from the sink and handing it to the girl. Shiloh gently took it from her to wipe her mouth.

"I think I'm getting sick," Shiloh's raspy voice filled the room. Paisley rolled her eyes.

"No duh," the smaller girl shook her head and offered the girl her hand. Laughing softly, Shiloh stood up and flushed the toilet, hugging her hands around her torso.

"You should lay down," Paisley nodded, grabbing Shiloh's hand and trying to lead her down the hallway. The green eyed girl paused though, glancing back at the studio.

"I need to finish..." Shiloh mumbled and shook her head. "It was almost done."

"It can wait," Paisley gave her a stern look, not taking no for an answer. Sighing in defeat, Shiloh trailed behind Paisley down the hallway.

Paisley paused once they made it to the bedroom. Studying Shiloh, she realized how much the older girl was shivering.

"Here," Paisley said softly, stepping forwards and helping Shiloh shed her flannels. She tossed them aside, peeling off Shiloh's white t-shirt and balling it up to wipe the excess paint off of her face and hands.

She signaled for Shiloh to stay where she was and disappeared into the closet. Moments later, the smaller girl reappeared with her blue New York hoodie and handed it to her wife.

"It is your favorite color, and it is super warm," Paisley explained, earning a soft smile from the girl. She stood on her tiptoes to help Shiloh pull the sweatshirt on.

"Here," Paisley motioned for her to wait. She hurried over to the bed, pulling the blankets back and fluffing up the pillows before leaning them against the headboard. "Lay down."

"Paisley, you really don't-,"

"Lo," Paisley crossed her arms and raised an eyebrow at the girl. And so Shiloh complied, partly because Paisley meant business, but also partly because her protectiveness was adorably cute.

"Wait here," Paisley nodded quickly before disappearing out of the room. Shiloh had to admit, she was cold. Which is why she pulled the blankets over her legs once she laid back on the bed.

Paisley reappeared a few minutes later with the same tray she had brought before. Sitting on the edge of the bed, she gave the girl leaning against the headboard a shy smile.

"I reheated it," she explained, carefully scooting back so she was facing Shiloh. "You should try... to eat something," she bit her lip. Wolf hopped up onto the bed to inspect what was going on.

"Here," Paisley gently held out the cup of tea, nodding towards Shiloh hopefully. "It is the sleepy tea. The kind you like, remember?"

"Yeah," Shiloh laughed softly, finding Paisley extremely endearing. She took the mug from the smaller girl's hands and held it in her own.

"I also brought this," Paisley explained as Shiloh began to sip at her tea. She held out a damp cloth, pointing to Shiloh's forehead. "This is supposed to help, right?"

In any other situation, with any other person, Shiloh would refuse to be taken care of like this. Showing weakness wasn't really her thing. She didn't like burdening people.

But with Paisley, it was different. It always had been. Paisley never treated her with annoyance or impatience. Paisley never treated her like a burden. Paisley treated her like someone she loved, and made it clear that she genuinely cared about the girl. Maybe even more than herself. Which is why Shiloh didn't protest when the smaller girl scooted forward and gently laid the cloth across her forehead.

"Is there anything else you need?" Paisley asked, tilting her head to the side. "Water? Juice? More crackers? If I call Ryland maybe she could go to t-,"

"I'm fine, Paisley," Shiloh laughed softly, shaking her head. "You've taken good enough care of me."

"I think we have applesauce. Or... or yogurt, or-,"

"Just come lay with me," Shiloh said quietly, setting her mug on the nightstand and scooting over to make room for the girl. Paisley could tell simply by the rawness of the girl's voice that she was sick.

"I made you something!" Paisley exclaimed, scrambling to grab her phone from the nightstand before joining Shiloh under the covers.

As she attempted to snuggle up next to the girl, she was taken by surprise when Shiloh scooted even further away from her.

"I don't want you getting sick," Shiloh explained, shifting her position slightly. Paisley furrowed her eyebrows together and shook her head.

"I do not care," she nodded firmly, reaching out and pulling Shiloh closer. She could tell Shiloh was cold by the way she was hugging the hoodie tightly to her chest, but it was opposite in contrast to the way she felt. Paisley could practically feel the heat radiating off of the girl.

"I learned a song on the piano. Maia helped me," Paisley explained, tapping through her phone until she pulled up a video. Holding her phone hesitantly, she bit her lip before handing it to Shiloh. "It is not good, but..."

"I'm sure it's great," Shiloh laughed, coughing a few times before composing herself.

Her lips spread into a loving smile when she pressed play and a nervous Paisley appeared on the screen, lent forwards and balancing the camera on a stack of books behind the piano. Her hair was in a messy braid that Shiloh had done the night before, and a few pieces of hair stuck out here and there, falling down in front of her face.

In the video, the small girl took a deep breath, glancing at the camera once more before placing her fingers on the keys. She mumbled something to herself, biting her bottom lip in concentration before pressing the first note.

From then on, it was easy to see that Paisley became more comfortable. She nodded each time she hit a note, which Shiloh found adorable. The green eyed girl was taken by surprise when the girl in the video took a deep breath and began singing.

The girl lingered for a few moments after hitting the last note, taking a deep breath before glancing up at the camera with a shy smile. She leaned forward to turn off the camera, ending the video.

Shiloh couldn't wipe the affectionate smile off her face as she turned to look at the small girl next to her. Embarrassed, Paisley had buried her face into Shiloh's neck.

"I didn't know you could sing," Shiloh said softly, reaching out to run her fingers through her wife's hair. Paisley bit her lip and looked up.

"Maia made me," she admitted, shaking her head. "The song had words. It did not sound good unless we used them."

"You know I love you, right?" Shiloh whispered, realizing just how much she adored the smaller girl in front of her. "You know I'd do anything for you?"

"I..." Paisley's face grew red and she resorted to hiding in Shiloh's shoulder once again, making the older girl laugh.

"You know that, Paisley?" Shiloh asked again, nudging her shoulder slightly. Paisley just giggled and nodded her head.

"But not as much as I love you."

CHAPTER 27

"Are you sure you're okay?"

Two days had passed since Shiloh's sporadic fever. Luckily it had been nothing major, but Paisley had still forced her to take it easy. Nothing would stop Shiloh from going to Vanessa and Ryland's Halloween party, though.

"I'm positive, babe," Shiloh shook her head and laughed softly at her wife's protectiveness. "I told you already, if I start feeling sick, I'll make sure you're the first person that knows."

"Good," Paisley nodded curtly. "Now get out of the room so I can change."

Laughing, Shiloh grabbed her bag of things before disappearing into the bathroom across the hallway. For some reason, Paisley had insisted on getting her costume with Ryland instead of Shiloh. She wanted it to be a surprise.

Shiloh had opted for something simple, donning a black dress, a red cape, and vampire teeth. It had taken her a while to convince Paisley that she was just pretending to be something evil, and not actually encouraging vampires.

It didn't take her long to change into her costume. She ran a straightener through her hair a few times and applied her makeup slightly heavier around her eyes. When she finished, she looked in the mirror and gave her reflection a small nod of approval.

"All done!" Shiloh called, leaning against the doorframe of the bathroom and running her fingers through her hair. She heard rustling on the other side of the door and waited as Paisley rushed to put the finishing touches on her costume.

"Ready?" Paisley giggled from the bedroom. Shiloh couldn't help but laugh softly, hearing the excitement laced in her wife's voice.

"Come on out," Shiloh watched as the door slowly opened and Paisley peered out.

"Count me down," the smaller girl whispered. Shiloh raised her eyebrows and gave in, motioning for Paisley to close the door once more.

"Presenting the wonderful, the beautiful, the magical, the ethereal, the most adorable girl in the world, the l-,"

"Faster!" Paisley cut off Shiloh's dramatic speech, bursting into laughter from behind the door.

"Fine," Shiloh rolled her eyes and feigned disappointment, making Paisley laugh even harder. "In three... two... one!"

Paisley pushed the door open and padded into the hallway, a shy smile on her face. The first thing Shiloh noticed were the sparkly blue wings on her back. Paisley wore a simple white dress underneath them. And as always, her white converse. She spun around in a circle once and looked at Shiloh hopefully.

"You're a beautiful butterfly," Shiloh laughed softly, giving Paisley a soft smile. She grew confused when the smaller girl paused and looked at her confusedly.

"I am a fairy," Paisley corrected her, a shy smile on her face. "Is it that hard to tell?" she asked, growing worried.

Shiloh quickly shook her head, grabbing Paisley's hand and gently guiding her into the bathroom. The smaller girl looked at her in confusion.

"You're a beautiful fairy," Shiloh reassured her, squeezing her hand. "But I know just the trick to pull your outfit together." Gently, she lifted her wife up by the hips and places her on the counter. Paisley giggled.

"Don't ask me why I have this," the dark haired girl laughed as she pulled out her makeup bag. "But I'm glad I do, because it comes in handy on nights like tonight."

Paisley watched as Shiloh dug through the bag and retrieved a small stick of roll on glitter. She couldn't help how wide her eyes grew, and she clapped her hands in excitement, making Shiloh laugh.

"Hold still," Shiloh said softly, cupping her wife's cheek and leaning in. Paisley's eyes fluttered closed, and she felt Shiloh gently dab some of the shimmer around the outer corners of her eyes and eyelids.

"Keep em' shut," Shiloh added, digging through her bag once more until she found her eyeliner. Tediously, she leaned in and winged a thin line on each eye. Just before Paisley opened her eyes once more, the green eyed girl placed a quick kiss on her lips.

Giggling, Paisley opened her eyes and turned around to look at her reflection in the mirror. She gasped, leaning closer and closing one eye at a time. It was perfect.

"I love it," she laughed softly, turning back to Shiloh and returning her kiss. "Now people will not think I am a butterfly." She nodded curtly and hopped off of the counter.

Taking a few steps back, the smaller girl took the time to admire Shiloh's outfit. The dress fit her amazingly, and she couldn't deny that Shiloh made a pretty good looking vampire.

"The vampire and the fairy," Shiloh laughed, catching sight of both of their reflections in the mirror. "I think this is pretty accurate, don't you?"

"Except you are not evil," Paisley corrected her with a soft laugh. She became distracted by her wings, moving her shoulders slightly and watching in the mirror as they bobbed up and down. Shiloh watched, attempting to stifle her laughter.

"C'mon, goofball, they want us there early to help set up and stuff," Shiloh laughed and ruffled Paisley's hair. The smaller girl feigned shock, leaping forwards and jumping on Shiloh's back once she turned around.

"Oh, what are you now? A monster fairy?" Shiloh laughed and shook the smaller girl off of her back. Paisley giggled, slipping past Shiloh and into the foyer as the older girl grabbed the car keys.

"Maybe," Paisley winked, fixing her wings as they walked to the car. Shiloh couldn't help but laugh. Paisley made her do that often.

"I'm in love with a monster?" Shiloh gasped dramatically. Paisley turned around and eyed her wife questioningly.

"Have you looked at yourself lately?" she raised an eyebrow. Shiloh just rolled her eyes, making a mental note to keep Paisley away from Ryland that night.

"Where are all the kids?" Paisley asked, looking out the window at the empty sidewalks as Shiloh drove. The green eyed girl shrugged.

"It's not dark enough out yet," Shiloh explained, turning onto one of the main roads. "I remember when I was a kid, though. I'd be ready to go trick or treating as soon as I woke up. It was torture to have to wait until it got dark. And once I was out, I didn't want to come back in. My parents practically had to drag me."

She glanced over at Paisley, who had her eyebrows furrowed in concentration. The smaller girl ran a hand through her hair and tilted her head to the side.

"I... I remember bits and pieces," Paisley said softly, looking over at Shiloh as she thought. "It is... blurry. Like... some of it I can not remember." Shiloh nodded in understanding and reached over to take her wife's hand.

"Take your time," Shiloh said quietly as they pulled onto the highway. Paisley took a deep breath and spent a minute or two in comfortable silence. It had already gotten dark, and Shiloh made sure to turn her headlights on.

"I was a black cat one year," the smaller girl nodded, remembering her costume. "I had a tail and everything."

"I was a witch for like... 3 years in a row," Shiloh laughed. "That's not as bad as Tara, though. She literally refused to be anything but a princess."

"I was a princess once. I think," Paisley nodded, a look of confusion across her face. Shiloh glanced over at her and raised an eyebrow.

Suddenly, Paisley's eyes widened and she shot upwards. "Lo!"

Following her eyes, Shiloh was blinded by the brake lights of the cars in front of them coming to an abrupt stop. The green eyed girl reacted quickly, swerving onto the shoulder and slamming on her brakes.

Their car jolted forwards as they came to a stop. Paisley pushed both hands against the dashboard to brace herself, as Shiloh pressed both of her feet against the brake with all her might. The car rocked backwards once them came to a halt, and there was a lingering silence between them.

"Oh my god," Shiloh put the car in park and caught her breath, turning to Paisley. "Are you okay? Are you hurt?"

She breathed a sigh of relief when the brown eyed girl shook her head. The smaller girl was visibly shaken up, but nothing besides that. Shiloh silently thanked the gods.

"What was that?" Paisley's shaky voice spoke up. Both girls leaned forwards. Paisley must had caught sight of something, because moments later she was unbuckling her seatbelt and hopping out of the car.

Shiloh quickly followed, glancing at the road, which had cleared by now. The front wheels of her car were in the grass, but thankfully both passengers were unharmed.

"Why did all of those cars stop?" Shiloh scanned the highway as cars whizzed past them. Nothing looked any different. The red Volvo in front of them had already moved down the road. There was practically no evidence of what had just happened.

"Lo..." Paisley's voice appeared. It was laced with something Shiloh couldn't make out. Fear? Panic? Whatever it was, it sent the green eyed girl racing over to the other side of the car.

"What?" Shiloh asked immediately, catching her breath. Paisley took a shaky breath and lifted her arm, pointing forwards. Shiloh followed her direction and felt her heart drop.

About a hundred yards away lay an overturned minivan. It was black, almost invisible in the lingering darkness. Shiloh couldn't tell much from far away, but it was clear to see that the car was totaled.

"Fucking bastards just kept driving," Shiloh cursed under her breath and shook her head.

"It is smoking," Paisley whispered. Her face was drained of all color and she stood frozen, still pointing to the van.

"Shit, okay," Shiloh shook her head as her mind caught up to her body. "Stay back," she warned the smaller girl, circling around the car and digging through her purse until she found her phone. Dialing 911, she held it against her ear and quickly made her way around the other side of the car.

Paisley was gone.

Shiloh knew this feeling all too well. Her heart sped up in her chest, heightening her anxiety. She looked around furiously, trying to figure out what had happened to the smaller girl.

"Pais!"

"Nine one one, what's your emergency?"

Shiloh cursed under her breath, holding her phone against her ear.

"I, uh, there's an accident. A car one. A bad one," she stuttered, cursing herself for being so idiotic. She circled the car and desperately looked for Paisley as she gave the dispatcher their information.

"Yeah, yeah, I'll leave the flashers on," Shiloh held the phone against her ear with her shoulder as she leaned into the car and pressed a button. Moments later, the headlights and taillights of her car were flashing to alert the police and surrounding cars of the accident.

Shiloh hung up the phone and tossed it aside, feeling her panic heightening with each second that Paisley didn't reappear.

"Paisley!" she cried out, cupping her hands to make her voice travel further. Just as she was about to call her name once more, she heard something in the distance. The green eyed girl paused and listened, struggling to hear against the sound of her heart pounding in her ears. A faint sound caught her attention.

Crying.

Shiloh took a few steps towards the noise, using the flashers to try and locate the sound of the crying. Something sparkled in the distance. Shiloh caught sight of the glimmer of Paisley's fairy wings just by the smoking van, and before she even had time to think she was hopping over the guard rail and running through the field towards them.

"Paisley!" she called. The small brown eyed girl's head shot up and she hurried over to her as the crying increased. Shiloh struggled to see, but once Paisley got close enough the flashing lights of her car allowed her to make out a smaller figure in the girl's arms - the source of the crying.

"Lo…" was all Paisley could breathe out while trying to catch her breath. Unsure of what else to do, Shiloh grabbed her wife's shoulder and quickly led her back to the edge of the guard rail.

"What the hell were you thinking?" Shiloh yelled, taking Paisley by surprise. "You could've gotten k-,"

She's interrupted by a distant rumbling noise and a loud burst of smoke from the van in the field, followed by the blaring sound of its car alarm. Shiloh and Paisley meet eyes fearfully.

Unsure of what to say, Paisley nodded down to the small child in her arms before looking back up at Shiloh pleadingly. The green eyed girl finally realized what had happened and felt her breath get caught in her throat.

"Oh my god," Shiloh's eyes widened. Paisley bit her lip.

"Oh god, okay, I... come here," Shiloh circled behind Paisley and helped her climb over the metal guard rail. The child in Paisley's arms was still sobbing violently, and it took everything in Shiloh not to simply start crying along with them.

"Sit down," Shiloh pointed to the patch of grass along the side of the road, unsure of what else to do. She helped Paisley sit down slowly and knelt down beside her to get a better look at the small person in her arms.

"Is it hurt?" Shiloh asked, biting her lip. Uncertainty flickered in Paisley's eyes.

Shiloh scooted closer. Upon further inspection, she realized the small girl was dressed in a pastel pink leotard and tutu, with her hair tightly pulled back into a small bun on the top of her head.

What really caught her attention, though, was the fact that the smaller child was practically drenched in gasoline. Both Shiloh and Paisley could smell it, it had even seeped though her clothes and onto Paisley's dress.

"Blood," Paisley whispered, unable to form any other words. Shiloh followed her line of sight and spotted the small scrape on the girl's head. But besides that, she appeared to be unharmed.

Shedding her costume cape, Shiloh used the edge of it to dab at the cut on the side of the girl's head. She'd yet to lift her head from Paisley's shoulder, and her arms were wrapped so tightly around the girl's neck that Shiloh wasn't sure how they were going to get her off.

"There are more," Paisley whispered, glancing back at the car. "Lo, there are more."

"More people?"

Paisley nodded and took a deep breath. "But... but they are..." She glanced down at the child in her arms and shook her head, not wanting to say it out loud.

"Are you sure?" Shiloh asked quietly. Paisley nodded.

"I know what it looks like," the brown eyed girl whispered, sending another pang of guilt to Shiloh's chest.

The 911 operator had instructed her not to approach the car since it was visibly smoking, and Shiloh was overwhelmingly thankful that Paisley had resurfaced unscathed.

The small girl was still crying. Violent, raw sobs shook her whole body and Paisley had to hold her tightly against her chest with both arms.

As Shiloh heard sirens approaching in the distance, she collapsed on the grass next to Paisley, letting out the breath she had seemed to be holding since she'd had to slam on the brakes.

This was going to be a long night.

CHAPTER 28

Shiloh felt like she was in a dream.

Her heart was still beating violently against her chest from when she was forced to swerve off the road. She glanced back at their car, eternally thankful that they hadn't gotten in an accident.

Unfortunately, the people in the black minivan couldn't say the same. Shiloh glanced back at the overturned car which was now completely enveloped in smoke. Everything seemed to be moving in slow motion.

She reached out and grabbed onto her wife's shoulder as the blaring sound of sirens approached them. They were blinded by the lights as a firetruck skidded to a halt at the side of the road and men immediately began hurrying over to the overturned car.

It was so loud that Shiloh could barely tell if the smaller girl in Paisley's arms was still crying. All three of them now reeked of gasoline but Shiloh didn't even notice. She was only worried about Paisley and the small child that her wife had practically torn out of the totaled car.

"Is everything alright ladies?"

Paisley and Shiloh both jumped when they were approached by a man in uniform, and Shiloh quickly got up to help her wife to her feet. The girl in Paisley's arms held even tighter to her, refusing to lift her face from her shoulder as she cried helplessly.

"I'm assuming you called this in?" he asked, and Shiloh nodded slowly. Before he could say anything else, though, one of the firefighters jogged over to them.

"There's signs of a child in there but there's no child within the radius of the c—," he started, but cut his sentence short when Shiloh cleared her throat and nodded toward the girl in Paisley's arms.

"Oh my god," the man called one of the paramedics over. "Is she hurt? Did she walk to you?"

Paisley's eyes widened and she glanced at Shiloh for help. The green eyed girl quickly stepped forwards slightly in front of her wife and shook her head.

"She, uh, she heard crying and got her from the car," Shiloh explained, biting her lip. "She's not hurt as far as we can tell, except for this," she added, pointing to the small scrape on the girl's head to which the paramedic nodded.

"Boss, there's two passengers in there," another man appeared, pulling a mask off of his head. "It's not looking good."

"What do you mean?" the first officer asked. Shiloh and Paisley exchanged nervous glances.

"We can't find a pulse and Derek says it looks like the girl is pregnant."

"Take Rodrick back down with you and see if you can get a pulse going," the man's voice turned serious. "Go!" The firefighter quickly nodded and disappeared moments later. Paisley glanced at Shiloh, anxiety flickering in her eyes.

"Thank you for calling this in," the man turned back to them. The lights flickered against his face and made him look even more intimidating. "If you don't have any other information for us, you're free to leave."

"Here," a paramedic approached them, holding out his hands towards Paisley. She glanced at Shiloh worriedly and didn't make a move, so he took this as a sign to step forward and take the girl from her arms. As soon as he tried to pry her away, though, the child started crying even harder and struggled to cling onto Paisley.

"I-I can hold her," Paisley spoke up, glancing at the officers and then to her wife for help. Shiloh nodded quickly.

"We have to check her out to make sure she's not injured," the paramedic explained, looking to the other officer. "I can take you guys up in the ambulance."

Shiloh was surprised when Paisley nodded, holding tightly to the girl in her arms who was still crying fearfully. The sound made her feel increasingly guilty, and she glanced over where the firefighters had begun sawing off the roof of the car to get inside. She shuddered.

"Lo," Paisley whispered, gaining Shiloh's attention again. The green eyed girl jogged over to catch up with her wife, who was following the man over to the back of the ambulance.

"Are you okay?" Shiloh whispered once she caught up with Paisley. The smaller girl eyed her questioningly before nodding and biting her lip.

Both Shiloh and the paramedic helped Paisley climb into the back of the ambulance with the girl in her arms. Shiloh hopped up afterwards, intent on making sure that both girls were okay.

Shiloh and Paisley both sat down on a small metal bench, watching as the man unlocked drawers in search of something. He groaned and shook his head, turning back around.

"I'll be right back," he explained before hopping back down out of the vehicle and disappearing. The girl in Paisley's arms was still crying, and Shiloh could tell it was worrying Paisley.

"Hey," Shiloh whispered, reaching out and placing a hand on Paisley's shoulder. "Breathe. We're gonna be alright."

Paisley bit her lip and looked up at her wife, nodding softly. Shiloh gave her a tired smile. She was taken by surprise when Paisley cleared her throat and began to sing softly.

Shiloh watched quietly as Paisley sung. The small child in her arms surprisingly began to relax slightly, worn out from all the crying. Scooting closer, Shiloh reached out and placed a hand on the little girl's back.

When the man appeared back in the ambulance with a briefcase-type container, Paisley ignored his presence and continued to sing softly. She could feel the girl calming down in her arms.

Shiloh, however, grew confused when the man began closing the two large back doors. She sat up slightly and raised her eyebrows.

"What are you doing?" she asked worriedly. The man turned around with a solemn expression on his face and Shiloh realized.

"They won't be needing an ambulance," he explained, confirming the news for Shiloh. Her heart dropped in her chest and she glanced over at Paisley and the child, who was completely unaware of her parent's fate. She swallowed the lump in her throat.

Shiloh felt the engine roar to life once the back doors were closed and locked. Her eyes widened but the man quickly beat her to saying something.

"They're towing your car to the hospital for you," he explained, walking over to Paisley and carefully freeing the small girl's arm. She didn't protest, but she didn't lift her head from Paisley's shoulder either. Paisley was still singing quietly, focused on keeping the small child comforted.

"What about her?" Shiloh asked, knowing that the man would know what she was talking about. As he took the smaller girl's blood pressure, he glanced over at Shiloh and shrugged guiltily.

"That's not my job," he explained, checking the blood pressure and nodding once when it was normal. He peeled the velcro from around the girl's arm and got to work on cleaning off the small gash on the side of her head. "They'll probably call the closest relative and take if from there."

Shiloh nodded, leaning back in her seat slightly and placing a hand on Paisley's shoulder to keep her steady as they turned off of the highway. She'd never ridden in an ambulance before and she wondered how many times Paisley had.

"I have two kids of my own at home," the man spoke up, cutting the tense silence. "I can't imagine something like this every happening to them."

Paisley glanced over at Shiloh with worry in her eyes, nodding towards the child in her arms. Without even using words, Shiloh could tell it was killing her that the smaller girl was still so upset. She gave Paisley a small smile and squeezed her shoulder.

"She's just shaken up," Shiloh whispered, leaning closer to Paisley. "Don't worry." Paisley gave her a nervous smile before nodding.

The ride in the ambulance seemed to go by in a flash, and soon Shiloh was helping Paisley back down to the ground. They had been taken to the emergency entrance of the hospital and directed over to a few of the officers that had been at the scene of the accident.

They all paused and stopped talking when Shiloh and Paisley approached them, the smaller child in their arms.

It was then that Shiloh realized that the system was human. She'd heard about these kind of accidents on TV, but she never faced the reality of it until she witnessed something as tragic as the smaller girl that clung to Paisley. It made her feel sick to her stomach.

"What are we supposed to do?" Shiloh spoke up when she realized no one else was. The officers all appeared to be almost as lost as she was, and they looked over at Paisley and the small girl. Luckily, one stepped forwards.

"The first step for us is to identify the other two passengers in the car," he explained. "We have a room set up for her where a nurse will look over her until we see what we can do next." Shiloh nodded softly.

"No."

All heads turned to Paisley, who was looking at them with furrowed eyebrows. The girl shook her head. "We will stay," she met Shiloh's eyes, almost as if she was telling her instead of offering.

"I, uh..." Shiloh stuttered. Paisley looked at her pleadingly and Shiloh sighed. "We can stay with her for now, I mean, if that's okay."

The officer thought about this for a few moments before nodding. Shiloh noticed how Paisley seemed to relax slightly. "She's comfortable with you for whatever reason, and I guess her comfort is what matters the most right now," he nodded. "I can get one of the nurses to lead you to the room."

Shiloh followed Paisley down the long, bright hallway. She studied the child now in better lighting, noticing just how ashen her face is. She realized it wasn't just the child when she looked down at her arms. Her and Paisley were covered in soot aswell.

Shiloh stopped the nurse once they got to the room, reaching into her pocket and retrieving her keys. "There's a black Toyota that they towed here.... could you possibly bring me the navy bag that's in the backseat? We were supposed to be going to a party and now we're.... you know. There's just a change of clothes and s-,"

"Sure thing," the nurse smiled and took the keys. "I'll leave the room across the hall open for you, too. There's a bigger sink and I figured you could use it to wash up."

"Thank you so much," Shiloh replied, breathing in a sigh of relief. The nurse gave her a small smile and held up the keys before disappearing down the hallway.

When Shiloh turned back around, she was shocked at the sight before her. Paisley sat on the hospital bed with her legs crossed, but what really caught Shiloh's attention was the small child now sitting in Paisley's lap, looking timidly around the bright room.

"Oh my god," Shiloh whispered, closing the door behind her as she entered the room. Paisley met her eyes, and Shiloh could see a glimmer of hope in them. Shiloh, however, was panicked.

"What do we do?" Shiloh's eyes widened. "Is she okay? Is she hurt? Can she talk? I mean... why are we here?" she shook her head and leaned against the wall to catch her breath. Paisley watched in confusion.

Shiloh lifted her head when Paisley started signing again, watching as her wife rubbed the smaller girl's back gently to keep her calm.

Noticing how bloodshot her eyes were, Shiloh sighed, walking over to the counter and dampening a paper towel. She walked over to the bed, giving the child a comforting smile before leaning forward and gently wiping the ash and soot off of her face.

The smaller girl watched her silently with wide eyes, and Shiloh realized she reminded her of a doe eyed baby deer. Small and timid.

As Shiloh gently dabbed at the sensitive skin under the child's cheeks, she realized that she must have a soft spot for brown eyes. She glanced over at Paisley and wondered what would become of the small child.

CHAPTER 29

Shiloh wasn't sure what she was supposed to do. Paisley was still holding onto the smaller girl, who had a look of plain terror in her eyes as she looked around the bright hospital room.

Finally, Shiloh snapped to her senses when the nurse reentered the room, holding her leather backpack. The green eyed girl hurried to retrieve it from her, thanking her over and over.

When they were left alone in the hospital room once again, Shiloh dug through her bag and bit her lip. The smaller girl was still covered in gasoline and the smell was so strong that Shiloh was beginning to feel sick

"Pais," she whispered, nudging Paisley's shoulder. "She's covered in stuff. We need to clean up." She motioned to Paisley's arms, which were also covered in soot. Paisley nodded softly in agreement, although she wasn't sure what she could do about it.

"Uh," Shiloh bit her lip, bending down so she was at eye level with the small girl in Paisley's lap. "Hi sweetie," she said quietly, placing a hand on her knee. "Is it okay if we take you across the hallway to get washed up? We can help you get changed into something a lot more comfortable."

"And we can watch a movie," Paisley added, her eyes landing on the television on the corner of the room. Shiloh gave her a thumbs up.

The small child looked back and forth between the couple with wide eyes. Shiloh could see the confusion etched in her face and felt her heart ache for the little girl.

"It is okay," Paisley spoke up, keeping her voice calm and placing a hand on the child's back. "You are safe here. I promise."

"She's right," Shiloh nodded. "We're really fun people." She could've sworn she saw the tiniest hint of a smile flash across the girl's face, but she wasn't sure.

"So do you want to go wash off all this stinky stuff?" Shiloh repeated her question, crinkling her nose slightly and holding out her palms to show the ash on them. This time, they earned a small, tedious nod from the smaller child.

"Good choice," Shiloh laughed softly, doing her best to keep the mood light. She figured the longer they could keep the girl distracted, the better.

"Here," Shiloh grabbed the bag and helped Paisley get off the bed with the smaller girl in her arms. Shiloh could tell how tired the child was simply by the way she laid her head on Paisley's shoulder as soon as the girl stood up.

Shiloh led her wife into the door across the hallway, flicking on the light switch and scanning the small room. There was no bed, only a large metal sink that she figured could function as a bathtub for the younger girl. She set her bag down on the ground and made sure to close the door behind them.

She could tell Paisley was still a bit shaken up from the accident, and she knew she had to step up and be positive for the both of them. She motioned for Paisley to set the little girl on the counter next to the sink, which she did.

"I see you're a ballerina," Shiloh smiled softly, pointing to the smaller girl's costume. Her dark caramel hair was pulled back into a tight bun, and she adorned a pastel pink leotard and tutu. There was only one ballerina slipper on her foot, though, and Shiloh realized the other must have fallen off back at the scene of the accident.

"Do you like to dance?" she asked, scooting over to the sink and turning on the water. As if Paisley read her mind, the brown eyed girl searched through the cabinets before handing Shiloh a small container of soap.

The smaller girl on the counter nodded, watching Shiloh intently. Shiloh realized that she wasn't too keen on talking anytime soon, which she understood. She knew how to hold one-sided conversations, though. She'd done it with Paisley many times before.

"I wish I could dance," Shiloh laughed, experimenting with the hot and cold water until it was just the right temperature. Paisley stood next to her, watching quietly. "Whenever I try to dance, I end up breaking things."

The child just stared at her and Paisley, watching as Paisley used a rag to clog up the sink.

"Tough crowd," Shiloh whispered, waiting until the sink filled up slightly to add bubbles. Before she could say anyone else, Paisley spoke up.

"Can I help you take off your ballerina dress?" she asked softly, crouching down in front of the younger girl. "Then you can be a mermaid."

This earned a shy nod from the girl, to which Paisley gently lifted her onto the ground and helped her shimmy out of her Halloween costume. She glanced at Shiloh, unsure of what she what supposed to do with the dirty clothes.

"Uh," Shiloh bit her lip, looking in the cabinets until she found a garbage bag. "Just toss them in there for now."

Paisley did so, setting it aside and turning back to the smaller girl in front of her. Noting the bun on the top of her head, Paisley realized her hair was wet from the gasoline as well.

"I brought shampoo and stuff in our bag incase we stayed the night at the apartment," Shiloh informed her, almost as if she had read her mind. Paisley nodded, giving her wife a soft smile.

"Is it okay if I take your hair out?" Paisley asked carefully, pointing the small bun on the girl's head. "But Lo can braid it after," she added and pointed to the green eyed girl at the sink. "She is good at that. She braids my hair."

Once the smaller girl gave her a soft nod, Paisley helped undo the bobby pins from her hair and let the girl's soft caramel waves fall down to just above her shoulders. She gave her soft smile, taking the girl back into her arms when she stood up.

"Ready to be a mermaid?" Paisley asked, looking down at the girl before glancing up to Shiloh nervously. The green eyed girl gave her a soft nod, letting her know she was doing well.

Paisley gently lowered the smaller girl into the bathtub, relieved when the child just watched as Shiloh dug through her bag to retrieve the shampoo and conditioner she'd brought with them.

Using one of the paper cups from the dispenser on the wall, Shiloh gently began wetting the small girl's hair. She glanced at Paisley, who was looking down at her own hands and grimacing.

"Paper towels and water," Shiloh spoke up, earning a confused look from the other girl. "There's a change of clothes in the bag. That's all we have for now."

Understanding, Paisley moved over to the other side of the sink and began wiping the soot and ash off of her arms. Shiloh continued to gently wash the little girl's hair, rinsing off her own arms in the process.

About fifteen minutes later, all three girls made their way back into the hospital room. Paisley and Shiloh both donned t-shirts and pajama pants, which was the only thing Shiloh had packed for the apartment.

Luckily, they had a few extra things packed, and now the smaller girl sat in the middle of the large hospital bed. She wore one of Shiloh's gray t-shirts, which fit more like a dress on her.

The nurse had left two trays of food and a few random oddities such as diapers and socks outside their door. Paisley sat on the bed beside the smaller girl while Shiloh sat in front of her, attempting to coax her into eating something.

"Mashed potatoes?" Shiloh offered again, even though the smaller child had basically turned down everything on the plate. She sighed when the girl shook her head slowly.

"Ice cream?" Paisley spoke up, grabbing the small plastic cup from the tray. Shiloh shook her head quickly, knowing ice cream wasn't the ideal meal. But when the smaller girl nodded almost immediately, Shiloh couldn't help but give in.

Shiloh wasn't quite sure why they were still there. The accident hadn't been their fault. They'd literally just been two bystanders that witnessed it. But Paisley was immersed in making sure the smaller child was okay, and Shiloh knew she couldn't get in her way.

Just as Paisley was opening the small ice cream cup, there was a light knock at the door. Shiloh looked up as the nurse slipped into the room, giving them a sympathetic smile.

"I'm told they still haven't identified the other two passengers in the car," she nodded, a slight frown on her face.

"There's a social worker coming for her in the morning," the woman explained, nodding towards the younger girl. "Obviously once they get in touch with her family we'll know more. But you guys are free to leave whenever y-,"

"No."

Shiloh could have predicted what Paisley was going to say. She glanced back at her wife, who had placed a protective hand on the smaller girl's shoulder. Luckily, the child was too invested in her ice cream to notice.

"What she means i-," Shiloh began, but was interrupted once more.

"We will stay," Paisley nodded with finality.

Sighing, Shiloh turned back to the nurse with an apologetic smile. Luckily, the woman was understanding.

Shiloh realized that in these types of situations, people tended to band together. Her and Paisley could have been two complete strangers, but yet here they were, watching over the smaller girl. But since the child was growing comfortable with them, no one had the heart to send them away.

"How long do we plan on staying here?" Shiloh asked once the nurse left the room once more. Paisley met her eyes, and Shiloh saw the compassion present in them.

"Would you want to be alone?" Paisley asked, raising her eyebrows at her wife.

"What?" Shiloh grew confused. Paisley sighed and nodded towards the little girl.

"If you were her... would you want to be alone?" Paisley repeated her question, looking back up at Shiloh.

It all clicked for the green eyed girl when she saw the longing in Paisley's eyes. Her wife was giving the girl what she hadn't had as a child. Someone who was there for her.

Shiloh felt a pang in her chest at the thought of a tiny Paisley in a similar situation. She decided not to question her wife anymore.

"I'm on your side," Shiloh whispered, giving Paisley a soft smile. "I'm here." The brown eyed girl looked up when Shiloh squeezed her shoulder gently, and nodded quietly in understanding.

Shiloh was taken by surprise when the small girl on the bed turned around and tugged on her sleeve. Shiloh met her eyes, and the child pointed hopefully to the TV, glancing between her and Paisley.

"You want to watch something?" Shiloh asked, glancing at Paisley who had an excited smile on her face. The small child nodded hopefully.

"Pais," Shiloh whispered, nudging her wife's shoulder. "When we came in a saw a room down the hallway with bookshelves full of movies. Do you want to go grab a few?"

Paisley nodded quickly, remembering seeing the room herself when they had came in. She gave Shiloh a soft smile before disappearing out of the room.

Shiloh scooted back on the bed, observing the younger girl who was looking around the room absentmindedly. She took the opportunity to see if she could get her to speak.

"Do you have a name, little one?" Shiloh asked, reaching out and brushing the girl's wet hair out of her face.

The smaller child just stared up at Shiloh quietly, her expressive brown eyes filled with uneasiness. Sighing, Shiloh shook her head.

"It's okay, sweetie," Shiloh reached out and rubbed her arm to try and comfort her. "We'll start off with my name, yeah? How about that?" She gave the girl a soft smile. "My name's Shiloh."

Moments later, the smaller girl was crawling forwards, claiming her spot in Shiloh's lap. The older girl was surprised at first, unsure of how to react, but when the small child curled up in her lap and wrapped her arms around Shiloh's own, she relaxed slightly and couldn't help the soft smile on her face.

Paisley reappeared a few minutes later, struggling to carry a large stack of DVDs. Shiloh had to stifle her laughter when they all came tumbling down onto the bed.

The smaller girl immediately latched onto Lilo and Stitch, offering it to Paisley with hopeful eyes.

Thirty minutes into the movie, the smaller girl was fast asleep in Shiloh's lap, clinging onto her arm for security. The green eyed girl was following in her footsteps, unable to keep her eyes open.

Paisley, however, sat in one of the chairs beside the bed. She kept her eyes on the two girls, ignoring the movie and forcing herself to stay awake. Her only concern right now was to make sure that the smaller girl was okay, no matter what it took.

C H A P T E R   3 0

Paisley didn't sleep at all that night.

Shiloh did, however. Paisley had propped up a pillow against the head of the bed and gently moved Shiloh back, out of her slumped position. The girl in her lap was fast asleep, holding onto Shiloh's arm.

Paisley was tired, sure. Exhausted was a better word. But she wasn't going to sleep, because she needed to make sure that they were okay. And she couldn't do that if her eyes were closed.

She wasn't sure what time it was, but she knew it was morning when the smaller child stirred awake. Paisley noticed something moving out of the corner of her eye and watched as the girl's eyelashes fluttered open softly.

A look of terror flashed across the small child's face. She was in a new place, she wasn't home. And then she remembered the events of the night before. Paralyzed by fear, she burst into tears.

Paisley's eyes widened when the child started crying. Shiloh didn't stir awake, though, so she quickly hopped to her feet, lifting the girl out of her wife's lap and into her own arms.

"I got you," Paisley whispered, rocking back and forth slightly to calm to smaller girl down. She balanced her on her hip and used her free hand to reach up and brush her wavy hair out of her face, gently wiping the girl's cheeks with her thumb. "No one is gonna hurt you. I promise."

Sniffing, the child gazed up at Paisley. Her bottom lip jutted out slightly and Paisley could tell how hard she was trying to stop crying.

The brown eyed girl sat down on the edge of the bed, holding the girl in her lap and rubbing small circles in her back to try and calm her down.

Shiloh had stirred awake by this time, and she slowly sat up, watching as Paisley sang softly to the younger girl. There was a knock at the door just as Paisley looked back and realized her wife was awake.

It was the same nurse as before, but accompanying her was another, older woman holding what appeared to be a briefcase. The nurse gave Shiloh a friendly smile, allowing the woman to enter the room before closing the door behind her.

"Hi," the woman smiled, walking over to Shiloh and extending her hand. "I'm Georgia. I'm the social worker who's been assigned to her case."

Shiloh shook her hand, noticing how the woman eyed the girl in Paisley's arms. It didn't go unnoticed by Paisley, either, who scooted back slightly and tightened her grip on the girl.

"I'm Shiloh. She's Paisley," the green eyed girl nodded towards her wife. Paisley just nodded slowly.

"They've identified the parents," the woman explained, sitting down on one of the plastic chairs and pulling a stack of papers from her briefcase. "Malachi and Rebecca Allen."

"Parents of a 3 year old daughter," she motioned to the girl in Paisley's arms. "With one on the way." Shiloh bit her lip. "Unfortunately, only one survived the accident." She nodded towards the child, and Shiloh felt her stomach drop in her chest.

"Obviously our first order of business is to get her into a permanent living situation as quickly as we can," the woman explained. Shiloh nodded.

"The only problem with that is that the only living family she has left is her 78 year old grandfather with Alzheimer's," she held up the papers to show them.

Shiloh and Paisley exchanged glances, both feeling a pang of sadness for the small child.

"But, I made a few calls, and I was able to find a group home that can take her in until we can find her a more permanent living situation," the woman nodded. Shiloh's jaw clenched.

"A group home?" she asked, raising her eyebrows. "For a three year old?"

"It's the best we could do given the circumstances," the woman attempted to explain, but Shiloh shook her head.

"You're positive she has no family? No family friends?" Shiloh refused to believe the older woman.

"Honey, I've done as much as I can," the woman shook her head. "I assure you, the group home will be fine until we can place her in a b-,"

"Fine?" Shiloh raised her voice, taking Paisley by surprise. "You're really going to settle for 'fine' for a child? A living child? You really want to mess her up at this young?" She sat up taller.

"I don't know what you expect me to do," the woman looked back and forth between the two girls. "I'm only doing my job."

"You need to do more than just your job," Shiloh shook her head, standing up and motioning to the girl in Paisley's arms. "That is a life, not just another number on your stupid paycheck. That's a living, breathing human with an entire future ahead of her. You're in charge of her future and she has no control over it. You have to be her voice. And right now it just sounds like you're settling."

"Again, I don't know what you expect me to do," the woman shook her head.

Shiloh could feel it. She didn't even have to look to know that Paisley's eyes were looking at her pleadingly. She sighed, taking a deep breath before sitting back down on the bed.

"Well, what about us?" Shiloh spoke up, taking even Paisley by surprise.

The woman grew confused. "What about you?"

"What if we take her?" Shiloh bit her lip, running a hand through her hair. She wasn't used to doing these kind of things. But something inside of her was pushing her.

"You can't just 'take' her," the woman laughed at Shiloh's words, which only angered the green eyed girl more. "You'd either have to apply for adoption, which is a long process. Or you'd have to have a foster license."

"How do you get a foster license?" Shiloh asked. Paisley watched her intently from her spot on the bed, holding the timid child protectively in her arms.

"It's a case by case basis. Sometimes i-,"

"Well how do we get one?" Shiloh interrupted her, making Paisley struggle not to laugh from behind her.

"You have to apply for one, it's a pretty complicated p-,"

"How do we apply?" Shiloh asked once more, ignoring the annoyed look on the woman's face. That wasn't her concern.

"Give me a moment," the woman sighed, grabbing her things and slipping back into the hallway. As soon as the door shut, Shiloh groaned and fell back onto the bed.

"What are you doing?" Paisley whispered in confusion.

Shiloh sat up, turning to Paisley and biting her lip. "I don't even know," she laughed nervously and shook her head.

"You really want to... you know?" Paisley nodded down to the girl in her arms.

"I, uh," Shiloh swallowed the lump in her throat. "I mean, I thought you... I just..."

"Lo," Paisley laughed, placing a hand on her wife's arm to try and calm her down. "Do you want to?"

Shiloh took a deep breath before nodding softly. "Toby and Maia said there's never a right time. And... and she needs someone, you know? I know it's a rush decision but I've always wanted kids and I assumed you did too and m-,"

"Okay," Paisley interrupted her, squeezing her hand. "Me too."

"Wait, really?" Shiloh's eyes widened in shock. Paisley laughed softly and nodded. A slow realization washed over them and Shiloh let out a deep breath.

"We are doing this?" Paisley asked, looking down at the girl in her arms and then back up at Shiloh hopefully.

Her wife nodded softly. "We're sure gonna try."

Before either of them could say anything else, the woman reentered the room, hanging up her phone and putting it in her pocket. The couple exchanged nervous glances.

"So," the woman took a deep breath, sitting back down. "I just made a few calls, and if you really are serious about this, we can make a few exceptions for this case and you will have a license within a week."

"But, in the time inbetween, she will have to stay at the group home," the woman explained, handing Shiloh a paper before she could interrupt. "It's rated wonderfully, and there's always more than enough staff with the children. I've sent kids there before." Shiloh nodded slowly.

"But I need to make sure you're 100% serious about this," the woman nodded. "It's a big commitment you're making." Shiloh and Paisley exchanged glances.

"Yes," Paisley spoke up, nodding confidently. "We want this."

"Alright," the woman smiled, clasping her hands together. "A woman from the group home is on her way now to pick her up. In the meantime, I'm going to run and print out some of the papers that I need you to sign." She grabbed her things, heading towards the door.

"Wait!" Shiloh called out, causing the woman to pause and turn around.

"What's her name?" Shiloh asked shyly, biting her lip. The woman laughed softly and glanced down at one of the papers in her hand.

"Presley. Presley Rose."

The woman nodded once more before exiting the room, leaving Shiloh and Paisley to glance at each other.

"Presley Rose," Shiloh repeated the name, a soft smile on her face. The smaller girl in Paisley's lap looked up, meeting Shiloh's eyes quietly.

"Little flower," Paisley whispered, combing her fingers through the girl's hair.

Shiloh laughed softly to herself, reaching over and squeezing Paisley's hand. She knew their way of doing things might be unconventional, but that's how it always was for them. Everything good that happened to them came abruptly and unexpectedly. And like Maia said, sometimes the best things come in the form of a surprise.

————————————

"I do not know what I am doing."

Shiloh groaned, setting the screwdriver in her hand down and nodding in agreement. "You'd think they would make these things easier to put together," she laughed softly.

Paisley nodded in agreement. They'd been struggling to put together the toddler bed for too long. She set down the large piece of wood and joined Shiloh on the floor, laughing softly to herself.

"How are we going to do this?" Shiloh sat up, shaking her head. "We can't even put a bed together, how the hell are we supposed t—,"

"Woah," Paisley quickly sat up next to her wife, grabbing her hand. "It is just a bed."

"Yeah, but how are we going to take care of a kid? How are w-?" she started, but Paisley interrupted her.

"Together," Paisley whispered, squeezing Shiloh's hand. "Just like we do everything else."

Shiloh took a deep breath and nodded. "Right," she whispered, looking around the small spare bedroom they'd been converting into Presley's room. "Together."

"Like always," Paisley smiled softly. Shiloh watched as her wife got to her feet, scanning the room and nodding. "I will call Toby."

"Wait," Shiloh shook her head and quickly got up to follow her wife into the kitchen. "We haven't told them yet, we haven't… oh my god, we haven't told anyone…"

"Lo," Paisley laughed, amused by the girl's tendency to overthink everything. "Breathe. Do you want to tell them today?"

Following her wife's advice, Shiloh took a deep breath and thought for a few moments. She needed to stop overreacting. "Yeah," she nodded, reaching out and squeezing Paisley's shoulder. "But we have to do it like we always do."

"Right," Paisley nodded, a mischievous smirk forming on her face.

Half an hour later, a worried Maia and Toby pulled in front of their house after receiving a phone call from Shiloh, saying there was an emergency. Shiloh quickly let them into the house.

"What's going on?" Maia asked, holding a sleeping Lucas in her arms.

"Over here," Shiloh shook her head, feigning anxiousness. She led them down the hallway to the previous empty spare bedroom, opening the door and watching as the couple's faces contorted in confusion.

"We need help," Paisley slid past them into the room and pointed to the pieces of the bed. "I can not build."

"What are you talking about?" Maia furrowed her eyebrows together and passed Lucas off to Toby. She took a few steps forward, scanning the room. "What is this?"

"How the hell did you get pregnant that quick?" Toby's eyes widened.

At that point, both girls dropped their act and burst into laughter. Shiloh quickly shook her head, holding out a hand to explain herself.

"There was an accident on Halloween," she explained, feeling Paisley grab her hand. "We pulled over to call the police. Well, I called. She ran," Shiloh pointed to Paisley.

"There was a kid in the car. Three year old girl," Shiloh continued once the couple nodded, still somewhat confused. "Paisley got her out and then we just... we just sort of ended up staying with her at the hospital and making sure she was okay."

"They wanted to take her to a group home," Paisley spoke up.

"Yeah," Shiloh nodded. "She didn't have any family that could take her in. And I sort of flipped out and now... well, we've been running around the past few days getting background checks and clearances of health, and... yeah, if all goes well after the home inspection..."

"We have our license and we pick her up on Friday," Paisley finished her sentence.

The young couple watched as Maia and Toby exchanged glances. Shiloh bit her lip, feeling Paisley squeeze her hand lightly for reassurance.

"Well when do we get to meet her?" Maia asked, tilting her head to the side with a soft smile. "What's her name?"

"Presley," Shiloh breathed a sigh of relief. "Presley Rose."

"Little flower," Paisley added quietly.

"Ryland's gonna flip," Toby laughed. "That poor child is going to be so overwhelmed when she and Nessa meet her."

Shiloh and Paisley exchanged glances, a soft smile on each of their faces. Shiloh locked their pinkies together and nodded softly at her wife. Paisley got the message.

Things would be alright.

CHAPTER 31

"We are back!"

Paisley's voice echoed throughout the small house as she carried two heavy plastic bags into the foyer. She set them down on the floor, hurrying back out to help Shiloh, who was half carrying, half dragging a large box down the sidewalk.

"What color did you decide on?" Maia asked, joining Paisley as she began to retrieve more bags from the car.

"We didn't," Shiloh laughed, earning a confused expression from the other girl. She grabbed the last two bags from the trunk and followed the other girls into the house.

"I thought that was the main point of this shopping trip? To get paint?" Maia asked, tilting her head to the side. Paisley and Shiloh exchanged glances.

"We did, but..." Shiloh shook her head.

"We could not agree," Paisley nodded. The smaller girl bent down, digging through the bags until she found all four cans of paint. She grabbed one and held it up, showing Maia proudly.

"See? This is the perfect color," Paisley nodded, a wide smile on her face. Maia studied the can of bright yellow paint, glancing over at Shiloh, who shook her head.

"But see, I think this color suits the room better," Shiloh nodded, bending down to retrieve a can of sky blue paint. Paisley giggled at their playful banter.

"So you bought both?" Maia raised an eyebrow. "Those two colors aren't that aesthetically pleasing together, you know..."

"Your poor child is going to think she lives in a Best Buy," Toby nodded, appearing by Maia's side with Lucas in his arms. Paisley laughed and shook her head.

"We got both to test out," Shiloh shrugged. "We figured you guys could break the tie for us."

"Sounds simple enough," Toby nodded, handing Lucas off to Maia and brushing his hands off on his jeans. "We got everything moved out of the room and tarped down. So we're ready when you are."

"Awesome," Shiloh laughed, grabbing another can of paint and following everyone into the bedroom. Paisley did the same, setting the cans down on the middle of the floor and looking around.

"Okay. So obviously we need to pick a color first," Toby laughed. Maia nodded in agreement, sitting down in the corner to keep Lucas entertained.

"Right," Shiloh nodded and dug through the bags, pulling out two paintbrushes and handing one to Paisley. "I guess we'll just test them out and see what they think," she nodded to the smaller girl.

Paisley immediately got to work, which required a bit of Toby's assistance to get the paint cans open. Once she did, she dipped the smaller brush in the bright yellow paint and chose her spot on the wall. Keeping it simple, she painted a small square and filled it in.

Taking a step back, Paisley smiled. She glanced at Toby and Maia, who were looking back and forth from her to Shiloh.

"I still like the blue better," Shiloh nodded, standing back to look at the small flower she doodled in the blue paint.

"I agree with Shiloh," Maia said softly, biting her lip. "Sorry, Paisley."

"Yellow is better," Paisley huffed playfully, a small smile of amusement on her face.

"Me and Lucas side with Paisley," Toby added. He raised both his hand and the child's hand, making Paisley laugh even harder. Maia rolled her eyes.

"Lucas doesn't count," Shiloh shook her head.

"Yeah, he's like... half a person," Maia agreed.

"Well then that's still half a vote more than you," Toby wiggled his eyebrows playfully. Shiloh and Maia exchanged glances.

"I have nothing against yellow," Shiloh sighed, turning around to look at the square Paisley had painted. "It's just... too... bright."

"What is wrong with bright?" Paisley tilted her head to the side. "Bright means happy. We want her to be happy, right?"

"Okay, you make a good argument," Shiloh sighed, but shook her head. "But blue is calming and relaxing."

"So it's between a bright and happy room, or a calming and relaxing room," Toby nods from his spot against the wall.

"Why can't we have both?" Shiloh turned back to the sample of paint on her wall and furrowed her eyebrows. Meanwhile, Paisley's face lit up.

"If we do one wall yellow and one wall blue, it would just look too confusing," Shiloh nodded, shaking her head and turning back to Maia and Toby. "So we have to pick o-Paisley!"

Shiloh's jaw dropped to the floor when she saw her wife sitting cross legged on the floor, carefully pouring equal amounts of blue and yellow into one of the large paint pans.

"What are you doing?" Toby furrowed his eyebrows while Shiloh just stood frozen in confusion. Paisley had a mischievous smile on her face as she leaned over to grab one of the wooden mixing sticks.

"We can have both," Paisley nodded softly, mixing the two colors together in a tin. Shiloh's shock slowly faded as the yellow and blue faded into a darker shade of green. "See?"

"Luckily, you're in the presence of someone who actually paid attention during the colors unit," Maia laughed softly, passing Lucas off to Toby and moving to the center of the room. They watched as she took the smaller can of white paint they purchased for the trim and added a tiny amount to the green mixture.

She continued adding small intervals of each color until she was pleased with the outcome - a light shade of mint green.

"Perfect," Paisley whispered. She glanced over at Shiloh for approval.

"That's better than the color I chose in the first place," Shiloh nodded. Paisley clapped her hands together in excitement, feeling Shiloh place a hand on her shoulder and give it a small squeeze. There was an air of nervous excitement between them, with only two days left until Friday.

Shiloh couldn't sleep on Thursday night.

It was the busiest week of her life. Her and Paisley had to rush to get everything in check to make sure they got their license. Background checks, doctor's appointments, and home inspections took up nearly all of their time.

Any other free time they had was dedicated to making sure they had everything they needed. Their kitchen was stock piled with food after two separate grocery trips. The second had been a result of Shiloh panicking and running out to the store at 8am to make sure they had absolutely everything they needed.

The entire house had to be childproofed, which was harder than they thought. They didn't realize how many things they had laying around that could be potentially dangerous.

And finally, the bedroom. Which for some reason, Shiloh couldn't get out of her mind. Along with a million other things. She didn't realize how much actually went into taking care of a child.

Glancing over at Paisley, who had shifted in her sleep and now had one leg halfway off the bed, Shiloh realized she wasn't going to get much sleep if she continued to lay there and let her thoughts race. So instead, the green eyed girl pushed herself out of bed, making sure not to disturb her wife (or Wolf).

She made her way down the hallway and into the art studio, humming softly to herself as she gathered her paints together and dispersed even amounts onto her palette. She grabbed two brushes and tucked one behind each ear. Instead of going to her easel, though, she made her way back across the hallway and into the newly painted bedroom.

Presley's bedroom was painted the soft mint green color they'd created. In the room now sat a small white toddler bed, along with a matching bookshelf and toy chest. The room had everything that they needed, but Shiloh couldn't help but feel like something was missing.

That's where Shiloh came in.

It just sort of happened. One minute she was standing in front of the wall, and the next, she was dipping her brush into the palette and painting.

Painting helped her think. Shiloh wasn't sure how to explain it, but it just did. It was a step by step process, and somehow she was able to untangle her own thoughts as she did so.

She did a lot of thinking as she painted. The biggest thing on her mind was Presley, though. She put herself in the little girl's position, trying to envision would it would be like to lose her parents at such a young age and then be in the hands of the state.

It made her angry, in a way. That the child had no control over where she ended up. If Shiloh and Paisley hadn't been there, where would she have gone? Shiloh didn't like to think about it. She rarely got angry, but when a child was put at risk, she wouldn't hesitate to throw a few punches.

And then she thought about her and Paisley. Were they going to be good parents? She knew without a doubt that Paisley would be. Paisley was always putting others in front of herself. Give her a child, and she would immediately protect it. It was as if it were her instinct.

Shiloh wondered about herself, though, which she figured every new parent must have done at one point or another. In a day, she would be responsible for another life. She'd be responsible for taking care of a child and teaching her how to be a good person. She and Paisley would be the people that shaped someone else's future. And it terrified her, because she didn't want to do something wrong.

"Lo...?"

Shiloh jumped when she heard a sleepy Paisley whisper her name from the doorway. Turning around, she was met with her wife, clad in only a t-shirt and underwear and running a hand through her tousled hair.

"What are you doing?" the smaller girl asked, tilting her head to the side and rubbing her eyes. Shiloh shrugged softly.

"Painting," she pointed to the wall. "And thinking."

"Painting and thinking," Paisley nodded, repeating Shiloh's words. She padded forwards, yawning and sitting down on the small bed to watch her wife. "Thinking about what?"

Shiloh shrugged. "Painting."

"Painting and thinking about painting," Paisley giggled, shaking her head. "What else?"

Shiloh looked over at her wife, giving her a soft smile. "I'm thinking about tomorrow, I guess."

"Oh," Paisley nodded in realization. "Bad or good?"

"Just thoughts," Shiloh said softly, holding her paintbrush in her mouth and running a hand through her hair. "Just... thoughts," she nodded again.

"What are you pa-?"

"Do you think I'll be a good mother?" Shiloh turned around, cutting Paisley off. The smaller girl clamped her jaw shut and looked at her wife in surprise.

"I'm serious," Shiloh sighed, sitting down on the bed next to Paisley. "Like... I'm just scared I'm going to screw up or something. Or say the wrong thing... or... I don't know..."

"Hey," Paisley whispered, reaching out and squeezing Shiloh's hand. "I have been with you for a long time, right?" Shiloh nodded in confusion.

"And I had the choice.... I had the choice to leave whenever I wanted," Paisley explained, biting her lip and trying to string her words together. "But... but I did not. And I do not want to."

"I am lucky," Paisley pointed to herself. "And she will be lucky," she motioned around the room before pressing her finger against Shiloh's chest. "Because of you."

"You do not have to be perfect," Paisley continued. She took both of Shiloh's hands in her own and gave her a soft smile. "It is okay to mess up. Because then... then they know you are... are human," she nodded quietly.

"I do not think Presley will expect us to be perfect," the smaller girl bit her lip. "But she needs us. And maybe we need her. Right? We help each other. That is how it always is."

"Yeah," Shiloh nodded, taking in everything Paisley had just said. "Are you nervous?" she asked, tilting her head to the side slightly.

"Of course," Paisley laughed softly, as if Shiloh had just asked the most ridiculous question in existence. "Who would not be?" Shiloh shrugged.

"But... but when I think about getting nervous, I realize that she is probably just as nervous as we are," Paisley explained, pausing for a moment to think. "Or more."

There were a few seconds of silence between them as Shiloh thought about what her wife had just said. She'd never thought about it that way. Paisley's perspective on things always gave her such a relieving clarity.

"I love you," Shiloh whispered, squeezing Paisley's hand. The smaller girl didn't need a sign to know that Shiloh had understood what she said. "I love you and I'm nervous as hell... but I'm excited. And I'm ready."

"I love you too," Paisley nodded, a shy smile on her face. She yawned, leaning her head against Shiloh's shoulder and looking at the mural she'd painted on the wall.

There was a large tower, and inside of it was a princess dressed in bright yellow gowns. But this wasn't a bad tower, either, because the princess was happy. In blue gowns, with dark hair, was another princess beside her. And Paisley didn't think the emerald green eyes were a coincidence.

"I love it," Paisley nodded, pointing to the painting. "It is perfect."

"Like you," Shiloh laughed, setting her paints aside and scooping Paisley up into her arms. "Except you're way better than a few globs of paint." Paisley giggled, wrapping her arms around her wife's neck.

"It's our last night we have alone, you know," Shiloh whispered, raising an eyebrow. Moments later, Paisley's lips were crashing against hers, and she hurried to turn the light out as they headed back down the hallway.

CHAPTER 32

Shiloh woke up the next morning to the alarm on her phone blaring. Paisley, however, was fast asleep. The green eyed girl groaned, rolling over and attempting to blindly silence her phone, which only resulted in it falling off of the dresser.

Mumbling profanity under her breath, Shiloh groggily threw the covers off of her legs and leaned off of the bed to retrieve her phone, successfully silencing the alarm before rolling back under the covers.

She turned over, propping herself up on one elbow and admiring her wife's sleeping face. Tangled under the white sheets with the gentle sunlight caressing her skin, Paisley looked like an angel. Peace in its purest form.

Shiloh couldn't stop herself from reaching out and tucking a loose strand of hair behind her wife's ear. Paisley's chest rose and fell slowly, and Shiloh found herself subconsciously mimicking her breathing.

The green eyed girl ran her thumb across Paisley's cheek, pressing a kiss to her forehead before retracting her hand. She would be perfectly content with lying like that forever, but they had things to get done today.

It was Friday.

When Shiloh pulled away, she saw a hint of a smile dance over Paisley's lips. She couldn't help but laugh, reaching out and running her fingers down her wife's arm.

"Babe, it's time to get up," she whispered, continuing to trail her fingertips over the girl's skin and forming goosebumps. Paisley laughed softly, her eyes fluttering open to find Shiloh's and giving her a sleepy smile.

"It is early," Paisley yawned, rubbing her eyes and looking around the room.

"Do you know what today is?" Shiloh asked. She tilted her head to the side, waiting for the smaller girl to realize. Paisley looked at her in confusion.

"Friday," the girl nodded. "It is F-Oh!" she sat up quickly, causing Shiloh to burst into laughter. Paisley couldn't help but giggle alongside her.

"It is Friday," Paisley nodded, her voice softening slightly. "We get Presley today."

"But first, we drive," Shiloh nodded, causing Paisley to groan and faceplant back on the bed. She mumbled something against her pillow, which Shiloh knew was referring to the three hour drive they had ahead of them. The social worker had neglected to mention the fact that the group home Presley was staying at was in another state.

"You better be ready in an hour, goofball," Shiloh laughed, leaning down to steal a quick kiss before grabbing her change of clothes and disappearing across the hall into the bathroom.

A few minutes after Shiloh shed her clothes and stepped under the stream of hot water, she felt a pair of arms gently wrap around the waist and join her in the shower. She turned around, catching Paisley mid-yawn, which made them both laugh.

"Good thing I'm the one driving," Shiloh teased, leaning forward and pressing a soft kiss to the bridge of her wife's nose.

Pretty soon, the couple was pulling out of their driveway just as the sun made its way above the trees. Paisley sat cross legged in the passenger seat, a blanket in her lap and a banana in her hand.

"Are you nervous?" the smaller girl asked, looking over at Shiloh who had one hand on the wheel and the other clutching a coffee mug.

Shiloh shrugged, taking a sip of coffee and offering some to Paisley, who grimaced and shook her head. Shiloh didn't understand how her wife could be awake this early without coffee. It was a necessity of hers.

"I'm more excited right now," Shiloh nodded. "I think we've got this."

"Yeah," Paisley smiled softly, taking a bite of her banana and reaching for Shiloh's phone. "Should we call your mom and dad?"

The girls had decided that they wouldn't tell Shiloh's parents until the day they brought Presley home. It was nothing against them, but they just didn't want any outside forces affecting their decision. It was something they needed to do on their own.

Shiloh bit her lip, glancing over at Paisley who had her finger hovered over their contact number and was waiting for an answer.

"The sooner the better," Shiloh nodded, causing Paisley to grow confused.

"What?" the smaller girl asked, raising an eyebrow.

"I'm just nervous about what they're going to say," Shiloh admitted, setting her coffee down and running a hand through her hair. "What if they get mad at me?"

"Us," Paisley corrected her. "If they do… it is not our fault. And… and they will just have to deal with it," she nodded firmly. Shiloh nearly choked on her coffee at her wife's bluntness.

"Then I guess there's only one thing left to do…" Shiloh nodded softly. Paisley gave her a soft smile before pressing the call button on the phone and plugging it into the car. The two girls made eye contact with one another when the first ring echoed throughout the car.

"Hello?" Shiloh's mother picked up on the second ring. Shiloh set her coffee down so she could reach over and lace their fingers together. Paisley gave her hand a reassuring squeeze.

"Mom?" Shiloh raised her voice so she could be heard.

"Shiloh?" her mother replied, confusion in her voice. "Hey sweetie, what are you doing up so early?"

"I'm currently driving," the dark haired girl laughed. "Paisley's here too. Is dad with you?"

"Hi Paisley!" her mother chimed, earning a shy 'hi' from the brown eyed girl. "Yeah, he's right here. We're eating breakfast, should I put you on speaker?"

"Sure," Shiloh nodded, feeling Paisley absentmindedly playing with her fingers. "We, uh, we kind of have something to tell you guys."

"Okay, you're on speaker!"

"Colette, you don't have to yell so they can hear you all the way from Miami," her father's voice appeared, making Shiloh laugh. "What's up girls?"

"We have something to tell you," Shiloh swallowed hard.

"Is it bad?" Matthew immediately replied. Both girls quickly shook their heads until they realized that they couldn't be seen.

"It's not bad, promise," Shiloh glanced over at Paisley. "You just... you can't be mad. Promise you won't be mad?"

Paisley couldn't help but giggle, watching as Shiloh suddenly seemed to take the role of a daughter, instead of the one in charge.

"Well now you've got me worried," Colette spoke up. "What's going on?"

"You didn't promise," Shiloh rebutted, biting her lip.

251

"We won't be mad, Shiloh, what's up?" her father asked. The two wives glanced at one another, debating over who should break the news.

"We are driving," Paisley nodded softly. "We are driving to....?" she turned to Shiloh in confusion.

"Connecticut," Shiloh whispered.

"We are driving to Connecticut," Paisley giggled. "There... there is someone there. Someone waiting for us."

"Her name is Presley," Shiloh jumped in. "Presley Rose."

"Little flower," Paisley whispered with a soft smile on her face. "She is three years old."

"And... well," Shiloh flashed a nervous smile in her wife's direction. "We're her foster parents."

There were a few seconds of silence on the other line, and Shiloh tightened her grip on Paisley's hand. She was hoping for her parent's approval.

"Her what?"

Shiloh's eyes widened. "Her foster parents," she said nervously. Paisley just ran her thumb over the back of the girl's hand.

"We're going to be grandparents?" her mother's voice was laced with shock. Shiloh still couldn't decipher if they were upset or not.

"Well, yeah," the green eyed girl nodded. "I mean, the plan is to eventually adopt her if all goes well."

"We will," Paisley added, glancing at Shiloh. "We do not give up on people." Shiloh flashed her a soft smile.

"Well this is news," her mother laughed.

"I'm sorry, we j-," Shiloh began.

"Don't be sorry," Colette interrupted her with a soft laugh. "We're just... I'm going to have a 3 year old granddaughter and I don't know anything about her. Tell me about her."

Shiloh and Paisley exchanged glances, a soft smile on both of their faces. As Shiloh began explaining what had happened over the course of the week, Paisley sat back in her seat and watched her wife talk. Things were going to be alright. They always were.

"Pais."

"Psst, Pais."

"Paisley."

"Paisley Lowe-Everest!"

Paisley's eyes fluttered open and she looked up at Shiloh, who was leaning over the center dashboard. One of her hands was still holding Paisley's, and she reached out to cup her wife's cheek softly.

"We're here," Shiloh whispered. Paisley's eyes shot back open and she sat up slightly.

"We are?" she asked, turning to look out the window. Sure enough, they were parked in front of a large white house. "It is pretty," Paisley noted, admiring the red and orange leaves that were scattered over the trees.

"Ready?" Shiloh asked, pulling the keys out of the ignition and swinging them around her finger. Nervous yet excited, Paisley nodded softly and swung her legs out of the car.

They walked up the long stone pathway to the front door. There was a nervousness in the air, but Paisley reached out and squeezed Shiloh's hand before ringing the doorbell.

A minute or so later, the door was opened to reveal an older woman. She had a small boy in one arm, resting on her hip, and a sippie cup in the other. She smiled widely as soon as she saw the girls.

"Come on in," she smiled brightly and held the door open for the two girls. "You must be Shiloh and Paisley?"

"That's us," Shiloh nodded, taking in the large house as the closed the door behind them. There were drawings taped to the walls, and various toys lying here and there. Both girls jumped when two boys raced past them, kicking a soccer ball across the foyer.

"Boys! What did I tell you?" the woman called after them, shaking her head and laughing as she turned back to the two girls. "She's upstairs, you can come with me."

Shiloh and Paisley were led down a long hallway, up a large staircase, and down yet another hallway. The woman stopped them, though, before they reached the doors at the end of the hall.

"We found out that her house was up for foreclosure before the accident," the woman said softly, nodding her head. "One of the girls took her back there to see if she wanted anything, which... we really weren't supposed to do, but... I mean, if there's any way we can do to comfort the kids obviously that's our first priority."

"She kept going back to her bed, though. There was something she wanted from her bed," the woman kept her voice down. "She wouldn't tell us what, though. But then one of the girls asked about a blanket, and she got real excited. We looked all over the place but it wasn't there, and her social worked told me they'd found one in the car... but it wasn't... salvageable. She didn't want anything else from the house. That blanket must've been her comfort item," the woman sighed, frowning.

"Oh, and she hasn't really... talked.... to any of us," the woman added. Shiloh nodded softly, squeezing Paisley's hand when she felt her wife tense up.

"We had a therapist come in and work with her, but he told me it's normal for kids her age to isolate themselves after a traumatic event," she explained. "He said it shouldn't last long."

Both girls nodded, exchanging glances as the woman led them down to the last door of the hallway. She opened the door for them, revealing a light pink bedroom.

"I'll leave you guys alone for a bit while I go put this one down for a nap," she gave them a soft smile and nodded to the boy in her arms, before heading back down the hallway. Shiloh squeezed Paisley's hand and led her into the bedroom.

There were three beds, but only one was occupied. The small, caramel haired girl they'd last seen a week ago sat cross legged in the middle. She had a sketchpad in her lap and a collection of crayons spread out in front of her.

"Hey little one," Shiloh said softly, kneeling down beside the bed. She squeezed Paisley's hand, prompting for her wife to do the same. "Remember us?"

The small girl looked over at them. Her expressive brown eyes scanned them for a few moments before she nodded quickly. An excited smile formed on her face, causing Shiloh and Paisley to look at each other in relief. It had been the first time they'd seen her smile.

"Do you understand what's happening today?" Shiloh asked, tilting her head to the side slightly. Paisley bit her lip.

The little girl's eyebrows stitched together and she thought for a few moments. Her face lit up and she nodded, flipping through her sketchbook until she landed on the page she wanted. Shyly, she offered the paper to Paisley.

Paisley gently took the paper from the child, holding it in front of her so Shiloh could see. Drawn in crayon were three figures. Two big, and one small. They all had blue wings, Shiloh realized, the same as the ones Paisley had worn Halloween night.

"Is that us?" Paisley asked, a soft smile on her face. The girl nodded softly.

"You know, I have a very important question to ask you," Shiloh nodded. Paisley looked at her questioningly, but Shiloh continued. She wanted the girl to feel like she had some say in the matter. "Would you like to come home with us?"

"And be a part of our family?" Paisley asked, catching on to what Shiloh was doing. The small child looked back and forth between them before crawling forwards and hopping off the bed. Paisley and Shiloh exchanged worried glances when the girl quickly hurried out of the room.

Just as they were about to go after her, small footsteps echoed down the hallway and reappeared in the doorway. The small girl ran back over to them, holding up her shoes and looking at them hopefully.

"I guess that's a yes," Shiloh whispered, making Paisley giggle.

C H A P T E R 3 3

"Thank you!"

Shiloh waved softly to the woman at the door as they made their way back down the front porch steps. Presley was in Paisley's arms, looking ahead nervously as they said goodbye to the members of the group home and hello to a future that was entirely unknown.

"We've got a long drive ahead of us," Shiloh laughed, glancing at the younger girl who looked over at her quietly. Paisley nodded.

"I can sit in the back," she offered once they got to the car. "Here," she turned to Presley, using her free hand to open the door and gently setting the girl in the car seat. Shiloh silently applauded herself for remembering that they needed one.

"Lo," Paisley whispered, glancing back at Shiloh and then nodding into the car. "How do I do this?"

"Do what?" Shiloh slid beside her, where Paisley held the seatbelt. She looked at her wife in confusion before looking back at Presley.

"Oh god," Shiloh shook her head, gently scooting Paisley aside so she could take the seatbelt from her. "I... uh... like this, maybe?" She attempted to hook the seatbelt under the arms of the seat. Presley just watched her in confusion.

The youngest girl reached out, taking the buckle from Shiloh and almost effortlessly securing it across her lap. When the seatbelt clicked to secure that it was shut, Shiloh couldn't help but laugh softly.

"Looks like we could learn a thing or two from you," Shiloh gave the girl a soft smile.

It was easy to tell that Presley was nervous. She had her arms hugged tightly around her torso and her wide eyes were looking around timidly.

Fifteen minutes into the drive, though, Presley was fast asleep.

Paisley quickly shed her jacket, folding it up into a makeshift pillow and gently sliding it under the smaller girl's head before crawling up front into the passenger seat.

"Do you think she'll be okay?" Shiloh asked quietly, glancing in the rear view mirror and catching a sight of the sleeping girl. Her heart ached knowing the things she'd been through.

"Does she know?" Paisley asked, confusing Shiloh even more.

"Know what?" the green eyed girl glanced over at Paisley as they drove. Her wife bit her lip, thinking for a few moments before sighing.

"They never told me," Paisley sat cross legged on the passenger seat. "About my parents."

"When the accident happened?" Shiloh raised an eyebrow.

"Ever," Paisley explained. "Everyone was too... scared. To tell me. They just expected me to know."

"That they died?"

Paisley nodded softly. "No one... explained it. I thought it was a lot of different things. I had to figure it out on my own."

"So you think we should try to explain it to her?" Shiloh asked, reaching over and taking Paisley's hand in her own. The smaller girl thought for a few moments.

"That is what I would have wanted," the brown eyed girl nodded slowly, absentmindedly playing with Shiloh's fingers. "Do you think so?"

"I think we at least owe her an explanation," Shiloh nodded. "And just make sure she knows that if she has questions - whether it be now or when she's older - that we're here to answer them."

"I like that," Paisley smiled softly.

They drove for about an hour longer. Paisley took over playlist duty, but ended up falling asleep halfway through. Glancing in the rear view mirror, Shiloh found Presley still asleep, now hugging Paisley's jacket against her chest.

Eventually, hunger got the better of Shiloh, and she pulled over at the first drive thru she could find. Hoping that Presley was fine with chicken nuggets, she drove for a little bit longer until she found the small park she'd noticed on the way there.

"Pais."

"Baaaabe," Shiloh hummed, squeezing Paisley's hand and nudging her shoulder lightly. The girl in the passenger seat stirred slightly before reaching up and wiping her eyes.

"Are we home yet?" Paisley mumbled groggily, yawning before looking over at Shiloh. Her eyebrows furrowed in confusion when she didn't recognize the surroundings.

"Not yet," Shiloh shook her head. "Are you hungry?" she asked, holding up the brown paper bag of food. Paisley's eyes shot open and she nodded quickly, making Shiloh laugh.

"Here," Shiloh handed Paisley the bag. "I'll grab Presley."

Shiloh circled around to the back of the car, carefully unbuckling the smaller girl's seatbelt. As she pried Presley out of the car seat, the child stirred awake and sleepily wrapped her arms around Shiloh's neck. The brown eyed girl yawned quietly, resting her head on Shiloh's shoulder.

"We got you something to eat," Shiloh said softly, closing the door behind her and following Paisley over to a picnic table set in the shade under a tree. "Are you hungry?"

Presley nodded against Shiloh's shoulder before lifting her head and studying their surroundings. Her face softened slightly, and Shiloh thanked the universe that it was a nice day out.

"Here," Shiloh laughed softly, setting the girl down on the top of the picnic table where she immediately sat cross legged. "Are chicken nuggets okay?"

The caramel haired girl nodded, allowing Shiloh to breathe a sigh of relief. As they divided out their food, Presley seemed to devour hers before Shiloh even got a chance to take a bite of her sandwich.

When the smaller girl was finished, Paisley noticed how she kept glancing over at the playground beside them.

"You can go play, if you want," Paisley said softly. The smaller girl nodded hopefully, even looking at Shiloh for approval before climbing down from the table and venturing over to the small playground.

Shiloh sighed, watching as Presley nudged a rock with her foot. "I wish she'd talk to us."

"She will," Paisley shrugged. "Her... her brain has to think, first. It does not know what to say yet. But it will," she nodded reassuringly. The brown eyed girl spoke as if she had no doubt in the world, which comforted Shiloh.

"I don't think she likes me," Shiloh whispered, biting her lip. To her confusion, Paisley laughed.

"You think too much," her wife shook her head. "She is a kid. They like everyone. She gave you wings, too. You are special. She is going to remember you because you are helping her."

"Do you remember the people who helped you?" Shiloh asked curiously.

Paisley nodded. "My teacher. She made me food to take home… for a long time. And my aunt had friends at church. They would watch me on Sundays. I remember them."

"I'm glad you understand what she's going through," Shiloh sighed, resting her elbow on the table and laying her head in her hand. "This is all new to me."

"That is why we are a team," Paisley shrugged. "You know some, and I know some. Together we are better. You and me."

"Me and you," Shiloh whispered, feeling Paisley place a hand overtop hers.

Small footsteps turned their attention behind them, where Presley padded back to the table. She held up a dandelion, showing the girls the fluffy white plant.

Paisley's face lit up and she glanced at Shiloh. Gently, she took the flower from the girl and examined it.

"Can we talk to you?" Paisley asked, scooting over and patting the bench beside her. Curious, the smaller girl crawled up beside her and rested her arms on the table, laying her head on top of them and looking at them quietly.

"Do you know why you are with us?" Paisley asked, biting her lip. She glanced at Shiloh, who gave her foot a supportive nudge under the table.

Presley nodded slowly, still confused by Paisley's question.

"You know your parents died?" Paisley asked carefully. The smaller girl nodded once more.

"Do you know what it means when you die?" Shiloh spoke up. Presley lifted her head to look at the older girl and her small eyebrows knitted together slightly, as if she was just now considering this for the first time.

"It means a lot of things to a lot of different people," Shiloh nodded. "Sometimes it's a sad thing to think about. Does thinking about your parents make you sad?"

The smaller girl sat up, looking down at her hands in her lap and nodding shyly.

"It is okay," Paisley nodded. "Being sad is okay sometimes." She tapped the girl's shoulder gently to get her attention before holding up the dandelion between them.

"When someone dies, it is hard to understand," Paisley glanced over at Shiloh for a moment. "Because one minute they are there... but then they are gone." She turned away, taking a deep breath before blowing on the dandelion, sending the white flakes scattering into the wind.

"And it is hard," Paisley turned back, biting her lip. "Because no matter what you do, you can not bring them back. And sometimes we do not... we do not know why they got taken away from us."

"But it is like a dandelion," Paisley nodded, holding up the empty stem. "One may be gone, but it left behind many of seeds," she pointed in the direction where she had blown the flower. "So it will... it will not really be gone. It will only grow."

Shiloh gave Paisley a soft smile from across the table and reached over to brush Presley's hair out of her face. "I know it's hard to understand why your parents are gone, and it's okay to be sad. It's okay to have questions, but that's what we're here for now," she nodded to Paisley.

"But even if it feels like you lost them, you didn't. They're right here," she reached out, taking Presley's hand and guiding her to rest it on her heart. "They love you so so so so much. And even though their bodies are gone, their love will never leave."

The tiny brown eyed girl looked back and forth between them slowly. Paisley noticed how her bottom lip was quivering slightly and she opened her arms. "It is okay," she whispered, just as Presley scooted forward and allowed Paisley to pull her into her lap.

"Well great, we made her cry," Shiloh whispered, biting her lip as Paisley held the smaller girl in her arms.

Her wife shook her head, rubbing Presley's back and meeting Shiloh's eyes. "She is learning to understand, it is okay," she said softly. "Sometimes it is sad."

Shiloh watched Paisley comfort the smaller girl, not saying anything, but just holding her. It started to click for Shiloh. Presley just needed someone. Sure, they could talk for her for as long as they wanted, but at the end of the day, what she needed the most was someone to be there for her.

Paisley stood up carefully, nodding softly at Shiloh. Once they threw away their trash, they headed back to the car. With only an hour left in their drive, both girls were anxious to get home and get settled in.

Paisley sat in the back seat with Presley, trying to entertain the girl by pointing to different things out the window as they drove. This grew old after only ten minutes, though, so Paisley resorted to her backup plan.

She leaned forward, grabbing Shiloh's phone and plugging it into the stereo. Shiloh glanced at her in confusion. Giving her wife a soft smile, Paisley put their music on shuffle.

As the first song began playing, Shiloh and Paisley immediately made eye contact through the rear view mirror, a knowing smile on both of their faces. Paisley leaned back against the seat and looked out the window, letting the familiar song fill the silence. The same song that they'd goofed around to at the old apartment, and the same song they'd belt out singing time and time again filled the car.

They immediately stopped though, when they heard something they'd never heard before. Giggling. Paisley's head snapped over to look at Presley, who was amused by their antics. The older girl couldn't help but laugh along with her.

Shiloh met her eyes through the rearview mirror, giving her wife a thankful smile before turning her eyes back to the road. Maybe this was their song. Maybe that was why it stayed the same, even if things around them were changing.

C H A P T E R   3 4

"Do you want to hold my hand?"

Paisley looked down at the younger girl standing next to her in the driveway, whose brown eyes were taking in the quaint white house that stood tall before them. Presley glanced up at Paisley, and then to her outstretched hand. She reached up and wrapped her small fingers around Paisley's thumb gently.

"This is your home now, too," Paisley said softly, squatting down next to the smaller girl to try and look at the house from her level. "It is not a big fancy mansion... but... it is home," Paisley nodded.

"Ready?" Shiloh appeared behind them, holding the pink duffel bag with Presley's belongings over her shoulder. Paisley nodded, standing up and leading the smaller girl up the front porch steps.

When Shiloh unlocked the door, Paisley held out a hand to keep her from entering. She nudged the door open with her foot, allowing Presley to shyly peer into the house. A few moments later, the smaller girl glanced up at Paisley, tugging on her thumb to tell her that she wanted to go inside.

Shiloh looked at Paisley in shock, but the brown eyed girl just giggled softly, allowing Presley to lead the way inside.

"It is about... being able to do it on your own," Paisley turned to Shiloh as the green eyed girl closed the door behind them. "To feel like... you have a choice."

"Control," Shiloh nodded softly. Paisley flashed her a small smile before turning her attention back to Presley, who was looking around with a hint of curiosity glimmering in her eyes.

"You can look around, if you want," Paisley laughed softly. Without letting go of her hand, Presley took a few shy steps forwards. Paisley followed her as she peered into the living room while Shiloh disappeared down the hallway to put her bags away.

"This is the living room," Paisley nodded, allowing Presley to lead her around the room as she checked out everything it had to offer. "The kitchen is over there."

Presley allowed Paisley to lead her into the kitchen, showing her around. They walked through the master bedroom, the dining room, the art studio, and eventually down the hallway where Shiloh rejoined them.

"Last stop, little one," Shiloh laughed softly, squatting down next to the girl and brushing her hair out of her face. "Do you know what this is?"

Presley turned to look at Shiloh, shaking her head slowly. Shiloh saw the curiosity in her eyes, so she nodded towards the door. "Take a look, then."

There was a hint of a smile on Presley's face upon Shiloh's words. She looked at them for approval before reaching out and pushing the door open.

When the colorful room was revealed, the smaller girl took the couple by surprise when she turned around and looked at them in confusion.

"That's yours," Shiloh whispered, nudging her forwards gently. "Go ahead."

Immediately, the smaller girl's face lit up. She looked back and forth from Shiloh to Paisley, as if she were trying to make sure they were telling the truth. A wide smile spread across her face once the reality set in and she turned back to the room, pulling Paisley forwards with her as she ventured inside.

Shiloh and Paisley exchanged glances, a relieved smile on both of their faces. Presley dropped Paisley's finger and began looking around the room, taking the time to study everything, especially the scene Shiloh had painted on the wall.

Both girls grew confused when something seemed to have startled Presley. Just as they were about to say something, the smaller girl giggled, pointing to the fluffy white tail that stuck out from underneath the bed.

Paisley rolled her eyes lightheartedly, moving forwards and kneeling down beside the bed. "That is Wolf," she explained, drumming her fingers on the carpet beside her to try and gain his attention. "He is nice, do not worry."

"Come here, doofus," Paisley giggled, patting the floor and watching as Wolf carefully creeped out from underneath the bed.

"He is blind," Paisley explained, motioning for Presley to sit down beside her. "Here," she held out her hand and let Wolf sniff it. "Let him smell your hand so he knows you are a nice person."

Presley glanced up at Paisley with a soft smile on her face before holding out her hand. The white cat took a step forwards and sniffed it, proceeding to rub against it only moments later. Presley giggled excitedly.

"He likes you," Paisley smiled, glancing back at Shiloh who was watching the interaction between the two from the doorway. "You just have to be slow with him, because he can not see you."

Presley nodded, gently smoothing out the cat's fur and giggling when he willingly lay out on the floor, yawning widely.

"Okay, that's unfair," Shiloh laughed from the doorway. "We've only been here five minutes and he already likes her more than he likes me." Paisley just giggled and crinkled her nose.

———————————

"Dinner's ready!"

Shiloh turned off the stove, setting her wooden spoon down and retrieving three bowls from the pantry. As she added equal amounts of pasta into each bowl, she heard giggling coming from down the hallway.

"Pais! Food!" she called louder, laughing softly to herself. A few moments later, she heard the bedroom door open and close. Paisley appeared at the entrance to the kitchen, and tiny footsteps followed behind her.

"Is that my paintbrush?" Shiloh asked once she turned around to face her wife, who had a plastic tiara on the top of her head.

"No," Paisley shook her head, a small smile on her face. "It is a wand," she nodded, moving the paintbrush in a spiral motion in front of her.

"Okay, well just… make sure you put the wand back away from where it came from," Shiloh laughed, shaking her head and handing Paisley a bowl.

Soon Paisley traded her wand for a spoon, and somehow all three girls ended up sitting on the floor in the living room while old Friends reruns played on the TV.

Paisley had suggested this so Presley wouldn't feel the pressure to talk at the dinner table, but Shiloh also knew the girl simply wanted to watch her favorite TV show. Even though Presley didn't quite understand what was going on, she'd giggle at the parts that she found funny, which in turn would make Paisley laugh, which would lead to Shiloh watching them both with an affectionate smile on her face.

"All done?" Paisley asked once Presley set her bowl down in front of her. When the smaller girl nodded, Paisley hopped to her feet to bring all three of their bowls back into the kitchen.

When she returned, Paisley found Presley now curled up in Shiloh's lap, sucking her thumb and keeping her eyes trained on the TV. Shiloh glanced up at her wife, giving her a soft smile and holding out her arm. Paisley sat down next to her, leaning into her side and resuming the episode.

Not even a full episode had passed before Presley was fast asleep in Shiloh's arms. The green eyed girl nudged Paisley with her elbow, taking her attention away from the TV and nodding towards the sleeping girl.

"We did good," Paisley giggled, turning off the TV and leaning over to kiss Shiloh's cheek. "Do you think so?"

Shiloh nodded softly, laughing softly when Paisley yawned and rubbed her eyes. "Did it wear you out?"

"A little," Paisley admitted, giggling and pushing herself up to her feet. She offered a hand out to Shiloh, helping her wife up and following the dark haired girl down the hallway.

"This is weird," Shiloh whispered, carrying Presley into the mint green bedroom and bending down to turn on the nightlight. Paisley furrowed her eyebrows.

"What do you mean?" the brown eyed girl asked, tilting her head to the side.

"Just... I don't know," Shiloh laughed, gently lying Presley's sleeping form down on the bed and pulling the blanket over her. "I never imagined any of this would happen to us when we first met."

"Neither did I," Paisley shook her head. "All I wanted was a bed." The brown eyed girl giggled and approached Shiloh from behind, wrapping her arms around her waist and resting her head on her shoulder. "I am glad it happened, though."

"Me too," Shiloh whispered, leaning down to smooth Presley's hair out of her face before turning her head to kiss Paisley on the cheek. "I wouldn't trade it for the world."

"Sleep tight," Shiloh said softly, running her thumb across Presley's cheek. Paisley circled around to the other side of the bed, kneeling down and pressing a soft kiss to the child's forehead.

"Goodnight, little flower," Paisley whispered, standing back to her feet and looking back once more before following Shiloh out of the bedroom.

Thirty minutes later, Shiloh lay back in the bed with a book in her hands. Paisley peered into the room from the hallway, clad in only a large t-shirt and underwear with a toothbrush handing out of her mouth. She noticed how Shiloh was struggling to keep her eyes open and couldn't help but laugh softly.

After rinsing out her mouth and washing her face, Paisley padded into the bedroom and crawled into bed beside her wife. She propped herself up on her elbow, reaching out and taking the book from Shiloh's hands.

"Hey," the green eyed girl mumbled, furrowing her eyebrows together. "I was reading that."

"No you weren't," Paisley giggled, earning a defiant mumble from Shiloh when she put the book on the nightstand.

"I love youuu," the smaller girl hummed, flashing her a shy smile before reaching over to turn off the lights.

"Come cuddle," Shiloh mumbled against her pillow, rolling over and holding out her arms from the smaller girl. Paisley giggled and immediately obeyed.

With one arm draped across Shiloh's stomach and the other snaked up her sleeve, Paisley laid her head on Shiloh's chest as the green eyed girl's breathing turned rhythmic.

Paisley didn't fall asleep, though. She tried to, but her thought were on the smaller girl across the hall. So about half an hour later, she carefully untangled herself from Shiloh.

The minute she quietly opened the door to Presley's room, she knew the smaller girl was awake. The nightlight dimly lit the room and she made out the smaller girl's tiny figure sitting in the corner of her bed that rested against the wall.

"Hey, it is just me," Paisley whispered, walking over slowly and sitting down on the edge of the bed. "Scared?" she asked quietly.

This earned a slow nod from the girl, who had the blanket clutched against her chest. Biting her lip, Paisley scooted back further on the small bed and patted the space beside her. Presley's eyes flickered up to hers before she abandoned the blanket and crawled into Paisley's lap.

"I have something for you," Paisley said softly, keeping one of her hands behind her back. Presley looked up at her in confusion, and Paisley held the object out in front of them.

"His name is Sunny," Paisley nodded, placing the yellow stuffed dog in Presley's lap. "He was my best friend when I was little... and... and maybe he can be yours, too," she smiled.

"And his name is Sunny like the sun. So he keeps all the darkness away," she nodded softly.

A soft smile crept its way onto the small doe eyed girl's face. She took the stuffed animal from Paisley and examined it carefully before hugging it tight against her chest. Paisley watched her in adoration.

A few moments later, though, the smaller girl looked up at Paisley with a conflicted expression on her face. Paisley seemed to know exactly what was wrong, though, because she simply shook her head and gave the girl a reassuring smile.

"You are welcome," she nodded softly. "Thank you, you're welcome," she added, making Presley giggle.

The smaller girl hugged the stuffed animal to her chest, smiling softly. Paisley noted how she yawned, and realized the smaller girl must still be exhausted.

"I know a way to keep the monsters out," Paisley spoke up, earning a curious expression from the smaller girl.

Taking the blanket that had fallen on the floor, Paisley scooped Presley up into her lap and lay back on the bed. Making the smaller girl laugh, she shook out the blanket and pulled it overtop of them, curling up her legs so they were completely covered under the sheet.

"It is like a fort," Paisley nodded. "It keeps the monsters out."

The smaller girl giggled, lying down beside Paisley and hugging Sunny inbetween them. Noticing how she yawned, Paisley wrapped an arm around her and pulled her into her side.

"Go to sleep, little flower," the older girl whispered, kissing Presley's forehead. "I will keep the monsters away."

With Presley's small fingers curled around Paisley's thumb, and Paisley's arm wrapped protectively around Presley, both girls were fast asleep within ten minutes.

CHAPTER 35

Shiloh was awoken the next morning by something poking her cheek. She mumbled a few words under her breath, rolling over and burying her head into the pillow. It only continued, though. So she eventually gave up.

"Baaaabe," Shiloh yawned, lifting her head and wiping her eyes. But instead of Paisley, she came face to face with Wolf, who proceeded to nudge her hand with his nose.

"You're not my wife," Shiloh mumbled, shaking her head and looking around the room in a daze.

Wait, where was Paisley?

Furrowing her eyebrows together, the green eyed girl pulled the covers off of her legs and quickly tugged on a pair of pajama pants. She had a feeling as to where Paisley might be.

As she walked down the hallway, she realized how much had changed in the years her and Paisley had been together. If she had woken up to an empty bed three years ago, she would have been set into a panic.

But now, as she pushed open the door to Presley's room, she realized she didn't have to panic anymore. Because there laid Paisley, fast asleep with Presley in her arms.

Shiloh struggled to fight back her smile at the sight. Presley had one hand curled around Paisley's thumb, and the other hugging Sunny to her side. They both looked so peaceful, so unaffected by anything that could be plaguing the world around them.

The green eyed girl quietly moved closer, laying the blanket back over them and brushing Paisley's hair out of her face.

It was almost as if in this moment, she realized this was hers. She didn't have to worry about losing people anymore.

As she quietly exited the room and closed the door, she noticed how much things had changed. The same fear she used to have when leaving Paisley alone wasn't there. Paisley could take care of herself, Shiloh trusted her in that way.

Granted, she never did like leaving Paisley. But now she knew she would always be there. It was no longer a choice of Paisley needing her. It was a choice of Paisley choosing her. And the smaller brown eyed girl had made that perfectly clear.

Paisley was her's and she was Paisley's. They didn't have to question it anymore. Shiloh had held her breath for years, and now it was as if she letting out the greatest sigh of relief.

She'd do it all again, though. She'd do it all again in the heartbeat. You wouldn't have to ask her twice. It was Paisley. Of course she'd choose her. She'd choose her over and over again, in any lifetime, no matter what. That's just how it was.

Running a hand through her tousled hair, Shiloh brushed her teeth and washed her face, which served to wake her up right away. After feeding Wolf, she wandered into the kitchen and searched through the pantry.

Somehow, ten minutes later, she found herself measuring out a fourth cup of vegetable oil and adding it to the bowl. She set the oven to preheat, and just as she was about to turn back to the pantry, she caught sight of something out of the corner of her eye.

A small head with two expressive brown eyes peered into the kitchen, and Shiloh paused, tilting her head to the side.

"Hey bug," she smiled softly, squatting down and holding out her hand. "Did you sleep well?"

Nodding softly, the smaller girl stepped out from behind the wall, clutching Sunny in one hand and padding over to Shiloh. The green eyed girl knelt down, pulling Presley into a hug and brushing her hair out of her face.

"Is Paisley still asleep?" Shiloh asked, laughing softly when Presley nodded and pointed back in the direction of the bedroom.

Shiloh glanced at the oven before turning back to Presley. "Are you hungry, little one?" she asked, placing a hand on her shoulder. The smaller girl nodded and looked at her hopefully, which was enough of an answer for Shiloh.

"Wanna help me make muffins?" the green eyed girl asked, pointing to the stove. When Presley nodded, Shiloh gently picked her up, placing her on the counter so her small legs hung down and rested against the cabinets.

"Here," Shiloh laughed softly, opening a container of blueberries and placing them in front of the girl. "Throw a handful or two of those in there."

Looking at Shiloh for approval, Presley gathered a few blueberries and plopped them into the bowl. Shiloh grabbed one for herself, tossing it in the air and catching it in her mouth. When Presley giggled, Shiloh offered her one.

"Now what do we need?" Shiloh mumbled to herself, turning back to the recipe book and scanning the page with her finger. "Two eggs. Think we can handle that, kiddo?" she laughed, turning back to Presley, who watched her as she retrieved two eggs from the fridge.

"Do you know how to crack an egg?" Shiloh asked, turning to Presley. When the child shook her head, Shiloh nodded softly and placed the second egg on the counter.

"Watch what I do, okay?" Shiloh gave her a small smile before tapping the egg on the side of the counter and cracking it into the bowl. Presley leaned forwards to watch.

"Now you have to be very gentle," Shiloh warned her before handing her the second egg. "Just make a little crack in it and I'll pull it apart for you, sound good?"

Nodding, Presley carefully tapped the egg on the edge of the bowl until it had cracked slightly. With a proud smile on her face, she held it up to Shiloh, who proceeded to crack it the rest of the way into the bowl and throw the shell away.

"Good job," she laughed softly and gave Presley a high five after rinsing off her hands. "Here, you can stir it while I get the pan ready," she nodded, handing the girl a spoon.

Pretty soon, the muffins were in the oven and the timer was set for fifteen minutes. Yawning, Shiloh leaned against the counter next to Presley and gave the girl a soft smile. "Hey, wanna know a secret?"

Meanwhile, Paisley was awoken by a beam of sunlight breaking through the window and shining across her pillow. Her eyes fluttered open and she groaned, rolling back over and covering her face with her arm.

Moments later, though, something caught her attention. Wiping her eyes, she sat up and grew excited when she realized Shiloh must be making food. But looking around the room, she also grew concerned because Presley was nowhere to be found. So she quickly got to her feet and hurried into her kitchen.

As soon as she entered the room, she was met with a smirking Shiloh and a giggling Presley, who was sitting on the counter with a container of blueberries in her lap. Paisley furrowed her eyebrows together in confusion.

"See, I told you she'd wake up once she smelled food," Shiloh laughed softly and nudged the smaller girl's shoulder. Realizing why they were laughing, Paisley halfheartedly rolled her eyes and wandered over to peer in the oven.

"Morning, sleepyhead," Shiloh laughed, walking up behind Paisley and wrapping her arms around her waist. "I saw you played a little game of musical beds last night, yeah?"

Paisley couldn't help but laugh, turning her head to kiss Shiloh's cheek. "I had to show her how to keep away the monsters," Paisley nodded, turning and looking in Presley's direction.

"That's what I figured," Shiloh laughed softly. Paisley gave her a sleepy smile before walking over to Presley and stealing a blueberry, which made the girl laugh.

"Good morning, little flower," Paisley said softly, still somewhat groggy from sleep. "Did you sleep well?"

Presley nodded, setting the blueberries aside and holding out her arms. Paisley looked at Shiloh in confusion.

"She wants to be picked up," Shiloh whispered, laughing when a look of realization spread across her wife's face. The brown eyed girl scooped Presley up into her arms, balancing her on her hip and smiling softly at the small girl.

"You can go set the table," Shiloh nodded, pointing to the oven. "I'll bring them in when they're done."

Only a few minutes later, all three girls sat at the table eating breakfast. The comfortable silence was interrupted by the buzzing of Shiloh's phone, though, and she hopped up to get it from the counter.

"It's Vanessa," she whispered, looking at Paisley nervously. The brown eyed girl's eyes widened and she glanced at Presley, who was too busy picking at her muffin to care.

The two girls had been on the way to Ryland and Vanessa's Halloween party when the accident threw their plans off track. In the hospital room, Shiloh had texted the girls to let them know they wouldn't be able to make it to the party. She hadn't really paid her phone much attention for the rest of the night, and only got their questions in the morning.

When she was questioned, Shiloh simply told them that they were both too exhausted to make it. But now, they could only make excuses for so long. Especially now that there was a third member of the family sitting at the table.

"I'll see what she wants," Shiloh nodded quickly, giving Paisley a nervous smile before answering the phone.

"Hey, Nessa. What's up?" she leaned against the counter, nervously awaiting her friend's response. Paisley watched anxiously.

"Shy? Hey, where have you been?"

"I, uh, busy," Shiloh stumbled over her words, shaking her head at her own incompetence. "Why'd you call so early?"

"You're asking me," Vanessa laughed, and Shiloh could hear the girl yawn over the line. "Leah just called and woke me up. I thought you'd still be asleep. She says she has something to tell us all."

"She what?" Shiloh furrowed her eyebrows and tilted her head to the side. Paisley even raised an eyebrow.

"I don't know. She just said she wants to see us all today. Maybe we could like... go out to lunch or something?"

Shiloh glanced at Paisley, and then to Presley. She bit her lip.

"I, uh, well, maybe you guys should like... come over here?" Shiloh spoke nervously. "We kind of have something to tell you guys, too."

"Oh god," Vanessa laughed. "Y'all better not be ditching us. Good luck finding two better looking dance majors in New Y-,"

"We're not," Shiloh shook her head, too nervous to joke around. "Just... can you meet us over here sometime today? I'll even make lunch or something."

"Should I be worried?" Vanessa asked, sensing the anxiety in Shiloh's tone.

"No! No. It's fine. Everything's fine," Shiloh nodded quickly, causing Paisley to tilt her head to the side. "Everything's just fine and dandy."

"Alright, so now I'm worried," Vanessa laughed. "We'll be over as soon as I can get Ryland to get her fat ass out of bed!" she raised her voice at the end, calling to the light haired girl in the other room. Shiloh couldn't help but laugh.

"I'll let Leah know, too," Vanessa added. Shiloh thanked her, saying her goodbyes before hanging up and collapsing back into her chair nervously. Even Presley, who had been previously distracted by her muffin, looked up at the dark haired girl in confusion.

"Leah has news. We have news. They're all coming over," Shiloh bit her lip and looked at Paisley from across the table. "What the hell are they going to say about this?"

"What do you think they are going to say?" Paisley laughed and shook her head. "Do you know Ryland?"

"I know you got way too much attitude from her," Shiloh teased. "What do you mean?"

"She will go crazy," Paisley laughed softly, but grew confused when Shiloh's eyes widened. "No, Lo, the good kind of crazy," she quickly added.

"You think?"

"Duh," Paisley giggled, glancing at Presley who seemed to be enjoying their playful banter. "It is Ryland. She is a kid."

"Oh, right," Shiloh nodded softly. She picked at her food, thinking for a few moments before turning to Presley. "Hey, kiddo, is it cool with you if we have some friends over today?"

"They are nice people," Paisley added. "Leah is tiny just like you."

The small doe eyed girl looked back and forth between the couple, thinking it over for a few moments before nodding softly.

Shiloh and Paisley exchanged glances. They both knew they were nervous for their friend's reactions, even if they weren't willing to admit it.

CHAPTER 36

"C'mon, kiddo," Shiloh laughed softly when Presley attempted to feed the last of her muffin to Wolf. "Let's get you dressed."

"Pais, can you get out the stuff for pasta salad and see if we have enough rolls for sandwiches?" Shiloh asked, balancing Presley on one hip and walking over to kiss her wife on the cheek. "I'll come help you once I'm done."

"Got it," Paisley giggled and crinkled her nose. Shiloh stole one more kiss before disappearing down the hallway with Presley.

She glanced at the smaller girl, who seemed to be content in just observing everything around her. Shiloh was anxious to see when the child would talk, but she also understood how important it was to be patient in these types of situations.

It was all about control, she'd figured out. When Paisley went silent, it had been when everything else around her spiraled out of control and she felt as if she was losing grip on reality. But the one thing she could control was her words. Shiloh figured that it was probably the same for Presley.

"I, uh, I put the clothes you brought with you away," Shiloh nodded, setting Presley down in front of the dresser. "It's sorta chilly outside so let's pick out something that'll keep you nice and warm, yeah?"

Ten minutes later, Presley stood in front of Shiloh, donned in black leggings and a knitted white sweater. Shiloh helped her slide her small hand through the second sleeve before sitting back on the bed and giving her a small smile.

"Now let's do something about your hair, yeah?" Shiloh laughed and ruffled the smaller girl's wavy hair that had been tousled in her sleep. "C'mere, bug," she scooted back on the bed and patted the space in front of her.

Presley shyly crawled onto the bed, allowing Shiloh to guide her to sit in front of her so she could smooth out her hair.

"I figure I should tell you a bit about who's coming over today just so you can be a little prepared," Shiloh laughed softly, combing her fingers through the girl's caramel waves.

"You'll like Leah. She's super sweet. Plus she's really good at baking," Shiloh nodded. "She's the oldest out of all of us so she's the one that usually keeps everyone out of trouble." Presley giggled softly.

"Then there's Ryland and Vanessa. They're dancers, kinda like you were when you dressed up on Halloween, remember?" Shiloh asked, beginning to part the girl's hair. Presley nodded.

"Except they like hip hop more, I think. Sometimes they can be kinda loud. Well, mostly Ryland. But they're super fun. Ryland loves little kids like you," Shiloh laughed quietly. "But just stick by my side if you get overwhelmed or anything, yeah?"

Once the smaller girl nodded, Shiloh smiled and tied off a section of caramel hair on the girl's head. "All done," she whispered, turning Presley around and fixing the two pigtails she had gathered on either side of her head.

"Well look at you, little one, you look so beautiful," Shiloh nodded. The smaller girl smiled shyly, reaching up to run her small fingers through the pigtails. She shook her head, giggling when her hair bounced back and forth.

"Now c'mon, let's go brush our teeth and then help Pais get lunch ready," Shiloh smiled, nudging Presley in the direction of the bathroom.

Meanwhile, Paisley stood in the kitchen carefully slicing up a tomato. She paused when she heard small footsteps behind her, feeling something tug at her sleeve. When she looked down, Presley stood beside her with her hands stretched out towards the older girl.

"You want to help?" Paisley asked, setting the knife down and bending down to pick up the smaller girl. Presley nodded, and Paisley glanced around the kitchen in thought.

"Here," Paisley nodded softly, setting Presley down on the counter and keeping an eye on her while she grabbed a bag of grapes and a large bowl. Setting them in front of the girl, she opened the bag and popped one into her own mouth. "Can you pull these off the stem and put them in here?" Paisley asked, pointing to the bowl.

Shiloh appeared in the kitchen soon after, taking over Paisley's job so the smaller girl could have her turn to get dressed. The green eyed girl glanced over at Presley, who seemed to put one grape in her mouth for every one she put in the bowl.

"Hey," Shiloh whispered, gaining the girl's attention and grabbing a grape. She opened her mouth and then pointed to Presley. "Catch."

The smaller girl smiled softly, opening her mouth and tilting her head back. Shiloh tossed the grape in her direction, but it bounced off her chin and landed on the floor. Presley burst into laughter.

"C'mon, try again," Shiloh giggled, grabbing another grape and taking a step backwards. This time, when she tossed the grape, it flew over Presley's head and bounced across the floor. Landing right at Paisley's feet.

"Lo," Paisley giggled, shaking her head. "They are almost here," she bit her lip and glanced at the door. Both girls were suddenly reminded of why their friends were coming over, and they quickly hurried to finish getting the meal ready.

Sure enough, only a little while later, the sound of Ryland's car could be heard in the driveway. When she beeped, it only confirmed who it was. Shiloh quickly rushed to set the last plate on the table before looking at Paisley in panic, who was holding Presley.

"What are we gonna do?" Shiloh whispered, her eyes widening. Paisley simply shook her head.

"You go," she nodded softly and bit her lip. "I will stay in here."

"I, uh…" Shiloh glanced between the door and Paisley when the doorbell rang a few moments later. "Okay. You just…. you just don't freak out."

"I am not the one that is freaking out, Lo," Paisley giggled, raising an eyebrow at her wife. Shaking it off, the green eyed girl quickly ran a hand through her hair and jogged over to the door.

She opened it slightly, immediately greeted by her three best friends. Before she had a chance to invite them inside, Shiloh slipped out onto the front porch and closed the door behind them. This earned a look of confusion from all three girls.

"I, uh, I… okay," Shiloh stammered, shaking her head and holding up her hands to try and keep her friends' questions at bay. "Me and Paisley… we… we kind of did something crazy," she confessed, biting her lip.

"What's new?" Leah laughed, trying to ease Shiloh's nervousness.

The dark haired girl shook her head. "It's, uh, kinda big," she nodded and glanced back at the door. "So… there's someone in there that we want you to meet."

"Quit with the dramatics, Shy, you know we love puppies," Ryland laughed, brushing past Shiloh and entering the house before the green eyed girl had a chance to argue.

"See, I told you it was a p—," Ryland froze when her eyes landed on Paisley. More specifically, the small child that was hiding behind Paisley's legs. "A…. a human?"

All three girls turned to look at Shiloh for some sort of explanation. All the darker haired girl could offer them was a nervous smile and a soft shrug.

"Is this like... babysitting or something?" Vanessa laughed, raising an eyebrow. "I'm confused."

"Not really," Shiloh bit her lip.

"She is ours," Paisley spoke up, kneeling down next to the small child and pulling her into her side. There was an air of protectiveness in her actions, but also one of possession. As if she were claiming the small child as her own.

"What?" All three girls spoke at the same time and whipped their heads back around to face Paisley, whose eyes widened.

"On Halloween," Shiloh whispered, turning their attention back to her. "There was an accident and she... well, she survived. But..."

"Oh," Leah suddenly understood, looking back and forth from the two girls.

"Oh?" Ryland furrowed her eyebrows. Vanessa nodded in agreement, unsure of what Shiloh was hinting at. Moments later, though, when Leah stood on her tiptoes to whisper something into both of the girls' ears, their eyed widened in realization.

"Oh my god," Vanessa whispered.

"Yeah," Shiloh bit her lip, unsure of what else to say. She glanced over at Presley, who was studying the three girls with wide eyes.

Before anyone could say anything else, Leah donned a wide smile and clapped her hands together. The oldest girl bent down next to Paisley, giving the small child beside her a warm smile. "Hey cutie," she said softly. "My name's Leah. What's yours?"

Presley just looked at the girl nervously before scooting closer to Paisley. Leah gave Paisley a look of confusion.

"She does not talk," Paisley shrugged, trying not to put pressure on the younger girl. "But it is okay," she added before standing up with Presley in her arms.

"Her name is Presley," Shiloh spoke up. "Presley Rose."

"Little flower," Paisley nodded, reaching up and twirling one of the smaller girl's pigtails around her finger. Presley giggled, causing all of the other girls to look at her.

"This is for real?" Ryland asked, turning back to Shiloh.

"It is," the green eyed girl nodded. She wasn't sure how her friends were going to react, but she was relieved when Ryland just nodded with a soft smile on her face.

"Y'all are like freaking superheroes," Vanessa laughed.

"Presley..." Ryland spoke the name aloud for the first time, causing the child to turn and look in her direction. "It fits you, kid. I like it." The smaller girl smiled shyly, holding onto Paisley.

"I'm Ryland," the light haired girl continued. "But now it's Aunt Ryland to you," she nodded, making Paisley laugh. "I'm the person you come to whenever you wanna have some fun."

"She's three!" Leah gasped, playfully smacking Ryland's shoulder. This resulted in Presley bursting into laughter, followed by Paisley.

"Don't you dare start hitting each other just to make the kid laugh," Vanessa stepped in, separating Ryland and Leah with a soft laugh. "Let's at least eat before we kill each other."

"Lunch is in here," Shiloh nodded, giving Paisley a quick kiss on the cheek before leading all of the other girls to the kitchen table.

Only a few minutes later, all the girls sat in a circle around the table. Presley was squished inbetween Paisley and Ryland, who kept passing her cheese to give to Wolf under the table.

"This kind of stuff only happens to you guys, I swear," Vanessa laughed, nodding to the couple across the table. "We literally had no idea it was something like this."

"I thought you guys got a puppy," Ryland nodded, taking a bite of her sandwich.

"Yeah, this is way better than my engagement," Leah laughed, shaking her head and grabbing another handful of grapes from the bowl across the table.

Everyone's heads snapped up the moment they heard Leah's words. Eyes widening, Shiloh and Paisley exchanged shocked glances.

"Plus, you didn't even t—woah," Leah paused when she looked back up and found everyone's eyes on her. Even Presley.

"You got engaged?" Paisley was the first to speak up, excitement laced in her words. Leah's face turned bright red and she quickly swiped her hands under the table.

"I-I forgot I hadn't told you yet," she mumbled, looking away bashfully. "It happened last night.

The only thing that could be heard next was the collective screeching of chairs against the floor as all of the girls hopped out of their seats and crowded around Leah.

"Tell us everything," Ryland squealed, grabbing Leah's hand and studying the ring. A collective gasp echoed from around her, and even Presley climbed out of her seat to hurry over and see what all of the commotion was about.

Leah laughed bashfully, her face turning bright red. "It was nothing huge," she shook her head. "We went to this haunted cornmaze, and it was super dark, and I got separated from him somehow," she explained.

"But then I heard him calling my name so I followed his voice and I turned the corner and suddenly there were all these candles and he..." she laughed, shaking her head. "He just asked me to marry him," the smaller girl shrugged, excitement in her words.

"I'm so happy for you!" Shiloh squealed, pulling Leah into a tight hug. Paisley did the same, smiling in excitement.

"Damn it," Ryland whispered, causing the other four girls to grow confused. They all looked back at the light haired girl questioningly.

"Well now it's between me and Vanessa to see who gets married last!" Ryland shook her head, pointing to the dark skinned girl next to her. Everyone else burst into laughter, even Presley who wasn't quite sure what they were laughing about.

"Gotta put yourself out there, Ryland," Shiloh teased playfully, throwing an arm around her friend's shoulders. "Maybe Pais can hook you up with some hot preschool parents."

"No thanks," Ryland shook her head, nudging Shiloh playfully. "Being an aunt is hard enough as it is."

CHAPTER 37

In Shiloh's mind, things were working out pretty well for them.

She sat on the back porch swing, watching Paisley, Ryland, and Vanessa all scramble to find a hiding spot in their large backyard. Meanwhile, Leah and Presley were around the side of the house, waiting for Leah to count to 30.

Her friends had actually been okay with the fact that they'd welcomed Presley into their home. Shiloh knew she should have known all along that they would be accepting, but they had kept it as a pretty big secret. Thankfully, their friends had accepted with a smile, as they always seemed to do.

Shiloh was still scared, though. And she knew Paisley was as well, even if she didn't vocalize it at the time. Shiloh could tell by the way that her wife would pause for a few moments, watching as Presley scurried after Ryland. She could see the uneasiness in her eyes. She'd had those moments too.

Presley hadn't been with them for more than a week, but Shiloh found herself faced with the daunting realization that they were now responsible for a child. A living, breathing human. Relying on them. And it was their job to make sure she was happy.

And since neither of them had been handed a step-by-step manual on how to raise a child, both Shiloh and Paisley couldn't help but feel a little overwhelmed. They had agreed on taking it day by day, but they both knew well enough that one another still had the thought in the back of her mind.

There was also the fact that Presley wasn't technically theirs. Legally, she was still a child of the state. Yes, they were fostering her. Yes, she was living with them. Yes, they considered her a member of the family. But, yes, the government could very well take her away from them at any moment. So things weren't exactly perfect yet.

"Help me, Lo!"

Shiloh was snapped out of her thoughts when Paisley practically hopped in her lap, throwing her arms around her wife's neck. At first the dark haired girl was startled, but when she heard Presley giggling from behind her, Shiloh lifted her head to find the smaller girl tapping Paisley's shoulder over and over.

"Is she it?" Shiloh laughed, raising an eyebrow at the tiny girl. Presley looked up, giggled, and nodded quickly. Paisley groaned dramatically into Shiloh's shoulder.

"Someone's a sore loser," Ryland teased, appearing from her hiding spot and jogging over to the porch. "You've gotta count to 30, Paisley. It's only fair."

Paisley simply giggled, shaking her head and hiding her face in her hair. Shiloh couldn't help but laugh, and she stood up, sliding Paisley off of her lap and letting the girl gain her balance back on her feet.

"Come on, Pais," Shiloh sighed, nudging her wife's shoulder. "I'll count with you."

Pretty soon, Shiloh and Paisley were knelt behind the side of the house, facing the wall making sure they couldn't see the backyard.

"We're supposed to start counting now," Shiloh whispered, laughing softly. Paisley just nodded.

"I know," the smaller girl replied, continuing to stay quiet and look at the wall in front of her. Shiloh grew confused.

"Well then what are you doing?" she laughed and raised an eyebrow.

"Worrying," Paisley admitted, sitting down cross legged in the grass and running a hand through her hair. Now even more confused, Shiloh sat down beside her and studied her wife's facial expressions, trying to figure out what was bothering her.

"Worrying about what?" Shiloh asked softly, reaching out and placing a hand on Paisley's knee. The girl stayed silent for a few moments, but placed her hand on top of Shiloh's to let her know she wasn't ignoring her.

"I am scared," Paisley confessed, finally meeting Shiloh's eyes. Just as Shiloh opened her mouth to reply, Paisley held up a finger to signal for her to wait. Shiloh paused, allowing her wife to think for a few more moments.

"I had a mom and a dad," Paisley spoke up once more, only confusing Shiloh even further. "I had a mom and a dad, and so did Presley. But now... she has us."

"And?" Shiloh asked, tilting her head to the side. "We'll be her legal guardians once we adopt her."

"I know, but..." Paisley paused, biting her lip. "But she will have us. A mom and a mom. Not a mom and a dad."

"So?"

"It is different," Paisley nodded hesitantly.

"Is that bad?" Shiloh asked, still confused. Paisley just sighed and looked away.

"That is what I was asking you, Lo," Paisley shook her head. "Is that bad?"

"Having parents?" Shiloh couldn't seem to understand what Paisley was alluding to. Growing frustrated, the smaller girl shook her head once more.

"Having a mom and a mom. Instead of a dad," Paisley mumbled, unsure whether or not she was overthinking things.

Shiloh slowly realized what her wife had been hinting at, and softly squeezed her hand to let her know she understood. She paused for a moment, taking a deep breath and thinking about what she should say.

"It shouldn't matter, right?" Shiloh finally spoke up, easing Paisley's nerves. "I mean, gender doesn't change much. There's people who identify as a gender that's different from the one assigned to them at birth, and there's people who don't even belong to a gender. But that doesn't change who they are as a person, you know?"

Paisley watched Shiloh talk, somewhat surprised at how passionately she was speaking about this. If Paisley didn't believe Shiloh's words alone, she was sure convinced by the way the raven haired girl's eyes ignited with a fire that couldn't be faked.

"Your soul... the core of your being... the things you believe and the things you say... those don't have a label on them. And that's what matters," Shiloh nodded, meeting Paisley's eyes.

"Plus, just because someone has a mom and a dad, doesn't mean they're good parents," the green eyed girl added, taking Paisley's hand into her lap and absentmindedly trailing her fingers up and down her arm. "I mean, look at your uncle. Yeah, he was a guy. But he sort of sucked as a role model. And even if he was a woman, that wouldn't change anything. I think you would have been happier with two of your aunt instead of him, am I right?"

Shiloh looked to Paisley for an answer, earning a slow, hesitant nod from the girl - which became more confident when Paisley began to realize everything Shiloh had said.

"Gender is stupid, anyway," Shiloh added, rolling her eyes. "You're telling me just because I was born a certain way that I'm not allowed to like sports? Or cut my hair short? Bullshit. That can't stop me."

"I like your hair long," Paisley whispered, reaching out and twirling a strand of Shiloh's hair around her finger. There was a gentleness in her words, as if Shiloh had spoken so truly that she didn't even need to think twice.

That was what worked between them. Paisley just got it. They were on the same wavelength. Shiloh didn't have to struggle to explain things to her. Paisley understood. And even before Paisley could talk much, Shiloh understood.

"I know you do," Shiloh laughed softly, reaching up and lacing her fingers with Paisley's other hand. "It was just an example."

"So you think we can do this?" Paisley whispered, meeting Shiloh's eyes once more. She earned a small smile from her wife.

"Of course we can, goofball," Shiloh reached out and tucked a loose strand of hair behind her wife's ear. "Parenthood should be a breeze compared to what you've been through."

"And we're a team. No matter what happens, we can get through it together," Shiloh nodded. She held up her pinkie finger inbetween them, giving Paisley a shy smile. "You and me?"

Paisley couldn't help but giggle at the age old gesture. With a crooked smile and a soft nod, she brought her hand up and interlocked her pinkie finger with Shiloh's.

"Me and you," the smaller girl whispered, her brown eyes flickering up to meet Shiloh's. Paisley leaned in and abandoned their pinkies.

Just as Shiloh was about to turn to bring her lips against Paisley's, the smaller girl giggled mischievously and pressed a quick kiss to her cheek. Hopping up to her feet, the smaller girl held a hand out for Shiloh.

"Tease," Shiloh mumbled half heartedly. She reluctantly took Paisley's hand, being pulled up to her feet. Just as she attempted to steal another kiss, Paisley turned her head out of the way and cupped her hands around her mouth.

"Ready or not, here we come!" the smaller girl yelled out, turning back to Shiloh with an apologetic smile. She grabbed Shiloh's hand and looked at her hopefully.

"Once our friends leave," she whispered, giving Shiloh a soft nod before turning to lead them around the back of the house. Before she could even take a step, though, someone's voice rang out from the backyard.

"Took you long enough!"

Shiloh and Paisley exchanged questioning glances.

"Shit."

"I think we found Ryland," Paisley whispered, causing both of them to burst into laughter. The smaller girl gave her wife one last kiss on the cheek before jogging around the back of the house to find her friend.

A few hours and two boxes of pizza later, the couple found themselves waving goodbye to their friends as they drove away. Shiloh stood next to Paisley in the driveway with a sleeping Presley in her arms, who had fallen asleep while hiding behind a tree.

"Looks like it's bedtime," Shiloh laughed softly and turned to Paisley once their friends' cars were out of sight. She looked down at the small girl in her arms, who had her head laid on her shoulder.

"Not for us," Paisley nodded softly, winking subtly at Shiloh before grabbing her free hand and leading her into the house.

The raven haired girl raised an eyebrow, following her wife into the house. She made sure to stay quiet as Paisley led them down the dimly lit hallway and into Presley's bedroom.

After struggling to change Presley into her pajamas while keeping her asleep, the two girls tucked her in and kissed her goodnight. Paisley disappeared into the shower, and Shiloh got ready for bed before curling up on the couch and absentmindedly flipping through the TV channels.

She was nearly falling asleep when a shift in the couch pulled her out of her daze. Paisley laughed softly, moving to straddle Shiloh with one knee on either side of her lap. The green eyed girl looked up at her, her breath catching in her throat when she saw how naturally beautiful Paisley was.

No matter how many times she saw her wife, she was shocked over and over by her beauty. Her eyes sparkled with an essence that reflected the light in her soul.

Over the years, Shiloh had learned the map of Paisley's eyes, revealing the girl inside and out. And yet she never grew bored. Nothing ever got old. Even hearing Paisley's name made her heart flutter. That's just how it had always been.

"Hi," Shiloh whispered, finally finding her words. The girl above her giggled, leaning forwards and letting her hair hang down the side of her face.

"Hi," Paisley smiled softly. She wrapped her arms around Shiloh's neck, gently pressing her forehead against the girl's. "Can I kiss you?"

"Yeah," Shiloh nodded slowly. "You don't have to ask before you kiss me. You can always kiss me. Whenever. It's you. I'll always say yes."

Paisley paused, somewhat taken aback by Shiloh's words. Her lips slowly curved into a smile, though, and she nodded slowly.

"Good," the smaller girl whispered, her eyes flickering down to Shiloh's mouth. Meeting the girl's green eyes once more, Paisley slowly leaned down and connected their lips in a soft, yet needy kiss.

Shiloh felt fireworks practically erupt on the back of her eyelids, and she brought her hands up to rest them on Paisley's hips. The smaller girl pulled away for a second, meeting Shiloh's eyes for approval before initiating another kiss. This one was deeper, more passionate.

Feeling Shiloh's hands tug on the bottom of her shirt softly, Paisley abruptly broke the kiss, which caused Shiloh to look up at her in confusion. The smaller girl placed her hands on top of Shiloh's, lowering them back down to her waist and shaking her head.

"You are tired," Paisley whispered. "I just want to kiss you. I…" she bit her lip, trying to find the right words. "I want to be close to you."

"That sounds stupid," Paisley shook her head with a frustrated sigh. "I just… I…"

The smaller girl was cut off by Shiloh, who wrapped one arm around her waist and brought her free hand up to place a finger over Paisley's lips, silencing her.

"I do too," the raven haired girl nodded, running a thumb over Paisley's cheek. Paisley blushed, Shiloh's touch sending shivers down her spine.

"I will not ask this time," she nodded with a soft smile, making Shiloh laugh quietly. She was cut off by her wife's lips, though, to which she wrapped both arms around the smaller girl's waist and pulled her even closer.

"I love you," Paisley whispered when the kiss broke, catching her breath before bringing Shiloh's lips to hers once again.

"I love you too."

CHAPTER 38

Shiloh couldn't sleep.

Even when she was younger, her mother always warned her that she was a very empathetic person. It was both a blessing and a curse. Shiloh felt for others so heavily that at times she felt as if she was going through just as much pain as them.

That's how it had been with Paisley when she had first showed up at the apartment. Shiloh only began to care even more as the smaller girl's past had been revealed. Now, her empathy had manifested itself into her diehard protectiveness of her wife.

But tonight, her mind wasn't on Paisley. The brown eyed girl was curled up contently in bed beside Shiloh, fast asleep. She was in Shiloh's arms. Shiloh didn't have to worry about her.

Instead, the green eyed girl's thoughts were with the youngest member of the household, whom they had put to bed a few hours ago.

It was hard for her to try and understand how the child was feeling. Did she understand? Shiloh sighed, staring up at the ceiling and biting her lip.

She had to understand, Shiloh thought back to what Paisley had said. Presley must have a general idea of what had happened. She might not have grasped it fully, but it was hard to misinterpret what the smaller girl had gone through.

Groaning, Shiloh rolled over on her side and closed her eyes. Sleep didn't come easy, though. It wasn't easy for her to relax knowing that there was someone she cared for that wasn't as happy as they could possibly be.

So, with a frustrated sigh, Shiloh slowly peeled Paisley's arms from around her torso and slithered out of the bed.

Making sure to stay quiet, she slowly padded out of the bedroom and headed down the hallway. Her art studio always seemed to provide her comfort.

Before she could make it all the way down the hallway, though, something else caught her attention. The door to her right was cracked open slightly, and there was just enough light for her to see two small brown eyes peering up at her.

As soon as she raised a questioning eyebrow, the smaller girl panicked and moments later the bedroom door was pulled shut. Furrowing her eyebrows together, Shiloh tilted her head to the side and placed a hand on the doorknob.

"There's nothing to be afraid of, you know," she whispered softly, slowly turning the doorknob and pulling it open slightly. Presley gazed up at her, hesitance flickering in her eyes.

"I'm not a bad guy," Shiloh said quietly, squatting down and holding out her hand for the smaller girl. "What's wrong, baby? C'mere."

Presley looked at Shiloh shyly, and the green eyed girl noticed how badly her bottom lip was quivering. Ignoring Shiloh's hand, the tiny girl walked forwards and straight into her arms, clinging onto the older girl.

Shiloh was startled by the child's actions, especially when she felt Presley's hands begin to shake as the tears finally spilled over.

Almost instinctively, the green eyed girl wrapped her arms around the younger girl, holding her close against her chest. Ignoring the fact that they were in the middle of the hallway, she sat down and pulled Presley into her lap.

"I know, sweetie," Shiloh whispered, feeling her heart breaking over the distraught child in her arms. "It's not as scary as it seems right now. I promise."

Presley just held onto her tighter. Something about the fact that the child refused to let go sent chills down Shiloh's spine. As if she was scared of what would happen if she let go.

"Do you wanna talk about it?" Shiloh asked, unsure how she was supposed to handle these sorts of things. Gently, she placed her hands on Presley's shoulders and separated them so she could study the girl's face. Small hands rose up to wipe her tear strained cheeks and the small child shook her head timidly.

"Do you, uh, do you wanna try and go back to sleep, maybe?" Shiloh offered, pointing towards the bedroom. Presley looked at the door for a moment, contemplating the offer before shaking her head once more.

Shiloh bit her lip, having run out of options. Sniffing, the smaller girl in her lap held tightly to the sleeves of Shiloh's shirt, looking at her pleadingly. The green eyed girl thought for a few moments before nodding softly.

"Wanna know a secret?" Shiloh asked quietly, reaching out to brush the child's tousled hair out of her face.

Presley just stared at Shiloh hopefully.

"Well, I couldn't sleep either," Shiloh spoke, running a hand through her hair nervously. "But I, uh, I paint or something when I can't sleep. It calms me down and sometimes it scares the annoying thoughts away for long enough so that I can fall asleep... Do you wanna help me?"

The smaller girl studied Shiloh's face for a few moments, wiping her tired eyes before nodding slowly. Somewhat relieved, Shiloh gave her a soft smile and stood up carefully, adjusting Presley in her arms.

"Crying helps sometimes," Shiloh continued, pushing the door to her studio open with her hip. "But there's other things that can help, too. The thing about crying is that it gets your feelings out, but then they disappear. When you put your feelings into art, you always have a reminder of the things you've felt and the things you've conquered. I like that a little more, I guess."

Part of Shiloh knew that Presley might not exactly understand, but part of her was also talking to herself.

Shiloh set the younger girl down on a small wooden stool next to her easel. Furrowing her eyebrows, she paused to scan the room.

"Uh, here," Shiloh moved the unfinished painting off of her easel and rummaged through the closet until she pulled out a blank canvas. Setting it down on the easel, she took a step back and thought for a few moments.

"Sometimes the best way to paint is to not have a plan," Shiloh spoke up, causing Presley to look over at her curiously. The child's tears had subsided, but her eyes were still glassy. "I know that sounds funny, but sometimes your soul knows better than your mind. And your soul is what drives your art."

"Here," she smiled softly, handing Presley a paintbrush. The younger girl took it into her tiny hands, studying it for a few moments.

"Gimme a second," Shiloh nodded. Turning around, the green eyed girl quickly added a variety of paints into her palette and held it out between them. "Have at it, kiddo."

Tentatively, Presley held out the paintbrush and dipped the tip into the section of orange paint. Lifting it back up, she held it in front of her face hesitantly before looking at Shiloh, unsure of what to do.

"Here," Shiloh laughed softly, taking a brush of her own and dipping it into the light green paint. "Let's paint some flowers. Flowers are easy, right?"

Dragging her brush across the canvas, Shiloh added a few flicks of a darker green. Presley watched in awe as the older girl almost effortlessly painted a stem and leaves in the middle of the canvas.

"Your turn," Shiloh nodded, tapping the top of the stem with her finger. "The petals are the prettiest part."

The green eyed girl watched as Presley studied the canvas, holding out her brush carefully. With shy, shaky movements, the small child brought her brush against the canvas. Shiloh watched patiently, giving Presley a reassuring smile when the small child looked up at her for approval.

"Beautiful," Shiloh nodded softly once Presley drew the brush back. "Wanna do another?"

The green eyed girl couldn't help but be comforted when Presley nodded almost instantly and looked up at her with a shy smile.

───────────────

Paisley awoke the next morning to the ding of the toaster from the kitchen, automatically confusing her. When she realized she was in bed alone, the smaller girl furrowed her eyebrows and rolled out of bed, keeping her blanket wrapped around her shoulders.

"Lo?" she yawned, padding into the kitchen and rubbing her eyes. There stood her wife, attempting to spread jelly onto a piece of toast with one hand, and holding a sleeping Presley against her torso with the other.

Shiloh jumped slightly when she heard Paisley's voice, turning around to see her wife standing in the entrance of the kitchen, hugging a blanket around her shoulders and looking adorably sleepy. Her lips curved into a tired smile, and the brunette tilted her head to the side in question.

"Oh," Shiloh whispered, realizing Paisley was referring to the smaller girl in her arms. "She fell asleep while we were painting and I didn't want to risk waking her up by putting her down," she said quietly, trying not to speak too loudly.

"Painting?" Paisley laughed softly, tilting her head to the side. "When were you painting?"

"A few hours ago," Shiloh shrugged, yawning and struggling to pull another piece of bread out of the bag. Paisley quickly moved forward, pulling her hand away and offering to do it for her.

"I got it," the smaller girl giggled, squeezing Shiloh's hand before placing two more slices of bread into the toaster. Turning back to Shiloh, the brown eyed girl studied her appearance. "Did you sleep?" she asked, although she already knew the answer.

Looking guilty, the green eyed girl shook her head slowly.

"Why not?" Paisley asked quietly, flinching when the toast popped out of the toaster. Shiloh grabbed her hand, squeezing it to calm her down before shrugging.

"Just worried, I guess," she admitted, leaning against the counter and watching as her wife focused on spreading butter onto the slices of toast. "And then Presley was crying, and I tried to cheer her up. She fell asleep again but I couldn't."

"Oh," Paisley nodded slowly, thinking for a few moments. "I could tell."

"I look that bad?"

"No," Paisley giggled, shaking her head and turning around to face her wife. "You look beautiful. But... but... you did not plug the toaster in..." she mumbled, trying to fight back a smile when Shiloh brought her hand up to her forehead and groaned.

"It is okay," the smaller girl laughed. She reached up, cupping her hand over Shiloh's cheek and smiling softly. "Go rest. I will finish this," she nodded towards the counter.

Too tired to argue, Shiloh nodded. She placed a sleepy kiss on her wife's lips before trudging over to the couch, Presley still in her arms.

Paisley knew she didn't have to bother to remake the breakfast, because by the time she cleaned up the counter, Shiloh was fast asleep on the couch with Presley in her arms.

An affectionate smile formed on Paisley's face when she saw the sight. Quietly, she reached out to trace her fingers over Shiloh's cheek, taking a few moments to enjoy how peaceful her wife appeared in her sleep. Paisley knew Shiloh was worried about how things would turn out. But Paisley also knew that her wife tended to stress herself out over the tiniest of things.

"I love you, Lo," the smaller girl whispered. Her small hands cupped Shiloh's cheeks and she pressed a soft kiss to her forehead, pulling back for a few moments to study the girl's face before heading off down the hallway.

Just as she was about to slip into the bathroom to shower, something caught her attention from across the hallway. The door to Shiloh's studio was jutted open slightly, and a flash of color made the smaller girl furrow her eyebrows. The painting Shiloh had been working on the night before had been in black and white.

Abandoning the bathroom, Paisley crossed the hallway and quietly slipped into the studio. Her eyes widened when she saw the small canvas resting on the easel. A wave of nostalgia washed over her and she gently took the canvas into her hands.

A countless amount of childish flowers were scattered across the canvas in an array of colors. Paisley could recognize which brush strokes belonged to Shiloh, and which ones belonged to Presley. There was something so simple about it. Shiloh had always used to doodle flowers when she was bored. Something about the simple repetition must have calmed her down.

With a soft smile on her face, Paisley set the painting back onto the canvas and made her way back into the living room. Just as she sat down on the couch, the smaller girl in Shiloh's arms began to stir awake.

Paisley immediately noticed the panicked expression on the child's face, and she quickly reached out to place a hand on her shoulder. Presley turned to look at her, her face immediately softening when she realized where she was.

"Morning, little flower," Paisley said softly, standing up and lifting Presley into her own arms, careful not to disturb Shiloh. "Are you hungry?"

CHAPTER 39

Things started to change a few days later.

Paisley had been outside in the cool November air, finally getting around to taking down their Halloween decorations. Presley was taking a nap, and Shiloh was supposed to be on the phone with Toby going over the final touches on one of their recent projects.

The brown eyed girl was startled, however, when Shiloh came barreling through the front door and onto the front porch. Paisley nearly fell off the small stepladder she had been balancing on, and she quickly grabbed onto the railing to keep her footing.

"You need to come inside," Shiloh looked at her with wide eyes, and an expression Paisley couldn't quite read. "Now."

The younger girl grew confused, quickly hopping off of the ladder and looking at Shiloh in confusion. Her wife didn't offer her an explanation, though. Before Paisley could open her mouth, the green eyed girl had disappeared back into the house.

Furrowing her eyebrows together, Paisley quickly tossed the decorations in her hands aside and hurried inside.

"Lo?" she called out, seeing no sign of her wife. She made her way over to the hallway and wrung out her hands nervously.

She had to cup her hands over her mouth to keep herself from gasping when Shiloh quickly hopped out from behind the wall and grabbed Paisley's hand.

"Shh," the raven haired girl met Paisley's eyes. "Listen."

Confused but comforted by the fact that Shiloh was there, Paisley knelt down next to the girl in the middle of the hallway. She sent her wife a questioning look, but moments later something else caught her attention.

"Oh let me be... your teddy bear,"

Paisley and Shiloh exchanged glances. The smaller girl's eyebrows stitched together and she shook her head, not recognizing the voice.

"She's singing," Shiloh whispered, pointing to Presley's door that was cracked open slightly.

"That is Presley?" Paisley's jaw dropped open in shock, Shiloh's sudden burst of energy was now making sense. The raven haired girl nodded, holding up a finger to keep Paisley quiet when the tiny voice sung the same line again.

"I think I know where she got her name," Shiloh spoke up after a few moments of silence, keeping her voice low and turning to Paisley. "That's an Elvis song."

"Elvis Presley?" Paisley raised an eyebrow and thought for a few moments. Shiloh giggled softly when she saw the realization spread across her wife's face.

"Don't," Shiloh quickly grabbed Paisley's hand when the girl began to rise to her feet. Confused, Paisley paused, turning to Shiloh and tilting her head to the side.

"We shouldn't be listening," Shiloh bit her lip, nodding towards the door. "She'll talk to us when she's ready, right? I... I just want to do this the right way."

"Oh," Paisley whispered, gently kneeling back down. "You are right, Lo," she nodded. The brown eyed girl glanced back at Presley's door. "Do you think she hates us?"

Shiloh couldn't help but laugh at Paisley's question, and she shook her head. Grabbing her wife's hand, she led them both into the living room, collapsing back on the couch and pulling Paisley down beside her. "Why would she hate us?"

"I-I do not know," Paisley shrugged, instinctively curling up in Shiloh's side. "I just... I do not want to mess up."

"Oh," Shiloh nodded slowly, understanding what Paisley meant. "Well, me neither. We've just got to try our best. That's all we can do."

"What if it is not good enough?" the brown eyed girl bit her lip, looking over at Shiloh worriedly.

"I think with someone who cares as much as you do, she'll be just fine," Shiloh laughed softly, reaching over and smoothing out Paisley's hair.

"That is you, silly," Paisley mumbled against Shiloh's side, leaning her head against her shoulder. "She is lucky. Cause' of you, Lo."

"Cause' of both of us," Shiloh nodded. She found Paisley's hand and laced their fingers together. "She'll talk when she's ready, whenever that may be."

Luckily for both girls, they didn't have to wait much longer.

Everyone ended up going to bed early that night. Even Shiloh. She and Paisley were bundled up under the covers in their bedroom, legs entwined and fingers laced together.

For some reason, sleep came easily for Shiloh that night. Which is why she wasn't awoken by the storm that made its way through the night, lighting up the house with the occasional flicker of lightning.

A tug on Shiloh's sleeve brought her out of her slumber, and the green eyed girl groggily brought her hands up to wipe her eyes. She turned to look at Paisley to see what she had wanted, but grew confused when she found her wife was still fast asleep.

Something else that caught her attention, though, was a small voice that pierced the peaceful silence.

"Mommy?"

"Wha...?" Shiloh mumbled, turning her head to look in the direction of the voice. Lighting flickered through the window, lighting the room for just a moment, and allowing

Shiloh to see the outline of the little girl standing timidly beside the bed, clutching a stuffed dog against her chest with small hands.

Shiloh's face immediately froze when Presley's words registered with her. Upon seeing Shiloh's reaction, the smaller girl realized what she had said, and her eyes widened in fear.

"I, uh," Shiloh stammered over her words, unsure of what to do. Biting her lip, she turned over and grabbed Paisley's shoulder to shake her awake.

"Pais," she whispered. There was enough concern in her voice to cause her wife to practically shoot up out of bed, looking at Shiloh in confusion as she wiped her tired eyes.

"What?" her wife whispered, looking at Shiloh worriedly. The green eyed girl nodded behind her, directing Paisley's attention to the smaller girl standing at the edge of the bed, bottom lip quivering.

"She spoke," Shiloh whispered between gritted teeth, keeping her voice almost silent. "She called me mommy."

"I'm sorry," the smaller girl at the end of the bed whimpered, becoming aware of what she had said and shaking her head timidly.

"No," Paisley quickly shook her head, crawling to the edge of the bed and holding out her hands towards the smaller girl. "Do not be sorry," she said softly. "What is wrong?"

"I-I don't like storms," Presley's tiny voice filled the air, taking both Shiloh and Paisley by surprise. "I wanna g-go home," her voice cracked slightly and she hugged Sunny tighter against her chest.

Shiloh and Paisley both exchanged glances. On one hand, they were both relieved that the smaller girl had finally spoken to them. But on the other hand, they were both now faced with another problem. One that they both weren't quite sure how to handle.

"C'mere," Shiloh whispered, sitting up and patting the space beside her. Hesitantly, the tiny child crawled up on the bed and sat in the space between Paisley and Shiloh. Paisley immediately pulled Presley into her lap, holding onto the small child protectively.

"Storms can be scary sometimes," Shiloh said softly, reaching out and brushing Presley's tousled hair out of her face. As if on cue, a large clap of thunder made both Presley and Paisley jump. The tiny brown eyed girl held onto the fabric of Paisley's sleeves timidly.

"But sometimes it's less scary if you think about it," Shiloh shrugged, turning to glance out the window for a moment. "Even the sky has to get sad and angry and let all its feelings out sometimes. Just like us."

"Yeah," Paisley whispered, nodding in agreement. "You do not have to feel bad for... for feeling," she shrugged softly. Presley turned to look up at her, watching Paisley intently. "If you ignore your feelings... they do not go away. They get worse. And then it is a hurricane... not just a storm."

"I'm sorry," Presley spoke again, sniffing and turning back to Shiloh.

"Sorry for what, bug?" Shiloh tilted her head to the side. Paisley loved watching the way Shiloh treated Presley so gently. Concern radiated in the green eyed girl's features.

"You're not my mommy," Presley mumbled. The small caramel haired girl shook her head and brought her hands up to wipe her eyes, looking down at her lap shyly.

"Oh, no," Shiloh shook her head. She reached out, lifting Presley's chin gently so the smaller girl would look up at her. "I know I'm not, babes. It was an accident. That's okay."

"Paisley and I aren't here to replace your mom and dad," Shiloh added softly, glancing up at Paisley for a moment, met with her wife's soft smile. "We're just.... we're just here for whatever you need us for."

"You can call us whatever you want," the green eyed girl nodded. "We're here to watch over you and take care of you but we're also here to be your friends, yeah? You're a part of our family now."

"Family?" Presley's voice was small and raspy, fitting her petite disposition. She looked back and forth from Shiloh and Paisley, a flicker of curiosity in her eyes.

"Yeah," Shiloh laughed softly. "I mean, if that's okay with you," she added, looking over at Paisley, who was running her fingers through Presley's hair.

"You'll take real good care of me?" Presley tilted her head to the side, her expressive eyes studying the two girls beside her. "I don't wanna leave again."

Shiloh glanced up at Paisley, who gave her a soft nod.

"We aren't going anywhere, kiddo," Shiloh smiled softly, squeezing Paisley's hand and holding out her pinkie. "Promise."

"Promise," Paisley added, doing the same and holding her pinkie out beside Shiloh's.

Smiling for the first time that night, Presley interlocked both of her pinkies with the girls and looked up at them shyly.

"A kiss makes it official," Paisley added softly, leaning down and kissing her hand. Shiloh gave her wife a small smile before doing the same. Presley watched them, giggling quietly.

Lighting flashed through the room once more but no one flinched. Instead, Presley crawled forwards to kiss both of the girl's hands before unlocking their fingers, looking up at them hopefully.

"I don't wanna sleep all alone..." the tiny brown eyed girl mumbled. She glanced towards the door, shivering slightly. Shiloh and Paisley both exchanged glances.

"The more the merrier," Shiloh laughed, scooting back on the bed and motioning for Paisley to follow. Presley watched them quietly for a few moments, sitting at the end of the bed while Shiloh pulled the blankets over her feet.

"C'mon, little one," Shiloh smiled, holding out a hand towards the smaller girl. "You need your sleep."

A soft smile made its way onto Presley's face, and she quickly crawled to the top of the bed to join them, along with the yellow stuffed dog that seemed to accompany her everywhere.

Once all three girls were lying back under the blankets, Paisley bit her lip, rolling over on her side and studying Shiloh, who was gazing up at the ceiling quietly.

"Lo?" Paisley whispered, reaching out over Presley and finding Shiloh's hand. The small child between them looked back and forth quietly.

"Yeah?" Shiloh's raspy voice filled the silence, and she turned slightly to look at Paisley.

"I-I, uh…" Paisley bit her lip, looking down at her hands. "Do you wanna sing?"

Shiloh couldn't help but giggle, raising an eyebrow at her wife. "I dunno, do you want me to?"

"Yeah," Paisley mumbled, a shy smile on her face. Presley giggled, watching the exchange between them.

"Well then," Shiloh giggled, propping herself up on one elbow and planting a kiss on Paisley and Presley's forehead before laying back down. "Only for you."

CHAPTER 40

Paisley realized very quickly that once they got Presley to start talking, it would be difficult for her to stop.

"What's that?" the tiny girl asked, pointing to the box of cereal Paisley had brought over from the kitchen. Presley was seated in the dining room, sitting on a small booster seat so that she could reach the table.

"Fruit loops," Paisley read off the front of the box, nodding softly. "Are these okay? We are out of muffins...." She set the box down on the table, biting her lip.

"I like these," Presley nodded, giving Paisley a crooked smile. She lifted her bowl in the air, looking at the girl hopefully.

"Good," Paisley giggled, opening the box and carefully pouring a small amount of cereal into the bowl. She slipped back into the kitchen, putting the box back in its place and retrieving a jug of milk.

Paisley paused when she walked back into the dining room to find the cereal dumped out of the bowl. She raised an eyebrow, watching as Presley carefully separated the pieces of cereal into separate piles. One for each color.

"What are you doing?" Paisley asked, tilting her head to the side.

Presley paused, a blue fruit loop in her fingers. She looked up at Paisley and then back down at the cereal. "Putting them with their friends," she nodded, continuing to organize the small pieces.

"Oh," Paisley laughed softly. The brown eyed girl sat down at the table, watching as Presley carefully added a blue fruit loop to the blue pile.

"Close your eyes," Presley giggled, looking up at Paisley. The older girl raised an eyebrow, but did as she was told.

Paisley waited as she heard Presley lean over the table, pressing something against her lips. "Eat it," the small child giggled, poking Paisley's cheek with her other hand.

Trusting the girl, Paisley opened her mouth and allowed her to place a single piece of cereal on her tongue. Opening her eyes, Paisley chewed for a few moments, giving Presley a questioning look.

"What color does it taste like?" Presley giggled, sitting up in her seat slightly and looking at Paisley with a curious expression on her face.

"Color?" Paisley laughed and raised an eyebrow. "How do you taste a color?"

The tiny girl giggled, plucking a blue fruit loop from the pile and popping it into her mouth. "Like this!" she smiled widely. "It's blue."

"What does blue taste like?" Paisley asked, a soft smile forming on her lips. Presley paused, debating this for a few moments.

"The sky," she giggled, clasping her hands together.

"What does the sky taste like?" Paisley couldn't help but laugh, watching as Presley's expression fell slightly as she pondered her question.

"Like blue fruit loops," the caramel girl finally spoke up, giggling and offering Paisley a piece of cereal from the pile.

"Makes sense," Paisley smiled softly to herself, enjoying the smaller girl's conversation. She accepted the offering, popping the piece of cereal into her mouth.

"Can he try?"

Paisley lifted her head, looking at Presley who was pointing to something below them. Glancing down, Paisley giggled when she saw Wolf circling around their feet. "Sure."

Smiling excitedly, Presley carefully selected an orange fruit loop and set it down on the floor in front of Wolf. Paisley then snapped her fingers, gaining his attention and making him sniff the piece of food on the floor.

Instead of eating it, though, the large white cat tapped it with his paw, sending it scattering across the floor. Turning playful, Wolf pounced forwards, causing the small piece of food to fly under the table.

Presley burst into laugher, finding Wolf's antics amusing. "You're supposed to eat it, silly!" she giggled, leaning her head under the table and watching as the cat pawed at the piece of cereal.

"He is crazy," Paisley laughed softly, an affectionate smile spreading across her face.

"What's your favorite color?" Presley turned back to Paisley, surprising the girl by changing the subject so suddenly. Laughing softly, Paisley shrugged.

"Yellow," she nodded, giving Presley a small smile. "What is yours?"

"I don't have one," Presley glanced back down at Wolf.

"Why not?" Paisley raised an eyebrow.

"Cause' I don't want the other ones to get jealous," Presley nodded confidently. "I don't wanna make em' sad."

"Oh," Paisley giggled, amused by Presley's logic.

"On my birthday my cake had rainbows on it," Presley remembered, sitting up straighter and nodding excitedly at Paisley. "It was this big," she explained happily, holding out her hands.

Meanwhile, Shiloh had been stirred awake from all the commotion in the dining room. At first, she was confused when she woke up alone, but she quickly remembered the events of the night before.

Hearing Paisley and Presley's soft voices coming from the dining room caused a small smile to spread across her face. Everything was starting to feel normal again.

Yawning, the green eyed girl brushed her hair out of her face and wandered into the dining room. She leaned against the doorway, watching as Paisley attempted to toss a piece of cereal into her mouth. It bounced off of her nose and rolled onto the floor.

Not yet aware of Shiloh's presence, Paisley giggled and grabbed another fruit loop. But when she saw Presley's gaze was focused elsewhere, she turned around to look where the other girl was looking.

"Morning," Shiloh laughed softly, her voice quiet and raspy from just waking up. Her lips curved into a soft smile when Paisley laughed quietly.

"Hi," Paisley giggled, glancing back at Presley. "We were eating breakfast."

"I see that," Shiloh laughed, leaning against the back of Paisley's chair and placing a kiss into the top of her wife's head. She reached over Paisley's shoulder to check the smaller girl's phone, furrowing her eyebrows when she realized what day it was.

"Shoot," the green eyed girl whispered under her breath, running a hand through her hair and standing back up. "I told Toby we'd watch Lucas today while he drove Maia up to see her mom..." she bit her lip.

Paisley nodded softly and glanced at Presley, who was looking at them both curiously. Standing up, Paisley gave Shiloh a soft smile.

"I can get us ready," she nodded in Presley's direction. "Call Maia and tell her we will be there soon."

"Have I ever told you I love you?" Shiloh laughed softly, leaning in and kissing Paisley's cheek. She was relieved that Paisley didn't mind that she'd had something scheduled for them. Her wife just smiled, looking down to hide the blush on her cheeks.

"Good morning, kiddo," Shiloh smiled, turning to Presley and bending down to match her height. She ruffled her caramel color hair, earning a shy giggle from the girl. "You're gonna meet some new friends today. I know they've been dying to meet you."

"Are they nice?" Presley asked, a curious smile on her face. Paisley nodded from behind Shiloh.

"Super nice," Paisley laughed softly, slipping past Shiloh and gently taking Presley into her own arms. "But we have to hurry up and get ready, because they will be waiting for us."

Shooting Shiloh a soft smile, Paisley gave her a quick kiss on the cheek before disappearing out of the dining room, taking Presley into the bedroom to get ready.

Not soon after, Shiloh was dressed and waiting on the couch for the other two girls to finish getting ready. Quick footsteps brought her attention away from her phone, and she looked up just in time to see Presley hop into the living room. The smaller girl was adorning a bright yellow sweater, which fit her like a dress. Shiloh realized it must have been Paisley's.

"You're s'posta to help me with my hair," Presley said shyly, standing in front of Shiloh and tilting her head to the side. "I don't know how'ta do it."

"C'mere, goof," Shiloh laughed, setting her coffee aside and pulling Presley into her lap. Almost effortlessly, she pulled the girl's hair up into a loose bun, securing it quickly and turning on her phone's camera so Presley could see herself. "Like it?"

Presley simply giggled, making a funny face at herself in the camera and looking up at Shiloh with a wide smile on her face.

"I'll take that as a yes," Shiloh laughed, sliding her phone into her pocket and hopping to her feet. She scooped Presley into her arms, making the smaller girl laugh.

Raising an eyebrow, Shiloh spun around in a circle with the child in her grip, causing her to laugh even harder. Laughing along with her, Shiloh flipped Presley upside down and pinched her stomach, making the smaller girl squeal playfully.

When Shiloh pulled her back upright, she was met with her wife leaning against the doorway, an eyebrow raised.

"We are going to be late," Paisley scolded her half heartedly. Presley looked back and forth between the girls.

"Party pooper," Shiloh mumbled, pouting playfully. Presley giggled, keeping her arms wrapped around Shiloh's neck as the girl bent down to retrieve her bag from beside the door.

"How is her mom doing?" Paisley asked, slipping on her shoes and shivering in the chilly fall air as they walked out to the car. Shiloh glanced at her wife, passing Presley over to Paisley so she could buckle her in to the car seat.

"I don't know," Shiloh bit her lip, sliding into the driver's side of the car. "Toby says Maia doesn't talk much about it."

"Oh," Paisley nodded softly, helping Presley get adjusted in the back of the car and hurrying to buckle herself into the passenger seat. "Do you think she is....? She is...."

"I don't think she's doing well," Shiloh whispered. "I've never seen Maia so upset over something."

Paisley nodded quietly, relaxing back into her seat and letting her thoughts wander as they made the drive to their friend's home.

Once they finally arrived to Maia and Toby's house, Paisley hurried around the back of the car to take Presley into her own arms. She could sense that the smaller girl was shy, especially around new people.

They'd become so acquainted with their friends that it was normal for them to let themselves into their house. Shiloh held the door open for Paisley, slipping into the house behind her.

The moment they stepped into the living room, they were practically swept up in a tornado. Lucas was immediately passed into Shiloh's arms by Maia, who didn't even acknowledge the girls as she quickly gathered her things and slipped past them out the door.

"Ignore her," Toby appeared, almost out of nowhere, carefully handing a list of phone numbers to Shiloh and giving her an apologetic smile. "She's just stressed."

The green eyed girl nodded, adjusting a sleeping Lucas in her arms and looking down at the paper in her hands. Meanwhile, Toby gave Presley a small wave, smiling at the small child.

"We'll have more time to get acquainted later," he nodded in Presley's direction, acknowledging Paisley with a quick smile. "Wish us luck," he laughed nervously, giving the girls one last wave before slipping out the door.

"What's he need a wish for?" Presley broke the silence as the door was pulled shut, leaving the three girls alone with a sleeping Lucas. Paisley set her down, allowing her to study the unfamiliar room.

"I-I, uh," Shiloh stumbled over her words, still confused by how worried Maia had appeared. "I don't kn-,"

"Sometimes people make wishes when they need a reason to keep believing," Paisley said softly, interrupting Shiloh. "Sometimes it is all they have to hold onto."

"If you wish on a shooting star, it always comes true," Presley nodded excitedly, a small smile on her face. She turned to look out the window, frowning when she realized it wasn't nighttime.

Shiloh reached over and squeezed Paisley's hand, causing the smaller girl to look up at her with a soft smile.

The green eyed girl knew well enough that Paisley had relied on only wishes for a long period of time.

And Paisley smiled back at Shiloh, because she knew her wish had come true.

Shiloh was distracted by a tug on her sleeve, bringing her attention away from Paisley and down to Presley, who was looking up at her hopefully.

"What's his name?" the girl whispered, pointing to the sleeping boy in Shiloh's arms.

"Lucas," Shiloh said softly, kneeling down next to Presley. "He's gonna be a year old soon," she added with a shy smile.

"Why's he sleepin'?" Presley tilted her head to the side, reaching out and feeling the sleeping child's hair. "Is he a baby?"

"Kinda," Shiloh giggled, looking up at Paisley who was just as amused by the situation.

"He needs to wake up," Presley nodded, sure of herself. "I wanna play with him."

Shiloh and Paisley exchanged glances, hoping the rest of the day would go this smoothly.

CHAPTER 41

"He's awake!"

Shiloh groaned half heartedly, rolling over on the couch and glancing at Paisley, who had her eyes trained on the television.

"You said that last time, goofball," Shiloh rubbed her eyes. She'd nearly fallen asleep herself.

They'd been at Maia and Toby's house for a little over an hour now. Lucas still hadn't woken up, and Presley had taken the job of guarding his crib while he slept.

"Hims has his eyes open!" the little girl protested, bounding back into the living room and looking at Shiloh hopefully. Paisley giggled, turning to Shiloh and giving her the same expectant look as Presley was.

"You better be telling the truth," Shiloh teased, reaching out and ruffling Presley's hair. The smaller girl seemed to be in a better mood today. Part of Shiloh wondered if it was because she'd finally spoken to them.

Turns out, Presley wasn't lying. When Shiloh entered the nursery, Lucas was standing up in his crib with a sleepy smile on his face.

"See?" Presley smiled proudly, tugging on Shiloh's sleeve. "Can I play with him now?"

"He's gotta eat first, goof," Shiloh laughed, gently lifting Lucas from the crib and holding him against her hip. "Then we can play."

"What's he eat?" Presley asked, tilting her head to the side and following Shiloh as she made her way into the kitchen. "Can I help you?"

"I guess that depends on what Maia's left out for him," Shiloh smiled softly, still getting used to Presley's tiny voice.

It was quiet and raspy - different than what Shiloh would have imagined - but it fit her perfectly.

"Here," Shiloh carefully lowered Lucas into his high chair, pulling it over by the table. "He likes bananas. Let's give him a banana."

"Right, bud?" Shiloh crinkled her nose, bending down and giving Lucas a goofy smile. The small boy giggled, drumming his hands on the tray of the highchair.

Shiloh kept an eye on Presley, who was making silly faces at Lucas, while she sliced up the banana. Pulling up a chair in front of his high chair, Shiloh sat down and placed the bowl of banana slices on her lap.

"Wanna give him one?" Shiloh turned to Presley and nodded towards the bowl. Smiling shyly, the smaller girl carefully picked up a slice of the fruit and held it out in front of Lucas.

"It's a banana...na," Presley giggled softly, wiggling the food to catch his attention. Shiloh watched as the smaller boy accepted the piece of banana from Presley, bringing it to his mouth with a closed fist.

"I think he likes it," Presley whispered, looking up at Shiloh and smiling hopefully. Laughing, the green eyed girl gave her a soft nod.

"I think so too," she whispered back. This earned a crooked smile from Presley, who clapped her hands together and carefully handed Lucas another piece of banana.

Meanwhile, Paisley leaned against the archway that entered into the kitchen, watching the interaction between Shiloh and Presley. There was a tenderness in Shiloh that she'd never experienced with anyone else. To Paisley, Shiloh was an angel on earth.

It was present in all of her actions. Shiloh truly was ethereal, from the way she spoke to the way she treated others. Paisley was proud of herself for realizing that from the start - and holding onto that fact even when she seemed to lose everything else.

"I like babies," Presley spoke up quietly, waiting to feed Lucas another banana slice. Shiloh smiled softly, looking down at the smaller girl.

"You do?"

"Mhm," Presley nodded, handing the slice to Lucas and giggling to herself when he reached for it eagerly. "Mommy says that's what makes a good big sister."

Presley didn't notice the way Shiloh's entire body tensed up. The bowl of food nearly fell out of the girl's lap and her heart sped up at the realization.

Fortunately, Paisley had overheard, and the brown eyed girl quickly hurried over to Shiloh's side. Placing a hand on her wife's shoulder, Paisley gained Shiloh's attention. A worried look was plastered on her wife's face and Paisley struggled to not do the same.

As soon as Shiloh saw Paisley, she quickly got up, knowing Presley was distracted by feeding Lucas. Grabbing her wife's hand, she tugged her into the back of the room and looked at her anxiously.

"Oh my god," Shiloh whispered, bringing her hands up to her forehead and shaking her head. "She just... oh my god, I just-,"

"Lo," Paisley shook her head, placing a hand on Shiloh's arm to try and calm her down. "Breathe."

"How do you expect me to breathe when she just said t-!" Shiloh began, raising her voice. She quickly hushed herself when she saw Paisley flinch, moving backwards slightly.

"Shit," Shiloh cursed under her breath, shaking her head once more and grabbing Paisley's hand. "I didn't mean to-,"

"It is fine," Paisley nodded slowly, taking a step closer to the girl and making sure Presley couldn't hear them. "Do you... do you know what to do?"

Swallowing hard, Shiloh shook her head, looking at Paisley with worry flickering in her eyes. "I can't do this," she mumbled under her breath, beginning to overthink things. "I don't know what I'm supposed to do... what do we tell her, what do we-?"

"Lo," Paisley hissed under her breath, grabbing Shiloh's wrist and glaring at her wife. The green eyed girl froze, realizing two pairs of eyes were on them from across the room.

"Fuck," Shiloh cursed to herself, biting her lip and glancing at Paisley.

Before she could say anything, Paisley squeezed Shiloh's hand. The younger girl crossed the room, kneeling down next to Presley and watching as the tiny caramel haired girl handed another slice of banana to Lucas.

"What else do big sisters do?" Paisley asked quietly, taking Presley's attention away from Lucas and onto the older girl knelt beside her.

"Lots'a stuff," Presley nodded softly and turned to face Paisley.

"Like what?" Paisley tilted her head to the side.

"Like... like sing songs," the smaller girl smiled slightly. "And tell bedtime stories. And play a ton of games."

"You sound like a really good big sister," Paisley laughed softly, watching as Presley handed the last slice of banana to Lucas.

"Yeah," Presley smiled. She giggled when Lucas eagerly retrieved the food from her hand, bringing it to his mouth happily. "Are you a big sister?" she asked after a few seconds of silence, tilting her head to the side as she turned to face the older girl.

"No," Paisley shook her head slightly. "It is just me," she shrugged. Presley nodded.

"Me too," the tiny girl shrugged, reaching out and letting Lucas wrap his small fingers around her hand. "It's just me too."

At this point, Paisley glanced back at Shiloh, who raised an eyebrow at her.

"Do angel babies have big sisters?"

Paisley's attention was drawn back to the small girl, who now had her eyes fixed fully on her. "What?"

"Angel babies," Presley nodded, as if it was common knowledge. "Do they have brothers and sisters?"

"Of course," Paisley shrugged, retrieving Lucas's plastic cup from the counter and setting it on his tray. "Nothing can take away brothers or sisters. Or moms or dads. They will always be special to you... no matter what."

"I lied."

"You what?" Paisley raised an eyebrow at the smaller girl.

"I have an angel brother," Presley nodded, rubbing her eyes with her tiny hands. "And an angel mommy and an angel daddy."

Glancing back at Shiloh for a moment, Paisley bit her lip. "So that means you are a big sister," she spoke up a few seconds later. Presley thought this over for a moment before nodding.

"I am?" the smaller girl's eyes widened.

"You are," Paisley smiled softly.

With a wide smile, Presley simply giggled and clapped her hands together before turning back to Lucas. She drummed her tiny fingers on his tray before looking at Paisley hopefully. "Can we play with him now?"

Looking at Shiloh one last time, Paisley nodded softly. "I think so," she smiled, standing up and lifting the small boy out of his high chair.

"C'mon, Lo!" Presley smiled happily, running over to Shiloh's side and grabbing her hand. "We can play with the baby now!"

Paisley and Shiloh both exchanged glances, giggling at Presley's use of her nickname. Pressing a quick kiss to her wife's cheek, Paisley carried Lucas back into the living room, with Presley following right behind her.

Paisley did a lot of thinking at night.

She figured that because it was bright during the daytime, her mind was distracted because there was so much to do, and so much to look at. But when it got dark, she was no longer driven by sight, which is when her thoughts liked to consume her.

Not that it was a bad thing. Paisley liked thinking. That's how she figured things out. It was just that she would have really liked to sleep at that moment, but her thoughts were keeping her awake.

Toby had called around dinnertime to ask them if they could stay the night with Lucas. Maia's mom wasn't doing well. The doctors had told them it was just a matter of time.

Shiloh fell asleep practically as soon as she'd gotten off the phone with Maia. After dinner they'd put on a movie, and Shiloh was out before the opening credits were over.

Presley, however, was insistent on staying up until Lucas was put to bed. Since Shiloh was asleep, Paisley had quietly crept past her with Lucas in her arms, lying Lucas in his crib and allowing Presley to say goodnight.

Now, Presley was fast asleep on the couch next to Shiloh, with one hand hooked around the green eyed girl's arm.

Paisley, however, was too wired to sleep. She tried watching part of the Disney movie Presley had picked out, but her mind kept pulling her back to the events earlier that day.

There were some nights where her past haunted her more than others. Unfortunately, due to the fact that she couldn't sleep, that night became one of those nights. The small brown eyed girl curled up in the corner of the couch, eyes fixed on the static of the television in the otherwise dark room.

Just as she had almost fallen asleep, a movement on the couch next to her caught her attention. Lifting her head, Paisley could make out the faint outline of someone stirring awake. Presley.

The tiny brown eyed girl looked around the room worriedly until her eyes landed on Paisley. With watery eyes, Presley quickly crawled over to her side of the couch, looking at Paisley pleadingly.

Paisley instantly knew that someone was wrong. She quickly reached out, placing a gentle hand on Presley's arm to make sure she was okay with being touched before pulling the smaller child into her lap.

"Little flower?" Paisley tilted her head to the side, keeping her voice quiet. "What is wrong?"

"They took em' away," the smaller girl sniffed, bringing her small hands up to rub at her eyes. Confused, Paisley held the smaller girl in her arms and bit her lip.

"Took who away?"

"Mommy," Presley's voice quivered. "And daddy. And brother.... And I-I didn't even get to see him..."

"Oh," Paisley whispered, the smaller girl's words slowly sinking in. Biting her lip, she simply nodded softly. "They took mine too."

"They did?" the smaller girl moved her hands away from her face and looked up at Paisley curiously.

"Yeah," the brown eyed girl nodded slowly, thinking over her words. "It is not fun."

"How far away are the angels?" Presley asked, looking up at Paisley with a hopeful glimmer in her eyes.

There were a few moments of silence between the girls, where Paisley seriously pondered her question. She bit her lip, turning to the smaller girl and then glancing out the window.

"Can I tell you a secret?" Paisley asked, keeping her voice low. Presley almost immediately nodded.

"Okay," Paisley nodded softly, standing up and taking Presley into her arms. Quietly, as to not to disturb Shiloh, Paisley carried the smaller girl across the living room and out the back door.

The faint echo of crickets could be heard in the chilly fall air, and Paisley immediately shivered. Luckily, they were dressed for the weather, so when Paisley set Presley down in the grass, the smaller girl looked up at her in confusion.

"You have to lie down," Paisley laughed softly, sitting down and laying back. She patted the space next to her, and soon she was joined by Presley, lying on her back and looking at Paisley.

"What's the secret?" the smaller girl asked, tilting her head to the side. Paisley simply pointed up to the sky.

"See those things?" Paisley asked, keeping her eyes trained on the dark night sky above them.

"The stars?"

"Yeah," Paisley nodded.

"I see em'," Presley whispered, looking back to Paisley in confusion.

"That is how you can see the angels," Paisley pointed upwards, tracing the constellations with her fingers. "They are holes. In heaven. So the angels can see us, and shine light on us, even when it is dark."

"Really?" Presley's eyes widened and she drew in a deep breath, quickly turning to look back up at the sky. "They're all the way up there?"

"Yep," Paisley nodded, a small smile tugging at her lips. "But guess what?"

"What?" Presley looked back to Paisley, hanging onto every word she spoke.

"Ghosts are real too," Paisley whispered. "But... but not scary ghosts. Good ghosts. Everyone leaves behind ghosts. Even if they are gone, their ghosts are still here."

"Where?" the smaller girl's eyes widened.

"Everywhere," Paisley giggled, still looking up at the stars. "When you listen to a song they liked, or... or sleep with a blanket they loved. They are there. You can feel them. So they can not really be gone."

"But I can't see them," Presley whispered, squinting her eyes and lifting her head slightly to look up at the sky.

"Just because you can not see, does not mean something does not exist," Paisley shrugged. "I know I love my mom and dad. I always will. And... and I do not think I would love them this much if they were not still out there... somewhere."

"I love em' a whole lot."

"Your parents?" Paisley whispered, turning her head slightly to look at the younger girl.

"Yeah," Presley nodded slowly. "I wish they coulda' seen you."

"They made you pretty awesome," Paisley laughed softly, feeling the smaller girl nuzzle into her side.

"Yeah," Presley giggled, yawning softly. "They woulda' thought you were awesome too. Super awesome."

"Really?" Paisley tilted her head to the side. When she didn't receive an answer, she turned to look at Presley. The smaller girl had her thumb in her mouth, and her eyelids were just fluttering closed.

Laughing softly to herself, Paisley sat up carefully and took the tired girl into her arms. "I guess that question will have to wait," she giggled, feeling Presley's head rest gently on her shoulder.

Just as she turned around, she caught sight of someone standing in the doorway. Taking a few steps forward, Paisley felt her heart clench when she saw Maia watching them with tear stained cheeks.

CHAPTER 42

Paisley's heart dropped.

Before she could say anything, Maia quietly slipped back into the house. Biting her lip and looking at the sleeping girl in her arms, Paisley hurried back inside as well.

She heard movement in the kitchen, and quickly laid Presley's sleeping figure beside Shiloh so she could slip into the other room. Her eyes then met Maia's, and she tilted her head to the side, almost in a silent question.

All she was met with was a soft nod from the other girl, to which Paisley immediately opened her arms and looked at Maia hopefully. Moments later, she wrapped her arms around the distraught girl in a hug, feeling her heart break for her friend.

"I am sorry," Paisley whispered, unsure of what else to say. Toby, who was on his phone by the counter, gave Paisley a sad smile over his wife's shoulder. Paisley would never point it out, but she could tell he had been crying as well.

"It's okay," Maia's voice wavered slightly when they pulled away from the hug. She wiped her eyes, shaking her head. "She handled it better than any of us."

"You did not lose her," Paisley spoke up following a few moments of silence between them. "You... you may think you did, but you will see. You can not lose people. Love.... it can not be broken. Trust me."

"Thank you," Maia whispered, pulling Paisley into another hug. Shocked, the smaller brown eyed girl quickly wiped a tear that had fallen from her own eye.

"What the fuck are y-?" The moment was interrupted by a groggy Shiloh, who wandered into the room and quickly cupped her hands over her mouth when she saw a distressed Maia and teary eyed Paisley in front of her.

"What's going on?" the dark haired girl rubbed her eyes and blinked a few times to let them adjust to the light. When Paisley met her eyes pleadingly, Shiloh furrowed her eyebrows and turned to Maia, which was when she realized.

"Oh," the green eyed girl whispered. "Oh."

"Yeah," Maia mumbled, glancing back at Toby who was watching their interaction. "We just got back... I-I... you guys can head home now."

"No," Shiloh and Paisley spoke up at the same time, surprising one another. They had both seen how stressed Maia had been before. Shaking her head, Shiloh stepped forward and pulled the girl into a hug.

"You've been through a lot today," the green eyed girl said softly, comforting her friend. "Sleep in tomorrow. Both of you," she pulled away and pointed towards Toby. "We'll take care of Lucas." Paisley nodded softly in agreement.

"Thank you," Maia whispered, biting her lip. "Was he okay tonight?"

"More than okay," Shiloh laughed softly and glanced back into the living room. "Presley seemed to take a liking to him."

"Presley," Maia's eyebrows raised. "You guys having a kid is going to take me some getting used to."

"Where is she?" Toby asked, coming up behind Maia and placing his hands on her shoulders.

"Asleep," Shiloh nodded, glancing at the clock. "It's almost midnight."

"Yeaaaah," Paisley nodded, mid-yawn. Shiloh laughed and nudged her side softly.

"Get to bed, yeah?" Shiloh gave Maia a stern glare. The girl nodded, glancing up at Toby, who kissed her temple. "We'll see you in the morning."

After saying their goodnights, Shiloh collapsed back onto the couch in the living room, being careful not to disturb Presley. When Paisley didn't join her, though, the green eyed girl sat up once more.

"Pais?" she raised her voice slightly, but not enough to disturb anyone else. There were a few moments of silence, and then a small voice echoed from within the other room.

"In here."

Raising an eyebrow, Shiloh walked quietly back in the kitchen. The room was now dark, but she could make out her wife's small figure in the moonlight that shone through the sliding glass door.

"Aren't you tired?" the green eyed girl asked, taking a few steps forwards. Paisley had her back turned to the girl, her palms pressed against the cool glass as she gazed up at the sky.

"Yeah," Paisley admitted, feeling Shiloh walk to stand beside her. Biting her lip, she shivered slightly.

"Then come to bed," the girl replied quietly, giving Paisley a look of confusion. "It's getting late."

"I know," the smaller girl mumbled, shaking her head and pressing her fingertips against the glass. "I-I... I..."

Upon hearing her wife's voice shake, Shiloh grew confused. Carefully, she placed a hand on Paisley's shoulder. "What's wrong?"

"I do not want to lose all this," Paisley admitted, finally turning to face Shiloh. Her eyes skitted downwards shyly.

"Lose this?" Shiloh grew concerned, trailing her fingers down Paisley's arm and taking her hand into her own. "Why would you lose this?"

"I-I do not know," the smaller girl shook her head. "Everyone has been losing people and... I-I just do not want things to change." She squeezed her eyes shut, fighting back tears. "I like how things are now."

"Babe," Shiloh whispered, shaking her head and moving forward to cup Paisley's face in her hands. "You can't waste your time worrying about things you can't change."

"I c-can not help it," Paisley sniffed, her eyes fluttering shut as Shiloh ran a thumb over her cheek.

"C'mere," Shiloh sighed, giving in and pulling the smaller girl into a hug. After a few moments of silence between them, Shiloh pulled away and met Paisley's eyes.

"Listen, I can't promise you that nothing will change," she said softly, lacing their fingers together and gently swinging their hands back and forth. "I wish I could. But what I can promise you is that I'll always be here. We're a team, remember? It's always going to be me and you. So even if everything around us changes, you still won't be able to get rid of me," she laughed softly, finding Paisley's pinky in the darkness and locking it with her own. "And that's a promise."

Laughing softly, Paisley wiped her eyes with her free hand and brought their interlocked fingers inbetween them so she could plant a kiss on the back of her hand.

"I will never leave," she nodded softly, turning back to the glass door and looking up at the sky. "You know that."

Wearing a soft, affectionate smile, Shiloh watched as Paisley gazed outside once more, her eyes fixed upwards. "What'cha looking at, babe?" she asked, pressing her hand against the glass and following Paisley's eyes.

"The stars," Paisley whispered, awe laced in her words. "I wish I could touch them."

"I don't think you'd want to do that," Shiloh laughed softly and shook her head. "They're like a thousand degrees hot or something."

"You know what I mean," Paisley giggled, nudging Shiloh's shoulder. "They are just so pretty. But they are far away."

"Want to hear a funny story?" Shiloh asked, a small smile playing on her lips. It was far past their usual bedtime, and she was beginning to become more careless with her words.

"What?" Paisley tilted her head to the side and glanced at her wife.

"You know how I used to tell you that I'd give you the stars?" Shiloh asked, biting her lip. Paisley nodded after thinking for a few moments.

"Well last year, I was trying to think of the best possible birthday present I could get you, right?"

"You got me speakers," Paisley remembered, nodding softly. "And the bracelet." She held up her wrist.

"Yeah, but that wasn't my original plan," Shiloh bit her lip and shook her head. "That was the backup plan."

"Then what was the original plan?" Paisley tilted her head to the side. Shiloh's cheeks flushed slightly and she looked away.

"It's kinda cheesy," Shiloh laughed, shaking her head. "I wanted to actually get you a star. They have these websites where you can literally buy a star and name it after someone, right?"

Paisley nodded softly.

"Well I wanted to name a star after you. So I filled out a form online and submitted it and everything and they send a certificate to your house," Shiloh sighed, shaking her head and rolling her eyes at herself. "Well I wasn't smart enough to double check the form when I filled it out on my phone."

"What do you mean?" the smaller girl tilted her head to the side.

"It autocorrected your name to Parsley," Shiloh mumbled.

"Huh?" Paisley raised an eyebrow.

"I bought a star and named it Parsley," Shiloh deadpanned, looking up and shaking her head. "Parsley."

Paisley struggled to hide her smile, looking up at her wife in disbelief. "Parsley?"

"Parsley."

"You named a star Parsley?" Paisley couldn't contain her laughter, and she cupped her hands over her mouth to try and hide her smile.

"Don't rub it in," Shiloh laughed, nudging her wife's shoulder and rolling her eyes playfully.

"Parsley Lowe," the smaller girl mumbled, hanging her head down to hide her laughter.

"That's why I had to run out in the middle of the night with Ryland to get your actual present," Shiloh laughed, tapping on the small pearl bracelet that Paisley wore on her wrist.

"You are cute," Paisley giggled, leaning into Shiloh's side and resting her head on the girl's shoulder. "Is Parsley out there?" she asked, tracing her fingers up the cool glass.

"Huh?"

"Where is Parsley?" Paisley giggled, pointing up to the sky. "Do you know where it is?"

"I-I, uh," Shiloh cleared her throat, looking down at her feet. She knew exactly where the star was. She had memorized the coordinates and practiced finding the star before to show Paisley on her last birthday, although her plans were changed after her little mistake.

"Here," Shiloh whispered, gently taking Paisley's hand in hers and bending her fingers into a pointing motion. Pressing their fingers against the glass, she carefully guided them upwards.

"The north star is the brightest," she said softly, moving behind her wife and resting her chin on her shoulder. "You have to find it first. Moving her hand to the side slightly, she stopped and tapped her finger against the glass. "There."

"Now Paisley-Parsley-is pretty hard to find. I picked one of the tiniest stars because I know you like to give love to the things that sometimes people tend to overlook," Shiloh explained. "See these three stars that make a triangle?" She moved her finger to the side slightly.

"Yeah," Paisley whispered, feeling Shiloh wrap her free arm around her waist and lean her head against her own. "Well, Parsley is right inbetween them. Right... there," she placed Paisley's finger against the glass. "See it?"

Leaning forwards slightly, Paisley could make out the small glimmer of a star right atop the space where her finger sat. Eyes widening, she turned back to Shiloh with a soft smile on her face.

"That is Parsley?"

"Unfortunately," Shiloh laughed, earning a soft nudge from her wife, who immediately turned back to the glass door to gaze up at the sky again.

"I love it," Paisley whispered, nodding softly. "It is our star."

"Our star?" Shiloh raised an eyebrow.

"Yeah," Paisley giggled, turning back around and looking up at Shiloh with a playful look on her face. "Even though it is named Parsley."

"Everybody makes mistakes," Shiloh huffed half heartedly, reaching up and ruffling Paisley's hair. "Some are just... more permanent than others."

"It is okay," Paisley laughed, leaning against Shiloh's side and gazing up at her adoringly. She'd come to learn that her wife looked exceptionally beautiful in the moonlight. It made her eyes light up like the ocean during a thunderstorm. There was something so captivating about her. "I will still love you."

"I'm honored," Shiloh laughed, turning her head slightly to kiss Paisley's cheek. Noticing how her wife yawned softly and rubbed her eyes, Shiloh squinted and glanced at the clock.

"I think it's time we got some sleep," Shiloh whispered, turning Paisley to face her. Wrapping one arm under Paisley's shoulders, she laughed softly. "Hop up."

"Huh?" Paisley tilted her head to the side. "What are you-woah!" She hurried to grab onto Shiloh's shoulders as the other girl hoisted her up into her arms.

"C'mon, Parsley," Shiloh giggled, carrying her wife bridal style into the living room, where Presley remained fast asleep. "You need your beauty rest."

Shiloh set Paisley down, falling back onto the couch and pulling her wife into the space beside her. Almost immediately, Paisley curled up in her side, letting out a small kittenish yawn.

"Goodnight, Lo," Paisley whispered, smiling to herself when she felt Shiloh lace her fingers together. "You will always be my star."

CHAPTER 43

"You are supposed to stir it."

"I am?"

"Yeah," Paisley giggled, raising an eyebrow at Shiloh, who was rushing to bring the last of the dishes over to the table.

"Shit," the green eyed girl shook her head, biting her lip and glancing back at the kitchen.

"I will do it," Paisley nodded quickly. "You go get Presley dressed."

"You're the best," Shiloh breathed a sigh of relief, quickly untying her apron and planting a quick kiss on her wife's cheek as she hurried back into the living room to retrieve the youngest member of the family.

Paisley, however, remained in the kitchen. Bringing her hand up to press against her cheek, she smiled softly. The brown eyed girl couldn't help but laugh when Shiloh scooped Presley off of her spot on the couch, playfully spinning the smaller girl around before disappearing down the hallway.

Quickly snapping back into reality, Paisley hurried back over to the stove. It was Thanksgiving Day, and they were expecting their guests any minute now.

As if one cue, just as Paisley brought the last few platters over to the dining room table, the doorbell echoed throughout the house.

"Got it!" Paisley called down the hallway before jogging over to the door. She peered out the window first, smiling widely when she saw Leah and Troy on the other side. She quickly pulled open the door, allowing Troy inside, who carried the turkey in a large container.

"Hey Paisley," Leah smiled, pulling the brown eyed girl into a hug. "Where's Shiloh?"

"She is getting Presley ready," Paisley nodded, closing the door behind the girl once she entered the house.

As if on cue, small footsteps bounded out of the hallway and into the foyer. Presley slid to a stop in front of Paisley, looking up at her with a shy smile.

"Wait!" Shiloh's voice rang from the other end of the hallway. The green eyed girl soon appeared into the foyer, a white scrunchie in her hand. "Pigtail down!" she cried dramatically, kneeling down next to Presley so she could secure the other half of her hair up into a wavy pigtail. The smaller girl giggled, crinkling her nose and looking at the girl beside her.

"There we go," Shiloh laughed, smoothing out the smaller girl's hair. "You look beautiful."

"I do?" Presley turned to face Shiloh and tilted her head to the side.

"Of course you do," Shiloh laughed, standing up and running a hand through her own hair. "You're glowing. I think that's your color."

"I picked it out myself," Presley nodded proudly, spinning around in the pastel green dress that she adorned.

A little over ten minutes later, Maia and Toby arrived, and everyone was seated around the dining room table. With the exception of Ryland and Vanessa, who always seemed to show up late to every event.

"So when's the wedding?" Shiloh asked, giving Leah a soft smile from across the table. Everybody else nodded in interest, except for Paisley and Presley, who were too busy trying to convince Lucas to try cranberry sauce.

"We're aiming for June of next year," Leah smiled shyly, glancing at Troy, who sat beside her. "We wanted to do something pretty small on the beach with just our closest family and friends."

"We'd rather save the money we'd use on a huge wedding and put it towards the honeymoon," Troy nodded. Shiloh bit her lip, glancing at Paisley, who was still failing at making a spoonful of cranberry sauce look appealing to the toddler.

"Where are you going?" Maia asked, nudging Toby's side to get him to pay attention.

"Paris," Leah failed to hide her excitement, replying quicker than everyone expected. "I know it's cheesy, but..."

"Paris sounds awesome," Maia laughed, shaking her head and dismissing the girl's claim. "I've always wanted to see the Eiffel Tower."

"Where did you two go on your honeymoon?" Troy asked, looking between Maia and Toby. The two exchanged glances, trying to stifle their laughter.

"Burger King," Maia laughed and shook her head.

"Burger King?" Leah raised an eyebrow in confusion.

"It's pretty hard to go on a honeymoon when you're both broke, in college, and one of you is pregnant," Maia explained, pointing to Lucas and then back to herself. "We eloped, got burger king, and then went home and went to bed," she shrugged with a laugh.

"We went camping that weekend, though," Toby added, making Maia laugh even harder.

"I could care less about that kind of stuff," Maia shrugged. "We'll have plenty of time to travel once Lucas is older. Toby needs someone besides me to do all the crazy stuff with."

"Like skydiving," her husband nodded.

"Anything but skydiving," Maia shook her head and shot him a half-hearted glare.

"Climbing Everest?"

"Shut up," Maia laughed, shoving Toby playfully. "We'll cross that bridge when we get there."

"What about you two?" Leah nodded to Shiloh. "Are you guys ever going to go on a honeymoon?"

"Hopefully," Shiloh laughed, glancing at Paisley who was now helping Presley cut her turkey into small pieces. "I haven't thought about it in a while."

"Where do you want to go?"

"Oh god, I don't know," Shiloh shook her head. "Good question."

Before anyone had a chance to say anything else, the doorbell caught everyone's attention. All the members at the table exchanged knowing glances, and Paisley quickly hopped her feet to go let their final guests into the house.

"Sorry we're late," Vanessa appeared in the dining room moments later. "We wanted to make a pumpkin pie but then Ryland fell asleep when she was supposed to be watching it and then the smoke alarm went off and then-"

"We brought ice cream?" Ryland held up a plastic bag from the grocery store with a hopeful smile.

"Toss it in the fridge and sit down before your food gets cold," Shiloh laughed, scooting her chair closer to Paisley's to make room for everyone at the table.

"So what's new?" Ryland asked once everyone was seated around the table, reaching over to grab a spoonful of mashed potatoes. "It feels like we haven't seen you guys in forever."

"Can I have more milk?" Presley asked, holding up her cup and turning to Shiloh and Paisley hopefully. "Please?"

Before either of the wives could respond, they were distracted by Vanessa's fork clattering against her plate and Ryland practically choking on a mouthful of her drink.

"She talked!" Ryland hopped to her feet, pointing to a very confused Presley, who shyly set her cup back down on the table.

"Yeah?" Shiloh raised an eyebrow, exchanging confused glances with her wife. "That's a thing she does."

"You never told us," Vanessa spoke up, shaking her head with wide eyes.

"Yes we did," Paisley's voice appeared from beside Shiloh, tilting her head to the side slightly. "I texted you," she retrieved her phone out of her pocket and began looking for the text conversation.

Vanessa and Ryland's eyes both went wide, and the two girls exchanged knowing glances.

"My phone broke," Vanessa shook her head, turning back to the girls. "A new one's supposed to come in the mail next week."

"How did you break it again?" Paisley asked, laughing softly.

"I-I, uh," Vanessa bit her lip and glanced at Ryland once more. "I just... did," she shrugged, shaking her head.

"Wait, but since when did she start talking?" Ryland interrupted them, changing the subject. Meanwhile, Leah hopped up to get Presley the refill she'd so patiently been waiting for.

"She just..." Shiloh glanced at the smaller girl. "She just did," the green eyed girl shrugged. "She needed a little time, that's all," she smiled, reaching over and ruffling the smaller girl's hair.

"You should really take better care of your phone," Paisley spoke up, nodding in Vanessa's direction. This caused Ryland to burst into laughter, earning a glare from the dark skinned girl.

"Thank you," Presley spoke up once more when Leah returned with her cup, placing it down in front of her. Ryland

and Vanessa both gaped at the smaller girl. They weren't used to hearing her voice.

"Do you know our names?" Ryland spoke up, sitting back down at the table and giving Presley a soft smile. The smaller girl across the table furrowed her eyebrows together, struggling to remember. Luckily, Paisley leaned over and whispered something in her ear.

"Rya!" Presley nodded, smiling proudly. She grew confused when everyone else at the table burst into laughter.

"It's Ryland, goofball," Shiloh giggled, correcting the smaller girl.

"Ryland," Presley said the name slowly, correcting herself and looking up hopefully.

"And that's Vanessa," Shiloh added, pointing to the other girl. Presley nodded softly.

"Vanessa," she repeated. "Ryland... and Vanessa," she pointed to each girl with a shy smile.

"You got it," Ryland laughed, holding out her fist across the table. This earned a confused look from Presley, who held up her own fist and examined it.

"I'm ashamed, Chanch," Ryland scoffed, shaking her head and looking at Paisley playfully. Paisley's eyes widened and she tapped Presley's shoulder, pointing to Ryland's fist.

"You are supposed to bump it," Paisley whispered to the smaller girl. Presley tilted her head to the side, but proceeded to gently tap her fist against Ryland's. The light haired girl immediately brought her hand up and made an exploding noise, which earned a shy giggle from the smaller girl.

"There we go," Ryland laughed, giving the girl a small smile and sitting back down at the table.

"Run, Paisley!"

"I got it!" Paisley called, jogging down the yard and keeping her eye on the football that flew towards her. Just as she thought she would catch it, Vanessa practically appeared out of nowhere, jumping in front of her and snatching it out of thin air.

"I do not got it," Paisley giggled, sliding to a stop and hurrying to chase after Vanessa, who was now running down to the opposite end of the yard.

Seconds before the girl scored a touchdown, Ryland came flying past Paisley, practically tackling Vanessa to the ground.

"Dammit, Ryland!" the girl huffed, but failed to hold back laughter as she laid back on the grass. Paisley caught up to them, struggling to catch her breath and bursting into laughter beside them.

"No cursing around the children," Toby teased, jogging over and retrieving the ball from the ground. He pointed towards the back porch, where Presley and Lucas sat on a blanket atop the grass, with Wolf spread out beside them.

While everyone else began another game of football, Paisley padded over to the porch, having noticed the lack of a certain green eyed girl. Quietly, she slipped into the house and paused to listen for a few moments.

Sure enough, there was soft music coming from down the hallway. She should've known. With a shy smile, Paisley quietly made her way to the art studio, opening the door slowly and peering in.

Shiloh sat on a stool in front of the window with her sketchbook in her lap. Quietly, as to not disturb the girl, Paisley took a few steps forwards and peered over her shoulder. A soft smile spread across her face when she saw Shiloh's sketch: a portrait of Presley and Lucas on the grass in light pencil.

Shiloh looked up, watching through the window as Presley burst into laughter when Lucas attempted to stand up and stumbled back onto his bottom. The green eyed girl giggled softly to herself, shaking her head and looking back down at her sketchbook.

"We are adopting her, you know."

"I know," Shiloh said softly, keeping her eyes on the page. She wasn't even started by Paisley's voice. She had sensed her presence since her wife walked into the room.

"Huh?" Paisley tilted her head to the side, taken aback by Shiloh's response. She moved to sit on the windowsill, making sure not to block Shiloh's view. "You know?"

"You said it yourself," Shiloh shrugged, closing her sketchbook and setting it aside. "We don't give up on people, right?"

"Right," Paisley nodded softly, looking at Shiloh with a curious expression on her face.

"Well then," Shiloh got up, moving over to her desk and filing through her drawers. "Whenever you're ready, Mrs. Everest-Lowe," she smiled softly, handing a collection of papers to her wife, who took them questioningly.

Paisley scanned the papers for a few moments before looking up at Shiloh in shock. "You signed them already?"

"I mean, I-I, yeah," Shiloh paused, looking at Paisley and biting her lip. "I did the night we stayed over at Maia's. It doesn't happen right away, I mean, she has to live with us for six months before we can have an adoption hearing but I just figured… you know, I hope you're not mad, I didn't mean t-,"

"I am not mad," Paisley giggled, standing up and placing her hand on Shiloh's arm. "Do you have a pen?"

"Wait, really?" Shiloh asked, perking up slightly and looking at Paisley with a glimmer of hope in her eyes.

"I need a pen to sign it," Paisley held up the papers, using her pointer finger as a fake pen to try to show Shiloh what she meant.

"Oh, right," Shiloh shook her head, hurrying over to her desk and digging through her papers until she retrieved a pen. "Here."

"Thanks," Paisley giggled, taking the pen from her flustered wife and leaning down to sign the papers against the windowsill. After a few minutes of paging through the papers and adding her signature in all the empty lines, Paisley recapped the pen and looked back up at her wife. "Is that it?"

"I've got a few phone calls to make in the morning, but... yeah," Shiloh nodded with a soft smile. "That's it."

Clapping her hands together, Paisley hopped to her feet and pressed a quick kiss to her wife's lips. "I love you, Lo," Paisley whispered, nodding softly. "I do not think I say it enough."

"Feel free to say it some more, then," Shiloh teased, crinkling her nose at the smaller girl and pulling her into her side. Both the girls' attention was caught by the group outside.

Toby had tossed the football to Presley before snatching her up and placing her on his shoulders. She was now giggling and holding on for dear life as he jogged down to the end of the yard. Paisley laughed softly when he prompted the girl to spike the ball, and Presley tossed it down to the ground.

Even from all the way inside, the two girls could hear their friends cheering for the smaller girl, who wore a huge smile on her face. It was contagious.

"Happy Thanksgiving," Paisley whispered, leaning her head on Shiloh's shoulder. She let out a deep breath, watching as Presley retrieved the football from the ground and tossed it to Ryland.

"Happy Thanksgiving to you," Shiloh giggled. "I love you too, by the way. Thanks for giving me something to be thankful for."

CHAPTER 44

"Please?"

"Yeah, c'mon guys, please?"

"It's just one day. You won't even know she's gone."

Paisley and Shiloh exchanged glances, surrounded by their friends' pleas. Paisley raised a questioning eyebrow to her wife, and was met with a shrug from the dark haired girl.

"We can handle a child for 24 hours," Ryland scoffed, shaking her head at her friends' hesitancy. "You just feed it, water it, and take it on a walk twice a day. It's not that hard."

It'd been a little over a week since Thanksgiving, and the couple had earned two extra visitors for the time being. Due to a plumbing issue at their apartment, Vanessa and Ryland had jumped at the opportunity to spend a few days with the tiny family.

Presley adored the two girls. It was obvious. They brought out her outgoing side. Just the night before, they'd conducted an impromptu karaoke session in the living room, which ended in a broken lamp and a million apologies from a guilty Ryland.

And now, Vanessa and Ryland had conducted a master plan. They wanted to take Presley to the city to see a ballet. Which meant they'd spend the night at a hotel to avoid traffic on the way home.

However, this resulted in a wary Paisley and a hesitant Shiloh. They'd yet to let Presley out of their sight since she'd come to live with them, and they were both nervous to do so.

"What's the worst that could happen?" Vanessa looked at the girls, raising an eyebrow. "It's a ballet. Not a heavy metal mosh pit."

"Someone's ballet shoe could fly off and hit you in the face," Shiloh nodded, convinced by her argument. "Or there could be an earthquake."

"There could just as easily be an earthquake here, smartass," Ryland quipped back half heartedly, giving her friend a knowing smirk. Paisley and Shiloh looked at one another once more.

"I don't know, Ryland," Shiloh sighed and shook her head. "Can't you guys find something else to do?"

"Come on, Shiloh," Vanessa laughed. "You get her every day. We're just asking for one night of auntie time. Besides, you two should jump at the chance to have the house all to yourse-,"

"I'm ready!"

Presley's voice rang out from her bedroom, interrupting the girls. The small girl bounded into the living room, donning a pink leotard and tutu, along with small pink ballet flats (on the wrong feet). Shiloh had to scramble to catch the little girl, who practically leapt into her arms.

"Woah there, lovebug," Shiloh laughed, moving to sit Presley on her hip. "Where'd you get that?"

"Rya gave it to me," Presley nodded, pointing the girl that stood a few feet away from them. "She said we're going to see the ballerinas."

Shiloh and Paisley's eyes both landed on a guilty looking Ryland, whose eyes had widened slightly.

"You told her already?" Shiloh asked, raising an eyebrow.

"I couldn't resist!" Ryland held up her hands as if she were surrendering, making Paisley laugh. "Plus I didn't know you'd be so uptight."

"I am not uptight," Shiloh argued, shaking her head. When the other girls struggled to stifle their laughter, the dark haired girl looked at her wife in confusion.

"You kinda are, Lo," Paisley said softly, placing a hand on Shiloh's shoulder. "But only sometimes," she added with a nervous smile.

"I am not uptight," Shiloh mumbled under her breath, shaking her head. Paisley giggled, looking down at her feet shyly.

"I expect lots of pictures," Shiloh spoke after a few seconds of silence, looking back to a hopeful Ryland and Vanessa. "And if you stay up late, you're dealing with her tomorrow if she's grumpy."

"So that's a yes?" Ryland's face lit up, exchanging excited looks with Vanessa.

"Only because I'm not uptight," Shiloh raised a teasing eyebrow at her friends. Paisley giggled, reaching over and squeezing Shiloh's hand. Vanessa and Ryland immediately celebrated, high fiving one another and pulling both girls into a hug.

"It's a yes!" Presley smiled widely, not quite sure what it meant - but knowing that it had made everyone happy. Giggling, the smaller girl threw her arms around Shiloh's neck and hugged her tight. "Thank you, mommy!"

Presley didn't even notice how all four girls froze and exchanged shocked glances. Instead, she leaned over and grabbed onto Paisley, planting a soft kiss on her cheek.

"Rya? Can you do my hair like a ballerina?" the smaller girl tilted her head to the side, squirming out of Shiloh's arms and padding over to the light haired girl.

Shooting the green eyed girl a soft smile, Ryland nodded and turned her attention back to Presley. "Let's go get a brush, Parsley."

"It's Presley!" the smaller girl giggled and ran down the hallway after Ryland, who was followed by Vanessa.

"Whatever you say, Parsley," Ryland quipped back, making the smaller girl laugh even harder. Moments later, only Shiloh and Paisley were left in the living room.

"She called you mommy," Paisley whispered, tapping Shiloh's arm and gaining the green eyed girl's attention.

"I know," Shiloh said softly, still somewhat in shock. "Wait, really?"

"Yeah," Paisley giggled, moving in front of her wife to gain her full attention. "Are you okay?"

"Yeah, just... wow," Shiloh laughed, shaking her head and finally meeting Paisley's eyes. "I wasn't expecting that."

"Me neither," Paisley bit her lip. "We should pack her bag."

Simply nodding, Paisley squeezed Shiloh's shoulder before disappearing down the hallway and leaving Shiloh by herself. Somewhat confused, the girl raised an eyebrow before shrugging it off and following after her wife.

"Goodbye, little flower," Paisley whispered, kneeling down next to Presley and kidding her forehead. "Have fun."

"Take care of Ryland," Shiloh teased, bending down and lifting up Presley to hug her. "We'll see you tomorrow, okay?"

"I'll remember it all so I can tell you everything!" Presley nodded happily as Shiloh helped her get buckled into her car seat. "Don't forget about me!"

Shiloh neglected to notice how Paisley tensed up behind her. Laughing softly, the green eyed girl nodded and kissed Presley's forehead. "I won't, bug."

"Do not get into trouble," Paisley turned to Ryland, looking at her seriously. "And do not be stupid." There was an edge in her voice that surprised even Ryland, and before anyone could say anything, Paisley gave Presley one last wave and disappeared up the walkway and back into the house.

"What was that about?" Vanessa asked, pulling Shiloh into a goodbye hug.

"M'not sure," Shiloh shrugged, just as confused by her wife's actions. "Have fun, yeah?"

"Duh," Ryland laughed, nudging Shiloh's shoulder. "Don't worry too much."

"I'm not uptight," Shiloh reminded her, giving them a small wave and watching from the sidewalk as Ryland's truck disappeared down the road. Presley waved until Shiloh was out of sight, making the green eyed girl laugh softly to herself.

Shiloh ran a hand through her hair and wandered into the kitchen once she was back inside. She found Paisley at the sink, scrubbing at the dishes they had yet to clean from last night's dinner.

"Here," Shiloh grabbed a dish towel and held out her hand. "You wash, I'll dry."

"I have got it," Paisley mumbled. Instead of handing the dish to Shiloh, she took the rag from Shiloh and hastily dried the plate in her hand, shuffling across the kitchen to put it away.

Taken aback by her actions, Shiloh moved forward to begin scrubbing the dishes in the sink, but Paisley appeared at her side once more and took the plates out of her hand.

"I said I got it," the smaller girl refused to make eye contact with her.

"I'm just trying to help," Shiloh laughed nervously, taking a step backwards. "Sorry."

"It is fine," Paisley's voice was quiet. The smaller girl continued her work at the sink, keeping her eyes off of Shiloh.

Still as confused as ever, Shiloh stepped forwards and placed a gentle hand on Paisley's arm. "Are you okay?"

"I am fine!" Paisley snapped, turning around and looking at Shiloh. "I am just trying to clean." She stressed her words, furrowing her eyebrows together and turning back to the sink.

"You aren't acting 'fine'," Shiloh quipped back, raising an eyebrow. "What's with the attitude?"

Shiloh regretted her words as soon at they left her mouth, because moments later there was a clatter of dishes in the sink and Paisley threw her washcloth aside.

"Can I please just... just clean... in peace?!" Paisley raised her voice, growing even more frustrated when she stumbled over her words.

Hurt and confused, Shiloh just nodded, taking a small step backwards. "I'll be in the studio," she said softly, giving Paisley a hopeful smile. Instead, her wife just huffed and turned back to the sink.

Biting her lip, Shiloh forced herself to keep quiet. She knew something was wrong, but she knew better than to push it out of the girl. Disappearing down the hallway, she attempted to busy herself in the studio. Although it wasn't that easy when both Presley and Paisley occupied her nervous thoughts.

Finally, about an hour (and a lot of crumpled sketches) later, Shiloh gave up on drawing when she heard the sound of the bedroom door. Hoping that Paisley was in a better mood, Shiloh quickly cleaned up and slipped down the hallway.

When Shiloh entered the bedroom, Paisley didn't even acknowledge her. The brown eyed girl was tugging on an old t-shirt, combing her fingers through her wavy hair.

"Anything from Ryland or Nessa?" Shiloh asked, hoping to create conversation. Paisley paused, turning around and looking at the girl.

"They would text us in the group," the smaller girl muttered, turning back to the mirror. Biting her lip, Shiloh simply nodded.

"Did they tell you when the show was supposed to start?" Shiloh spoke up once more, glancing at the clock.

"I do not know!" Paisley snapped back, startling Shiloh and causing her to hop up from the bed.

"I was just asking a question," Shiloh muttered, shaking her head. "What is your problem tonight?"

"Why... why do you think there is a problem?!" Paisley gave up on trying to pull her hair into a ponytail, throwing her hands down at her sides and turning to Shiloh in frustration. "There is not a problem!"

"Obviously there is," Shiloh motioned to the girl. "Something's got you all worked up."

"Why do you care so much?!" Paisley shook her head and met Shiloh's eyes for a split second.

"Why do you think?!" Now it was Shiloh's turn to raise her voice, tossing her hands up in the air. She was growing frustrated with Paisley's sudden change in mood. "You're my wife, for fucks sake!"

Paisley paused for a moment, realizing just how worked up she'd managed to make Shiloh. She quickly shook her head, though. "Stop asking questions!"

"Fine!" Shiloh threw her hands up as if she were surrendering and turned away. Grabbing her phone, the green eyed girl lay back on the bed and remained silent.

"Fine!" Paisley huffed, turning back to the mirror and hastily pulling her hair back in a ponytail. Shiloh glanced up from her spot on the bed, unable to bite her tongue.

"Fine," the green eyed girl mumbled under her breath. Paisley whipped her head around to glare at Shiloh before throwing her hands down at her side and moving towards the door.

"Fine," Paisley raised her voice loud enough for Shiloh to hear her before storming out of the room and slamming the door shut behind her.

Shiloh would be lying if she said she didn't jump when the door slammed shut. The green eyed girl sat up slightly, surprised by Paisley's actions. (And ultimately regretting her own.)

Meanwhile, Paisley had come to a stop at the end of the hallway, realizing she had no clue where she was going. Pausing, the brown eyed girl glanced back at the bedroom door and sighed.

Just as Shiloh had gotten off of the bed to go after Paisley, the bedroom door flew back open and the brown eyed girl reappeared in the doorway.

"I do not like fighting," Paisley breathed out, shaking her head quickly. Feeling guilty, the smaller girl couldn't bring herself to meet Shiloh's eyes.

Now even more confused, Shiloh nodded and stood up slowly. "Me neither," the green eyed girl confessed. "Are you okay?"

"I am sorry," Paisley mumbled, finally looking up slowly and wringing her hands out nervously.

"Don't be," Shiloh shook her head. "It's my fault."

"No it is not," Paisley replied quickly.

"Yes it is," Shiloh quipped back. She paused, though, realizing she was starting another argument. "We're both sorry."

"Yeah..." Paisley whispered and hung her head down. Noticing the smaller girl's change in mood, Shiloh sat down on the bed and held out a hand.

"C'mere," the green eyed girl whispered, patting the space beside her.

Paisley quickly hurried over to the bed. Instead of sitting beside the green eyed girl, Paisley crawled onto her lap, pressing a gentle kiss to Shiloh's cheek. "Let's not fight anymore."

Shiloh just giggled softly, wrapping her arms around Paisley's waist and holding her close. "Deal," she whispered.

After a few moments of silence, Paisley lifted her head. "She called you mommy," the brown eyed girl whispered, biting her lip.

Confused, Shiloh nodded softly. "Yeah…?"

"Who does she think I am?" the smaller girl mumbled under her breath. Shiloh raised an eyebrow.

"What do you mean?"

"If she called you mommy… what does she think I am?" Paisley ran a hand through her hair and looked down at the ground.

"Just as important as me," Shiloh replied almost immediately, shocked when she found out what Paisley's doubts had been. "You really think she loves me any more than she loves you?"

"I dunno," Paisley mumbled, shrugging her shoulders.

"Hey, look at me," Shiloh reached up and cupped Paisley's cheek, tilting her chin so their eyes met. "Do you see yourself? Do you realize how amazing you are?"

"That kid adores you, Pais," Shiloh laughed softly and shook her head. "Just like I do. And if you don't see that, then you've just got to trust me. It's pretty hard not to love you."

Before Paisley could open her mouth to respond, a buzzing noise from the bedside table caught their attention. Shiloh reached over, unlocking her phone and smiling softly when she saw what was on the screen.

"See for yourself," Shiloh whispered, gently handing the phone to her wife. Furrowing her eyebrows, Paisley held the phone between them.

[Vanessa - 7:39] We were ten minutes late because she insisted on buying these for her mommies.

Attached was a picture of Presley seated at the ballet, adorned in her tutu ensemble and sucking her thumb. Her eyes were focused on the stage, and in her free hand was a bouquet of yellow roses.

"They are yellow," Paisley whispered, a small smile spreading across her face as she turned the phone to show the picture to Shiloh.

"I wonder why," Shiloh teased, placing the phone back on the nightstand and crinkling her nose at the girl. "You'll see one day, Paisley. One day you'll realize how amazing you truly are. For now I'll just have to keep reminding you."

C H A P T E R   4 5

It was never easy to get used to a goodbye. Paisley never could.

They came so unexpectedly. Every time, Paisley thought that things were just lining up to be perfect. And every time, it hurt in all the same ways.

It was the first day of December. They were supposed to celebrate. Shiloh had even gone out the night before and gotten whipped cream so she could put smiley faces on their pancakes. She set her alarm for extra early so she could be up before both Paisley and Presley.

Which is why she was surprised when her wife's worried voice brought her out of her slumber.

"Lo."

Even in her half conscious state, Shiloh knew something was wrong. She quickly opened her eyes, peering up at her wife in confusion. "Huh?"

"He is sick."

Furrowing her eyebrows, Shiloh sat up. "Who?"

"Wolf," Paisley's voice lowered and she nodded to the bundle of blankets in her arms. Shiloh shivered.

"How?"

"He just is," Paisley shook her head, wanting none of Shiloh's questions. "I need help."

"Let me see him," Shiloh said softly, holding out her hands. She could see the concern in her wife's face, prodding her to handle him with the utmost care when Paisley passed him into her arms.

"H-he did not eat last night. Or this morning," Paisley mumbled, slowly sitting down beside Shiloh on the bed and watching as she carefully studied the old white cat. "He did not even want to go outside when I opened the door."

"That's odd," Shiloh whispered, carefully, pressing her fingers around his neck and realizing the cat's breathing was slowed. "Where'd you find him?"

"Hiding," Paisley nodded, reaching out and placing her hand atop Shiloh's. "Under the couch. What do we do, Lo?"

It was at this point that Shiloh became aware of the small pair of eyes watching them. She turned around and glanced at the doorway, where Presley stood in her light blue pajamas, sucking her thumb and gazing at them worriedly.

"I'll call the vet," Shiloh nodded, adjusting the sick animal in her arms. "I need you to go and get Presley dressed just in case we have to go, yeah?"

"Yeah," Paisley whispered, standing up slowly and glancing towards the door.

"Hey," Shiloh paused to reach out and grab Paisley's hand. She met her eyes, giving her a soft smile. "It's all gonna be fine."

It wasn't fine, unfortunately.

"FIP. Feline Infection Peritonitis," the veterinarian explained, turning back from the computer to face the small family standing in front of her. Presley was in Shiloh's arms, petting the white cat that lay on the table in front of them.

"What do we need to do?" Shiloh asked, glancing over at Paisley. Her wife was standing a step behind them, somewhat wary of the room they were in. She never did like doctor's offices of any kind.

"Well, you have two choices," the woman abandoned the clipboard in her arms and leaned her elbows against the cold metal table. "You can either take him home with you and let nature take its course, or you can save him a few days of suffering and put him to sleep."

"Wait," Shiloh's heart dropped in her chest when she heard Paisley draw in a sharp breath. "What about medicine? Or surgery?"

"It doesn't exist," the woman shook her head, giving them a sympathetic look. "The virus acts fast. It doesn't respond to any type of treatment. I wish I could-,"

"Home," Paisley's voice deadpanned from behind them, making both Shiloh and Presley look back at her in shock.

"What?" Shiloh raised an eyebrow at her wife.

"I want to take him home," Paisley nodded once. Shiloh saw her hands balled into fists at her sides. But she also saw how Paisley was struggling to keep them from shaking.

Shiloh could tell just by the look on the veterinarian's face that Paisley's request wasn't the desirable one. She bit her lip and turned back to her wife, adjusting Presley in her arms.

"Paisley, I—,"

"No, Shiloh," Paisley's eyes narrowed and she shook her head. "We are going home."

"No we aren't, Paisley," Shiloh raised her voice slightly, which caused Presley to look at her in shock. Even Paisley tensed up in front of them.

Shiloh set Presley down, urging her to go keep Wolf company while she pulled Paisley out in the hallway. Her wife looked at her in confusion. And although she tried to keep a brave face, Shiloh could tell Paisley was struggling to grip the reality of the situation.

"Taking him back home would be selfish," Shiloh sighed, shaking her head and reaching out to place a hand on Paisley's arm. "He's already sick. You heard her say how cats hide their sickness until they can't handle it anymore."

"But I—,"

"Pais," Shiloh whispered, taking a step forward and lacing their fingers together. Her free hand rested on

Paisley's shoulder gently. "I'm not going to watch you be miserable for the next few days because you can't do anything to help him. I know you. I know how you are."

"This was not supposed to happen," Paisley let out a long breath and hung her head down. Shiloh felt her heart pang for the smaller girl. "He was supposed to live."

"Nothing lives forever, babe," Shiloh gently cupped Paisley's cheek and brought her eyes back up to meet hers. "He has nine lives anyway, remember? He's a cat." She offered her wife a soft smile, which was only received with a scowl and a turn of the head.

Sighing, Shiloh pulled her hands away. "Listen, Paisley," she shook her head. "It's your decision. I'm not going to try and stop you if you want to take him home. I'm just trying to think about what's best for him." She took a step backwards and nodded toward the door. "Think about it for a few minutes and come let me know when you've decided, okay?"

Paisley just nodded softly, and Shiloh gave her one last soft wave before disappearing back into the room. Presley now sat on the cold metal table, holding Wolf carefully in her lap. Her big brown eyes flickered up to meet Shiloh's when the girl came back into the room.

"It's not a busy day. I'll give you a few minutes," the vet nodded, giving the green eyed girl a sympathetic smile.

Once she exited the room, Shiloh pulled a chair over beside Presley and sat down with a soft sigh. The brown eyed girl had her eyes focused on Wolf, and Shiloh simply watched as Presley petted him gently.

"You'll say hi to em' for me, won't you?"

Presley's voice was soft, taking Shiloh by surprise. Just as she raised her head to question the smaller girl, she realized the question hadn't been aimed at her.

"You know, my mommy and daddy?" Presley whispered, leaning down slightly. "And you'll tell them I miss em' an awful lot? My brother, too. Promise you'll take real good care of em' for me? And you can tell them all about my new family so they don't have to worry too much. Can you do that?"

"I think he can," Shiloh whispered, reaching over and squeezing Presley's hand.

"You do?" Presley looked up to meet Shiloh's eyes this time, tilting her head to the side.

"I do," Shiloh laughed softly. "Do you know what's happening, kiddo?" she added in a more serious tone, studying the small girl intently.

"Mhm," Presley nodded quickly. "Hims is leaving us," she shrugged, taking Shiloh by surprise. "He did all his good deeds."

"Good deeds?" now it was Shiloh's turn to ask a question. Presley simply nodded and continued petting Wolf.

"Daddy said that's why Jakey had to leave. Cause' he already did at the good things here, and there was no more good things left for him to do," she paused and looked up at Shiloh. "What good things did Wolf do?"

"He was not scared."

Both girls paused and glanced towards the door, where Paisley stood tentatively. Shiloh watched as her wife slowly walked over to join them, wringing her hands together nervously.

"When there were bad things," Paisley explained, joining them at the metal operating table and reaching out to smooth out his fur. "Even when I cried. Or yelled. Or broke things. He was not scared of me."

"Lo helped the bad things go away," Paisley nodded softly. "But when they were still here, he helped to make me forget about them for a while."

"You didn't give up on him," Shiloh nodded, remembering how Paisley had latched onto the small, disheveled kitten that no one else had wanted. "Because of that, he didn't give up on you."

"We do not give up on people," Paisley whispered, her eyes flickering over to meet Shiloh's for a split second before looking back down at Wolf. "He does not have eyes, but I think he can see."

"I do not want him to hurt, Lo," Paisley sighed, allowing Shiloh to pull her into her lap. "I do not want him to."

"Do you mean...?" Shiloh paused her sentence when Paisley simply nodded softly.

Five minutes later, all three girls watched as the veterinarian prepared the needle across the room. One of Paisley's hands was laced with Shiloh's, and the other was gently stroking Wolf's fur.

"Thank you for keeping us company, Wolf," Paisley's voice wavered slightly and Shiloh was surprised she was keeping her composure. "I hope you had fun while you were here."

Just as the vet approached them with the needle, Presley's eyes widened.

"Wait!" the smaller girl shook her head and tugged on the woman's jacket, leaning up to whisper something into her ear. The woman nodded in understanding, and moments later Wolf was being transferred from Presley's arms and into Paisley's.

The small brown eyed girl just nodded slowly, cradling him in her arms and taking a deep breath. Once she was sure Paisley was okay, Shiloh gave the veterinarian a soft nod. Both girls held their own breath as the woman carefully injected the medicine into his neck.

"I am sorry," Paisley whispered under her breath, sitting down with the limp animal in her arms and somehow managing to fight back tears. Even Presley, who was normally very talkative, remained quiet and watched as

Paisley held the animal in her arms until she was sure he'd fallen asleep.

In some ways, she was thankful for goodbyes. Sometimes even the simple act of saying goodbye had been taken from her. She didn't even remember the last thing she said to her parents. Or her aunt.

It still hurts, though, she realized. It made her feel hollow, and numb, which is why she didn't even remember Shiloh helping her back up to her feet and out to the car. She didn't remember the drive home. Everything was fuzzy from then on out, until she woke up in her bed a few hours later.

The first thing she saw was her wife's soft green eyes gazing down at her. Reaching up to rub her own eyes, Paisley sat up slightly and gazed at Shiloh in confusion.

"You fell asleep in the car," Shiloh explained, answering Paisley's unspoken question. "So did Presley. She's still asleep, I think," she glanced back at the door before nodding softly.

"I had a weird dream," Paisley mumbled, sitting up and rubbing at her eyes once more. "Wolf-,"

"Babe," Shiloh's face fell slightly, and she reached out to find Paisley's hand. "It wasn't a dream."

"Oh," was all Paisley could manage to whisper. "It was not?"

"I wish it was," Shiloh sighed, feeling Paisley's shoulders slump beside her.

"I was wishing it was, too," Paisley squeezed her eyes shut for a few seconds before drawing in a deep breath. "Did you cry?"

"A little," Shiloh admitted, brushing the hair out of Paisley's face and looking at her gently. "Did you?"

Paisley shook her head.

Sighing, Shiloh simply nodded and brought her hand up to cup Paisley's cheek. She ran her thumb over the smooth skin and pressed a kiss to Paisley's forehead. "Do you want to?"

Shiloh already knew the answer. As soon as Paisley nodded, she was being pulled into Shiloh's arms.

The tears that she'd been holding in since that morning finally spilled over, and Paisley buried her head in Shiloh's shoulder as the green eyed girl lay them back on the bed.

"I love you, okay?" Shiloh whispered, rubbing small circles in the girl's back. "I know it may not matter much right now, but I do. And I'll lay here with you as long as you want."

"I-I love you too," Paisley's voice wavered and she lifted her head, wiping the tears from her face with the back of her hands. "It always matters, Lo. It will always matter." She sniffed, curling into Shiloh's side and allowing the green eyed girl to move her hair out of her face.

"If it makes you feel any better, Presley's practically made him her honorary guardian angel," Shiloh laughed softly. Surprisingly, this earned a quiet laugh from her wife as well.

"He was a good birthday present, you know," Paisley whispered. "You both did not give up on me. Thank you for that."

C H A P T E R   4 6

Waking up early had become a habit for Shiloh. Ever since Paisley had come into her life, she was always the first one awake. Like a guard dog, almost. She liked having the first hour or so of quiet to herself.

Today was different, though. And Shiloh knew well enough why she woke up with a sinking feeling in her stomach.

Paisley knew, too, because while Shiloh was waiting for her coffee to warm up, she heard quiet footsteps enter the kitchen behind her. A small blanket was wrapped around her shoulders, and Paisley leaned over her shoulder to press a soft kiss to her cheek before padding over to get her own breakfast.

"You're up early," Shiloh commented, even though she knew why. Paisley was aware of this, too, because the brown eyed girl simply shrugged her shoulders as she poured herself a glass of orange juice.

"Could not sleep," Paisley offered Shiloh a nervous glance while the green eyed girl retrieved her mug and cradled it between her hands. "I know you were in the studio last night."

Shiloh nodded, confirming Paisley's suspicions. "Couldn't sleep," she laughed weakly, leaning back against the counter and watching as the steam from her coffee drew patterns in the cold morning air. "Looks like we're in the same boat."

"You okay?" Shiloh set her mug aside and held out one of her arms, opening the blanket and offering Paisley the space beside her. Her wife simply nodded, yawned, and shuffled across the kitchen to lean against the green eyed girl's side.

"It does not get easier," Paisley admitted. Shiloh studied her wife, who pushed her tousled hair out of her face and shook her head. "Life... does not get easier. We just get used to it."

"Hey now," Shiloh sighed. It'd been a tough few days for them. Paisley especially. First Wolf's death and now... well, today.

"We get tougher, Paisley," her voice softened, and she gained Paisley's attention by using her full name. "That sounds more noble. It doesn't get easier, but we learn how to throw a few punches. Some more than others."

"She is too young," Paisley sighed. She understood Shiloh's words, she really did. But sometimes it was so much easier for her to sulk in her worries than to take the green eyed girl's advice. "It is not fair. It never is."

"I'd change it if I could, babe," Shiloh reached out and gently slid Paisley's glass out of her hands so she could lace their fingers together. "And I know you'd do the same in a heartbeat. But we can't. We can wish as hard as we want, but sometimes things don't turn out the way people think they should."

"I remember what it was like," Paisley simply nodded instead of acknowledging Shiloh's words. "Everyone... everyone was waiting for me to cry. But I did not."

"Crying isn't weakness, you know."

"I know," Paisley shook her head. "But... I was thinking a lot. Because I wondered if all those people were crying because they were really sad for them, or... or because they were sad that they lost them. My cousin told me that he was going to miss them, and I remember thinking that he sounded pretty selfish."

"I was mad for a long time, too," the brown eyed girl paused for a few moments and watched as Shiloh took a sip from her mug, nodding for her to continue. "At them. But... but I think I was just mad because I was too scared of being sad. Because then it was real. And I did not want it to be real."

"Funerals are never fun," Shiloh agreed, running a hand through her hair. "You said it yourself. It's just a bunch of people gathering around and being sad together."

"I hate it," Paisley shook her head. Shiloh just nodded in agreement, wrapping an arm around Paisley's waist and resting her head on her shoulder.

"That's why today's going to be different," Shiloh shrugged. "I already asked Presley what she wanted to do to remember them. We decided we're going to plant flowers for by their graves and paint some rocks to place around them. I already got permission from the cemetery and everything."

There had never been an official 'funeral' for Presley's parents. Shiloh and Paisley had only received word that they'd been buried at a local cemetery, and a private donation had provided their headstones.

The two girls hadn't been sure how to approach the subject with Presley. In the end, they didn't need to, because Presley had been the one to bring it up.

Shiloh had thought the smaller girl was asleep in her lap while she was watching television. But when the smaller girl sat up and asked about what was happening to the people in black clothes on the screen, Shiloh had no other option but to explain to the smaller girl what a 'funeral' was.

She hadn't exactly understood it at first. But as Shiloh explained it to her, Presley had gone quiet. Later that night at the dinner table, she had asked when her parents' funeral was, taking both of the girls by surprise.

Unfortunately, that had happened only one day after Wolf's passing, and Paisley excused herself to wash the dishes. Shiloh understood, though, and proceeded to sit Presley down and help her come up with a special way that they could celebrate the lives of her parents.

And now here they were, on a chilly Saturday morning in December, standing in their kitchen and discussing the events that were to happen that afternoon.

"It is too cold," Paisley shook her head. "Everything will die."

"Have some faith in me, babe," Shiloh whispered, leaning over and kissing the corner of her wife's mouth. "Leah's letting us use her greenhouse over the winter, so we can go back and plant them in the summer. Plus, I already went out and bought a few trees that grow in this kind of weather."

"When did you do that?" Paisley raised an eyebrow.

"This morning," Shiloh laughed and ran a hand through her hair. "You don't have to worry about a thing, okay? I've got this. You just have to tag along and be your beautiful little self."

The brown eyed girl couldn't help but laugh, turning her head away from Shiloh to hide how pink her cheeks had grown.

"And after we finish visiting with her parents, we're going to come home and have hot cocoa and marshmallows and watch Toy Story," Shiloh added with a soft laugh, reaching out and squeezing Paisley's hand. "Presley says that was their favorite movie to watch together."

So a little over an hour later, the trio packed up in their small car and drove to the cemetery. Once they got there, Presley marched ahead of them in her brand new yellow winter coat. Her bright blue boots led them along the wrought iron fence, until Shiloh stopped them at the back corner of the cemetery and pointed out two small headstones.

"That's them?" the smaller girl stopped in her tracks, digging her shoes into the cracked soil and turning around to look up at Shiloh.

"That's them," Shiloh confirmed with a soft nod. She noticed Presley's hesitation and knelt down beside her. "What's on your mind, lovebug?"

"It's different," Presley glanced between the graves and Shiloh, and then up to Paisley who had caught up with them.

"What do you m-?"

"It is okay," Paisley cut Shiloh off, giving her an apologetic look before kneeling down beside Presley and placing a hand on the smaller girl's shoulder. "It is supposed to feel like that."

"Like what?" Shiloh whispered, a bit confused by Paisley's words. The brown eyed girl turned to her wife and pursed her lips in thought.

"Like seeing them is supposed to make it feel better," Paisley spoke up after a few moments of silence. "You... you expect it to feel the same as before. But it does not. It is different."

"It is not bad, though," Paisley turned back to Presley and squeezed her hand. "Sometimes different is okay."

"Oh," Presley nodded, tilting her head to the side. "Can I touch them?"

"The gravestones? Yeah," Shiloh laughed softly and nudged the smaller girl forwards. "Go ahead, babes. We're right behind you."

Shiloh and Paisley watched as the Presley glanced up at them once more, before quietly walking towards the two graves. They followed behind her, but Paisley grabbed Shiloh's hand to stop her, wanting to give the smaller girl her space.

They watched as Presley came to a stop in front of the graves, studied them, and then proceeded to sit down in front of them. The smaller girl pulled grass out of the ground with her fists, reaching up and sprinkling it overtop the graves.

Paisley couldn't help but laugh softly at the smaller girl's makeshift decoration.

"You good?" Shiloh asked, pausing to make sure Paisley was okay. And surprisingly, she was. The smaller girl simply nodded and took her hand, pulling her forward to join Presley by the graves.

The next hour or so was composed of Presley telling them stories, listing all her favorite memories with the two people who inhabited the graves. She sure could talk someone's ear off, but Paisley and Shiloh both listened intently. Because it mattered to her, it mattered to them.

"Lo, look," Paisley whispered, nudging her wife's side and pointing upwards. Confused, Shiloh raised her eyebrows and looked up in confusion.

"I don't see anyth-," Shiloh clamped her mouth shut when she felt something brush against her nose. Blinking a few times, she let her eyes adjust, only to realize it had started to snow softly.

"Oh," Shiloh giggled. Presley paused, looking at the girls in confusion and then looking up at the sky.

"What're you looking at?" she asked quietly, tilting her head to the side and crawling over to the green eyed girl. Shiloh just laughed, glancing at Paisley before reaching out and taking Presley's tiny hand. Turning it over, she watched as a snowflake fluttered down and landed on the girl's palm, staying for a moment before quickly melting against her warm skin. Presley's eyes widened.

"It's snowing!" the smaller girl squealed, jumping up to her feet in excitement. "That means it's Christmas!"

Shiloh and Paisley immediately exchanged concerned glances.

"It's not Christmas yet, goof," Shiloh laughed and shook her head. "Twenty five more days."

"Twenty five?" Presley's shoulders dropped and her bottom lip pouted. "But that's so many!"

"Not if you have just as much fun inbetween," Shiloh shrugged. Presley thought about this for a moment.

"Does that mean we can still have hot cocoa? Even though it's not Christmas yet?" she looked up hopefully, clasping her hands together and glancing back and forth from Shiloh to Paisley. "Please?"

"Will you settle for hot cocoa with marshmallows?" Shiloh teased, scooping down to pick Presley up and place her on her shoulders. The smaller girl squealed gleefully, pulling Shiloh's beanie off of her head and giggling as she placed it on her own.

"Lots and lot'sa marshmallows," she nodded excitedly, holding onto Shiloh as the green eyed girl began walking back the fence, leading them back towards the car. Paisley laughed, jogging up behind them and switching the beanie on Presley's head for the one on hers.

Two hours and a lot of hot cocoa later, Paisley sat on the couch, watching as Buzz Lightyear swooped in to save the day. Meanwhile, Presley was asleep in her lap, and Shiloh was asleep with her head on her wife's shoulder.

Paisley had nearly dozed off as well, until she felt the tiny girl stirring in her arms.

"Mama?"

Paisley paused, her attention being turned away from the movie and down to the girl in her arms. Instantly figuring that Presley was dreaming, Paisley shifted her position on the couch and turned down the TV slightly.

"Mama?" Presley's small voice was clearer now. And when Paisley looked down, she realized the smaller girl's eyes were fixed on her, gazing up at the girl expectantly.

She had been addressing her.

"Me?" Paisley was shocked, and she quickly blinked a few times to let her eyes adjust.

"Yes, you," Presley giggled. The smaller girl sat up, yawning and rubbing her eyes with her tiny hands. "I'm hungry."

"I-I... well... dinner," Paisley stumbled over her words, quickly shaking off her initial shock and excitement and giving the girl a small smile. "Let's go make dinner, little flower," she said softly, standing up and taking Presley into her own arms.

She could've sworn she saw Shiloh's lips curve into a smile as she carried the smaller girl into the kitchen.

C H A P T E R   4 7

"C'mon, goof," Shiloh laughed, rolling her eyes and pulling Presley away from the large mirror in the airport. "We're gonna miss our flight if you two don't hurry up."

"Party pooper," Paisley mumbled, getting up from her knees in front of the mirror and shooting Shiloh a playful look. The green eyed girl just scoffed half heartedly and nudged Paisley's suitcase towards her.

"If we miss this flight, you're losing your ride home," Shiloh teased, raising an eyebrow at her wife as she grabbed Presley before the smaller girl could become distracted by the gumball machine a few feet away. Presley giggled, holding tightly to the ladybug backpack in her arms and smiling excitedly up at Shiloh.

"How do they make the airplanes fly?" Presley asked, bouncing up and down in Shiloh's arms as the two girls jogged to their gate. They'd gotten distracted on the way there because Shiloh insisted on stopping and waiting for a small gopher to cross the street.

Not to mention, the three feet of snow on the ground that made traffic slow to almost a complete stop. Shiloh figured that's what they got for traveling a few days before Christmas.

"Magic," Shiloh laughed softly, using her free hand to fix the winter hat on the girl's head . Presley was practically hidden in her winter clothing, bundled behind her bright purple coat and boots, with a white scarf hanging from her neck. "I think they-crap, Pais!" she pointed towards the line of people boarding their plane.

They had to practically sprint to get in line at the gate. Setting Presley down, Shiloh quickly handed the two girls their tickets, nudging Presley forwards to hand it to the woman scanning them.

Looking up at Shiloh for approval, Presley clutched her ticket in her gloved hand and shyly held it out to the woman, who scanned it and gave the girl a small smile. Once Shiloh and Paisley did the same, they followed the crowd of people down the skywalk and found their seats in the middle of the plane.

"I want the window!" Presley glanced up at them excitedly. Shiloh just laughed, nudging her forwards and exchanging glances with Paisley when she realized they both couldn't sit next to the smaller girl.

"Go ahead," Shiloh laughed, moving aside so Paisley could take the seat inbetween them. She knew the girl had been excited about taking Presley on her first flight, even if she hadn't said it aloud.

"You sure?" Paisley raised an eyebrow and tilted her head to the side slightly.

Shiloh simply nodded. "As long as I get to sit next to one of you," she teased, nudging Paisley forwards. "We can switch on the way back if you want."

"I'm scared."

Presley's tiny voice interrupted their small discussion, and both girls paused to look at the girl in the seat. She'd pulled the blind on the window up, observed the wing of the plane, and then come to the realization that this is what would be taking them to Florida.

Exchanging glances, Shiloh quietly nudged Paisley into the row of chairs so she could take her seat on the end.

"Here," the green eyed girl reached into her backpack and pulled something out, reaching over and placing it in Presley's lap.

"Sunny?" the smaller girl's eyes lit up and she looked at Shiloh excitedly.

"I made sure you wouldn't forget him," Shiloh laughed and glanced at Paisley, who just smiled softly back at her.

"He'll keep us safe. He kept this one safe for a long time," she laughed and nodded towards Paisley.

Ten minutes after their flight took off, both Paisley and Presley (and Sunny) were fast asleep. Shiloh just admired the image of her small family, holding Paisley's hand in her own and watching as the city of New York disappeared beneath them.

"Do not be nervous," Paisley bent down next to Presley, watching as the smaller girl's eyes took in the large house in front of them. They'd abandoned their heavy winter clothing as soon as they got to the airport. And now they stood in the driveway of Shiloh's childhood home, arriving for yet another Christmas spent together. (And Shiloh and Paisley's first Christmas as a married couple.)

As Shiloh retrieved the bags from the back of their rental car, Paisley had noticed Presley's hesitation. "You think they will not like you, yeah?" Paisley tilted her head to the side in question. Presley simply nodded and tugged on the sleeves of her pink sweater.

"I thought the same thing," Paisley nodded. "But that is a secret," she added quickly, holding her finger up to her mouth and making Presley smile softly. "You do not have to worry, though. They made Shiloh. They are great people."

"A little help here, babe?" Shiloh called, struggling to lug all three of their suitcases up onto the sidewalk. Paisley gave Presley's shoulder a comforting squeeze before hopping back up to her feet to help her wife with their belongings.

"They'll love you, kiddo. They already do," Shiloh reassured Presley once they were standing on the front porch. Although Shiloh's parents had seen Presley over Facetime, the smaller girl was always considerably shy. This would be her first time meeting them in person. The small child just nodded, staying hidden behind Paisley's legs and peering out when Shiloh rang the doorbell.

Moments later, the door was pulled open, revealing a surprised Maggie. She looked at Shiloh and Paisley excitedly, before craning her neck to glance behind them, as if she were looking for something. "Where is she?"

Shiloh and Paisley exchanged glances, realizing who Maggie was talking about. Clearing her throat, Shiloh met Maggie's eyes and nodded towards the tiny girl peering out from behind Paisley's legs.

"Oh!" Maggie laughed, pushing past Shiloh and then kneeling down on the front porch so her height matched the tiny girl's. "You're Presley, right? I'm Maggie," she nodded quickly, an excited smile on her face. "I'm your aunt. But you don't have to call me that because I'm only 9, and 'Aunt Maggie' makes me sound super old. You saw me on Facetime, remember? I-,"

"Margaret Everest!" her mother's voice appeared behind them. "Don't overwhelm the poor thing," Colette laughed, now standing in the doorway. Shiloh's father soon appeared behind her.

"Sorry," Maggie laughed shyly, giving Presley a small smile before taking a few steps back. Presley just held onto Paisley's legs, studying the family in front of her.

"Hey, mom," Shiloh laughed, accepting her mother's hug and moving in to hug her dad. "It's been a while."

"Too long," Colette joked, pulling Paisley into a hug. "Did you do something different with your hair?" she addressed her daughter-in-law, making Paisley laugh softly.

"Washed it," the brown eyed girl shrugged. She watched as Colette's attention turned to the tiny girl holding tightly to her legs. When Presley realized the woman was looking at her, she quickly moved to hide further behind her mother.

"Hey," Shiloh quickly moved to squat down next to Presley. "You don't have to be shy, goofball. This is my mom," she gave her a small smile and motioned for her mother to kneel down next to them. "Can you say hi?"

Presley glanced between Shiloh and Paisley, and then back to Colette, who gave her a welcoming smile. The tiny brown eyed girl nodded, taking a small step out from behind Paisley and gently holding out her fist. "Hi," she said shyly, keeping her tiny fist extended between them. "You've gotta' bump it."

Colette paused before shooting Paisley a knowing look, making the girl laugh as if she'd been caught.

"Hi, Presley," Shiloh's mother laughed softly and gently tapped the smaller girl's fist. There were a few moments of hesitation, but eventually Presley couldn't resist. She pulled her fist back, making an exploding noise with her mouth and causing everyone around them to laugh.

"Do you like cookies?" Colette asked, winking at Shiloh before turning back to Presley. Once the smaller girl nodded shyly, the woman smiled. "I'm helping all the cousins bake cookies in the kitchen. Would you like to come help us? I sure would appreciate an extra set of hands."

Presley couldn't hide her excitement. She looked to both Shiloh and Paisley quickly, hoping for some sort of approval. Shiloh simply laughed and nudged her shoulder.

"Go ahead, bug. Me and mama are gonna go put our stuff away and then we'll be right down, okay?" Shiloh gave the girl a reassuring smile.

"Do you have sprinkles?" Presley asked, turning back to Colette and tilting her head to the side slightly.

"I think we do," Colette laughed and stood up, extending her hand. "Want to go check?"

"Duh," Presley giggled, abandoning her hiding place from behind Paisley's legs and taking Colette's hand, allowing the woman to lead her down the hallway and into the kitchen.

Shiloh and Paisley immediately exchanged knowing glances. "Ryland."

"Merry Christmas Eve Eve," Paisley giggled as she emerged from the bathroom, clad in one of Shiloh's band t-shirts. She wrung out her wet hair, yawning and glancing at the clock before collapsing on the bed beside her wife.

It was nearly eleven o'clock that same day. The rest of their night had consisted of squeezing around the dinner table with the members of Shiloh's family and getting caught up on what had been going on in everyone's lives. Daxton was looking at colleges, Tara was helping organize her school's dance, and Maggie had gushed about a new boy in her class.

Her parents had asked Paisley about the event at the school earlier that year, and the girl had been able to talk about it without breaking down. Shiloh kept their fingers laced together the entire time, though. Even Presley had stood up in her chair and sung Christmas carols to prove to everyone that she was the most excited for Christmas.

And now, they had put Presley to bed in Maggie's room and gotten unpacked in Shiloh's old bedroom, where they'd be staying for the week to celebrate Christmas with her family.

"I'm exhausted," Shiloh laughed, setting her book aside and pulling Paisley beside her. She remained silent for a moment, letting her eyes trace her childhood bedroom with a soft smile on her face.

"Me too," Paisley whispered, reaching over to turn out the light. "I love snow, but... I like the weather here, too," she admitted with a soft laugh. Shiloh tugged the blankets over them and nodded silently in agreement.

"I love you," Shiloh rasped softly, wrapping her arms around her wife's waist and tangling their legs together. Paisley sighed contently.

"I love you too," the brown eyed girl whispered. "Can you sing?"

"Only for you," Shiloh's voice appeared quietly, and Paisley couldn't help but smile. Soon, Shiloh's hushed singing lulled them both to sleep.

———————

Paisley wasn't sure how late it was when she was stirred awake. Blinking a few times, she turned her head to look at the door, which had opened slightly and caused a beam of light to stream straight across her face. Squinting her eyes, she realized that there was a small figure standing in the doorway.

"Presley?" Paisley asked softly, rubbing her eyes and pushing herself up with an arm. "Is that you?"

"Mama?"

Presley's voice was quiet and shaky, and Paisley immediately knew something was wrong. She sat up quickly, sitting on the edge of the bed and holding out her hands. "What is wrong, little flower?"

It was as if a switch was flipped. As soon as Presley confirmed it was Paisley, she quickly hurried into the room and stood hesitantly in front of her mother. "I miss them."

Paisley didn't need to ask to know what the girl was talking about. There was a long pause of silence, and she glanced over at Shiloh's sleeping figure. She wasn't sure what to say.

Presley didn't notice the hand that slipped out from beneath the blankets. Paisley did, though. Because when she felt something squeeze her hand, she looked down and realized Shiloh hadn't been asleep. Shiloh didn't move, though, and Paisley slowly realized her wife was telling her to do what she had to do.

So Paisley nodded softly, hopping to her feet and pulling on a pair of pajama pants. Presley watched in confusion as the older girl tugged on a pair of boots. "What're you doing?"

"I... I have something to show you," Paisley said softly, standing by the doorway and holding out her hand. Confused, but trusting in her, Presley took a few shy steps forward and allowed Paisley to lead her down the dark hallway, down the stairs, and to the front door.

"Where are we going?" the tiny girl asked, standing on one foot as Paisley helped her slip on her shoes. Paisley paused, glancing up at her and giving her a soft smile.

"For a walk," Paisley nodded. Presley didn't question her, hearing the sincerity in her voice. And soon, the smaller girl was following behind Paisley as they made their way down the sidewalk. Paisley seemed to know exactly where she was going, and Presley followed behind her curiously.

The streetlights lit the way for most of their walk, but soon Paisley veered off onto a smaller pathway and retrieved her phone flashlight from her pocket to light the way. Presley stuck close to her side, holding onto the sleeve of Paisley's hoodie and looking around curiously.

It was hard to see where they were going, but Paisley eventually found what she was looking for. Presley watched as the older girl knelt down and brushed off two plaques on the ground. Shivering, Paisley turned to Presley and shone the light on the graves. "I miss them, too."

It took Presley a few seconds to understand what Paisley had meant. Even Paisley was taken by surprise when the tiny girl practically lept into her arms and held her in a tight hug.

They remained like that for a few moments before Presley pulled away to sit down, carefully reaching out and feeling the cold marble of the graves. She turned to Paisley, tilting her head to the side slightly. "I bet they were super awesome," she nodded. "'Cause' they made you super awesome, too."

"They would have loved you, too," Paisley laughed softly. Moments later, Presley was crawling into her lap, huddling in her arms to stay warm. Paisley held her gently, hoping she'd done the right thing by bringing Presley here.

"You should sing em' a song," Presley whispered, breaking the silence between them. Paisley looked down at her, confused.

"Me?" She raised an eyebrow. "Why?"

"Because you're a good singer. And I like it when you sing in the car," Presley giggled, looking up at the girl hopefully. How was Paisley supposed to say no to that?

"Maybe just once," Paisley sighed softly, giving in. Smiling excitedly, Presley hugged Paisley's arm and looked up at her hopefully.

When Paisley crawled back into bed that night, she felt a pair of arms wrap around her waist and gently pull her closer. Shiloh burned her face in the girl's shoulder, holding her close and smiling softly.

The green eyed girl yawned tiredly, finding Paisley's hand and squeezing it gently. "I'm proud of you," she whispered, making Paisley's cheeks turn bright red. "I know they would be, too."

C H A P T E R   4 8

"Twas' the night before Christmas, when all through the house. Not a creature was stirring, not even a mouse."

Paisley sat on the floor in the living room in her Christmas pajama pants and one of Shiloh's black t-shirts. Presley was in her lap, donned in her colorful Christmas onesie, sucking her thumb, and clutching Sunny tight against her chest.

"The stockings were hung by the chimney with care, in hopes that St. Nicholas soon would be there."

Paisley and Presley were seated on the floor with the rest of the children, who were all looking up at Shiloh. The green eyed girl was sitting in the rocking chair, reading from a storybook and pausing to show the illustrations every time she turned a page.

The young couple had found themselves in charge of putting the children to bed while all the adults gathered in the basement to pass around a few drinks and celebrate. It'd been an exceptionally long day for Shiloh and Paisley, who made the mistake of waiting until Christmas Eve to get a majority of their shopping done.

Now, they'd assisted Daxton in helping them to light the fireplace, and gotten all the kids into their pajamas before gathering them in the living room to read a bedtime story.

"The children were nestled all snug in their beds, while visions of sugarplums danced in their heads."

Shiloh glanced up from the book, meeting Paisley's eyes and giving her a quick wink before turning the page. The brown eyed girl laughed, adjusting Presley in her lap and resting her chin atop the smaller girl's head.

As the story carried on, Presley was nearly falling asleep in Paisley's arms, but refused to let sleep overtake her before all of the other cousins were put to bed. Shiloh finally reached the last page of the story, and Presley hugged Sunny snugly against her chest.

"But I heard him exclaim, as he drove out of sight. 'Merry Christmas to all! And to all a good night!'"

Shiloh closed the book, smiling softly at one of her younger cousins who toddled towards her and held up his arms. After scooping him up into her lap, Shiloh glanced around the small circle of children gathered around her. "Are you guys ready for bed?"

"Is Santa comin'?" Presley yawned and looked up at Paisley quietly.

"I think so," Paisley couldn't help but giggle. "But you all have to be fast asleep first."

"Race you to bed!" one of the younger cousins hopped to his feet and dashed towards the stairs. Before Shiloh or Paisley had a chance to say anything, there was a stampede of children ascending up the staircase.

Presley glanced up, debating following them, but eventually deciding against it and lying her head back on Paisley's shoulder. The brown eyed girl stood up, holding a sleepy Presley, and gave Shiloh a soft smile. "That was easy."

"Tell me about it," Shiloh laughed and stole a quick kiss from Paisley before following them up the stairs. Paisley and Presley soon followed.

Ten minutes later, Presley was bundled under the covers on one of the air mattresses they'd blown up for the visiting family. As always, Sunny was nestled snugly between her shoulder and chin, and both Paisley and Shiloh sat on the edge of the bed.

"Santa's not gonna forget me, right?" Presley's small eyebrows furrowed in concern. "Does he know that we're in Florida?"

"Of course he does, goofball," Shiloh laughed, leaning down to kiss the tiny girl's forehead. "Trust me on this one."

"Promise?" Presley gazed up at her with hopefulness flickering in her eyes. She held slid her hand out from under the blankets and held out her pinky finger.

"Promise," Shiloh laughed softly and locked their fingers together. With her other hand, she found Paisley's pinky behind her and did the same. "Now get to bed so he'll get here quicker," she added with a playful smile.

"No, mommy, wait!" Presley grabbed Shiloh's wrist just as she moved to stand up, looking at her hopefully. "Can you sing? That way I'll fall asleep faster and then Santa will be here," she smiled shyly.

"Of course, babes," Shiloh glanced back to Paisley, mouthing 'only for you' before squeezing her wife's hand.

After their song, planting one last kiss on Presley's cheek, Shiloh and Paisley got up and quietly slipped out of the room, flicking the light off behind them.

After a long day of running back and forth, between cleaning and cooking and running errands, Shiloh was exhausted. It was assumed that Paisley would be, too. But long after Shiloh fell asleep, Paisley found herself still awake, tossing and turning and growing frustrated with herself.

Her thoughts were beginning to cycle around in circles. Groaning, the smaller girl flopped onto her back and covered her face with a pillow. She just wanted to sleep. She didn't want to think about this tonight.

She wasn't sure how much time had passed, all she knew was that it was now 11:28. She had stared at the digital clock beside the bed for too long, feeling an unexplainable tightness in her chest that wouldn't go away.

Eventually, realizing she didn't have any hope of falling asleep like this, Paisley rolled over on her side and pulled the covers down slightly. Shiloh's sleeping face appeared, and she took a few moments to appreciate how peaceful she looked. She always found it weird how she never thought she'd fall in love, and somehow she'd found Shiloh.

"Lo," she whispered tentatively. Her words were hesitant and barely audible. As expected, Shiloh remained fast asleep.

"I-I, uh..." Paisley cleared her throat, reaching out and giving her wife's shoulder a gentle nudge. "Lo," she repeated herself, raising her voice with slightly more assurance.

The dark haired girl didn't budge.

Knowing she'd wimp out if she didn't wake up soon, Paisley quickly cleared her throat and reached out to squeeze Shiloh's shoulder. "Shiloh."

Green eyes immediately fluttered open and looked up at her in confusion. Paisley was finally able to let out a sigh of relief. Even in her sleep, Shiloh knew something was serious when Paisley addressed her by her full name.

"Hm?" Shiloh mumbled sleepily, bringing her hands up to wipe her eyes and tilting her head to the side slightly. "Pais? What are you—?"

"I need to do something," Paisley blurted out, taking Shiloh by surprise. The green eyed girl sat up slightly, just now noticing how distraught her wife appeared. Concerned, she reached out to find Paisley's hand.

"Do what?"

"C-can we just....?" Paisley shook her head, taking a deep breath and meeting Shiloh's eyes once more. "Can we... go for a drive?"

And for some reason, Shiloh knew not to question it. Even Paisley was shocked when the green eyed girl just nodded, squeezing her hand before hopping out of bed to pull on a pair of pajama pants.

"Where do you want to go?" Shiloh asked, blindly searching for her keys on the nightstand. Paisley watched for a few seconds before quickly hopping to her feet and looking at Shiloh timidly.

"Somewhere. Anywhere," she shook her head and ran an anxious hand through her hair. "Just... just for more than..." she glanced over at the clock. 11:36. "For more than... twenty four minutes."

"What?" Shiloh paused to look where Paisley had been looking, raising a confused eyebrow at the clock. "Midnight?"

"Yes," Paisley simply nodded, feeling a rush of adrenaline surge through her. She tugged on her boots before standing the doorway and looking back at Shiloh, almost desperately. "I... I need to break the chain."

"Break the chain?" Shiloh asked, tilting her head to the side. She was confused, but she still followed Paisley quietly down the hallway and down to the front door. She paused, though, and grabbed Paisley's hand before she could open it. "Paisley, what's going on?"

Now it was Shiloh's turn to use first names. The smaller girl tensed, shivering and shaking her head.

"I... I need to know, Lo," she sighed, letting her hands fall to her sides. "Because.... They... it happened..." she pointed to the ground. "Today. And... I just..." she shook her head, bringing her hands up and holding tightly to her hair.

"Hey, breathe," Shiloh reminded her softly. "Breathe, Pais."

"I just... I have to know that it was not supposed to be me," Paisley admitted, feeling Shiloh run her thumb over the back of her hand. "They died and I... I sometimes think it was supposed to be me."

"Like... like the universe made a mistake or... or something," the smaller girl shook her head.

"You're not a mistake," Shiloh shook her head firmly.

"I-I know, but..." Paisley sighed. "I need to break the chain. I need to know if the universe hates me. Lo, I just... I have to know. I can not stop thinking about it. I-I know it is stupid... but—,

"It means something to you," Shiloh interrupted her, taking Paisley's hand off of the door handle and holding it between her own. She met Paisley's eyes, making the smaller girl shiver. "It isn't stupid if it means something to you."

Paisley looked down shyly, settling on giving the girl a soft nod. When Shiloh dropped her hand, she felt her heart drop along with it. That was, until she heard the quiet creak of the door being pulled open.

"C'mon, babe," Shiloh whispered, gently taking Paisley's hand in her own. "We have a chain to break."

And so they drove.

Shiloh started up the car, keeping her fingers laced with Paisley's the entire time. If it mattered to Paisley, it mattered to her. That's how it had always been. Love made her do crazy things, she supposed. Like going on drives at midnight.

"Twelve more minutes," Paisley whispered as they pulled out of the driveway. Shiloh simply nodded. Sometimes all Paisley needed was a hand to hold. Sometimes words didn't need to be exchanged between them.

They drove. And they drove and they drove. Nobody else was crazy enough to be out at midnight on Christmas Eve, and Shiloh realized just how beautiful the tipping point between today and tomorrow was.

"Three minutes," Paisley broke the silence between them. Shiloh wasn't even sure where they were anymore. She'd driven a few blocks and didn't recognize the neighborhood they were in. She felt Paisley's grip on her hand tighten when she pulled out onto a main road, but simply gave the girl's hand a reassuring squeeze.

"Two," Paisley whispered. Shiloh glanced over at her. Her wife's eyes were fixed to the small digital clock on the dashboard. It glowed an eerie blue, reflecting in Paisley's eyes.

"One."

Paisley's hand slipped out of Shiloh's as she clasped her own two hands together. Shiloh watched her, feeling her own heart start to race for some unknown reason. She glanced at the clock. 11:59.

In a last minute decision, Shiloh slowly began to press harder on the gas. They were on a long, open stretch of road, with no one around for miles. She saw Paisley tense beside her and bit her lip when she realized the smaller girl was counting softly under her breath.

When she heard a small 'ten' whispered from the seat beside her, Shiloh sped up the car even more. Paisley's eyes flickered over to look at her in worry, but Shiloh simply shook her head and motioned for her to keep counting.

"Nine." Shiloh rolled down the windows.

"Eight." Shiloh turned on the radio, turning it up so the music was practically pounding through her bloodstream.

Paisley continued whispering, feeling her heart practically beating out of her chest. The wind was whipping through her hair and she felt tears stinging in the corners of her eyes.

"Five, four, thr—,"

"It's midnight!" Paisley was cut off when Shiloh's voice rang out from beside her and the car suddenly swerved to the side of the road, coming to an abrupt stop on the shoulder. The smaller girl's eyes quickly flickered over to the clock.

12:00

Paisley wasn't sure if it was fear, adrenaline, or some greater force compelling her, but as soon as she saw those glowing blue numbers, she burst into tears.

Moments later, Shiloh was scrambling out of the driver's seat and sprinting around to Paisley's side of the car. Just as

Paisley had climbed to her feet, Shiloh was wrapping her in a bone crushing hug, picking her up and spinning her around in a circle.

"It's broken!" Shiloh laughed, letting out the breath she seemed to have been holding in the entire drive. "We broke the chain!"

Once Paisley's feet were planted back on the asphalt, she wiped her eyes and looked up at Shiloh with a look of sheer disbelief on her face. Maybe they were overreacting. But it meant something to her. The numbers on the clock stood for something far greater.

"You did it, Pais!" Shiloh smiled widely, pulling Paisley into her arms and holding her tightly. Paisley couldn't help but laugh. She felt lighter. She could breathe. Sometimes letting go took place in the form of midnight drives and wind blown hair.

"Are you crying?" Paisley asked, wiping her own tear filled eyes and taking a step back to look at Shiloh. Sure enough, the girl's green eyed were glistening with tears.

"A little," Shiloh laughed softly, reaching up to dry her eyes on the back of her sleeve. "If it matters to you, sometimes it matters even more to me."

"I…" Paisley was at a loss for words. She just stared at Shiloh for a few moments. "I love you," she breathed out, falling into yet another hug as her eyes welled up with a different kind of tears. The happy kind. The 'oh my god, I'm constantly falling in love with her' sort of tears.

And as their lips met on the side of the road at midnight, Paisley realized the universe must love her an awful lot if it kept someone like Shiloh by her side.

C H A P T E R   4 9

"I see Parsley."

Paisley whispered softly and pointed up at the sky, tracing the pathway from the north star to the small, almost invisible star that they'd come to recognize. The two girls now sat on top of the parked car, taking the time to appreciate the first few hours of quiet in the morning. They hadn't had much time together the past few days.

"Where?" Shiloh asked, leaning forwards and following Paisley's gaze. The smaller girl reached over, gently tilting Shiloh's head upwards. Pointing to the star, the smaller girl giggled when a soft 'oh' escaped past Shiloh's lips.

"Wait, that reminds me!" Shiloh gasped, startling Paisley beside her. The green eyed girl quickly moved to scramble off the top of the car. Paisley watched her in confusion, but Shiloh was already digging around in the car before she could ask any questions.

"What are you-?" Paisley was cut off when Shiloh hopped back up to her feet, hiding something behind her back and holding out her hand to help Paisley down from the roof of the car. The brown eyed girl raised a questioning eyebrow, hanging her legs down from the edge and allowing Shiloh to help her hop down to the ground. Brushing off her hands, she turned to her wife with a confused look on her face.

"Okay, so... I, uh, I don't really like giving presents in front of everyone," Shiloh stumbled over her words nervously. "I just-I'd rather have it be more private. I don't feel the need to show off... I mean, I want to show you off, but I just-," she grew frustrated with her inability to express herself and blushed nervously.

"I just wanted this to be an *us* kinda thing, if that makes sense," Shiloh laughed, rocking back and forth on her toes.

Both of her hands were holding something behind her back, and Paisley gave her a comforting smile. "I, uh, this is for you," Shiloh added after a few moments of silence, holding out a small box between them.

It made an odd rattling noise, and Paisley tilted her head to the side out of curiosity. Carefully, she took the box into her own hands, growing even more perplexed by the odd weight inside of it.

Shiloh bit her lip and watched nervously as the smaller girl pried the flaps of the box open with one hand. Paisley's face distorted slightly when she peered inside, finding only pieces of shattered glass. She looked up, tilting her head to the side once more. "I-I think it is broken, Lo," she said softly, not wanting to disappoint the older girl.

"Oh no, babe," Shiloh quickly shook her head and took a step forward, opening the box more and glancing back up at Paisley. "It's supposed to be like this. Do you know what it is?"

"Broken glass?" Paisley tried her best not to act confused, but she had no idea what was going on.

"Well, yeah," the green eyed girl laughed. "But it's more than just that. Do you know what it's from?"

Paisley simply shook her head.

"Okay, well, do you remember what we did after the wedding?" Shiloh asked, biting her lip and shaking the box slightly. The glass rattled around and Paisley studied it carefully.

"We did a lot of things, Lo," Paisley laughed quietly, reaching into the box and holding a piece of the glass up to the light carefully. Shiloh watched her with a soft smile. "I do not know."

"Think, Pais. On top of the mantle in the living room," Shiloh reminded her, watching as Paisley's face softened slightly.

"You broke the honeymoon jar?" Paisley's eyebrows raised and she looked at her wife in shock. "But I thought that is where we put the money for the honeymoon?"

"I broke it," Shiloh nodded slowly. Paisley's eyebrows furrowed together.

"Why would you do that?" the smaller girl asked, utterly confused and somewhat concerned that all the hours she'd spent counting coins had gone to waste.

"To get these," Shiloh struggled to hide her smile as she pulled something from the waistband of her pants and handed it to Paisley, taking the box from her hands and setting it down. When she stood back up, the girl's brown eyes were carefully scanning what she'd been handed.

"I... Iceland?" Paisley looked up at Shiloh. "What?"

"They're plane tickets," Shiloh laughed and flipped over the small papers in Paisley's hands.

"Wait... for us?" Paisley's eyes widened. "Plane tickets... for us... for Iceland?"

"There we go," Shiloh giggled and nodded. "I know Iceland sounds weird, but... I've kind of had this obsession with the Northern Lights ever since I was little... and, well, it's the perfect time to see them right now. And I really wanted to share that with you," she nodded quickly. "So I pulled a few strings...I just... the place I booked for us is absolutely incredible. There's so much to do and see. But if you don't want to, I can always f-,"

"Holy shit."

Shiloh's head shot up when she was interrupted, locking gazes with Paisley who was looking at her with wide eyes. She struggled to read her wife's expression for a few moments, and grew concerned when the smaller girl brought one of her hands up to press against her forehead.

"What's wrong?" Shiloh quickly stepped forward and placed a hand on Paisley's arm. "Are you okay?"

"Yeah, I... I think I..." Paisley paused, shaking her head and looking back at Shiloh with a look of awe on her face. "Sometimes I still remember things," she explained, rubbing her forehead and shaking her head. "You... you did a project on Iceland."

"I... yeah, I did," Shiloh laughed. She had completely forgotten about that small detail.

"I remember," Paisley smiled softly. "You said you wanted to go there more than anything."

"Yeah..." Shiloh bit her lip and looked down slightly. "I mean, I wasn't trying to be selfish by doing this... I just really wanted to surprise you, and I thought it'd be perfect for the both of us. I-,"

"Shh," Paisley giggled, placing a hand on Shiloh's arm. "Stop doubting yourself."

"So you like it?" Shiloh looked up hopefully.

Paisley couldn't help but laugh. "I love it."

"Even if I've wanted to go there forever?" Shiloh tilted her head to the side.

"Your dream is my dream," Paisley smiled softly and squeezed Shiloh's hand. "It is perfect, Lo. Absolutely perfect. Positive."

"In that case, there's one more thing," Shiloh bit her lip, taking the tickets from Paisley's hands and flipping them over.

"What?" the smaller girl raised an eyebrow.

"We leave tonight."

"What?!" Paisley gasped, her eyes darting up to meet Shiloh's as the green eyed girl bit her lip worriedly. "Tonight? But what about Presley?"

"I've got it all under control, babe," Shiloh laughed. "We already have our stuff with us. We leave tonight after Presley goes to sleep. Ryland and Nessa is down here visiting their family, too, so they're gonna fly back up with Pres and watch her until we get back. She can't wait."

"You told Presley?" Paisley gasped.

"She's a good secret keeper, what can I say?" Shiloh raised a playful eyebrow. "Is that okay with y—?"

"I can not wait!" Paisley squealed, engulfing Shiloh in a tight hug. "We are finally getting our honeymoon, Lo."

It was already 6am by the time the two girls quietly snuck back in the house. Struggling to hold in their laughter, they hurried back up to Shiloh's bedroom and burrowed back under the covers.

This didn't last long, though. Because only a little over an hour later, soft footsteps padded into the room and paused in front of the bed.

"Mommy?" Presley whispered, tapping Shiloh's shoulder.

Green eyed fluttered open and adjusted to the light, quickly realizing who had awoken her. Even on just a few hours of sleep, Shiloh's mood was through the roof. She smiled at the smaller girl and sat up slightly. "Morning, lovebug."

"Did Santa come?" the smaller girl's voice was soft, and she carefully climbed on the bed beside Shiloh.

"I bet he did," Shiloh giggled. "Once mama wakes up we can go and check."

Shiloh immediately saw the longing in Presley's eyes. Laughing, she shook her head and gave in. "Fine. Just this once we can wake her up, okay?"

Giggling, Presley nodded quickly and hurried off the bed, circling around to Paisley's side and looking at Shiloh once more. "Mama," she whispered, tapping Paisley's shoulder and tilting her head to the side. When Paisley remained fast asleep, Presley nudged her shoulder once more.

"It's gonna take more than that, kiddo," Shiloh laughed. The green eyed girl moved to kneel next to her wife, looking at Presley mischievously. "On the count of three, we tickle her. Okay?"

Presley nodded, giggling quietly when Shiloh held up her fingers and counted down softly. "Three, two... one!"

Within seconds, Paisley was squirming awake, looking at Shiloh in complete shock. Just as she was about to snap at her wife for waking her up so abruptly, she noticed the smaller girl giggling beside her and bouncing up and down in excitement.

"She's awake! Now we can go see if Santa came!" Presley squealed, hurrying towards the door. Shiloh shot Paisley an apologetic look.

"It was all her idea," Shiloh teased, kissing Paisley's cheek before slipping out of bed. "C'mon, babe. Santa came while we were asleep."

Soon enough, Shiloh, Paisley, Presley, and the rest of Shiloh's extended family were seated around the tree. Everyone was already passing around presents, and Shiloh had been extremely grateful when she realized even her aunts and uncles had placed a present under the tree for Presley.

Presley currently sat in Paisley's lap, flipping through a large sticker book she had gotten. Noticing this, Shiloh smiled softly and leaned over to whisper something in the smaller girl's ear. Immediately, Presley's face lit up and she hopped to her feet, giving Shiloh a thumbs up before scurrying out of the room.

"Wha...?" Paisley tilted her head to the side and looked at Shiloh in confusion. The green eyed girl simply signaled for her to wait, letting a few seconds of silence pass before she heard Presley's tiny footsteps reproaching down the hallway.

"Happy Birthday!" Presley smiled excitedly, hopping down beside Paisley and handing her a present wrapped in bright yellow wrapping paper. Shiloh leaned down and whispered something else in her ear.

"Happy Christmas!" the smaller girl giggled softly and looked at Paisley hopefully. "It's your present," she whispered.

"It is?" Paisley tilted her head to the side and looked to Shiloh, who simply gave her a soft nod.

"From me and Presley," Shiloh smiled, kissing Presley's forehead and pulling her into her lap. "Go ahead, babe. Open it."

A small smile spread across Paisley's face, and she carefully tore through the wrapping paper. She raised a curious eyebrow and studied the book in her hands. As soon as her eyes scanned over the title, she looked up at Shiloh in shock.

"What's it say?" Shiloh laughed softly and raised an eyebrow. Paisley bit her lip to try and hide her smile.

"The Adventures of Wolf and Flower Princess," Paisley giggled, running her fingers over the cover and looking at Shiloh in shock.

"Hey, don't look at me," Shiloh laughed and nodded to Presley. "This one was the creative genius behind it all."

Paisley flipped through the pages, giggling at the illustrations that were a mixture of Shiloh and Presley's handiwork. "I love it," she smiled. "Thank you," she leaned down and kissed Presley's cheek, ruffling her hair before moving up to cup Shiloh's cheek and place a gentle kiss to her lips.

"You have to open yours, now," Paisley nodded, setting her book down carefully and crawling over to retrieve something wrapped in silver wrapping paper and tucked underneath the tree. Shiloh watched as Paisley hurried back over to her and placed the small, rectangular box in her lap.

The two girls now sat alone in the back of the room, for Presley had been distracted by Maggie handing her a self-wrapped present. Shiloh smiled softly, turning the box around in her hands. "I thought we said no presents this year?"

"I have to get you a present," Paisley rolled her eyes. "You did not follow that rule, either."

Laughing softly, Shiloh reached out and squeezed Paisley's hand before carefully tearing at the wrapping paper. Paisley watched nervously as Shiloh opened the small box, becoming confused at the contents inside.

The green eyed girl carefully removed the silver flower, studying it in her hands and realizing it was a daisy.

"It is a flower," Paisley whispered with a soft nod. "For us."

"For us?" Shiloh tilted her head to the side.

"Yeah. For us," Paisley carefully took the metal flower from Shiloh's hands and studied it. "It... it is made out of titanium. Nothing can break it. Like us." Her eyes flickered up to meet Shiloh's hopefully. "Nothing can break us."

"Oh my god," Shiloh whispered, suddenly understanding the meaning Paisley had placed behind the flower. She took it back into her own hands, a bittersweet nostalgic feeling washing over her. "That's so... perfect."

"Really?" Paisley's eyes filled with hope and Shiloh laughed softly.

"Of course it is," she whispered. "How'd you find this?"

"I did not," Paisley shook her head. "I made it."

"You made it?"

"Yeah," Paisley nodded. "Maia and Toby helped me. It took a long time," she laughed softly.

"No one's ever done something so thoughtful for me," Shiloh whispered. Even if it was just a metal flower, the meaning and effort behind it made her heart swell. "Thank you."

"I wanted you to know," Paisley shrugged. "And this can help remind you. So you never forget."

"Thank you," Shiloh whispered, leaning over and cupping Paisley's cheek. "I love you."

"I love you too, Lo," Paisley giggled, kissing her quickly before they were interrupted by Presley hurrying over to show them the new stuffed animal she'd gotten.

"And you'll take lots of pictures for me?"

Shiloh and Paisley lay on her bed with Presley sandwiched in between them. All three girls were exhausted after the usual Christmas festivities. Now, they were spending time with Presley before they had to leave. Both girls were absolutely giddy with excitement over their honeymoon.

"Of course, goofball," Shiloh laughed, rolling over on her side and poking the tiny girl's nose. "Mama and I will call you every morning and tell you all about it."

"But not too early, right? Cause' Auntie Nessa says Rya sleeps a lot," Presley giggled, crinkling her nose and playfully pulling the covers up to hide her face.

"Not too early," Shiloh nodded, glancing at Paisley who was struggling to keep her eyes open. "Got it."

"You have to go on a plane in the dark?" Presley asked, tilting her head to the side.

"Yes ma'am," Shiloh nodded softly. "And when you wake up, Ryland and Vanessa will be here to pick you up. You'll have tons of fun with them."

"Yeah," Presley's face lit up. "They're super fun. Rya says I get to paint her nails. And that we're gonna have ice cream sundaes and watch movies all night."

Shiloh couldn't help but laugh, knowing that was exactly what Ryland would do. She reached out, smoothing Presley's hair out of her face. "That sounds like so much fun, babes."

"You're gonna come back for me, right?"

Even Paisley, who had been half asleep, raised her head upon hearing Presley's question. Immediately, she exchanged glances with Shiloh, who looked just as confused.

"Of course we will, Pres. You're our daughter," Shiloh laughed nervously. "We're always going to come back for you."

Paisley nodded in agreement. Both girls were taken by surprise when Presley shot up out of bed and looked back and forth from the two girls. A few seconds of silence passed before she finally turned back to Shiloh and tilted her head to the side. "I am?"

"Huh?"

"I'm your daughter?" Presley glanced back over at Paisley, who glanced at Shiloh. They both nodded.

"Well, yeah. That's you, kiddo," Shiloh laughed, reaching out and ruffling the smaller girl's hair. "You were meant to be with us. I have no doubt about it. We've just gotta wait a few months before it's official."

"For real?" Presley's eyes widened.

"For real," Paisley rasped, speaking up for the first time since they'd come into the room.

"Yeah, you're stuck with us," Shiloh giggled and proceeded to tickle the smaller girl until she fell back onto the bed.

"Now get to bed, little flower," Paisley whispered, pressing a kiss to Presley's cheek. "You have a busy day tomorrow."

"You should sing a bedtime song," Presley yawned, moving under the covers and looking up at the two girls hopefully. "I really like it when you do that."

Glancing over at Paisley and lacing their fingers together, Shiloh nodded softly. "Only for you," she said, almost inaudibly, so only her wife could hear her. Paisley struggled to hide her smile.

A little less than an hour later, Paisley was coaxed awake by Shiloh. Both girls had ended up falling asleep alongside Presley. Luckily, Shiloh had woken up with more than enough time for the to make it to the airport.

"Babe, c'mon," Shiloh giggled when Paisley groaned and rolled over to hide her face in the pillow.

"Pais, babe, we have a plane to catch," Shiloh sat down on the edge of the bed and gently brushed her wife's hair out of her face. "Remember?"

Shiloh rolled her eyes half heartedly when she heard muffled laughter against the pillow. Sighing, she stood up and scooped Paisley up into her arms. The smaller girl squealed, quickly clamping her mouth shut when she realized Presley was still asleep.

Carrying her wife bridal style, Shiloh set Paisley down on the hallway and gave her a soft smile. "C'mon, sleeping beauty, I have a honeymoon to attend. Care to join me?" she raised a playful eyebrow and held out her hand.

"It would be an honor," Paisley giggled, playing along and taking Shiloh's hand.

And so on that night, in the chilly winter air, Paisley and Shiloh disappeared down the hallway and down the front walkway to yet another adventure they'd never forget.

C H A P T E R   5 0

It was nearly eleven o'clock at night when a knock at the apartment door demanded Ryland's attention. Tossing her phone aside, the tall girl strolled over to the door and pulled it open with a soft smile.

There stood Shiloh and Paisley, arms piled full of bags, and hair tousled and wavy. Ryland raised an eyebrow. "You look like death."

"Thanks," Shiloh laughed, shaking her head. "Our flight got delayed twice. We're exhausted."

"Yeah, well, y—,"

"Mommy! Mama!" a tiny voice appeared from the other room. Moments later, quick footsteps echoed into the foyer and Shiloh had to drop her suitcase in order to catch the small girl who practically leapt into her arms.

"You came back!" Presley giggled, throwing her arms around Shiloh's neck and holding her tightly.

"I thought you were supposed to be in bed?" Shiloh raised an eyebrow at Ryland from over Presley's shoulder.

"I'm too excited," Presley smiled widely, reaching over to Paisley. Shiloh passed the small girl over to her wife, who quickly returned her hug and kissed the tiny girl's cheek.

"C'mon. The kid has a birthday in an hour. I figured it was only fair that she got to stay up until her parents got home, geez," Ryland chuckled, nudging Shiloh's shoulder.

Moments later, Presley was being passed back to Shiloh, and Paisley was tossing her suitcase aside. Shiloh raised an eyebrow, watching as her wife yawned, stretched out her arms, and trudged towards the staircase.

"I need a bed," Paisley mumbled, giving them a sleepy smile before slowly making her way up the stairs.

"You have to tell me all about it," Presley gushed, looking at Shiloh hopefully. And, as Shiloh had learned long ago, there was no saying no to that pleading pair of brown eyes.

"Well, what do you wanna hear about first?" Shiloh sighed, letting her bag slide off of her shoulder and lay near the door. Ryland gave the girl a soft smile before closing the door behind the green eyed girl, who was making her way over to the couch.

"Everything," Presley looked up at her with wide eyes. Sighing, Shiloh slumped back on the couch and pulled the smaller girl into her lap.

"Well, let's see..." she wiped her eyes, giving her daughter a kiss on the cheek before beginning her story.

"Shiloh."

"Shiloh... come on," Ryland huffed, grabbing the girl's shoulders and shaking her until green eyes fluttered open. The dark haired girl groaned, pushing Ryland off of her and looking around in confusion.

"It's 1am, Shy, I figured you'd be upstairs in bed by now," Ryland laughed under her breath before motioning to the smaller girl curled up against Shiloh's side.

"Oh, shit," the green eyed girl mumbled, wiping her eyes and glancing down at Presley, who was still fast asleep. Meanwhile, Ryland glanced at the doorway and then back to Shiloh.

"Get your butt upstairs, Everest," she laughed squeezing Shiloh's shoulder.

Nodding, the green eyed girl carefully scooped Presley up into her arms and carried them both upstairs. She was so exhausted that she didn't even think about anything else but collapsing onto the first bed she found.

"Mommy?"

Shiloh was awoken the next morning by Presley, who sat cross legged in front of her, gazing at her mother curiously.

"Hm?" Shiloh mumbled, blinking a few times to let her eyes adjust to the morning light that had made its way into the room. It took her a moment to realize where they were. Back in New York.

"Is it my birthday yet?" the tiny girl looked at her with hopefulness flickering in her eyes. A small smile made its way across Shiloh's face.

"I think it is, lovebug," she laughed, holding out her arms to the smaller girl. "C'mere."

Presley's face immediately broke out into a wide smile and she hurried across the bed, practically diving into Shiloh's arms and engulfing her into a hug. The green eyed girl fell backwards onto the bed, feeling Presley giggle against her shoulder.

"Happy birthday, Pres," Shiloh laughed softly, pushing herself back up and kissing the top of her daughter's head. "How's it feel to be 4 years old? I wanna hear all about it."

One thing Shiloh had decided as they embarked on this journey with Presley, was that she wanted her daughter to be a master in the art of self-expression. She wanted Presley to pay attention to detail, to question things... to tell stories. And so she did her best to encourage her daughter's active mind. Which is why she allowed Presley to tell her all about the vivid dream she'd had the night before.

"-and there was tons and tons of lights. Everywhere," the smaller girl giggled, stretching her arms out to show Shiloh.

"But then I woke up. And I had to wake you up to make sure it was my birthday." She giggled, clasping her hands together and looking at Shiloh happily.

"You've got a pretty awesome day ahead of you, don't you?" Shiloh raised an eyebrow. "How about you go wake up Ryland so we can all be ready for when your party guests get here?"

Presley's face lit up upon remembering her party, and she nodded excitedly. "Is Lucas going to be there, too?"

"You betcha'," Shiloh laughed when Presley hopped off of the bed, clapping her hands together before scurrying off down the hallway to awaken Ryland from her slumber.

Shiloh, on the other hand, ran a hand through her tousled morning hair and made her way downstairs. Vanessa's running shoes were nowhere to be found, meaning she had already gone out on a run.

However, there were a pair of bright yellow slippers in front of the stove in the kitchen, and Shiloh smiled contently when she realized who they belonged to. She was met with a wave of nostalgia, remembering the days she and Paisley had lived in this apartment along with their three roommates. Things had sure changed since then.

Paisley, clad in an oversized blue hoodie and pajama pants, stood in front of a glass bowl. She held an egg in her hand, studying it before glancing at the bowl once more. Shiloh raised an eyebrow.

"Good mornin'," she rasped, walking up behind her wife and wrapping her arms around her waist. "Sleep well?"

Startled, Paisley jumped at first. She nearly dropped the egg, but quickly realized who it was and laughed softly. "Kinda," she shrugged, turning her head to kiss Shiloh's cheek. "Did you?"

"Yeah," Shiloh yawned, making both of them laugh. She turned her attention to the bowl, glancing at the box of pancake mix and then back to Paisley. "Making breakfast?"

"I-I... yeah," Paisley sighed, holding up the egg and looking at Shiloh hopefully. "Help?"

Shiloh took the egg from her wife's hand and raised an eyebrow at her. "Crack it?"

"Yeah," Paisley laughed, hanging her head down and shrugging. "I jammed my finger in the door last night and... it hurts," she bit her lip and looked at Shiloh hopefully, quickly shoving her hands into her pockets.

"How many do you need?" Shiloh laughed, not thinking much of Paisley's clumsiness.

"Three," Paisley giggled, leaning against the island and watching as Shiloh took over cooking for her, cracking three eggs into the bowl and mixing it carefully.

"You excited for the party?" Shiloh asked, making light conversation as she poured some of the mix into the pan and let it sit. "Presley's currently waking the beast."

"Ryland?" Paisley couldn't help but laugh, playing with the sleeves of her hoodie. "When is everyone getting here?"

"Noon, I think," Shiloh nodded. She grew confused when moments later, Paisley gasped from behind her and quickly hopped to her feet.

"We have an hour, Lo," Paisley looked at her worriedly. Shiloh's eyes widened and she immediately turned to look at the clock, realizing what Paisley had said was true. Luckily, she quickly kicked into game mode.

"Girls!" Shiloh called, cupping her hands over her mouth. "We have an hour until everyone gets here!"

"Ryland! You're in charge of getting both of you dressed!" she added, glancing back to Paisley and biting her lip. "You finish making breakfast, Nessa's in charge of decorations as soon as she gets home. And I..." she bit her lip, glancing to Paisley. "I'll go get the cake and our... you know."

"I know," Paisley giggled, giving Shiloh a quick nod. "Hurry."

"Got it," Shiloh stole a quick kiss before grabbing her jacket and hurrying out the door.

Shiloh arrived back just in time.

"Got it?" Paisley asked, opening the door to find a breathless Shiloh. The green eyed girl quickly nodded, looking past Paisley to scan the apartment.

"Where is she?"

"Upstairs," Paisley nodded quickly. "Ryland is keeping her busy."

"Got it," Shiloh nodded, quickly hurrying into the laundry room to hide her belongings before reappearing in the kitchen with the cake, where Paisley quickly handed her a plate of pancakes.

"I will put it on the table. Eat," she nodded, giving Shiloh a stern look. The green eyed girl just nodded, quickly finding a fork and proceeding to scarf down her breakfast as fast as she could.

As soon as she was finished eating, Shiloh rushed upstairs to get dressed, nearly knocking over Vanessa who was stringing pink streamers around the railing. She flashed her friend an apologetic smile before hurrying into the bedroom.

Fifteen minutes later, Shiloh made her way downstairs just as their first guests arrived. Presley scrambled past her when they heard the knock at the door, clapping her hands excitedly.

"Lucas! Look! You have to come see my cake!" Presley exclaimed, looking up at Maia hopefully. Laughing, the girl set Lucas down on the ground and watched as Presley excitedly led him into the dining room.

"How was the honeymoon?" Maia asked, hugging Paisley before moving to hug Shiloh. The two girls exchanged glances, smiling softly.

"Amazing," Paisley nodded slowly. "It was so... breathtaking."

"Yeah," Shiloh laughed, scooting over and wrapping an arm around Paisley's waist. "It really was. I can't even find the words to describe it."

"Mama! Come look!"

Paisley glanced at Shiloh, laughing softly before squeezing her hand and disappearing into the other room.

A short while later, Leah and Troy arrived with a handful of presents, adding them to the pile and greeting Presley. Eventually, they all gathered around the dining room table while Shiloh and Paisley hurried to the door to pay and tip the delivery man. They returned with three boxes of pizza, dispersing slices to everyone at the table.

Finally, when they finished eating, Paisley and Shiloh both exchanged knowing glances. "Are you ready to open presents?" Shiloh asked, raising an eyebrow at Presley, whose head immediately shot up.

"Right now?" the smaller girl's eyes widened hopefully.

"Right now," Paisley laughed, nodding towards the collection of presents they had laid out against the wall.

"Me first! Me first!" Ryland raised her hand, hurrying over to collect her boxes. Rolling her eyes, Vanessa followed to help her.

"Don't be fooled," Vanessa laughed and shook her head. "This is from both of us."

Presley's eyes lit up and she took the small, rectangular gift from them. She glanced around at everyone quietly before tearing at the paper, tossing it aside to reveal a cream colored box. Everyone else looked at Ryland and Vanessa, curious to see what they'd given her.

Slowly, the tiny girl lifted the lid from the box. Moments later, her face lit up, and she gasped in excitement. Everyone else crowded closer to try and get a peek at what she'd received.

"They're beautiful," Presley whispered in awe, now holding up a pair of pastel pink ballet slippers. Everyone else turned to look at Ryland and Vanessa in confusion.

"Didn't you already get her a pair like... last month?" Leah asked, raising an eyebrow at their friends.

"Yeah, but those were fake ones," Vanessa laughed, shaking her head. "These? These are real."

"But they come with one condition," Ryland spoke up. This took Presley's attention away from the slippers, and the small girl looked up at Ryland curiously.

"You, my little friend, can wear those slippers as long as you agree to throw on a leotard and tights and attend ballet classes at the studio twice a week," Ryland wiggled her eyebrows at the smaller girl, whose eyes immediately widened.

"Can I, mommy?" Presley hopped out of her chair, looking at Paisley and Shiloh hopefully. "Mama, can I?"

Green eyes met brown eyes before they both nodded softly, causing Presley to gasp excitedly and dart over to crush both Ryland and Vanessa in a tight hug.

"I'm going to be a real ballerina," Presley breathed, a wide smile on her face as she clutched her new ballet shoes against her chest.

"You didn't have to do that," Shiloh whispered to Vanessa as Presley got Ryland's help putting on her slippers. Norman just shrugged and gave Shiloh a soft smile.

"We wanted to," she laughed, watching as Presley wiggled her toes impatiently before Ryland adjusted her shoes, giving her a thumbs up. The tiny girl spun around in a circle before clasping her hands together and climbing back up on her chair.

"I don't know how I'll ever be able to outdo that," Maia laughed, carrying a larger box over and setting it down in front of Presley. "But this is from me and Toby. Happy birthday, kid."

Presley smiled shyly, studying the shape of the box before ripping into it. Moments later, Shiloh was kneeling down next to her and looking up at Maia with a surprised smile on her face.

"What is it?" Presley asked, giggling softly.

"It's an easel," Shiloh explained, turning the box around and pointing to the picture on the front. "For you to paint on."

"Like mommy," Paisley spoke up, earning a shy smile from Shiloh.

"And it's the perfect size for you!" Shiloh laughed, reaching out to brush Presley's hair out of her face.

"Can I put it next to yours?" Presley asked with an excited smile, hopping out of her chair to get a closer look. "And can I paint with you?"

"Of course, bug," Shiloh giggled, mouthing a 'thank you' in Maia and Toby's direction. "I'll teach you everything there is to know."

"Thank you!" Presley smiled widely, hurrying over to hug both Maia and Toby. Meanwhile, Shiloh studied the easel even more, and Paisley had to remind her that it was a present for Presley and not her.

"Oh, one more thing," Maia added, nodding down at Presley. "Lucas has something for you. Sit back down and close your eyes."

Curious, Presley hurried back over to her chair and covered her eyes with her hands. "I'm closin' em'!" she giggled in anticipation. Maia knelt down in Lucas in her arms, and moments later Presley felt something being tugged onto her head.

"Go ahead and open them," Maia laughed softly, setting Lucas down. Presley opened her eyes, attempting to look up at her head and giggling when she realized she couldn't see it. She hopped out of her chair, running over to the mirror in the other room and gasping when she saw the pastel green beanie that sat atop her head.

"It's like mama's!" Presley beamed, running back into the dining room and looking at Paisley. "See, mama? It's like yours!"

"I see," Paisley giggled, kneeling down and fixing the beanie on her daughter's head. "You look adorable, little flower."

Meanwhile, Shiloh glanced over at Maia and raised a questioning eyebrow, simply earning a soft laugh from the other girl. "It was bound to happen eventually," Maia laughed, nudging her friend's shoulder.

"Thank you, Lukey," Presley giggled, grasping the toddler's face between her hands and pressing a quick kiss to his forehead. Paisley and Shiloh glanced at one another, feeling a wave of nostalgia rush over them.

CHAPTER 51

Meanwhile, Troy nudged Leah's side, making her quickly realize something and hurry to retrieve a small, flat box from the collection of gifts. Shiloh ushered Presley to go sit back down, and watched as Leah set the box in front of her with a soft smile.

"This is from us," she nodded back to Troy. Presley nodded, quickly tearing into the paper. Everyone watched as she pulled out a pink t-shirt with something written on the front. Confused, the smaller girl held it up and tilted her head to the side.

"What's it say, mama?" Presley asked, turning to Paisley who sat beside her. The small brunette scooted closer, narrowing her eyes to read it and gasping.

"No," Paisley's jaw dropped and she immediately turned to look at Leah, whose face grew bright red.

"What?" Ryland and Vanessa immediately grew confused, leaning over the table to try and read it. Shiloh hurried over to see what all the commotion was about.

"Best Aunt Ever," Shiloh read off the decorative lettering on the shirt, furrowing her eyebrows in confusion. A few moments later, everyone at the table was gasping and whipping their heads around to look at Leah.

"What's wrong?" Presley asked, still not understanding. Giggling, Paisley knelt down and whispered something in her ear.

"You're gonna have a baby?!" Presley practically leapt out of her chair, scrambling over to Leah and looking at her in shock. "You have to sit down! And…. and… wait here!"

While Presley disappeared out of the room, everyone else looked at Leah and Troy in shock.

"You're serious?" Vanessa asked, being the first one to break the silence. The moment Leah nodded, they were all smothering her in a large group hug.

"I'm so happy for you, oh my god," Shiloh laughed. "Do you-?"

"Be careful!" Presley's voice echoed around the room. "You're gonna hurt her!"

The moment everyone let go of Leah, Presley hurried over and took her hand, leading her over to a chair and making her sit down. "You've gotta drink lots of water," she nodded, handing Leah the water bottle she retrieved.

Shiloh and Paisley exchanged glances, enamored by Presley's concern for the older girl.

After things settled down and Leah explained how they had just found out, Shiloh and Paisley glanced at one another knowingly. Paisley smiled softly at her wife, nudging her side to signal for her to speak up.

"There's one more present," Shiloh added softly, drawing everyone's attention once more. Surprised, Presley looked up and tilted her head to the side in curiosity.

"Just... wait here," Shiloh pointed to Presley before slipping out of the room. In the meantime, everyone else turned to look at Paisley. Ryland raised an eyebrow at her brown eyed friend.

"Shh," Paisley shook her head, refusing to give her friends any answers. A minute or so later, Shiloh reappeared, carrying a large box wrapped in blue and yellow polka dotted wrapping paper. She carried it carefully, gently setting it down on the table in front of Presley.

"Slow, okay? Open it here," Shiloh explained, tapping the lid. Curious, Presley nodded, standing up in her chair and looking at Shiloh for approval before carefully lifting the lid from the top of the box.

"What?" Presley whispered, her jaw dropping open as she pushed the lid aside. Shiloh and Paisley both exchanged amused looks. "Is it real?" the smaller girl looked at Shiloh with wide eyes.

"Of course it is," Shiloh giggled, nodding towards the box. "Go on, Pres."

A wide smile formed on Presley's face as she carefully reached down into the box. A collective gasp echoed around the room when she gently lifted a small, brown and white colored kitten into her arms. Complete with a bright red bow around its neck.

Presley's face seemed to be permanently stuck in an expression of pure adoration, and she quickly turned to look at Shiloh and Paisley. "This is my present?" she asked, almost in disbelief.

The two girls exchanged glances, laughing softly. "He's all yours, kiddo," Shiloh nodded, unable to keep the smile off of her face when she saw how shocked Presley was.

"He's mine?"

"He is yours," Paisley giggled, amused by her disbelief. "We... we decided that Wolf needed someone to take over for him."

"He's mine?" Presley repeated herself, sitting down carefully and cradling the tiny animal in her arms. "What's his name?"

"That's up to you," Shiloh shot Paisley a smile before kneeling down beside Presley's chair and smoothing out the kitten's fur. "Your cat, your choice."

"Do you have any ideas?" Paisley added, kneeling beside Shiloh and resting her head on her wife's shoulder. She couldn't help but grow amused by how gentle Presley was being with the small animal.

The smaller girl paused to think for a few moments before her face lit up and she nodded quickly. "Elvis," she announced proudly, a shy smile on her face.

"Elvis," Shiloh laughed, shaking her head. "Presley and Elvis?"

"Perfect," Presley smiled widely, looking down at the tiny kitten and struggling to hold in her excitement. "He's perfect."

"We figured you'd like him," Shiloh smiled, reaching out to brush Presley's pigtails out of her face.

"Thank you sooooooo much," Presley giggled, looking back and forth between Shiloh and Paisley. She moved to get up, but quickly realized she couldn't hug them and hold Elvis at the same time. Giggling, she leaned in a placed a kiss on each of their cheeks before sitting back and giving them a shy smile.

"You are welcome, sooooo much," Paisley laughed, squeezing Presley's shoulder. "Happy birthday, little flower."

"Lucas, c'mere!" Presley glanced behind her and motioned for the toddler to come join her. "You've gotta' meet Elvis. Just be gentle, okay?"

Exchanging glances, Shiloh wrapped an arm around Paisley's waist and pulled her into her side, pressing a kiss to her wife's temple. Things were only going up from here.

"Holy shit, it's getting late," Shiloh spoke up, glancing at the clock from her seat at the dining room table. Presley's birthday lunch had ended up turning into a birthday dinner, and now it was nearly nine o'clock.

Everyone but Paisley and the kids were seated around the dining room table, making light conversation and remembering old stories. Meanwhile, Paisley had slipped off with Presley and Lucas to try out her new toys in the living room.

"We should get going," Maia laughed, sitting up and stretching out her arms. Leah and Troy both nodded in agreement, and soon everyone was heading into the living room to see the guests off.

"Oh my gosh," Maia whispered, putting out her arm to stop Shiloh. The green eyed girl raised an eyebrow, following Maia's gaze and cupping her hand over her mouth when she saw what the girl had been looking at.

A rerun of Friends was playing on the TV, but the audience was fast asleep. Paisley help Lucas in her lap, with body slumped over slightly and her head resting against the arm of the couch. Presley lay on the couch, curled up against Paisley and using her lap as a pillow. One of her hands was holding her thumb in her mouth, and the other was clutching Paisley's thumb.

"Long day," Toby chuckled, carefully bending down to retrieve his son from the couch without disturbing the other two girls. Shiloh and Maia exchanged glances, laughing softly at the sight.

"Text me when you get home, yeah?" Shiloh looked at both the couples as they stood in the doorway, who agreed quietly. "Thank you guys for coming. I know Presley loves having you guys around."

"And we loving having you around," Leah smiled softly. "All three of you. Take care, yeah?"

"You too," Shiloh laughed, rolling her eyes. "Troy, you make sure she doesn't stress herself out to much. Take care of your girl."

"Will do," the taller man laughed, squeezing Leah's shoulder.

After they all said their goodbyes, Vanessa and Ryland gave Shiloh a soft wave before disappearing upstairs and heading into their respective bedrooms.

Yawning, Shiloh made her way into the kitchen to begin cleaning up the dishes from that night. She was humming softly to herself when she heard quiet footsteps enter the room, and a pair of arms gently wrap around her waist.

"Finally decided to join us?" Shiloh teased, feeling Paisley sigh contently and rest her chin on her shoulder.

"I was tired," the smaller girl laughed quietly, shaking her head.

"Is Pres still asleep?" Shiloh asked, setting the dishes in the sink and turning around to face Paisley, resting her hands on her wife's shoulders. Paisley nodded, and Shiloh planted a soft kiss on her lips before nodding.

"I'm gonna take her up to bed and when I come back down we can finish cleaning up," Shiloh smiled, playfully curling a strand of Paisley's hair around her finger and kissing her cheek before slipping into the living room.

Scooping her sleeping daughter up from the couch, Shiloh quietly made her way upstairs and tucked Presley into the spare bedroom, kissing her forehead before changing into something more comfortable and heading back down the spiral staircase to join Paisley in the kitchen.

Before she could get to the kitchen, however, Paisley practically appeared out of nowhere and handed Shiloh her hoodie. Raising an eyebrow, the green eyed girl looked at her wife in confusion.

"Put it on," Paisley urged her, holding the hoodie out hopefully. "I want to go for a walk."

"Now?" Shiloh glanced at her phone. "It's almost ten."

"Yes, now," Paisley laughed nervously and bit her lip. "Please? I... I just... please?"

"Okay...?" Shiloh laughed, taking the hoodie and quickly shrugging it on. Paisley smiled hopefully, hurrying over to the door to tug her shoes on. Confused, but intrigued, Shiloh followed her and did the same.

"Where are we going?" Shiloh asked, hopping down the hallway after Paisley as she struggled to tug her boot on. Once she finally got it, she jogged to catch up to her wife, who was hurrying towards the front door of the building.

"The park," Paisley nodded, pushing through the large doors and shivering in the brisk winter air. Shiloh eventually fell into pace beside her, watching her wife in confusion.

"Why the park?" Shiloh asked, following Paisley across the dark street and down the narrow sidewalk. She shivered, realizing it was considerably colder there than it had been in Florida. Or Iceland, for that matter.

"Stop asking questions," Paisley laughed, hurrying ahead of Shiloh once more as they arrived at the stone pathway that led through the park. "You will see."

Amused, Shiloh hurried to keep up with Paisley, who was practically jogging by now. Confused but curious, Shiloh reached out to grab her shoulder. Paisley paused, turning around to look at her wife.

"What's going on?" Shiloh asked, suddenly growing concerned when she saw how nervous Paisley appeared. The smaller girl simply shook her head.

"Just a little bit further, Lo," Paisley shoved one of her hands in her pocket and grabbed Shiloh's hand with the other, leading her further down the parkway. Shiloh stayed quiet until they came to a stop in front of a familiar bench.

"Here," Paisley nodded, sitting down on the bench and pulling her legs underneath her. Even more intrigued, Shiloh sat down beside her and studied the surrounding area, which was dimly lit with the small lights that lined the pathway.

"What about it?" Shiloh asked, running a hand through her hair and looking around.

"This is where it all started," Paisley sighed, a small smile tugging at her lips. Shiloh tilted her head to the side.

"You mean...?"

"Us," Paisley nodded, confirming Shiloh's question. "It is like... our park. It is special to me."

"Me too, Pais," Shiloh laughed, scooting over and laying her arm across Paisley's shoulders. "Why'd you bring me out here in the freezing cold at night, though?"

"I did something crazy," Paisley blurted out, causing Shiloh to turn at look at her with concern flickering in her eyes. Biting her lip, Paisley looked down and toyed with the long sleeves of her hoodie.

"You what?" Shiloh asked, reaching out to tilt Paisley's chin so the girl would meet her eyes. "Paisley, what's going on?"

"It is nothing bad, Lo," Paisley laughed, brushing Shiloh's arm away. "Do not worry."

"Well then what is it?" Shiloh asked, growing even more confused. Taking a deep breath, the smaller girl turned to face Shiloh, pausing a moment to compose her thoughts.

"I, uh... Last night... I did something," Paisley bit her lip. "I could not sleep and I... I got Ryland to help me with something."

"With what?"

"I... I did... I got..." Paisley stumbled over her words, eventually growing frustrated and giving up on trying to explain herself. Instead, she freed her hand from her pocket and held it out in-between them, biting her lip and looking up at Shiloh.

"You hurt your finger?" Shiloh asked, eyeing the bandage on Paisley's finger. When she saw the hesitation in Paisley's face, her eyes were widening in realization a few moments later. "Oh."

"You really...?" Shiloh paused, reaching out and gently picking at the edge of the bandage. "Can I?" she asked, looking at Paisley for approval. Once the smaller girl nodded, Shiloh carefully peeled the wrap off of Paisley's hand.

"It is a star," Paisley whispered softly. Shiloh nodded, holding up Paisley's hand and studying the tiny, star shaped tattoo that sat just above where her pinky finger met her palm.

"I-I drew it... and then... Ryland took me out and we... yeah," Paisley laughed softly, growing shy. "I just... I wanted to have something. I named it Shiloh," her cheeks turned bright pink and she laughed shyly. "Because you are my star."

"I am?" Shiloh whispered, her eyes flickering up to meet Paisley's. The smaller girl nodded, laughing softly.

"Yeah," Paisley nodded. "You... when it is dark, you are still there. Like a star. I can always follow you when I need to go home. And... and I can always count on you to be there."

Paisley lifted her hand, looking at the tattoo and smiling softly. "I learned once that stars die. And that made me really... really sad. Because I do not think things that are that beautiful should ever disappear. But... but then I learned that even when stars die, we still see their light... for a long time. And... I think that makes a lot of sense," she paused, looking up at the sky and sighing softly.

"Because even if you are not next to me, I still feel you. I... I still see you in everything. I... I met you, and you changed me. It is like... like you came into my life and suddenly everything I love turned into you," Paisley blushed and looked down at her hands. "I hear you in music, I see you in the sky.... you are everywhere, Lo. You are my star."

"And... and sometimes I think I do not thank you enough," Paisley looked up, meeting Shiloh's eyes and laughing shyly. "Because you have done so much for me. And sometimes I do not think you understand... because I love you, I do, Lo. I am here because I love you. And I will always be here."

"You know I'd do it all over again, right?" Shiloh's voice was barely a whisper when she spoke up once more, feeling tears glistening in her eyes. "You know that, don't you Paisley? You know I don't regret a second that I've ever spent with you, right?"

"I-I..." Paisley bit her lip, growing shy and looking down at her hands. "You do?"

"I do, Paisley, I always will," Shiloh smiled softly and squeezed the girl's hand delicately. "I wish I could put into words just how much you've... you've made me feel... whole. It's like you came into my life and made everything complete and I hadn't even realized what I was missing. You filled the voids in me that I didn't even know existed. I owe you the world."

"You are the world," Paisley whispered, scooting into Shiloh's side and leaning her head on the green eyed girl's shoulder. "You really are, Lo. You have oceans in your eyes, the sky in your heart, and... and galaxies in your hands," she reached out, lacing their fingers together.

"You are my world," Shiloh said quietly, feeling Paisley relax into her side. And even though the world around them was frostbitten, Shiloh didn't feel so cold.

That's what love does to someone, Shiloh supposed. It filled up all the hollow spaces inside of her and made no room for the cold. And now with Paisley by her side, she knew she'd never be cold again.

In fact, she hadn't felt that cold for a while now.

EPILOGUE

June, The Following Year

"Mommy! Mommy! Did you see me?"

Smiling widely, Shiloh weaved through the crowds of people and knelt down, just in time for her daughter to come leaping into her arms. Laughing, the green eyed girl embraced the small girl and stood up, giving her a soft smile.

"There's my little ladybug," Shiloh laughed, looking down at her daughter, who had two red rosy cheeks painted on her face.

"Did you see me?" Presley asked, an excited smile spreading across her lips.

"I sure did, kiddo. Did you hear everyone clap for you?" Shiloh asked, reaching out and brushing Presley's hair out of her face. The smaller girl nodded excitedly, her ladybug antennas bouncing up and down atop her head.

"Where's mama?" Presley tilted her head to the side, giggling softly when her antennas bounced along with her.

"I think she's backstage, bug. Let's go find her," Shiloh laughed softly. Nodding, the tiny girl wiggled out of Shiloh's arms and hurried down the steps of the auditorium in search of her mother. The dark haired girl quickly followed.

"Slow down!" Shiloh laughed, weaving through the other parents and their children. Eventually, she lost sight of Presley, and she quickly slipped past the red velvet curtain and into the backstage area of the auditorium.

"There you are, little flower!"

Shiloh couldn't help the smile that spread across her face when she heard Paisley's voice echo throughout the room, watching as Presley hurried over to engulf the brown eyed woman in a hug.

"Did I do good, mama?" Presley asked, looking up at Paisley hopefully. The girl nodded, standing up with her daughter in her arms and poking her nose playfully.

"You did amazing," Paisley reassured her, balancing Presley on one hip and bending down to grab her bag. "Where is Lo?"

"Right here," Shiloh laughed softly, appearing beside Paisley and stealing a quick kiss on her wife's cheek. "Great play, babe. You make an awesome Narrator #2."

"Hush," Paisley laughed, nudging her wife's shoulder jokingly. She jumped when she heard a thud from behind her, and moments later she was passing Presley off to Shiloh so she could go reel in the group of preschoolers before they broke something expensive.

Glancing at the clock, Shiloh gasped. "Pais! C'mon, we've gotta go!"

"I have to get them back to the classroom," Paisley looked back at Shiloh, now with one child on her hip and two other preschoolers tugging at her sleeve.

"Go ahead," Shiloh laughed at the image, shaking her head. "I'll get this one ready," she nodded towards Presley, waiting for a thumbs up from Paisley before slipping down the backstage hallway and searching for the nearest bathroom.

"Are we going now?" Presley asked once Shiloh set her down on the counter, retrieving a wipe from her purse and gently scrubbing the stage makeup from her daughter's face.

"Yep," Shiloh gave the small girl an excited smile. "As soon as you get dressed and ready." She dug around in her bag until she found the change of clothes she had packed. In record time, Presley's ladybug costume was replaced with a blue floral dress, and her hair was pulled back into a small bun atop her head.

"I love dresses," Presley giggled, standing on the counter and turning around in front of the mirror while Shiloh quickly packed up their things.

"Are you excited?" Shiloh asked, raising a playful eyebrow. Presley giggled and nodded furiously.

"I'm super duper ex-woah! Mommy!" Presley squealed, giggling when Shiloh scooped her off of the counter and slung her over her shoulder, making the tiny girl laugh wildly.

"We've gotta find Mama," Shiloh laughed, helping the smaller girl get adjusted on her shoulders as she navigated her way down the school hallways. The parents and children were abuzz with excitement after the last day of school program, and Paisley had her hands full in her new position as a full time teacher's aide.

"Wrong way," Presley giggled, pointing in the direction Shiloh was supposed to be going. Laughing, the two finally found Paisley's classroom amongst the crowded hallways.

"Pais," Shiloh whispered, peeking her head into the room where Paisley was helping one of the boys zip up his jacket. "C'mon."

"I am hurrying," Paisley laughed softly, making her way across the room to grab her jacket before waving to the few remaining students, leaving them in the hands of the teacher.

"Hiya, pretty," Paisley smiled, reaching up and squeezing Presley's hand as she hurried to join them in the hallway. "Are you ready?"

"Is it gonna be scary?" Presley asked from her perch atop Shiloh's shoulders.

"Not at all, goof," Shiloh laughed, ducking them down under the doorframe as they made their way outside in the humid summer air. "All it is is a couple more pieces of paper to sign and then the state recognizes you as our actual daughter."

Presley giggled, holding onto the top of Shiloh's head as headed towards the car. Paisley handed the tiny girl off to Paisley as she quickly got adjusted in the driver's seat. Within minutes they were on the road.

Just as Paisley reached to turn on the radio, Presley's tiny voice made her think otherwise.

"Where's Sunny?"

Immediately, Shiloh and Paisley exchanged confused glances. "What?"

"I put hims right here," Presley nodded, sure of herself as she pointed to the pocket on the seat in front of her. "I put him here this morning so I wouldn't forget him."

Cursing under her breath, Shiloh shook her head. "I brought him back inside with me after I dropped you guys off so he wouldn't get lost."

"But I need him!" Presley gasped. "He was supposed to come with me!"

Biting her lip, Shiloh glanced at the clock and then turned to look at Paisley, who simply met her eyes and shrugged.

"I don't know if we'll have time to go back and g-,"

"Please, Mommy?" Presley met Shiloh's eyes hopefully through the rear view mirror. "He's me and Mama's good luck charm."

Sighing, Shiloh nodded softly. "Hold on," she warned them, abruptly turning off into the nearest driveway so they could turn around. Paisley couldn't help but laugh at how easily Shiloh had been swayed.

Thanks to Shiloh driving faster than usual, they arrived back at their house in no time, and Paisley was scurrying inside to retrieve their daughter's beloved stuffed animal. The moment she was back in the car, Shiloh was speeding off down the road, determined to make it to their appointment on time.

"What's it gonna be like?" Presley asked, now hugging Sunny contently against her chest. "Is there gonna be lots of people?"

"Nope," Shiloh shook her head. "Mama said you wanted it to be just the three of us, right?" Presley nodded softly from the backseat.

"Oh, babe, that reminds me," Shiloh remembered, glancing over at Paisley. "I told Toby we'd watch Lucas tomorrow. Maia has another doctor's appointment."

"Another?" Paisley asked, raising an eyebrow.

"Yeah. This pregnancy isn't treating her as well as her first," Shiloh laughed softly and shrugged. "Toby said they're trying to get her on medicine for her morning sickness."

"Oh, Pres, guess what me and Mama found out last night?" Shiloh added, an excited smile forming on her face as she glanced back at her daughter.

"What?" the smaller girl tilted her head to the side and looked at Shiloh inquisitively.

"Remember how Auntie Leah's gonna have a baby in October?"

"Yeah!" Presley smiled widely. "And it's gonna be best friends with Maia's baby!"

"Yes ma'am," Shiloh laughed. "Well, she called us last night after you went to bed, because they went to the baby doctor and figured out that their baby is gonna be a little girl," she glanced over at Paisley with a soft smile.

"It's a girl?!" Presley sat straight up in her seat and looked at Shiloh excitedly. "She's gonna have a little girl?"

"Yep," Shiloh laughed softly and reached over to squeeze Paisley's hand.

"That's so cool," Presley nodded, leaning back in her seat and looking out the car window. "Is Auntie Maia gonna have a girl, too?"

"They do not know yet," Paisley spoke up, turning around in her seat to reach back and smooth out Presley's hair. "They have to wait a little longer."

"Oh. Good," Presley nodded. "I want it to be a boy."

"You do?" Shiloh asked, raising an eyebrow. "Why?"

"Cause' I want a baby brother," Presley shrugged, hugging Sunny against her chest.

Upon hearing this, both Shiloh and Paisley exchanged confused glances. "Babes, their baby isn't going to be your sibling. It'll be more like a cousin. Like Luke is."

"I know," Presley shook her head. "I'm just pretending."

Shiloh and Paisley didn't have much time to analyze her comments, though, because moments later Shiloh was turning the car into a parking spot outside the building. Upon realizing this, Presley clapped her hands together and looked out the window in excitement.

"This is a big deal, you know," Shiloh said softly as she lifted Presley from her carseat. "It's a big day for you."

"I know, mommy," Presley giggled, holding onto Sunny and wrapping her arms around Shiloh's neck. "Mama already talked to me about it."

"She did?" Shiloh glanced over at Paisley and raised an eyebrow. "What'd she say?"

"Blood does not make a family," Presley nodded once. "Oh, and she said we could get ice cream after," she added hopefully, making Shiloh laugh softly. The green eyed girl glanced back at Paisley, reaching out and taking her hand.

"Ready to be a Everest-Lowe?" Shiloh asked, squeezing Paisley's hand and laughing when Presley nearly dropped Sunny from nodding so hard. Paisley caught up to them with a wide smile, feeling Shiloh wrap an arm around her shoulder as they made their way into the large building.

-

427

Shiloh stood a few steps back, watching as Paisley knelt down beside Presley and gave her a boost up to reach the judge's desk.

They were in a small room, surrounded by all sorts of official looking documents and such. The whole process had been quite different than Shiloh had expected. The judge was neither strict nor rigid. Instead, he had been warm and inviting, even entertaining Presley when she asked him if he got to 'hit the hammer on the desk.'

Now, Shiloh and Paisley had just signed the last documents, sealing the adoption. That was supposed to have been it, but Presley had also spoken up and questioned why she didn't get to sign anything. And surprisingly, the judge had simply laughed and drew a third line on the paper, handing the pen over to the small girl.

"Really?" Presley's eyes grew wide and she allowed Paisley to help her up to stand up on the chair, leaning over the desk and looking at the document that sat in front of her. It looked extremely official. The good kind of official, too. Shiloh planned on framing it and hanging it up as soon as possible.

"You wanted it to be official, didn't you?" the judge laughed. Presley nodded quickly, accepting the pen from his hand as if he might take the opportunity away from her. Biting her lip in concentration, the smaller girl leaned down, bringing the pen to the paper and carefully scrawling out her name.

A few moments later she paused, tilting her head to the side and looking back up at Paisley. She stood on her tiptoes to whisper something in the girl's ear.

"R-O-S-E," Paisley laughed softly, tracing the letters into the paper to help Presley spell out her middle name. The smaller girl moved to quickly finish her signature, pausing before deciding to add a small flower doodled at the end.

"There," Presley nodded proudly, standing back up and handing the pen over the desk. "It's perfect now." The smaller girl laughed shyly, hopping off of the chair and hurrying over to take back her place by Shiloh's side.

"That's it?" Shiloh asked, watching as the judge simply nodded and closed the drawers of his desk.

"That's it," he confirmed, laughing at her nervousness. "Congratulations."

"Mommy, we have to hurry!" Presley tugged on Shiloh's sleeve. "Remember?"

"Right," Shiloh nodded quickly, scooping her daughter up in her arms. "Pais, can you grab the stuff? I need to run and get her changed."

"Got it," Paisley laughed, watching as Shiloh quickly slipped out of the room with Presley in tow. When she turned back around, the judge raised an amused eyebrow at her.

"Busy schedule, I suppose?" he asked, chuckling and organizing the papers on his desk to hand over to her. Paisley just laughed softly and shrugged.

"Maybe," she ran a hand through her hair. "But I love her. I love them."

"Well, I'll tell you, that little girl is pretty lucky that you two just happened to be at the right place at the right time," he laughed, handing a folder of forms to Paisley. "I wish you all the best."

After thanking the man, Paisley hurried to gather their things and meet up with Shiloh and Presley, who now donned her favorite pink leotard and ballet slippers. Shiloh was hurrying behind the girl, attempting to stick yet another bobby pin into her bun before they made it out the door.

"Good, you're here," Shiloh laughed, immediately handing one of their bags off to Paisley and scooping a giggling Presley up into her arms so she could quickly secure her hair. Paisley couldn't help but laugh, watching her wife and daughter playfully bicker back and forth.

Eventually, they made their way back into the car. Presley wouldn't stop talking about the judge, and how she'd gotten to sign her name on her own adoption certificate. Shiloh and Paisley were both thankful that she felt that she had a say in the day's events. Neither of them could be happier with their small family.

"Pais, her hair," Shiloh sighed from the front seat, glancing into the rear view mirror at Presley. "It's already falling out."

"It is fine," Paisley giggled, raising an eyebrow at her wife. Shiloh glanced over at her though, and Paisley could tell by the look in her eyes that there wasn't any convincing her otherwise.

"Fine," Paisley rolled her eyes playfully, unbuckling her seatbelt and crawling into the backseat to fix Presley's hair.

"Play the song!" Presley smiled hopefully, clapping her hands together when Shiloh reached for the radio. Moments later, Anna Sun filled the car. Every single girl in the car couldn't help but sing along.

"Stay still," Paisley giggled, furrowing her eyebrows as she put the finishing touches on Presley's hair. Pretty soon, Shiloh was parking the car and Presley was scrambling out of the car, hopping onto the sidewalk and waiting for Paisley to follow.

"There you are," Ryland laughed once Shiloh held the door of the studio open for the two other girls. Presley immediately jumped into Ryland's arms to greet her, giggling when the light haired girl tossed her into the air.

"C'mon, Pais, class is starting," Ryland nodded, slumping the smaller girl over her shoulder and making her laugh even harder as she carried her down the hallway, forcing Presley to call out rushed goodbyes to both Paisley and Shiloh. The two girls exchanged amused glances.

"How'd it go?" Vanessa asked, who was seated behind the rectangular counter and filing through a stack of CDs.

430

While Shiloh engaged her friend in conversation, Paisley absentmindedly wandered into the viewing room, where the other parents sat and watched their children in class.

Paisley slipped in quietly, leaning against the wall and watching as Ryland nudged Presley to go join the few other children in their class. Paisley made sure she couldn't be seen - a lesson she and Shiloh had learned months ago when Presley caught sight of them through the window and insisted on making silly faces at them throughout the entire class.

She watched for a few minutes while Presley followed the teachers instructions, standing on her tiptoes and walking in wobbly circles. Paisley couldn't help but laugh, but she found the other parents even more amusing. One of the mothers insisted on banging on the window and scolding her child for not paying attention, which was when Paisley glanced back into the lobby and noticed a different set of eyes studying Shiloh.

She didn't know him, but she already didn't like him. He was leaning up against the wall by the door, obviously waiting for someone, but also not-so-subtly studying Shiloh, who was still talking to Vanessa with her elbows rested on the counter.

Paisley rarely got mad or annoyed, but this was an exception. Holding her chin up in the air, she made her way back into the lobby and slid into place beside Shiloh. The green eyed girl was too caught up in the conversation to pay much attention to this.

Furrowing her eyebrows, the smaller girl glanced back at the man, who quickly diverted his eyes back to his magazine to try and appear as if he hadn't been staring. Paisley mumbled a few words under her breath before turning back to Shiloh and snaking her arm around her waist.

When Shiloh didn't acknowledge Paisley's actions, the smaller girl huffed and scooted impossibly closer to her.

Shiloh nearly stumbled over, causing her to turn her head and raise a questioning eyebrow at the girl.

Smiling up at her innocently, Paisley hummed quietly and leaned her head on Shiloh's shoulder. The dark haired girl simply gave her a soft smile before turning her attention back to what Vanessa had to say.

Paisley glanced back at the man, who was doing a horrible job of hiding his amusement over Paisley's struggle to gain Shiloh's attention. So instead, the smaller girl gave up on being subtle. She slowly slid behind Shiloh, wrapping her arms around the girl's waist and resting her head atop her shoulder. Shiloh leaned her head against Paisley's, but for the small girl, that wasn't enough.

"Hi," Paisley whispered, pressing a kiss to the curve between Shiloh's neck and shoulder. That sure got her attention.

"Wh-wha..." Shiloh stuttered, turning her head to look at Paisley and forgetting about her previous conversation with Vanessa. Paisley internally celebrated her victory.

"Hi," Paisley repeated herself, a soft smile on her face. "I love you."

"I, uh, hi?" Shiloh laughed, feeling her cheeks flush red. "H-hi. I love you too?"

"Y'all can leave, you know," Vanessa spoke up, rolling on her chair behind the counter to retrieve a stack of papers and page through them. "You've got a few hours to kill. Ryland wants to take a couple of the kids out for pizza after class. You've been running back and forth all day, go home," she laughed, raising an eyebrow at Paisley.

That was enough for Shiloh, who jumped at the opportunity for some much needed down time. She nodded, finding Paisley's hand and lacing their fingers together. Paisley reveled in her victory, forcing herself not to stick her tongue out to the man as Shiloh said her goodbyes and absentmindedly ran her fingers up and down Paisley's forearm as she led her out of the studio and back to their car.

"What was that all about?" Shiloh asked, starting up the car and glancing over at her wife. Paisley paused, biting her lip and shrugging. She quickly changed the topic of conversation, and eventually the pair fell into comfortable silence on the drive home.

Once they got home, Paisley yawned, stretched out her arms, and hurried in front of Shiloh to open the door for her. As soon as they were inside, Elvis came bounding in from the hallway, rubbing against their legs and begging for attention.

Compared to Wolf, Elvis was the equivalent of a small child. While Wolf had been mostly calm and mellow, Elvis was extremely playful and adventurous. He was Presley's cat, though, so it worked for the two of them.

"I am tired," Paisley admitted, squatting down to pet Elvis's striped fur. "Take a nap with me?" she added hopefully, looking up at Shiloh.

Of course, there was no saying no to a pair of hopeful brown eyes, which is why only a short time later, Paisley was pulling Shiloh down to the space beside her on the bed. The brown eyed girl immediately curled up in her side, to which Shiloh sighed contently and lazily ran her fingers through Paisley's hair.

Shiloh did this all the time. She'd lay there quietly, waiting for Paisley's body to relax as her eyelids grew heavy, and she eventually fell asleep beside the green eyed girl. Shiloh, however, made no attempts to sleep. It was just a thing they did. Shiloh laid with Paisley until she fell asleep, and then Shiloh pressed a kiss to her forehead and disappeared down the hallway. She appreciated those quiet moments.

So now, Shiloh slipped into the studio, turning on the playlist Paisley had made her for Valentine's Day and flipping open to a clean page in her sketchbook. She wasn't sure what she wanted to draw. In fact, she'd been lacking inspiration for the past few weeks. It was typical for artists, but Shiloh still grew frustrated with herself.

She twirled the piece of charcoal between her fingers, biting her lip and leaning back against her chair as she surveyed the room, trying to gain ideas for something to draw. Eventually, she started scratching absentmindedly at her paper, giving up on finding an idea with any substance, and simply tracing the outline of the window in front of her.

Shiloh grew so lost in the music that she wasn't even aware how long she'd been in the room. Whenever she drew, painted, or even doodled on her notebooks, she blocked everything else out, getting completely immersed in her own little world.

Which was why she didn't even hear the small footsteps pad into the studio. Or see her wife, clad in one of her white t-shirts and hugging an old blanket around her shoulders, until Paisley yawned and sat down on the windowsill, brushing the curtains aside and gazing out at the sky.

Shiloh had just been perfecting the shadows on the lace curtains when she looked up to find something else in the way. Her first reaction was to gasp, which made Paisley jump and look back at her in confusion. Shiloh's eyes darted back down to her sketchbook, and back up to the scene that Paisley had just interrupted. The green eyed girl cursed under her breath.

"Did I do it again?" Paisley asked, eyes widening when she caught a glimpse of what Shiloh had been sketching. This wasn't the first time Paisley had accidentally ruined one of Shiloh's pieces. In fact, the couple joked about how often Paisley seemed to unknowingly reverse Shiloh's progress. It'd been a bad habit of hers since day one.

Something Shiloh had learned, though, was that the outcome somehow always ended up being better than anything she could have ever done on her own.

"I am so sorry," Paisley sighed, growing annoyed with herself as she moved to stand up. But Shiloh's eyes were on something else, and she quickly reached out to stop Paisley.

"No, stay there," Shiloh said quietly, grabbing Paisley's wrist to keep her from moving any further. "Just... just sit down," she laughed softly, placing her hands on Paisley's shoulders and directing the girl to sit back on the windowsill. "There. Just like that."

The tiny girl raised an eyebrow, but did as she was told. Shiloh didn't say anything else, she simply hurried back over to her chair, holding her pencil in her mouth and furrowing her eyebrows as she flipped to a new page and immediately brought her stick of charcoal down to the blank paper.

Every few moments Shiloh would look up, studying Paisley. Sometimes, her tense muscles would loosen up, and her eyes would trace the smaller girl's figure. She would genuinely forget what she was doing, getting lost by the way the gentle light from the setting sun made Paisley literally glow. She was an angel on earth, Shiloh was convinced.

Paisley just watched Shiloh, her expression softening as Shiloh's did. The brown eyed girl pulled her legs up underneath her on the wide windowsill, glancing outside every once in a while. But for the most part, she just watched Shiloh. That view was much better than anything on the other side of the window.

It was silent for a long time, until Shiloh's raspy voice finally spoke up and took Paisley by surprise.

"I hate telling you that you're beautiful," Shiloh mumbled under her breath, making Paisley look up at her in confusion.

"What?" the smaller girl asked quietly, tilting her head to the side. Shiloh just shook her head, running a hand through her hair and leaning closer to her paper to fill in the smaller details.

"I need to invent an entirely new language and dedicate it to you. I need better words," Shiloh continued, pausing to look up once more. "Calling you beautiful just seems shallow. It's surface level. It doesn't even touch on any of the things that make you the way you are."

"I do not know what you mean," Paisley said softly. The brown eyed girl bit her lip, watching as Shiloh simply shrugged and continued smudging the black charcoal against the paper.

"Yeah, sure, you're beautiful. But that's only talking about the physical. There's tons of beautiful people with ugly insides. But you... you're different," she paused, rubbing her upper lip, completely unaware of the now black smudge she'd wiped above it. "Beautiful doesn't even begin to encompass any of the things that made me fall in love with you."

"I mean... just..." she sighed, looking up at Paisley and shaking her head in disbelief. "Look at you. I fell in love with you because I realized that there was so much more to you than just the way you look."

"Like - your hands. I love them because they hold mine. I love them because you use them so delicately. Even when you're doing something as simple as holding a warm mug," Shiloh spoke as she drew, making Paisley's cheeks flush slightly red. "And yeah, sure, your eyes are the most calming shade of brown. But I'm more in love with the way they flutter shut when you're falling asleep on my shoulder. Or the way they gaze down at Presley with complete and utter adoration when she's going on and on about something that most people would just laugh off."

"I don't know, Paisley, it's just so hard to try and communicate to you how fucking unique you are," Shiloh shook her head. "I don't do a good enough job of it."

"You are kidding, right?" Paisley couldn't help but laugh. This caused Shiloh to look up at her with a raised eyebrow.

"You... you..." Paisley sighed, shaking her head and turning to face Shiloh. "You do not understand, do you? Nothing... nothing will ever make me feel as beautiful as I do when you look at me, Lo. That is all it takes."

Shiloh just studied Paisley for a few seconds before nodding, a shy smile forming on her face. For Paisley, that was enough to let her know that Shiloh understood.

The green eyed girl set the charcoal down on the table and held out her sketchpad, looking up at Paisley hopefully. "I finished."

Paisley leaned forwards, eventually sliding off the windowsill and padding over to study the finished drawing. Shiloh watched Paisley, as the smaller girl slowly drew her bottom lip between her teeth to try and fight the smile that was threatening to break out.

On the paper, decorated in contrasting light and dark charcoal, was Paisley, sitting serenely on the windowsill with the curtains fluttering beside her, sending rays of light spilling across her small figure.

"You are really good at that, you know," Paisley whispered, leaning her head against Shiloh's and sighing softly.

"I guess," Shiloh shrugged. "Drawing you has taught me one thing, though."

"What?" Paisley asked curiously.

"I'll never be able to be the artist I want to be," Shiloh closed the sketchbook gently and set it aside. Upon hearing this, Paisley tilted her head to the side.

"Art can't capture everything. Words can't capture everything. Even if I put them together and did everything I could, I could never even begin to recreate the things you make me feel. Or the light in your eyes when you're happy," Shiloh explained, standing up and brushing Paisley's hair out of her face. "But I've decided that it's okay. I'm alright with it now. I have you. That's all I'll ever need."

"I love you, you know," Paisley mumbled, leaning against Shiloh and hiding her head in the girl's shoulder to hide how much she was smiling. The green eyed girl couldn't help but laugh, separating them a few inches so she could reach up, cup the girl's cheek, and pull her in for a quick kiss.

"I hate to ruin the mood but we have to go get Presley," Shiloh whispered once the kiss broke, leaning her forehead against Paisley's and brushing her thumb across her cheek. The smaller girl just flashed her a small smile, stealing one more kiss and squeezing her wife's hand before hurrying out of the room to get their things together.

"Hold on, babe! I forgot something!" Shiloh called, hearing Paisley getting things together in the living room. She hurried to grab a change of clothes for Presley, shoving them in a bag before jogging in the kitchen to grab something quick to eat.

Holding an apple in her mouth, Shiloh hopped around, struggling to tug on her second shoe. Paisley entered the room, failing to hold back her laughter. Eventually, Shiloh stood up, running a hand through her hair and looking at Paisley. "We're gon'f be late," she mumbled after taking a bite of her apple, making Paisley laugh softly.

"Then hurry," the smaller girl shook her head playfully, moving a few steps forward and planting a kiss on her cheek before brushing past her, disappearing out the front door.

Shiloh, however, stood in the middle of the foyer for a few seconds. She paused to bring her hand to her cheek, feeling the flushed skin from where Paisley's lips had just been. A small smile spread over her lips, and she hurried to grab her bag and catch up to Paisley.

"Wait! Lo," Paisley paused moments before she got in the car, looking around for Shiloh. "Did you remember it?"

"Of course I did. Did you?" Shiloh asked, tossing her bag into the back of the car and glancing back to Paisley, who nodded quickly and hurried to slide into her seat. Minutes later, they were on the road on the way to pick up

Presley from dance class. (Singing along to the radio, nonetheless.)

-

"Mommy!" Presley smiled widely when she saw Shiloh wave to her from the door in the studio, prompting the smaller girl to say goodbye to her teacher and hurry over to greet the green eyed girl. The smaller girl was changed out of her leotard, now donning her floral dress, as well as her pastel green beanie that she practically refused to take off. "You missed it! Rya got us pizza!"

"I heard," Shiloh laughed, crinkling her nose playfully at the smaller girl. "Did you remember what I told you to bring?"

"Yeah! It's right h-," Presley paused, furrowing her eyebrows and turning back around. "There!" she laughed, hurrying over to the hooks by the door to retrieve her ladybug backpack, holding it up for Shiloh to see.

Meanwhile, Paisley had made her way over to the counter to get a schedule of Presley's upcoming classes from Ryland, who was currently working at the computer. Paisley waited as the paper printed out, scanning the room absentmindedly. Her eyes landed on the man from before, who seemed to be waiting for his daughter's class to end. She scowled.

"Oh yeah," Paisley raised her voice, turning to Ryland and nodding. "I am having a picnic with my wife. I love her."

Ryland raised her head, confused when Paisley practically blurted those words out of nowhere. She quickly realized, though, when her friend glanced behind her to the man, who was now looking at her in confusion.

"Subtle, chanch," Ryland whispered, rolling her eyes half heartedly. "You're not being subtle."

"Tomorrow is our anniversary," Paisley continued, ignoring Ryland behind the counter. "It has been a whole year since we got married."

Rolling her eyes and giving in, Ryland turned around to retrieve the papers from the printer and staple them together. "Only a year?" she asked, giving Paisley a look that read 'you owe me.' "It seems like it's been way longer than a year."

The smaller girl smiled triumphantly, drumming her fingers against the countertop. "Good. I want forever with her," she said, focusing less on the man behind her and more on the true meaning of her words.

"Take your papers, you weirdo," Ryland rolled her eyes playfully, handing Paisley the packet and turning back to the computer. At the same time, Paisley felt a small hand tug at her sleeve, and looked down to find Presley gazing up at her.

"Help?" Presley asked, tilting her head to the side and pointing to the candy jar that rested on the counter just out of her reach. "Please?"

Laughing softly, Paisley knelt down to pick the tiny girl up, holding her level with the counter while she dug around in the bowl, eventually choosing a lollipop and holding it up to show her mother. Paisley set her back down, turning and nearly running into Shiloh, who had just stolen a lollipop for herself.

"Ready?" the green eyed girl asked, donning a goofy smile as she ripped the wrapper off of her lollipop and popped it into her mouth. Paisley just nodded, laughing and letting Presley take her hand and excitedly pull her towards the door. They waved goodbye to Ryland one last time before heading towards the car.

-

"Are we there yet?" Presley asked, tilting her head to the side from her carseat. An hour drive seemed like an eternity for the smaller girl.

"Twenty more minutes," Shiloh reassured her from the back of the car.

"You said that last time!" Presley giggled, shaking her head.

"Okay, okay. For real this time," Shiloh couldn't help but laugh, holding up her pinky behind her to let the smaller girl know that she meant it. Presley pondered this for a few moments before leaning forward in her seat and locking their pinkies together.

Paisley watched the exchange between the two, a soft smile making it's way across her lips. She reached over, finding Shiloh's hand and interlocking the girl's fingers with her own. Without taking her eyes off the road, Shiloh squeezed her hand, and Paisley saw the corners of her lips rise into a soft smile.

Twenty minutes (and a few stops) later, the three girls were piling out of the small car. Presley immediately ran ahead of them, chasing after a brilliantly colored butterfly down the pathway. Paisley laughed, glancing back at Shiloh who was beginning to unpack the back of the car.

"Do you need help?" Presley hurried back over them, looking up at Shiloh hopefully. The green eyed girl gave her daughter a small smile, handing her a small tray of the brightly colored flowers they'd packed into the back of the car.

Paisley did the same, until eventually Shiloh could kick the car door shut and lead the way down the pathway. They walked for a while in silence, mostly because Presley was too busy trying to balance the flowers on both of her hands to talk.

"Right here, Pres," Shiloh nodded, pausing and waiting for the smaller girl to catch up to her. Presley followed her mothers' example, setting down the flowers at her feet and brushing off her hands, studying the area where they'd ended up at. She noticed the exchanged looks between Shiloh and Paisley, and the way Shiloh's cheeks blushed slightly.

"We're planting them here?" Presley asked, clasping her hands together and tilting her head to the side. When Shiloh nodded, she furrowed her eyebrows, thinking this over for a few minutes.

"Why?" the tiny brown eyed girl asked, looking back and forth between the two girls. This time, Shiloh and Paisley exchanged glances.

"It is our park," Paisley shrugged before handing Shiloh the shovel she'd been carrying.

"It is?" Presley tugged on her beanie and watched as the green eyed girl dug the shovel into the grass, working away at the dirt and tossing it aside. "Why do we have flowers?"

"To plant them," Shiloh spoke up. "Because it's springtime."

"Why?" Presley continued, hurrying to follow after Paisley, who knelt down beside the earth Shiloh had dug into and began pressing the flowers into the soil. "Why are we planting more flowers?"

"Because... because they are pretty," Paisley shrugged and patted the spot beside her for the tiny girl. "And sometimes.... people just need color around them. To keep everything from being gray."

"Oh," Presley hummed, thinking this over before nodding softly and hopping beside Paisley, eager to help her pat down the soil around the colorful flowers.

A short while, and a lot of dirt later, Paisley and Shiloh both rose up to their feet to admire their handiwork. Lining the pathway in the back corner of the park was an arrangement of colorful flowers. The two girls exchanged glances, to which Paisley smiled widely and clapped her hands together.

"It is perfect," Paisley nodded happily, scooting closer to Shiloh and resting her head on her shoulder.

"You missed a spot!" Presley gasped, hopping forwards and pointing to the gap in the middle of the circle, leaving a medium sized hole in the ground. Immediately, the smaller girl looked around for the last of the flowers, only to realize they'd planted all of the flowers they had bought.

"I know," Shiloh shrugged, bending down to retrieve something out of her bag. "Remember?"

"Oh, yeah!" Presley's eyes lit up and she scurried over to retrieve her own backpack, clutching it tightly against her chest and looking up at Shiloh in excitement. "Right now?"

"Right now," Shiloh confirmed, kneeling down in the grass and waiting for both Paisley and Presley to do the same. Then, she proceeded to place a small metal lockbox in-between that three of them, opening it up to reveal the empty insides.

"Do you know why we're doing this, Pres?" Shiloh asked, crossing her legs underneath her and holding her own backpack in her lap. Paisley was doing the same, leaning her head against Shiloh's shoulder as the tiny girl shook her head.

"Well, it's called a time capsule," Shiloh explained, holding up the box. "We wanted to do one cause' we figured we've all got a few special memories that we want to store away. And then we can come back and dig it up in a few years and revisit them."

"Also, sometimes it helps to say goodbye," Paisley spoke up. "To things that are not a part of your life anymore."

"Exactly," Shiloh nodded. "Like this," the green eyed girl said softly, pulling something out of her backpack. Paisley's eyes immediately widened when she saw it was a sketch of her.

"You are saying goodbye to me?" Paisley asked in confusion, looking at Shiloh worriedly. The green eyed girl quickly shook her head and placed a hand on Paisley's knee to calm her down.

"No, no," she couldn't help but laugh softly. "I'm talking about the drawing, babe. I'm not letting you go anywhere." She squeezed the smaller girl's hand.

"Do you remember what this is from?" Shiloh asked, holding up the pencil sketch between them. Presley leaned over to study it as well, tilting her head to the side. Paisley simply shook her head.

"I drew this while I was waiting on the steps of the courthouse, remember?" Shiloh's voice softened slightly, and she ran her fingers over the rushed drawing. Paisley paused, suddenly realizing why the drawing had seemed so familiar.

"I just... it doesn't look right anymore," Shiloh said after Paisley nodded slowly. "You've changed. Not just physically, either," she paused to hold the drawing beside Paisley's face and compare the two. "There's more light in your eyes now."

"So... yeah," Shiloh laughed softly, folding the drawing in two and placing it in the bottom of the box. "That's my contribution to the time capsule."

Paisley bit her lip to fight her smile, glancing at Shiloh and nodding softly. When she realized both pairs of eyes were on her, she laughed softly and dug around in her backpack for a few moments until she finally retrieved the item she'd been looking for.

"I brought two," Paisley added quietly. "I could not pick one."

Moments later, the smaller girl help up a light blue collar between them, studying it for a few moments. She smiled softly, tapping the small bell attached that emitted a faint ringing noise.

"Hey, that's Wolfie's!" Presley smiled widely, scooting closer to Paisley and tilting her head to the side.

"Yeah," Paisley nodded softly, glancing over at Shiloh who raised an eyebrow at her. "I just... figured it was a good way to remember him." She nodded once more before placing the collar in the box.

"And then..." Paisley paused, looking in her bag once more. "This," she nodded slowly, pulling out a book and tossing her bag aside. Both Shiloh and Presley looked at her in confusion.

"A book?" Shiloh asked, leaning closer to try and read the title. Paisley simply shook her head.

"It is what is inside," Paisley explained, slowly paging through the book until she found the page she needed, nodding softly and cracking the book fully open. While Presley's eyebrows furrowed together in confusion, Shiloh's jaw practically dropped.

"It just... felt wrong to throw them away," Paisley explained as she gently pressed her fingertips against the dried flowers. "They... they remind me of my lowest point..." she paused for a few moments. "But they do not mean much to me anymore, really. You were right, Lo... so much has changed."

"What are they?" Presley asked, gently tilting the book to get a better look at the flowers pressed between the pages.

"Flowers," Paisley laughed softly. "It is a long story."

"A long story," Shiloh spoke up, nodding softly. Paisley simply laughed, closed the book, and carefully placed it in the box, along with Shiloh's drawing and Wolf's collar.

"Is it my turn?" Presley asked, hugging her backpack to her chest and looking at them hopefully.

"It's all yours, kiddo," Shiloh laughed, reaching out to fix the green beanie that sat atop her daughter's head. Moments later, Presley was clapping her hands together and dug around in her backpack.

"Mama said to pick somethin' special to me, that I could say goodbye too, right?" Presley asked, looking up at Shiloh for approval. The green eyed girl glanced back at Paisley and smiled before nodding softly.

Giggling, Presley nodded, pushing her backpack aside and holding out her item. "I picked these, cause' I love em', but they don't fit right anymore," she smiled hopefully, showing her mothers the first pair of ballet slippers she'd ever received.

"You know what? That's perfect," Shiloh laughed, nudging the box towards Presley. "That way we can dig this up when you're a world famous ballerina and you can remember where you started," she smiled softly, leaning in and kissing the tiny girl's cheek. Paisley laughed softly from beside them.

"Rya says I'm not allowed to tell anybody but that I'm the bestest dancer in the class," Presley nodded, hugging the old ballet slippers to her chest before placing them into the box.

When Shiloh and Paisley both burst into laughter, Presley's eyes widened, and the small girl quickly brought her hands up to clap them over her mouth. "You can't tell her I told you that!"

"We won't," Shiloh managed to calm down her laughter. "We won't, Pres. Promise."

"She was not lying," Paisley leaned over and whispered in the smaller girl's ear, making her giggle.

"Well, that's our time capsule," Shiloh spoke up, nodding towards the box. "Ready to say goodbye for a while?"

Once Presley nodded, Paisley scooted forward and closed the box. Just as she was about to secure the lock shut, the tiny brown eyed girl practically rocketed up to her feet and shook her head quickly.

"Wait! I forgot something!" Presley exclaimed, startling Paisley and causing her to quickly pull her hands away from the box. Both Shiloh and Paisley watched in confusion as the tiny girl furiously dug through her backpack.

"This!" Presley hopped back to her feet and gently placed something in Shiloh's lap. "Auntie Nessa and Rya said I had to give it to you."

"What is i-?" Paisley began, but was cut off when Shiloh gasped from beside her.

"Oh my god, Pais, look," Shiloh breathed out, running her fingers over the smooth black cover of her old sketchbook. "Look what it is."

Paisley let out a small gasp, leaning against Shiloh's shoulder and watching as the green eyed girl opened the book, noticing the sticky note attached to the inside of the front cover.

Found this in the back of your old closet a while back. Figured you'd want to see it. (Don't worry, we didn't snoop.) - Ryland & Nessa

"I remember this," Paisley said softly. "You... you never went anywhere without it."

"Yeah," Shiloh laughed softly, glancing up at Presley and patting the space beside her. "Come look, babes. These are my old drawings."

"You made these?" Presley asked curiously, kneeling beside Shiloh and watching as the green eyed girl slowly paged through her collection of old sketches.

"A long time ago, yeah," Shiloh smiled softly, pulling Presley into her side and kissing the top of her head. "Even before you were born."

"That's old," Presley giggled, making Shiloh laugh. Paisley, however, ended up gasping moments later.

"Lo," she whispered, placing her hand on top of Shiloh's and pausing her motions on a particular page. When Shiloh looked down, she quickly realized why Paisley had reacted so strongly.

Half of the drawing was in pencil, obviously done by Shiloh. Heavily shaded leaves and stems lined the bottom of the page. However, this transitioned into a combination of crayon and marker, adding shaky, colorful flowers to the top of the stems.

Shiloh and Paisley exchanged glances. Paisley immediately brought her hand down to trace her old markings, feeling a wave of nostalgia wash over her. "I remember this," she nodded softly, looking up at Shiloh.

"Me too," the green eyed girl nodded. "This was from one of the first days you came to live with us. After... you know."

"I know," the brown eyed girl whispered, biting her lip. "Wow."

"Wow?"

"I think I knew I loved you... even then," Paisley whispered, nodding slowly. "Wow."

"Oh," was all Shiloh could manage to say, glancing up at Paisley, who met her eyes and smiled shyly.

Presley interrupted the silence, gently reaching out and pulling out a small square she'd noticed wedged between the pages. "What's this?" the small girl asked, holding it up and studying it.

"Huh?" Shiloh glanced over at her, raising an eyebrow when she realized what her daughter had found. "Oh, Pres, it's a picture," she nodded, tapping the other side of the paper for Presley to turn it over.

"Who is it?" the tiny girl asked, handing it to Shiloh and looking at her curiously. It took the green eyed girl a few moments to study the dark polariod, and Paisley was the first one to make out the slightly blurry image in the darkness.

"That is us," Paisley nodded quickly, tracing the outline of their figures to Shiloh. On the polaroid was a picture of both Shiloh and Paisley from years ago, both fast asleep and crammed into one of the old armchairs during their annual movie nights at the old apartment. Shiloh's eyes widened, realizing Leah must have taken the picture using her old camera.

"Woah," Shiloh whispered, laughing softly. "Look how little we were."

"That's you?" Presley asked, leaning over Shiloh's lap and pointing to the picture. Shiloh laughed and nodded slowly.

"That's Mama and I, see?" she asked, tracing the two figures in the picture just as Shiloh had done.

"It is?" Presley's face lit up and Shiloh allowed her to take the picture into her own hands and study it closely. The tiny girl nodded softly.

"Why are you smiling?" she asked, looking up in curiosity.

"Because I love her," Shiloh shrugged, feeling Paisley rest her head against her shoulder.

"You do?" Presley looked up with a inquisitive smile on her face. "Does she love you?"

"I sure hope so," the green eyed girl laughed. The wavy haired girl beside her simply giggled, leaning in and kissing her wife on the cheek.

"Of course I love her," Paisley spoke up. "We... we love each other an awful lot."

"Why?" Presley asked, tilting her head to the side.

This time, Shiloh and Paisley both exchanged glances. Once Paisley squeezed her hand, the green eyed girl sighed and closed the sketchbook. She placed it in the time capsule, closing it and locking it before turning to her daughter and taking her wife's hand in-between her own. She took a deep breath, feeling Paisley's eyes watching her lovingly, as they sat in the place where it had all begun.

"Well, I guess you could say it all started with a flower..."

a c k n o w l e d g e m e n t s

➤➤

Well this has been crazy.

Three books and a ton of stories later, here we are. As I'm writing this, it's been a little over a year since I posted the first chapter of Yellow up on Wattpad. Since then it's been this crazy whirlwind journey for me. I'm a completely different person than I was when I sat down and started writing this series. It's hard for me to wrap my mind around.

Something that sticks out in my mind is always listening to the album "Every Kingdom" by Ben Howard while writing chapter after chapter. The entire album brings me back to that time and if you listen to it, it gives you the same light and airy feeling I wanted the book to carry. The song Gracious from that album was even the first song Shiloh sang Paisley.

Continue to read and write, listen to music, hold onto hidden treasures, and hope for the best. I love you. Thanks for reading and sticking with me. Be nice to yourselves.

(Thank you, you're welcome.)

lena nottingham

my social media

wattpad - txrches
tumblr - txrches
twitter -@lenajfc

68471424R00274

Made in the USA
Middletown, DE
30 March 2018